STRAY CAT STRUT

STRAY CAT STRUT

BOOK 4

RAVENSDAGGER

Podium

Podium

STRAY CAT STRUT

Some kids thought they could be cool.

Like, if they trained hard, if they just found the right gear or made the right friends, if they were given an opportunity, they could grow up to be a badass motherfucker, chewing nails and spitting fire.

I was one of those kids. Daydreaming of being awesome, of kicking ass. I'd find some discarded samurai super-gun. I'd discover that my parents were linked to one of the cooler cartels somehow and they'd take me in. Maybe I'd just start my own gang with the kittens as recruits.

It was all stupid daydreaming.

Weird how life twisted things around sometimes.

I paused midstep, then stood a little straighter to look out the window. Earth was below me. Just . . . the entire planet, hanging there. The part below us was brightly lit, stark white clouds over dark greens and brilliant blues. The place where I'd spent my entire life.

"You okay?" Gomorrah asked. She had paused a few steps ahead, Deus Ex—still in her pajamas—by her side.

"Yeah," I said. "Just taking it all in." There was this weird feeling of vertigo, my stomach doing little flips as I took in the world below. It wasn't just the fear of the drop that had me feeling that way. A week ago, I'd been a nobody orphan; the kind of street trash that no one sensible gave a fuck about.

I'd come far in a few days.

"Let's keep moving," I said. "Clock's ticking, right?"

There were thirty-ish hours left until the apocalypse started.

The girls nodded, and we continued down the dark gray corridor of Deus Ex's home away from Earth. She stopped us in front of a pair of doors set against one wall: big bulkhead-looking things, like I'd expect to see in some futuristic submarine. "This is your way down," she said. "Get in, grab on, and then enjoy the ride."

The doors opened into rooms the size of broom cupboards, with slits against the walls and handles at about waist height. There was a sort of leaned-back chair at the rear too. "How, exactly, is this going to bring us back to Earth?" I asked.

"Gravity."

I shook my head and got into the pod first.

"See you groundside," Gomorrah said.

"Yeah," I replied. "Deus Ex, you'll keep in touch?"

The shorter girl shrugged. "I'm busy, but I might have a few hours to spare, yeah. The trip over to Mars takes a week or so. I'll be stuck in my ship that whole time with nothing to do but binge shows and take naps."

"While we'll be on Earth fighting for our lives?" I asked.

She shrugged. "Want to go fight for your life on Mars instead?"

"I think I'll take my chances down below," I said as I settled into the pod. The door closed with a heavy thump, and I felt it as the pressure changed. The walls unfolded, and clamps grabbed me around the waist and shins and arms. It was uncomfortable to be restricted so much.

Then the pod started to fill from the bottom up with some sort of goop. It rose and rose, cold as it seeped around my armor.

"What in the fuck is that?" I asked.

It's a heavily oxygenated shock-absorbing liquid. You should be able to breathe it, and it will diffuse any impacts so that they don't harm you.

Myalis was always so damned comforting. "That's real nice to hear," I said as the goop swelled up, then reached my arms. It was hard to move in, like gelatin. Then it swallowed my head, and I found myself holding my breath for a moment.

It didn't last long. I trusted Myalis, even if she was a bit strange at times.

The pod clunked, and the wall before me lit up. It was a screen, one that showed the inside of a tube.

Something clanged, and then the tube shot up while I went down.

Then we left the station. I glimpsed another pod falling a little bit above me before I was rotated around. Jets of some gas realigned my pod with little spurts, and then I was falling back down to Earth.

A lot of kids really wished that they'd grow up to be badasses. I had been one of them.

Now I was falling out of a samurai's space fortress back toward the Earth in a little metal casket moving so fast that the bottom of my pod lit on fire as it screeched through the air. A timer hovered on the edge of my vision, counting down to what might be the end of everything. There were few things as badass as what I was doing, I figured.

I would have traded it all for an afternoon spent cuddling in bed.

I held on while the pod shifted and rattled back down to Earth. My jaw started to hurt from being clamped so hard for so long.

Then something clunked, and for a heart-wrenching moment I thought I was fucked, but things started to slow down and the flames licking at the side of the pod gave way to hissing air and then clouds.

The next thing that I could see, once I was past the gray wall of cloud cover, was the tallest buildings in the city, reaching up toward me.

The sides of the pod opened and a set of thrusters fired off toward the ground, slowing me down further and pushing the drop pod toward a specific building.

The museum.

I landed with a heavy crunch and the front door of the pod blew off the side, all of the goop holding me in place sloughing off onto the landing zone right next to my home.

The clamps around my legs and arms and waist let go, and I found myself standing on the spot, entirely uncertain of what to do next.

Are you well?

"Uh," I said. I swallowed, let my heart settle for a moment, then winced as something crashed nearby. A second pod. Gomorrah had been sent to the same spot as I had.

I stepped out of the drop pod.

It was, of course, raining. For once that seemed to help, washing off the gunk clinging to my armor. Gomorrah stepped out of her pod and glanced around, then to me. "That was fun," she said.

"I don't know. I liked the space shuttle a lot more," I said.

She shrugged. "This was probably faster."

I couldn't help but laugh. A couple of minutes ago I was in space; now I was back on solid Earth. More or less. "Yeah, I guess so."

There were a couple of vans parked nearby. Hovervans, with their sides opened to reveal a bunch of tools within, and a few construction guys were there, tool belts around their waists, coffee cups in hand, and jaws slack as they stared at Gomorrah and me.

Guess we had made something of an entrance.

"You getting renovations done?" Gomorrah asked.

"Yeah. Setting the place up for the kittens. It's supposed to take a couple of weeks," I said.

Someone stepped out of the building, then ran over. I recognized him as the contractor in charge of stuff. He'd given me his name half a dozen times, and I forgot it every time. "Miss Stray Cat," he said, a bit out of breath. "I wasn't expecting you."

"I wasn't expecting to show up here either," I said. Did Deus Ex send me here on purpose, or was it just the nearest place with enough room to land?

"Are you here to see how the work's progressing?" he asked.

"Huh? No. I was just . . . in space. Uh. You know that matter reconfiguration machine, at the back?"

He nodded. "The one Raccoon is taking care of?"

Right, another loose end to take care of. "That's the one. Can a couple of your guys help Raccoon load these pods into it? I'm pretty sure they'll fit if you cut them up a bit." Would they even be able to do that? "If you can't, just leave them somewhere."

"Certainly, ma'am," he replied with an easy, if nervous, smile.

I nodded to him and turned toward Gomorrah. "Think you can get your car over?" I asked.

"The Fury is on its way already," she said. "What are you planning on doing?"

"Uh," I said. I was supposed to have a meeting with a nonprofit soon, to go over the making and distributing of prosthetics. I had to bully Burringham some more about the sewers. I had to check up on Raccoon, tell her about the prosthetic thing, and get her a proper place to stay. I'd been meaning to look into schooling for the kittens, maybe therapy? They definitely needed that.

Knowing that I had . . . about twenty-nine hours until the world went to shit kind of put a damper on all of my plans.

Deus Ex sent an itinerary. There are two meetings that will take place before the end of the deadline. I suspect that you'll want to attend both. The first is in five hours. A nighttime meeting with representatives from a few paramilitary groups and members of the city council and appropriately large corporate entities. The second is tomorrow morning, a meet-and-greet for all the samurai in the city. Seventeen have reserved places at the meeting so far. Both are organized by the Family.

"Interesting," Gomorrah said. So Myalis had been sending to her too. Good to know.

"That leaves us with a bit of time to take care of other things," I said. "Cool. Going to need every minute of that time."

CHAPTER ONE

FEED THE MACHINE

The bigger they are, the more they'll make fall.
Or something like that.
Look, I don't exactly read a lot of books, all right?
—Three Swipes, comment about the
unveiling of the Domus, 2052

"I'm heading home," Gomorrah said.

I glanced over to her. "Just like that?"

She shrugged. "We'll see each other in a few hours. The security around the church is tight, but it's not tight enough to stop a full-on invasion. I have a few hundred points to spare."

"That actually sounds like a decent idea," I said. I glanced at the museum. The interior had been torn apart already, with workers crawling all around the inside moving junk into containers and others bringing in new materials.

I could probably speed that up considerably.

The problem was that I could only do so for the topmost floor.

I stared around. The museum was on top of the shortest building in sight. Only thirteen floors tall. Most of the buildings around were twice that height; some more distant buildings were considerably taller than that.

"Cat?"

I spun around to face Gomorrah. "Sorry, head in the clouds," I said. "I might do something similar here."

"You'll want to reinforce the floors below too," Gomorrah said. "Keep that in mind."

"Right," I said.

She nodded, then awkwardly tapped me on the shoulder. "Well, I'll be seeing you in a little while. Try not to be late."

I chuckled. "Yeah, don't worry. See you at the meeting."

She nodded back and took off toward the edge of the landing pad. The Fury showed up almost the moment she reached the edge, the door sliding open so that she could slip into the driver's seat without having to miss a step. The car tipped away from the building, then shot off through the city.

"Myalis," I said.

Yes?

"I don't know where to begin."

Hesitation doesn't suit you. What are your current goals?

"I think we need to fortify the place. Make it so that the kittens and Lucy can stay here without being in any danger," I said. The current renovations were all about making it livable. That was probably a mistake. They'd make the place nice, I was sure, but they wouldn't make it alienproof.

There are catalogs for such things. Though you run into two possible issues.

"And those are?" I asked.

Time is the first obstacle. If you want to fortify the location rapidly, then you will need to pay an equivalent number of points to obtain materials that require less time to install. For example, a low-cost construction drone could build a decent fortification out of plainly available materials. It would mix its own cements, construct its own reinforcements, and build a secure area over time with commercially available materials.

"But that'll take time," I said.

Several weeks, for a location as large as this one. A drone of the sort could be ordered to assist human workers, improving on their designs and building things faster.

"And your faster solution?" I asked.

A prebuilt building could be purchased. In fact . . . this might be somewhat expensive, but if you tore apart the entire top floor of the building, you could purchase a new floor.

"Wait, like . . . the entire floor?"

You would need a construction drone to go over the anchoring points. But yes. It can be teleported in with nanometer precision. The same construction drone could be used to clear the top of the building, or at least assist the construction company on location in doing the same, and afterward it could work to reinforce the rest of the building.

"Huh," I said. It would save a lot of time. And I was willing to bet that anything I ordered from a catalog would look better and be tougher than anything the locals could build. "We'll need to account for the gun emplacement above, and for a few other things, I guess. Wires and pipes and all that."

That is true. I can draw up a blueprint for the contractors telling them what to leave in place and where.

I nodded. "How much would that cost?"

The construction drones would cost two hundred fifty points per unit. You only need the one for now, though I would suggest purchasing a second and third soon. The actual floor will depend entirely on what features you want. On the lower end, a simple building made of unhardened materials would cost one thousand two hundred points. The upper end is nearly limitless.

"We'll want something that covers the whole floor, with a landing pad and all. We need rooms for all the kittens, and a room for Lucy and me. Kitchen, bathrooms. You know, all that stuff. Uh, probably glass too? I don't want a bunker, you know?" I said. I was really just tossing ideas out as they came to me.

A tab opened in my augs, and a mockup for the top floor appeared, slowly spinning around. It was nice. A sharp slope, with long ledges next to the landing area and geometric lines cut into something that looked like metal plates, with a garden to one side and a second landing area near the roof next to the gun emplacement Longbow had left behind.

"That looks bigger than what we have now," I said.

We can't build down, so why not build up and out? This is all exterior architecture, without any furnishings on the inside. You will need to purchase those things yourself, though the fittings will all be in place.

"How much?" I asked.

Four thousand five hundred.

"Will it be tough?" I asked.

Reinforced titanium walls, designed for warships; a type of lightweight concrete made to endure extreme wear and tear; and transparent panels made of realigned crystal matrices. The entire thing would be quite difficult to damage.

I started walking toward the head contractor. "Send the blueprint to Lucy, get her input on things. She's got more of a head for that, and more time too. Tell her it's important." I flagged the older guy down and he jogged over, an eager smile on his face. At the same time, I sent a text to Raccoon, telling her to meet me in a few minutes.

The contractor's head bobbed up and down as I explained things to him. He seemed a little worried but eager to do whatever I told him to do, which was good enough for me.

At nearly the moment I was done with the guy, I got two texts. One was from Raccoon, telling me she'd be up in a minute. The other was from Lucy. She wanted to know if things were all right.

I sent her a quick *things are okay, talk later* while I stepped into the museum.

I paused and looked down at myself. My armor had changed to be an offensively bright yellow. "Uh," I said.

You're supposed to be wearing a high-visibility vest within the construction site. A helmet as well, but yours is of greater quality than the OSHA standard requires.

"So you made my armor turn yellow?" I asked.

It fits the requirements.

"It's bulletproof," I said.

Which also complies with security standards.

"Why do you even care about those?" I asked.

I don't. I just wanted to paint a yellow cat on your back.

I sighed. Some things didn't change. "You're such a pain in the ass," I said. I couldn't help the bit of humor that snuck into my voice, though. Myalis was probably trying to destress me a little.

The interior of the museum was a mess of torn-down walls, stacks of materials, and piles of trash that hadn't been picked up yet. The far end of the space wasn't so bad, though. I found some security cordon tape blocking access to the room where Lucy and I had placed the matter reconfiguration machine.

It still sat pretty in the end of the armory, big and shiny and . . . next to a row of stacked blocks?

I walked over to the blocks and knelt next to them. They were about ten centimeters long and two thick and wide, little rectangular blocks of different colors with letters engraved on their sides: *Fe, Co, Cr.* There were some little numbers too, but I glossed over those. Some of the blocks were clearly canisters too. Were those gases?

It seems that Raccoon has been busy.

"What are these?" I asked. The stacks were actually pretty large.

Elements. Purified and reconstituted into usable blocks for material printing. They're one of the possible end results that the reconfiguration machine can produce. An easy way to store metals, essentially.

I stood up and took in all the stacks of blocks. Some were by far more common than others. How much time had Rac spent feeding the machine?

"Well, that's something."

CHAPTER TWO

THE SCROUNGER

People used to mock preppers a lot. To be fair, the entire culture around the movement—if you can even call it a movement—was pretty strange. Paranoia that was being acted upon, lots of conspiracy theories, and strange people with too much time on their hands.

Then the aliens actually showed up, and the entire thing changed. Now it's less a fringe group and more just . . . something everyone with a lick of common sense does.

—Interview with Liz Maybirb,
Director of the Ready Community group, 2029

"Hey, boss!"

I jumped at the sound and turned to find a familiar face bouncing over to me. Raccoon looked healthy. Dirty, but healthy. She had overalls on, stained and covered in cuts and wrinkles. She was lugging around a backpack that looked like it would have been big on an adult man; it was huge on her and entirely filled with a clanging assortment of metal trash.

"Hey, Rac," I said. I placed the metal ingot I had back onto the pile and reached down to rub the kid's head.

She ducked under my hand and shot me a look that was soon replaced by a nearly feral grin. "You like my work so far?" she asked.

I glanced back at the stacks of metal. "So far you've been doing great," I said. "Is this all you've been doing?"

"Pretty much, yeah. Started with the trash in this building, and I've been expanding out. The best thing about trash is that it's a renewable resource. In a couple of days I can return to where I started, and there'll be a whole new heap of it to dive through, you know?"

"Sounds . . . handy?" I tried. Dumpster diving didn't sound like what I'd call a fun pastime. Or a safe one, for that matter. Then again, lately my newest hobby was making things that were trying to eat me explode, so I was going to keep my stone collection firmly inside my glass house. "I came over to see how you were doing, and to, ah, give you some news, I guess."

"What sort?" Rac asked. She slid past me and to the large machine dominating the end of the room. With practiced ease she opened the hopper at the back of it, slid her backpack off, then started filling the empty receptacle up with scrap. The machine hummed, and a large progress bar appeared on its main screen, with smaller bars beneath labeled with the names of metals.

"Well, first, we're going to tear apart most of the top floor of this building. I'm going to buy a new one outright. It'll be teleported in place. Should be pretty neat."

"Whoa," Rac said. "That does sound kind of awesome. Like just . . . zap-bang and there's a new building?"

"Part of a building," I said. "Just the topmost floors. I asked the building crew to move the matter reconfiguration machine over to the room where Longbow's gun is stored. I . . . need to send him a text about that, actually. Anyway, it should be safe."

"Am I gonna be out of work, then?" Rac asked.

"For a few hours, maybe," I said. "You have a place to sleep?"

"Usually just sleep there," Rac said. She gestured to a corner of the room. I hadn't really noticed the blankets in the corner. I'd kind of just assumed they were some random junk left behind. "I can find a place, don't worry."

"Right," I said. "You're welcome to stay here once everything's in place. Ah, that's the other thing. We're going to start producing prosthetics. Like, cheap but functional ones. I still need to talk to someone about that, but we'll probably start production tomorrow. It'll likely use up a lot of the materials you've collected."

The machine hissed, and the front opened to reveal a neat stack of bars next to some small, squarish tubes. Not all of them were metal. In fact, about half the ingots looked like they were plastic, and the tubes were clearly filled with some sort of liquid, or maybe gases?

It kind of made sense; if the machine was breaking scrap down to basic elements, then it would have to deal with some elements being liquid or gaseous or whatever.

"I can always collect more," Rac said. "It's not a big deal."

"Cool," I said. "Besides, it's for a good cause. You know, giving poor folks new limbs and shit?"

Rac nodded. I couldn't tell if she was happy about that or not, not while she was meticulously placing the ingots she got into neat stacks.

"One other thing, the world's going to end in, like, thirty-ish hours."

Rac's stack of plastic ingots crashed to the floor with a clatter. "It's gonna what?" she asked.

"Turns out the aliens have been building a lot of hidden hives, and they're all going to activate at about the same time. So we'll be dealing with a massive surge of Antithesis trying to attack . . . pretty much everyone everywhere, all at the same time."

"That's seriously fucked."

"I know," I agreed. "We're going to stop it, of course, but it's going to ruin a bunch of plans, I bet. It's why I want to fortify this place before we get flooded with aliens."

"Shit," Rac said. "You need help with anything?"

I was about to shake my head when I paused. "I might. Can you take care of shit here for me? At least until Lucy and the kittens move over? Also, I wouldn't mind one more person keeping the kittens safe."

Rac nodded, but her eyes narrowed and she looked at me judgingly. "You're not just saying that so that I'll stay with the other kids where I'll be safe, right?"

"No?"

"Uh-huh."

I grinned and jerked my head toward the door. "I've got some calls to make and some shit to look into. Stay safe, all right?"

"Yeah, yeah, no worries," Rac said. "I think I've got time for another scrap run before I need to find food."

We didn't really say goodbye. Neither of us was formal enough for that kind of thing. I just headed out and paused in the corridor just outside the room.

"I need to make a call," I muttered as I opened up a phone app from my augs. I paused. "Or maybe just send an email?"

To whom?

"Peter Silverbloom, the nonprofit guy."

He'd been pretty nice during our last meeting. Even if that meeting had lasted all of a few minutes. If he was as legit as he wanted to appear, then he'd be willing to bend a bit to let me help him better. Also, he knew a lot of the more community-based groups in the city. If anyone would know how to get people ready for the oncoming apocalypse, it would be him.

I decided to call him. It was less impersonal than an email or a message. That, and I wasn't so great with written words.

The line rang twice before Peter answered. "Hello?" he asked. He sounded out of breath.

"Hey, Peter, it's Cat," I said. "You all right?"

"Huh? Oh, yes. I had to jog a bit to catch the train. Sorry. I'm fine now. How can I help? Is this about the clinic?"

"Yeah, a bit," I said. "I'm getting things ready for that on my end, but we might have a bit of a problem."

"What sort?" Peter asked.

"You know those aliens that like eating people? We're about to get swarmed by a fuckload of them from all sides across the entire planet, all at once. We have maybe a day to really prepare for it. So I was thinking that maybe we should focus on that kind of thing. I still want to set up a clinic, but I was thinking of maybe having it be at my place? It'll be safer. I think a lot more people will be needing medical attention in the coming weeks."

"Uh," Peter said. "Are you serious?"

"Deadly, yeah."

"Dang."

I blinked. *Dang?* Really? This guy needed to be less nice. "Look, just call up whoever you think can help with this shit. I don't imagine things getting better anytime soon, but maybe we can soften the blow a bit."

"Will you be fighting?" he asked.

"Yeah. I don't know the details on that yet. We might need volunteers to man the walls. Or to build walls to man. It's going to be a whole thing."

"All right. I'll do what I can. Thanks for reaching out."

"You're welcome," I said. "Get me the stuff for that clinic . . . say tomorrow afternoon? My place should be built by then."

"All right. Thank you, Stray Cat."

I ended the call, then leaned against the nearest wall, just basking in the sounds of the construction crew tearing the place apart. There were so many things to take care of at once.

I couldn't wait for the Antithesis to arrive. At least then some of the weight on my shoulders would be lifted.

CHAPTER THREE

THE LITTLE MEET

In a world increasingly led by corporate and nongovernmental entities, it's becoming clear that in order to secure its personnel, obtain the funding needed to operate, and remain at the top in terms of lethality, the modern army will have no choice but to change its fundamental structure.

This isn't a new thing. Historically, many nations were protected by armed forces that had a more . . . mercenary edge to them. This is just a return to the good old days, when lining our pockets with coin was more important than decorating our chests with valor.

—General Blackmill, *Treaties on the Future of Armed Warfare*, 2026

Under any normal circumstance, I would have avoided the meeting like the plague.

Myalis had easy access to the guest list, and it wasn't inspiring. Of the nearly three hundred people in attendance, three quarters were the sort of people I wouldn't piss on if they spontaneously combusted.

Mostly, that number was made up of politicians from the city and the country and their entourages, and then there were a heap of C-suite representatives from just about every corporation that had business in the city. From what I could tell, the invitation, despite being sent out at the last minute, came with a sort of "you'd better be there" tone that everyone chose to respect.

The last quarter was the one I was most interested in. New Montreal had two dozen paramilitary groups based in it. Some of those were small, and most were just branches from one corporation or another, but others were more like Clenze Private Military, Inc. The same group that had cordoned off the incursion . . . was it just last week?

They wouldn't be alone; the rest of the guest list was made up of representatives of various police, EMT, and firefighting companies in the city, as well as a big group from the army.

I rode my hoverbike around the building that was hosting the event. It wasn't anything too special. A midtier hotel in one of the less busy parts of

New Montreal, which wasn't to say that the traffic wasn't awful, but it wasn't smack in the center of downtown.

I let the hoverbike guide itself to a landing spot inside the hotel on auto-pilot. I still wanted to learn how to fly the thing properly, but I had too many things on my mind all at the same time to really have time to worry about that.

"So, are the best of the best waiting for us already?" I asked as the bike slowed to a stop. There was a parking level right in the middle of the hotel, with car elevators to the side where people could park their vehicles and have them disappear below and out of sight until they called them back up. I didn't bother with any of that and just brought my bike over to the side of the nearest entrance and deployed the kickstands.

For a certain definition of "the best." It seems as though most corporations have heeded the call and have sent some representatives here, but only a few of them are actually what you would consider important members of the corporation. The political side of things is mostly filled with interns and assistants. Only the military and paramilitary representatives are actually well ranked.

I shifted my shoulders to loosen them a bit. I really needed to have Lucy play with my back some more to get rid of some of the stress. "Why are we only getting the dregs here?"

I suspect that the message calling for this assembly was couched in terms that suggested its importance but didn't divulge the entire truth of the incoming mass incursion.

"Trying to prevent people from panicking?" I asked. I'd heard that kind of excuse before. It made some sense, but it never entirely sat well with me.

It's more likely that it's to prevent people from trying to profit from the news.

That made a lot more sense.

I ignored the valets and hotel staff milling by the entrance. The place was nice, but it lacked the elegance and . . . classiness of the hotel that Deus Ex had dumped the kittens in. I wasn't exactly an expert in that kind of thing, though. The entrance was still nice. A tall ceiling, some benches with plants dotting the room here and there, and a long reception desk at the rear. It was all done up in chrome and black faux-marble. Very 2040s.

A hovering sign with arrows and QR codes floated in the middle of the lobby.

2000h—City/Corp-wide Announcement from Laserjack, hosted by the Family

2030h—Mixed Armed Forces Meeting, hosted by the Family

2100h—Open Forum on Contingencies and Collaterals, hosted by the Family

Looking at the QR codes automatically downloaded a map of the hotel, with the meeting rooms highlighted for me already. "Right," I muttered. "Who's Laserjack?"

A Vanguard member of the Family who generally works along the Eastern Seaboard of North America. He specializes in social technology.

"Not lasers?"

The name does seem to be somewhat misleading.

I hesitated. There was a large digital clock above the lobby counters that read 20:05. I wasn't exactly on time. Did I want to step into the political meeting now, or wait a bit and join the military meeting later?

I could do both meetings, but I wasn't sure if my patience would be able to handle that much sitting down and listening.

The choice was made for me. A woman in a uniform walked my way. She looked somewhat familiar, tall with orange hair, the Clenze logo on her breast. "Stray Cat," she said before snapping a quick salute. "Pleasure to meet you again."

"Uh, hey," I said. "You're . . . Major Hunt?" the woman towered a head above me, and even her happy grin didn't make her any less intimidating. Hell, I was the one in the power armor; it wasn't fair that she be scarier.

"You remember my name. It's an honor. We were told that there would be samurai in attendance, but I didn't expect this many."

"Well, I just know of two so far," I said.

She nodded. "Laserjack, Sam-o Ray, Cause Player, Grasshopper, Gomorrah, and now yourself. More firepower and danger in one location than I've ever personally witnessed."

"Gom's here?" I asked. That was great. I wasn't entirely sure if she would show up to the event at all. The only other samurai on that list that I recognized was Cause Player, and I hadn't seen him since the mini-incursion over in Black Bear.

"I believe she's waiting by the meeting room for the Mixed Armed Forces meeting," Major Hunt said. "Most of the other samurai are there, with the exception of Laserjack."

"Right, he's hosting that other meeting," I muttered. "Mind showing me the way to the fun meeting?"

"Certainly," Major Hunt said. "I just stopped to greet you. It behooves one to keep in touch with those who are particularly talented at killing xenos."

"Uh-huh," I agreed.

She started walking back across the room, as if expecting me to keep up. I had to jog to catch up. "Do you know what all of these meetings are about? This all seems rather unprecedented."

"You haven't heard yet?" I asked.

She shook her head. "We haven't. If the higher-ups know, then it hasn't been disseminated to my level yet."

"I guess it's just a small spoiler, then, since the whole meeting will be about it. We're expecting a mass incursion."

"Soon?"

"In a few dozen hours," I replied. "It's not going to be a normal one. No big rifts in the sky with aliens pouring out. Just a lot of aliens showing up all over and spreading."

"Like a stealth incursion?"

I nodded. "Like that, but everywhere and all at once. If we're not on top of it, we'll be dealing with hundreds of little hives across the world."

"That . . . is troublesome," she replied. "Depending on the severity, that could mean anything from a worldwide halt to all industry while the hives are burned out to a near-extinction-level event."

"I think the whole goal of these meetings is to try to encourage things to be on the less shit side of things," I said. "I figure with a dozen samurai at the helm, things are going to go pretty well, at least around New Montreal."

The major didn't say anything, not for a bit, but her brows did draw together. "Having more officers at the helm doesn't always help as much as you would think," she said. "Sometimes all that means is that there are more chances that everything will be pulled in the wrong direction."

With those ominous words hanging in the air, we arrived at the meeting room.

I was expecting some sort of auditorium, with seats lined up toward a stage.

Instead, the meeting was going to take place in a large room dominated by a huge oval table. About forty chairs sat around the table, with little microphones in front of them and a few pitchers of cool water set in strategic locations.

Some were filled already, by mercs and people in neat uniforms, and, of course, by a few samurai who couldn't help but stand out from the crowd.

I waved to Gomorrah, who was near the far wall, with Franny next to her, then continued to take in the room and its occupants.

The weight on my shoulders only grew heavier.

CHAPTER FOUR

HOW TO STALL THE END
OF THE WORLD

Words like "Caucasian" and "African American" became far too loaded and controversial, not to mention inaccurate as time progressed. So, in order to alleviate some of the issues that came from the use of these words, a system was created that properly categorized a person based on ethnicity, origin, and appearance.

It worked similar to the Dewey Decimal System that categorized books, with multiple sets of numbers meaning different things. The system could accurately convey a person's history and ethnicity in a single string of letters and numbers.

This was widely viewed as a terrible idea and was quickly discontinued.

—Lecture on the Sociological Impact of Titles in the Information Age,
Professor Adams, 2029

Major Hunt pointed to a seat near the middle of the table. There was a little hovering placard in front of it that had my name on it. Well, it said "Stray Cat," which was sort of my name, at least in present company. "That's your seat," she said.

"I guess so. Where are you sitting?" I asked.

"Back room. There's a feed of this meeting room. It's where all the less-important people are sitting and listening in," she said.

"A major doesn't rank high enough to participate?" I asked.

"Not here, no," she said. She smacked me on the shoulder before moving past. "Good luck, samurai. And remember, the first priority is making those xenos burn."

"Yeah, yeah," I said. I watched her go for a bit, then moved over to my designated seat. It happened to not be too far from Gomorrah's, so I was able to see her mask and nod as I sat. We were just far enough apart that conversation aloud would be awkward, though.

Gomorrah nodded back, then turned to Franny. "Want to go hang out in the back? I'm sure they'll make room for you."

"Better back there than up here," Franny said. She patted Gomorrah on the shoulder. "I'll see if they have anything worth eating around here. I'm feeling peckish."

Gomorrah whispered something back, but I chose not to listen in—that is, until she turned back toward me. "Did you handle everything that needed handling?"

"Not even half of it," I said. "You get your own stuff in order?"

Gomorrah took a deep breath, then let it out as a long-suffering sigh. "No. Not everyone took the news as well as I would have liked. Then again, I could hardly expect them to. The nuns are already run ragged taking care of the people we saved from the sewers. We're going to end up with a lot more people who need saving in the next few weeks."

"They do a lot of post-incursion stuff, right?"

Gomorrah nodded. "They're still sending some sisters out to deliver blankets and supplies to people from the last incursion. The timing here is kind of terrible."

"Huh, yeah, I guess. Anything I can do to help?"

"Kill the aliens fast?"

I chuckled, and a moment later, Gomorrah joined in. "Should have seen that answer coming," I said. "Hey, change of topic. You know any of the other samurai here?"

Gomorrah gestured to the end of the table. Cause Player was there. His armor had changed. It was still green, though a darker shade, and it looked a lot more streamlined and angular than last time. A bit more scuffed too. The number 117 was stenciled onto his right breastplate, and he seemed to be talking to a bluish hologram hovering over his hand.

"Right," I said. "Haven't seen him since Black Bear."

"It'll be nice to have him around," Gomorrah said. "He's versatile, and I think we might need that."

I nodded along. There were a few others in the room. One in the corner, lurking in the shadows. He, or at least I figured it was a he from the shoulders and stance, had form-fitting black armor on, with lots of belts and straps across his torso. He had a long polearm hanging over his shoulder too, some high-tech thing that I couldn't guess the function of.

"I don't know him," Gomorrah said as she followed my gaze. "The woman on the ceiling is Grasshopper."

"Ceiling?" I looked up, and blinked.

There was indeed someone squatting upside down on the ceiling. She wore light brown and beige armor, covered in little spikes. Her helmet had two large black spheres on the front. They looked like comically oversized eyes from below. She turned her head, almost mechanically, and faced me.

Grasshopper raised . . . lowered a hand, and waved.

I waved back.

"She's a range specialist," Gomorrah said. "Been around for a couple of years."

"Neat," I said. "Not a celebrity sort?"

Gomorrah shook her head. "She's known, but she doesn't run after attention. Mid–twenty thousands on the leaderboards."

That still placed her way higher than I was on the popularity charts.

"Who's he?" I asked, pointing to someone not too far away. I wasn't entirely sure if he was a samurai at all. He wore armor made of white plates, decorated by thin black lines that seemed to almost be painted on. They formed an intricate, almost tribal pattern across the armor. His helmet was on the table, leaving his long brown hair free.

He turned my way and grinned, showing off perfect teeth. "I'm Sam-o Ray," he said. "You can ask, I don't bite."

"Uh, hey," I said. "I'm Stray Cat."

"Pleasure to meet you, little sister!" he said. His voice was the kind that couldn't be contained, and it boomed out of him with genuine geniality.

"And I'm Gomorrah," Gomorrah replied. She nodded to him and he smiled right back, unaffected by the frowning mask she wore.

"Ah, I am meeting so many companions today. It's a good day, despite all the news, isn't it?"

"Uh, yeah, sure," I said. I didn't quite know how to deal with someone so optimistic and happy. Well, no, Lucy could be that way, but I wasn't going to deal with this guy the way I dealt with her. "So, those patterns on your armor, is that for, like, a shield or something?"

He blinked, then tilted his head back and laughed. "No! No no, little Stray Cat. These are my tatau. I have them printed onto my armor as they are on my skin. I would much prefer to be without the armor, but my pride won't stop a bite, and besides, it's cold around here."

"Huh, that's neat," I said.

Sam-o Ray nodded. "I thought so too."

I was going to ask him a few more questions, just shit to pass the time, when someone cleared their throat. A man was standing at the front of the table, gesturing to others to find their seats. He was a tall fellow, with a well-tailored suit and a crown sitting atop his head.

"Hello, everyone," he said. His voice was transmitted across the room to a few speakers tucked away in the corners. "My name is Jolly Monarch. I'll be the one directing this meeting."

Another samurai? He did have a few interesting scars on his face, but his darker skin hid them well. I guessed that the crown was something of a giveaway.

"We don't have all that much time, nor do I want this to go on for too long. As of right now, every hour we have has to be used to its utmost, and that means wasting as few as possible. For that reason, we won't be going over introductions and will begin right away. We're a few minutes ahead of schedule, but everyone who will be here is here already."

Jolly Monarch gestured, and a hologram flicked to life above the table: Earth, floating in empty space while rotating in a slow circle. Red dots started to appear on the surface, mostly around that big space that I vaguely recognized as Russia, then spreading out in every direction like a ripple. The last place to be covered in little dots was South America.

"Sometime in the next twenty-four hours, we expect to get hit by approximately three thousand stealth incursions."

"Fuck," someone lower down the table said.

Judging by the murmurs from the nonsamurai around us, they hadn't all gotten the memo. I glanced around, taking in a lot of people in suits and more in military-like uniforms. There had to be reps from half a dozen PMCs in the room.

"Our focus," Jolly Monarch said, "will be this area."

The holomap changed to a view of New Montreal from above, as well as a big circle around the city. It extended out maybe a hundred kilometers in diameter.

"The New Montreal area is, in terms of sheer space, minuscule. But it also represents the location where nearly a hundred million people live. Our task is to set up a defensive perimeter around the city to keep it safe while also preparing strike groups that will head out and destroy any hives in this area."

A second circle appeared, maybe twice the size of the first. As the hologram panned out, it overlapped with some other circles next to other cities to the south, east, and west.

"Now that we're all on the same page," Jolly Monarch started (it was pretty damned clear that we weren't, but he seemed eager to plow past) let's figure out exactly how we can stall the end of the world. Shall we?"

CHAPTER FIVE

LOGISTICS

A plan's complexity is tied to a logarithmic increase in the difficulty to provide logistical support to the pawns involved in said plan.
>
> —Tin Man, professional RTS player, 2025

It was incredible how a meeting that would literally determine whether hundreds of millions of people lived or died could devolve into something so incredibly boring in the span of a couple of minutes.

Jolly Monarch and his AI had scanned the environment around the city and had plotted out the best locations for fortifications, outposts, defensive structures, and rally points. The plan looked pretty sound to me, but a few of the generals and military sorts had questions about it.

The biggest problem was that the plan assumed that every available soldier, police officer, and hired gun in the city would be willing to man the walls. That was almost stupidly optimistic. Of the two dozen groups in the room, about a quarter were vocally reluctant to participate at all, another quarter would only work for good pay, and yet another quarter were being real quiet about their opinions, and I had the impression they were as likely to bolt as they were to stay and help.

Interestingly, the plan didn't give any of the samurai present fixed locations. Instead, we were told that we'd be called in, as available, to handle any large surges in the oncoming incursion. Jolly Monarch had some sort of Family-based system that could predict who would be best where, more or less.

So, I could expect to either volunteer to stem the tide or be called over to wherever things were at their worst to take some of the burden off the normal folks manning the walls.

The meeting was supposed to last an hour. By the third, I was practically nodding off in my seat.

Jolly Monarch knocked his knuckles on the table. I wasn't the only one to jump. "And that'll be the end for the meeting today. We have nearly every construction crew in the city heading to the outskirts in the morning. If things go well, by the end of next month there should be a wall all the way around New Montreal. Payments, shifts, and deployment orders will be sent out from the offices of the Family. Feel free to email us any additional concerns and needs."

The older samurai adjusted his crown, and then with a nod to the lot of us, he backed away from the table.

I was caught a bit flat-footed by the sudden end to the meeting.

Generals and PMC leaders stood up, some forming little cliques that whispered between each other. In the center of the room, an AR hologram of New Montreal continued to circle around slowly.

It only took me a moment to spot the museum. It was clear that the projection was somewhat real-time. Half the upper floor was outright missing, and I could make out tiny pixel-wide figures moving around.

The museum wasn't on the edges of New Montreal, but it wasn't in the center either. Jolly Monarch had highlighted areas of higher and lower risk, and we were bordering one of the higher-risk parts.

That last incursion a few days ago had wrecked that part of the city, and any defenses that might have been there were in bad need of replacement or repair.

"Cat?"

I glanced to the side and found Gomorrah standing next to me. "Hey," I said.

"You all right?" she asked.

I nodded. "Yeah, just a lot on my mind. Sorry. I think it'll get easier in a few days, you know?"

"Once all we have to worry about is an unending tide of man-eating monsters pouring out of the countryside to eat us all?" Gomorrah asked.

"Yeah. That's a lot easier to handle. Mentally, I mean. Just kill the aliens. No politics, no dealing with people, no making hard choices. Well, not super-hard choices, at least."

Gomorrah tilted her head to the side, just a little bit. It was a gesture I'd caught her doing a few times, her thinking pose. "I guess so. There is some beauty in simplicity. I'm not sure if it's okay to look forward to such a destructive event. But I'll admit that I'm itching for a fight too."

"More things to burn?" I asked.

She sniffed. "I'm not some barbarian."

"You're a burnbarian."

Gomorrah stared at me. I could feel the judgment wafting off the mask. *I can say with rigorous certitude: that was terrible.*

I chuckled and got to my feet. "Well, that lifted my spirits a little. So, you brought Franny along? Is this your idea of a date?"

"It's nothing like that. I think she was as nervous about staying at the church as I was. Heavy as the conversations here are, they're still less stressful than dealing with the people back home."

"Ouch," I said. "You need a place to stay? We can kick some of the kittens out of their room at the hotel."

"You'd evict a child from their room so that I have a place to stay?" Gomorrah asked. "I don't know if that's cruel or hospitable, honestly."

"I mean, you could have the couch too. They're kids, they can sleep on the floor."

"Truly you are the embodiment of motherliness," Gomorrah said.

I snorted. "Fuck off, I'd make a great parent and you know it."

"I shudder to imagine."

"So, that kind of shit aside, I think I've made up my mind. I'm going to be spending a whole lot of points tonight. Going to secure that museum, make it a safe spot for the kittens and Lucy. Maybe something of a base, you know?"

Gomorrah nodded. "That's not a terrible idea. I don't think this situation will end in us losing the city, but if it comes to a protracted siege, then a samurai-secured place or two wouldn't hurt." She went quiet for a moment until I received a call from her.

I answered while shutting off the exterior mics on my helmet. "Yeah?"

"Also, between you and me. I suspect the meeting tomorrow morning between all the local samurai will be putting a lot of pressure on us to perform the way the Family thinks is best. They can't force you to spend points you no longer have, though."

I hadn't considered that. For that matter, I didn't think the Family would really push us that hard. Then again, they did have something of a stick up their asses sometimes. "Thanks for the heads-up," I said. "I'm heading back there now."

Gomorrah nodded and extended a hand to shake.

I pulled her into a quick hug instead, with a few good pats on her back for good measure. "Give Franny a hug for me," I said as I started to head out.

I could feel her eyes rolling behind me.

Sam-o Ray gave me a nod on the way out, but other than that, no one slowed me down as I headed out of the hotel and to the parking garage where my hoverbike waited for me.

What sort of big purchases are you aiming to make?

"That depends, I guess. What's my point total at?"

Current Point Total: 10,494

I nodded as I swung a leg over the bike and made sure my coat was sitting right. "All right. First priority is the museum. I want it secure as hell. Did you get into contact with Lucy about it?"

She's been playing with designs for the last few hours, between watching over the kittens and asking me about your status. She has more or less chosen one design and has been making minimal adjustments to it for the past hour.

"Cool," I said. "Tell her to finish it up. We'll be installing it tonight. Right, after that . . . I want construction and repair drones. Maybe with their blueprints? I want to be able to fix up the rest of the building. It's less urgent, but it's still a priority."

You don't own the rest of the building. It's possible that the other owners will complain.

"Let them," I said.

Noted. A single construction drone provided with limitless resources could properly reinforce the tower in the span of several weeks.

"I want to do more than that," I said. "We need to do more, and faster. Turrets. We need a blueprint for something small and easy to install. Maybe something that doesn't need to be reloaded? Like lasers or something."

A small laser emplacement, with a solar cell for power generation and a connection to the city's grid might work. A blueprint can be drawn up for something small enough to be built from your fabrication machine.

"That sounds perfect," I said.

Though something so small will have a difficult time against anything in the third tier and above.

"That's fine. We'll upgrade things as we go." I shot out of the parking lot and beelined for the sky. "For now, let's just get a good, secure place where we won't have to worry about aliens."

CHAPTER SIX

KITTY CAT PALACE

There's value in memes, you know?

It's a bitch to quantify it, but it's there. Anything that's instantly recognizable by a large number of people has value. Maybe not value that can be instantly transformed into capital, but cultural and social value, and sometimes that can be worth a lot more than just money.

—"So You're a Meme, Now What?," pamphlet, 2024

I hovered over the museum, some hundred meters over the top of it, my arms crossed so that my elbows were leaning against the handlebars of my bike. Below me, the last of the contractors were moving away, large hovering dumpster trucks flying with all the skill and precision of whales while smaller hovercraft darted away.

Renovating the museum would take weeks.

Destroying it had taken hours.

The one was much easier than the other, and I bet if I were a more poetic sort of soul I'd find something meaningful to say about that.

"Is everything ready?" I asked.

It's unlikely. While the contractors are professionals, they were in a hurry to execute your orders.

"Then we'll start with the construction drones," I said. "Two of them should be enough, right?"

A single construction drone could, given materials and the infrastructure with which to recharge itself, rebuild this city from scratch. The issue is less the number of drones and more the amount of time you're willing to give them to work. And to preempt your question, since the work is mostly done I suspect it would take one drone approximately an hour to check and finalize the work. It would take two less than half that time.

"Less than half the time?" I asked.

The work-time-to-workers ratio isn't linear.

"All right," I said. I didn't quite get it, but I also didn't care enough to ask for a full-on explanation. "I'm going to need to unlock a new catalog or two, aren't I?"

In this case, it would actually be somewhat cheaper to just purchase one catalog with a wider range than two more-specific catalogs. The three things you're looking for—construction drones, turret emplacements, and specification-precise prebuilt structures—are all available in the Defensive Structures catalog. The catalog costs four hundred points to purchase.

"Steep," I muttered. "All right, let's do it."

New Purchase: Defensive Structures

Points Reduced from . . . 10,494 to . . . 10,094

I winced. My next purchase would drop me below ten thousand points. That sucked, but I could live with it. "All right, the drones next," I said as I shifted on my seat. It was a decently comfortable seat. Some sort of gel padding, if I had to guess. And my armor was decently comfortable too. Still didn't stop me from getting a bit sore from staying in the same position for so long.

I would suggest two Mark II Motherlode Construction Drones. They are fully autonomous vehicles that carry a load of smaller drones with them that can be deployed to fulfill smaller tasks while the main drone takes care of heavier lifting and resource management.

An alternate reality display opened over my cybernetic eye, and I took in a rotating image of the drone. It was an ugly, boxy thing, with a few thrusters on the sides for directional thrust and cutouts all over, likely hiding tools and the aforementioned mini-drones. Definitely one of those designs that was built purely for function over all else. "How much are they?" I asked.

Three hundred points each.

"More than my bike," I said. They could do a whole lot more than just fly around, though. It made sense. "Are they the only option?"

No, there are thousands of varieties of construction drones, though the variety mostly exists to cover a wide range of environments and possibilities. You don't need drones capable of operating underwater, in high-pressure environments, in combat, or in empty vacuum. After narrowing down the list, the Mark II Motherlode Construction Drones seem like the most cost-effective option based on your stated goals. There are cheaper alternatives as well, but you would sacrifice points for build time or convenience. If you want to shop for things yourself, I can assist you there. A lot of Vanguards enjoy the experience of looking for their own equipment.

I shook my head. "Nah, no thanks. That kind of shopping isn't my forte. Anyway, I've trusted you this far. Let's get those drones running."

Technically, they fly.

New Purchase: Mark II Motherlode Construction Drones

Points Reduced from . . . 10,094 to . . . 9,494

The drones appeared out of thin air with no more than a soap bubble's pop worth of noise: two big boxy bricks that clung to the air as if set there by the hand of some clumsy god.

The drones gently turned toward the museum, and then their sides opened and a dozen smaller, more skeletal drones fell out of them and took off toward the building.

Work will start immediately.

"Probably for the best," I said. The Motherlode drones dropped too, and I noticed a lot of eyes turning their way as they approached the museum. They were pretty attention-grabbing for large gray blocks.

Next up should be your largest expense yet.

"We'll want to keep a few hundred points for tomorrow. Just in case. Never know if I might need some very specific piece of equipment before all the fighting starts."

We can work around that. We also need to purchase the blueprints to the turrets that you wanted.

I nodded. "Yeah, good idea. Those'll cost a bit too, I bet."

We can save some points by only purchasing a turret blueprint from an existing catalog. Plasma-Casting Weaponry, Sun Watcher Technologies, and Stealth Technologies all have turret models that might fit all the criteria you're looking for.

"That would be nice. Anyway, the building first. Did Lucy finish up the design?"

She completed two designs. One she labeled as "Serious and Boring," the other as "Fun, Iconic, and Trendy and Cat Should Pick This One."

I rolled my eyes, but I couldn't help the smile that snuck up on me. "That does sound like Lucy's way of naming things. Let's start with the boring one first."

This is the Serious and Boring design.

My eyesight flickered over the museum, and then the building was complete. The addition was slightly opaque, and I could see vehicles moving through it. So just a projection, but a damned realistic one.

The top floor was now a sharp-edged box. The roof tapered in at the edges. There were added landing pads on the sides, as well as a few pillars that stuck out at an angle. "Are those turret emplacements?" I asked.

Indeed. They are there to give any turret placed within them a wide downward firing arc.

It looked pretty modern. Sleek and sharp. It contrasted a bit with the rest of the building, but not so much so that it looked wrong.

I couldn't see much of Lucy's touch in the design. Then I squinted and it was as if the outer walls melted away. The interior was spacious, with lots of rooms and a few corridors connecting everything together. Other than the bedrooms, most areas were open enough that there wouldn't be any places to hide. Lots of upper-floor balconies and half walls separating areas.

It was much bigger than the museum was. Not so much in width and length but in height. There was a dip on one end around Longbow's turret installation, but the rest was much taller. That would wreck his line of sight, I figured.

"All right," I said. "It looks perfectly acceptable. And yeah, a bit boring. What's the other one?"

The projection disappeared, and I found myself looking down at the torn-open top floor of the museum again for just a moment before a new projection flickered into place.

I closed my eyes and sighed. "Dammit, Lucy."

The building now looked like a giant cat.

It wasn't a furry, cartoony sort of cat. More like a sphynx. It was a bit blocky, and the shape was strange, but there was no denying that the entire floor was catlike. The front had a head looking out toward the edge of the city, with a landing space between two paws.

The worst thing was that it looked mostly functional. There were windows hidden along the sides where the walls jutted out as a series of angled panels that looked tough and also imitated fur a bit. The face had windows behind the eyes and what looked like study rooms once I looked past the walls, and the main body of the cat left plenty of room on the inside for living space. Not as much as the previous design, but still plenty.

If anything, I liked the interior of this design more. It was a bit less impersonal.

While the design is amusing, I want to note that I ensured that air circulation, living space arrangement, and defensive installations were optimized before it was finalized. I don't want to compromise too much for aesthetics.

"It looks a bit . . . dammit." I wanted to say "childish," but Lucy had been too clever by half for that. The building didn't look cartoonish at all. It could have been the top floor of a fancy casino, or maybe a themed hotel. "Does it have room for defenses? Like, offensive defenses?"

Panels opened along the cat's back, revealing hidden gun emplacements that were left empty.

Longbow's gun emplacement would have more room too, being right at the base of the cat's neck. It would block one angle of attack, but not the rest.

And the building would be iconic enough that people would know where to find me. Which wasn't a bad thing.

"How much is this thing?"

Seven thousand six hundred points.

"I can't believe I'm going to spend so much on a fucking meme."

CHAPTER SEVEN

HOME SWEET FORTRESS

If you look back at our records—which unfortunately only stretch back to the early 1900s reliably—then you can chart the size of the average person's home through time. It's pretty obvious that from the 1940s onward, the average size of a family's dwelling became significantly smaller year by year.

Now, in the early 2040s, a hundred years after the start of that decline in space, it isn't uncommon for the average person to have under a hundred square feet to call home.

—Quote from a Jon Mott YouTube video, 2042

I sent a text to the construction company foreman, asking him if the area was cleared. Then I sent another to Rac, to make sure she was safe. Apparently she was hanging out with the printer, which had been moved into the room where Longbow was storing his gun. I told her to stay there for the next few minutes. It wasn't far off and it was probably a safe spot for the moment.

And that was it for preparations.

"I think we're ready," I said.

The area is cleared of living people, the struts are cleared, and all structural points have been cleared by your new drones. It seems as though some of the metal used in the construction of the main building was predictably subpar, but it's all still well within tolerances.

"You mentioned the drones being able to fix stuff, right? We'll set them to upgrading the rest of the building later." I hovered down so that I was closer to the building. I couldn't call it the museum anymore, not when the entire top floor was gutted. "Let's do it," I said.

This was going to be, by far, my largest purchase yet. That was a lot of points gone, points I could have spent on guns and armor and toys. Still, it would provide something important. A place for the kittens to stay, a safe place for Lucy to live in. A home.

New Purchase: Custom Building
Points Reduced from . . . 9,494 to . . . 1,894
Such a small name for such a huge point sink.

I looked at the museum, waiting for something to happen. It seemed entirely unchanged, and I wondered if Myalis had made a mistake. "Hey, wher—"

There was a bang, like a car backfiring.

A huge sphynx now sat atop the building, a cloud of dust falling away from it. "Whoa," I said as I pulled my bike back. Everything sat pretty, though. No big explosions, no sudden collapse. I waited, expecting it all to crumble apart, but it held fast.

"Well, then," I breathed out.

Riding my hovercycle around, I flew to the front of the building and came to a gentle landing between the cat's forepaws. My bike's landing legs popped out and I slid off and stepped onto the landing pad.

The huge cat head had looked a bit silly on the plans, but from up close, towering above me, it was actually rather intimidating.

I didn't know if I really had time for a tour, but it would feel weird not to at least check the place out.

The cat's "mouth" had a large set of double doors in it, which slid open as I approached. There was a tiny lobby area, with room to take off shoes and hang up a jacket to the side, and a second set of doors leading deeper into the building. It made a lot of sense to me. It would keep out the cold better, it was a decent place to hide some anti-personnel defenses, and by the looks of it, the room was airtight, with some sort of air circulation system in place that was already humming nearly inaudibly when I stepped in.

"How well equipped is this place?" I asked.

There are hidden solar panels on the roof segments that provide enough power to supply the building's basic requirements. Lighting, temperature control, air filtration, and basic functions such as the automatic doors.

"Neat," I said. The entranceway led into a large room. There were spaces to the sides with half walls around them, like playpens almost. A long table sat in the center of the room, and there was a kitchen at the far back with an arched doorway leading into it.

Stairs rose and dropped to the sides, leading into the rest of the building.

The lower sections are homes; the upper floors have living spaces and access to your new armory and garage and to Longbow's weapons platform and your factory machine. The main bedroom is also on one of the upper floors.

"Nice," I said as I looked around. The walls were all done up in whites and grays, with a few neon splashes of color here and there to spice things up. Lots of RGB lighting, which was important.

I could imagine the kittens having a blast around here. It was definitely nicer than any place we'd ever lived in. Even the hotel wasn't as spacious.

"Bathrooms?" I asked.

Seven of them, including the one for the main bedroom.

"Damn," I muttered. "We're going to need some furniture and shit, aren't we? TVs to distract the kids . . . wifi."

There is internet access already. Though you are correct that there is a distinct lack of furniture. The rooms have beds built into the walls but otherwise lack any spaces to sit or work.

"I guess we'll have to figure that out as we go," I said. I poked into a room to one side and found a nice boxy room with a decently high ceiling, a small slit of a window looking out into the city, and not much else. It could serve as . . . anything, really. There was a lot of potential here.

I got a text from Raccoon and decided to put off visiting the rest of the place in favor of meeting her.

Taking the steps up two at a time, I wandered around the upper floor until I found the reinforced door leading into Longbow's weapons platform. I knocked twice before opening the door.

Rac was lying down on the floor, legs bent and one hand raised before her face. "Oh hey," she said. "Gimme a sec."

"You all right?" I asked.

"Yeah, middle of a game," she said. "The house here yet?"

"Uh, yeah," I said as I glanced past her. Her precious pile of metals and plastics and other materials was stacked up against one wall, and the printer was sitting in the middle of the room on a wooden pallet.

Rac waved her hands dismissively before her, and then she kipped up to her feet. "So what's the plan now?"

"For you?" I asked. "Simple. Myalis, did you narrow down a good turret blueprint?"

Indeed. Two of them, in fact. One I would suggest using around your new base, and another that is more mobile and easy to place, though they are weaker overall. The second requires significantly less maintenance and only needs some sunlight in order to recharge itself.

"Huh," I said. Two options wasn't bad. "What's the first one need, then?"

The first is from your Plasma-Casting Weaponry catalog. It requires more power and to have ammunition fed into it. Its destructive abilities are significantly greater, though. If you intend to protect your home against Antithesis in the third tier and up, then I would consider using these.

Two images of turrets hovered before me. I have to admit I was instantly enamored with the plasma turret. It was a big chonky boy, with a big barrel that had rings around it and a heavy base that looked like it was made to fit on a battleship.

The other turret looked fine. A box with a stubby barrel, some panels around it, and suction-cup-like legs. It was the off-brand IKEA of laser turrets.

"Can't you make that one look less lame?" I asked.

In trying to keep the price low, I forwent any attempt at making the design appealing. I can armor it up for a few points, perhaps add some glowing bits to it?

The design changed, gaining a bulkier frame with some inset holes that glowed from within. The barrel got a bit fatter, and the end of it now looked like the silhouette of a cat's head.

"Stupid, but somehow much better," I said.

What a wonderful way to add ten points to the cost of something. Do you approve of both?

"How dangerous are they?" I asked.

Both are fairly lethal. The laser turret can burn through most first-tier Antithesis in a matter of seconds. The plasma turret can fire a supersonic burst of plasma capable of denting modern tank armor. The fact that the projectile is burning at several thousand degrees Celsius might also add to its lethality. For both blueprints, it will cost you around four hundred and seventy points.

"All right, last big purchase of the day, then," I said.

New Purchase: Heavy Plasma Turret Emplacement Blueprint
Points Reduced from . . . 1,894 to . . . 1,594
New Purchase: Mobile Laser Defense Mechanism Blueprint
Points Reduced from . . . 1,594 to . . . 1,424

I clapped my hands. "All right, Rac, I've got some work for you. How do you feel about turning this place into a fortress that'd make any aliens think twice?"

CHAPTER EIGHT

THE CATS WHO WERE HERDED

The Family is a strange organization. It's one part a corporate entity whose existence revolves around assisting samurai and acting as a logistical support base for them, and one part a club for samurai to hang around at.

The organization is unique in several ways. Notably, it's one of the few corporations whose size has changed frequently over the years. The occasional death of high-ranking members costs the organization much power, but the influx of new members brings in more than enough to counterbalance the loss.

—The Observer's Report, "The Family," July 2047

When I was told that there'd be a meeting with a whole heap of samurai—hosted by the Family, no less—I was expecting something pretty extravagant as a venue. Maybe another hotel at worst. In my mind, though, I imagined I'd be visiting another space station or something equally awesome.

Lucy had been super jealous last night when I'd recounted my visit to Deus Ex's home. She spent more time asking about that than she did worrying about the massive, planetwide alien invasion that was about to go off right on top of us.

She really did have her priorities in order.

We spent a few hours in our PJs, just chatting until, between one blink and the next, I fell asleep. Lucy woke me up with fresh toast and slightly burnt eggs and a kiss that took my breath away.

I really wished that I were back home instead of here. Then again, Lucy was going to spend the day moving the kittens over to the new house, so even if I could stay, it wouldn't be all naps and shower sex.

I shook my head to refocus. As pleasant as those daydreams were, they weren't productive.

The Family had a building in New Montreal. A boxy thing, with no windows and what looked like thick walls. It would have stood out from the rest of the city based on its size alone. It was squat and short and entirely hidden from the main city. The base was placed on the ground, beneath the huge platforms that held up New Montreal.

I had to dip down below street level and along a main road that was filled with large cargo vehicles going back and forth to reach the base. I couldn't for the life of me figure out why they'd decided to build down there. Maybe privacy? But if they'd built above, where every other building in the city was, it would be much easier to slip in without notice.

Did they not have the budget for a nice place? I really doubted it. The Family had a bunch of samurai working for them; they could just kick some corporation out of one of the towers and take the spot over if they really wanted to.

I sighed. When did I start spending so much time thinking about real estate? It was such a boring, adult thing to think about.

My hoverbike glided toward the side of the building, and part of the wall slid to the side to let me into a large parking space.

A few of the cars here were definitely samurai-owned. The Fury was sitting pretty next to something that looked like a mechanical stingray, and next to that was a large bulbous vehicle covered in windows with a complex control seat in the middle of it.

I parked my bike in a free spot, then disembarked as a small head-sized drone hovered over to float near me. "Greetings, Miss Stray Cat. Are you here for the meet-and-greet?"

"I guess I am," I said.

The drone spun. "Please follow me."

I glanced around, but there weren't any other people around, just a well-maintained parking garage. I was spending a lot of time in those lately.

Following the drone, I stepped into an elevator, then waited as it shot down a few floors. Way faster and smoother than a normal elevator, I noticed idly. The doors opened, and the drone hovered out into a lobby. An archway to the side led into a large room with a hodgepodge of desks and seats and couches, all more or less pointing to a half stage at the end of the room.

There were samurai here already.

I recognized the girl in the green armor, Grasshopper, hanging off a wall in a weird squat, a can of soda in one hand with a straw leading up into her mask. She saw me staring and waved.

Sam-o Ray wasn't too far from the entrance, speaking with Gomorrah with wide, happy gestures.

Deeper in, I made out Jolly Monarch talking with a man in a neat suit who I didn't recognize.

There was another person I didn't recognize sitting toward the front of the room, a boy maybe a year older than me, in some fatigues and with a rifle across his lap. Cause Player was speaking to him, perched on a stool that looked reinforced.

"Hey," Gomorrah called out to me. "You showed up, and actually on time."

I sniffed as I walked over. "Why do you say that? I'm not late to stuff. I arrive when I arrive." I nodded to Sam-o Ray. "Hey, big guy, how're you doing?"

"Ah, I'm well, Stray Cat. From the sounds of it you live up to your name," he said with a grin. He had his helmet stuck to his belt, right next to a large handgun. I glanced around the room and noted a lot of guns and weapons just casually strapped on here and there.

"It's grown on me," I said. "If I can use it to get away with some shit, then it's all the better, right? Look at Gomorrah here, she can use her name to excuse her pyromania."

"I am not a pyromaniac," Gomorrah lied.

"Sure," I said. "So, when can we expect this thing to start?" I gestured vaguely toward the stage.

"Soon enough, I think," Sam-o Ray said. "I don't think we'll have more than twenty samurai showing up."

"Just twenty?" I asked.

That was a lot of samurai, more than usually gathered in any one place as far as I knew, but it was still just twenty people.

"More will show up once the action starts," he said. "But trying to wrangle us is like trying to wrangle cats. I think we're lucky that even this many will show up."

"Was that a cat pun?" I asked. I couldn't decide if I was offended or not.

He laughed. "No no, it's just the way it is. There aren't as many of us around as you'd think. And not all of us are keen for a big fight, you know?"

I glanced back as a few more samurai entered the room. Two that looked like they were in plain clothes, with only a couple of tools and guns to show that they weren't normal folks, and, behind those two, a young woman in an all-black goth-punk outfit walked into the room. She had a long polearm hanging off her back.

So, not everyone showing up looked like a total newbie samurai, but a lot of them were obviously not geared up for a big fight.

Then again, maybe they had very subtle gear. Not everyone needed power armor or flame-resistant nun outfits to get the job done.

The room wasn't even starting to feel crowded when someone clapped their hands at the front.

"Guess the show's about to begin," Sam-o Ray said as he glanced over. "Gonna find myself a seat before the good ones are all taken."

I nodded and followed Gomorrah to a sort of boxy couch off to one side.

It was strange having a room with a dozen different kinds of seats, but it did make it feel a little less like a formal meeting.

"Hello, everyone," the guy up front said, his voice carried around the room by a bunch of tiny speakers mounted near the ceiling. "I'm Laserjack, a midtier samurai and member of the Family. For the moment, I'm also in charge of New Montreal's response to the oncoming mass incursion, or at least the samurai-related part of that response. Do note that this does not mean that any of you answer to me. I'm just going to be doing my best to direct and guide you to where you're needed most. I can also be called upon in case you need support or additional equipment, or if you have important information to relay to the others."

He checked over the room to see if anyone had any complaints, then nodded.

"Good. Now, before anything else, we will all be working with each other a lot in the coming days. I thought it would be appropriate to go around and introduce ourselves. I know it's a bit . . . childish, but having a name to put to a face and an idea of each other's capabilities might help a lot down the line. I can start, of course!"

And with that, our strange little meeting began.

CHAPTER NINE

ROUNDTABLE

Host: So let me get this straight, there are two bodies here, right, but both of them are . . . are you?

Twinskull: That's right. I was twins before I became a samurai. And now, thanks to some protector technology, I combined my minds into one.

Host: So both of you—

Twinskull: There's only one of me. I just happen to have two brains and two bodies.

Host: That's incredible! Does it ever get weird, though?

Twinskull: Oh, all the time. I'm used to it now. Sometimes I still wonder which of my stomachs is growling, and seeing out of four eyes takes some getting used to. But it's really handy in a pinch.

—Live interview with Twinskull, July 2028

Laserjack was, I decided, a demented fuck.

No one should be able to stand in front of so many samurai with a shit-eating grin a moment after telling them that they'll all have to do some kindergarten-level self-introduction thing. His grin never even had the common decency to leave as he started.

"My name is Laserjack. I'm thirty-four, I have been a samurai for . . . oh, three years now? My specialties are social manipulation and amplified-light-based weaponry." He bowed his head. "Don't worry, I swear I'm not using any active manipulation equipment on anyone here."

"Fucking what?" a samurai flopped on a love seat behind me asked.

"It's true," Laserjack said. "I make a point of dealing honestly with fellow samurai. Now! Shall we go around willy-nilly and give the shy a way out of speaking, or maybe alphabetical order? We could even start from *J* and work our way around, give those poor *A*-name people a rest. Or we could start from one end of the room and work our way across!"

Someone near the front sighed, and I saw Jolly Monarch shaking his crowned head. "You're a piece of work, Jack," he said. "My name is Jolly Monarch. I'm a long-standing member of the Family. My specialty lies in drone control. Specifically a large number of highly disposable drones. I mostly serve as an information officer. If you have any questions, I always have an ear, no matter the subject."

"Was that a pun?" Gomorrah muttered just loud enough that I was able to pick it out.

Sam-o Ray bounced to his feet. At some point he'd replaced his helmet. "I won't let anyone accuse me of being shy. My name is Sam-o Ray. I specialize in heavy-ray weaponry. If radiation can hurt it, then I can melt it." He waved at the room, then sat right back down.

Cause Player raised a hand without standing. "I'm Cause Player. I do variable weaponry and armor. Mostly I stream all my fights. Hope no one minds."

A couple more samurai introduced themselves. One who looked like an office drone and a young woman in ratty leather armor with three arms.

"I'm Mnemonic. Data control, restoration, hardware hacking."

"I'm Nomad. No specialty. Just like moving around. Happened to be here."

Gomorrah and I looked at each other while a newbie samurai introduced himself—just some guy who had become a samurai in the last week and didn't have much to show for it yet. Not that I could cast stones; I hadn't been a samurai for any longer.

Sighing, I stood up. That fuck Laserjack just kept smiling. He had to know that there was some social pressure fuckery pushing us all to act. "I'm Stray Cat," I said. "I'm from around here. I do stealth and bombs."

"Those two don't go together," someone at the back said.

I half turned to see that it was that goth girl in the all-black armor. I shrugged, then made my armor go invisible as a wave, from my head down to the tip of my feet, just a hand-thick band of transparency. "It's the bomb you don't see that gets you," I said.

"All right," the girl said with a nod. She seemed satisfied enough with that.

Gomorrah stood up next while I sat back down. "Gomorrah, and yes, I'm a nun. My specialty is fire."

"Just fire?" Sam-o Ray asked. He obviously didn't mean it as an insult or anything, not judging by his tone. Just genuine, friendly curiosity.

"If it burns hot enough, it'll purify any problem," Gomorrah said.

The goth was next. I guessed that she was eager to speak up after her little quip earlier. "I'm Emoscythe Mordeath Noir," she said, entirely serious.

I turned in my chair to stare at her. Delivering a name like that, with a straight face, required some serious balls, or someone insane. After looking at her, arms crossed and shoulders set, I decided she might be a bit of both. "What's your gimmick?" I asked. She'd asked about mine, it was only fair.

"I cut things."

I bet she did.

A few seconds passed where no one said anything, and then one of the last samurai in the room who hadn't introduced themselves spoke up. "All right, Laserjack, everyone played your little game, can we move on?" she asked. It was the girl in the green armor.

"You're not going to introduce yourself?" Laserjack asked her.

I couldn't see her face, not through her strangely bug-eyed helmet, but I imagined her eyes were rolling. "I'm Grasshopper. I specialize in long-range ballistic strikes and in not being the center of attention. Happy?"

"You can't imagine," Laserjack said. "Any other takers? No? Well, then! Onward we go! Knowing each other will be somewhat important. While we won't be ordering any of you to go anywhere, we are setting up a system that will warn you of incoming threats."

Laserjack gestured, and I noticed that I received a ping.

Checking it now . . . it's clean. Just a non-updating file. One of my sibling AIs made it.

"You should have received a packet, if you have the hardware to receive it with. It's a map of the region and all the projected hot spots. In the coming days, we're expecting certain hives to become active. Some will head for the city; others will grow faster. Basically, we have a lot of places where having even one samurai could make a big difference, so we're setting up a system."

The wall behind him lit up with a similar map of the region, but this one had large circles on it. "We're giving you all access to our information network. Projected attack vectors, hive locations, and our best guess at the number of Antithesis you might encounter in any given fight and their troop composition. In exchange, we only ask that you keep us informed of which location you're hitting and when. That way we know where to reach you if you need backup, or if the situation changes."

"You won't be directing us at all?" Gomorrah asked.

"Not one whit!" Laserjack said. "If you want to hit a hive as a group, we have something akin to a group finder in place. If you want to help defend a wall or ambush a group of Antithesis or even just do nothing, then feel free to inform us and we'll keep our maps up to date. Mostly, we want to avoid two of you showing up where only one is needed, so the map will update to show you who is working where, who might be in need of assistance, and so on."

That sounded pretty reasonable.

Laserjack gestured to the map. "Areas in blue are fine; areas in yellow mark locations of suspected or possible Antithesis presence. Those of you who are used to doing cleanup work might want to focus on those areas. And the red areas."

He paused as part of the map lit up in red. Just a little sliver along the east side of the city, right where the blue smudge of a river passed.

"That map is live," he said.

"Ah, shit," someone who caught on faster than me said.

If that map was live, then that red smudge there meant trouble.

"Well, then," Laserjack said. "Looks like things have started! And a few hours early at that! Don't you love it when plans don't even manage to make it to first contact?"

Grasshopper stood up and started toward the door. "I live near there. I'll go take a look," she said before casually leaving.

I got up too. If things were starting now, then I wanted the kittens and Lucy moved before the air filled with panicking maniacs. "I'm heading out too. I'll use that system of yours, Laserjack, don't worry."

"Aww, I didn't even get to the parts where you can request orbital strikes. But yes, I suppose I can send the rest of my presentation over as a data packet. Good luck, samurai. Make sure the city doesn't burn!"

I snorted as I headed out, Gomorrah keeping pace with me.

This entire meeting hadn't gone how I expected it to, but maybe that was for the best.

It was nice to know that for the foreseeable future all I'd have to deal with was a flood of aliens to kill.

CHAPTER TEN

MARKETING YOUR WAY HOME

Work sucks.

A lot of people say it, but it's not true. Work itself isn't awful. It can be satisfying; it can be something you look forward to. Working with others you enjoy, creating something that will go down in history, becoming better and earning enough to live a comfortable life. There are a lot of reasons why work can be an enjoyable, fulfilling activity.

The problem is that in order to create work like that, the entire system needs to be willing to take big steps and make big sacrifices. Those cut into a company's profits, and a company only exists to generate profits.

So yeah, work doesn't suck, but yours probably does.

—Precision Headhunter Company CEO,
teleconference on the joys of work, 2024

I crashed into Lucy and pulled her to me.

My worries crashed into her too, like a freight train barreling down a slope at full speed, then meeting the face of a mountain.

She grabbed me closer, returning the hug even as I buried my face in the big mess that was her poofy hair. "I love you too," she said. As far as greetings went, it was just about perfect.

"Mm-hmm," I agreed. I pulled back enough to press my lips to hers. It wasn't a sexy kind of kiss, though, just contact, a reply, I guess.

Look, I was never good with the romance stuff.

"So, uh," I said. "The museum's a house now."

Lucy laughed. "Is it? You picked the giant cat shape, right?"

"It's kind of iconic," I said.

"Ironic, more like," she shot back before spinning out of my grasp. A few of the kittens were milling around. The Twins were in the kitchen space, barely visible over the island, and a few others were in the living room, a movie blaring on the big screen.

"Do you have a lot of things to pack away?" I asked. "The kittens?"

"A few things," she said. "You want to move us over?"

"Right away," I confirmed.

Her eyebrows shot up. "Really?"

"Yeah. There's aliens on the edge of the city already. I don't know if there are enough soldiers between them and us for me to be comfortable. The museum . . . ex-museum's probably safer than the hotel. Or it will be soon enough."

Lucy nodded. "I'll wrangle the kittens. It shouldn't be too hard; you know how kittens are when you show them a new box. We didn't come here with much."

"You're saying we won't strip the entire place for everything it's got?" I asked.

Lucy tapped her lower lip. "Do you think we can leave with the bed? And should I tell the kittens to leave anything that's nailed down?"

"I want the TV," Nose shouted from the living room. The little shit was listening in, huh?

"We can't sneak the TV out," I called back. "It won't fit in any bag . . . also, we don't have bags to begin with."

"I'll call the staff," Lucy said. "I'm pretty sure they have a sort of lost and found with old luggage we can take."

"They'll probably be happy to see the back of us," I said.

Lucy shook her head. "Oh no, no way. They've been using you for advertising since you got here. Bet the midlister management types are going to cry when we leave."

"Seriously?" I asked.

She shrugged. "They've been tasteful about it. They don't name you but it's, like, really obvious it's you. Plus their media feeds have been linking over to some paparazzi sorts that did take pictures of you. You know, hashtag StrayCatWasHere."

"Oh, fuck me," I muttered. I squeezed the bridge of my nose while shaking my head. In the end, though, it didn't really matter much. Corpos would corpo. "Well, whatever."

"You know, we could use that to our advantage," Lucy said.

"How?"

She gestured around the room. "This place is furnished. Ours isn't. Not much, anyway. We need beds, and a few appliances, entertainment stuff, tables, chairs, couches. You know, house stuff. The hotel happens to have a lot of that stuff."

"All right, so we steal it all on the way out?"

Lucy giggled. "I was thinking more about getting them to deliver it all for us. Maybe use some of their designers or whatever to make it all nice and neat at home."

"Uh," I said. "That sounds expensive."

Lucy nodded. "I bet. Millions, at the minimum. Probably more than we can afford. But you have something they want. The credibility of a samurai. And with the city about to get attacked, all those bougie rich sorts living on the outskirts will want to move inward to where it's safer."

I caught on. "I help them run an ad or something, maybe use my image, and they can claim that the place is safer. Then they'd help us get furniture and shit like that."

"Yeah," Lucy said. "I . . . have no idea who you'd need to talk to, to work all of that out, but it's an idea."

"It's a brilliant idea," I said.

For multiple reasons. It would keep Lucy busy and safe at home while getting us what we needed without spending points for it. I would even likely have a few extra turrets in a few days. I bet the hotel would be all over those.

"Yeah, that could work," I muttered. "Okay, we still need to move the kittens over, and sooner rather than later. Can you do that?"

"I'll have to rent a car or two," Lucy said. "We're not going to take the metro all the way over, are we?"

"Oh, fuck no," I said. Using public transportation was basically asking to get stabbed—or to lose a kitten somewhere along the way. Especially if news got out that the Antithesis were around and ready to chow down on some nice juicy civilians. Having the kittens caught in a panicking mob wasn't something I was keen on. "I'll give you a heap of money; just find a moving company, or rent a bus, or get, like, ten drivers to get the kittens and all the stuff over."

"If you're giving me the money," Lucy said, "that means that you're not going to be here."

I worked my jaw. "I mean, I guess I could stay," I said.

She shook her head, hand touching my arm carefully. "It's fine. Well, fine-ish. I'll still worry, but I know you well enough to know that you want to be out there. You'll stay safe?"

"I'll probably be working with Gomorrah," I said. "Maybe some of the other samurai I met today. We'll watch over each other's backs."

"All right," Lucy said.

I didn't tell her that I didn't even have an inkling of what the long-term plan was. The way things had been laid out had been almost entirely responsive, relying on defending the city instead of attacking the root of the problem.

That didn't bode well, but then, I probably didn't have the rank or power or whatever to casually fly around and take out entire hives.

I pecked Lucy on the cheek real fast. "I'll head out again, all right? I'll be back in a couple of hours. Text me if anything comes up. Anything at all. And feel free to remind people that if I have to fly back here, that means removing a samurai from an active battlefront that's literally at their front door and that I'll probably not be in the best of moods."

"Oh, you can come in, all pissed off and covered in alien gore, then be all sexy at them," Lucy said.

"Uh" was my reply.

Lucy nodded. "You know that righteous fury is kind of hot, right?"

I cleared my throat, pretended not to feel the warmth on my cheeks, and slapped my helmet back on. "Anyway, I need to head out," I said.

She grinned, because of course she did. We hugged again, and then Lucy gave me a farewell smack as I walked toward the door. "Be safe, all right?" Lucy asked.

I nodded. "I promise, I'll be as safe as I can be."

"You'd better," Lucy said. "I have an in with Gomorrah, and she'll tattle on you if you do anything too stupid."

"Hey! I never do anything stupid," I said.

Lucy smiled. "I love you, even if you're a bit stupid sometimes."

I left with a grin that wouldn't leave and a warm fuzzy feeling in my chest.

"Myalis, can you bring up that map?" I asked.

My vision split, part of it turning into the overhead color map of the region. More and more yellow stains were appearing around the city, mostly deep into the countryside. A few notes were already pinned on the map: requests for people to guard convoys of evacuees or supplies being pulled out of distant warehouses.

That one section that had gone red was back to being just yellow. I guessed that Grasshopper had arrived a while back and was taking care of things.

That still left a whole lot of work available.

I dialed up Gomorrah, and she answered before the first ring. "Hey," I said.

"Hey," she replied. "Done taking care of your girlfriend and many children?"

"They'll manage without me for a few hours," I said. "So, want to burn up some xenos?"

"I thought you'd never ask."

CHAPTER ELEVEN

GETTING READY TO GET HOT

Megacities have their place. We need them. Workers need to be close to factories and offices, homes need to be close to schools. Utilities and electricity are simpler to route when everything is close together, and of course, concentrating security makes it more viable. Shelters and overlapping gun emplacements mean that even with a higher concentration of people, a city is a safer place to be in during an incursion.

That's not to say there aren't any problems. Notably, how do you feed a hundred million people?

—Opening text from *Megaurban Development 101* textbook, fifth ed., 2039

I found a love seat tucked between two plants in the hotel lobby and sat back onto it. If I had to wait for Gomorrah to show up, I might as well be comfortable during the wait. "All right," I said as I looked over the map of New Montreal. "Looks like . . . Cause Player, Nomad, and one other who doesn't have an icon are dealing with that big orange lump along that highway there."

There were more and more yellow stains appearing around the map, mostly in areas that looked like forests or the like, but a few were showing up on the borders to some towns. The biggest, and the one where the map indicated three samurai were already waiting, was along the old Trans-Canadian Highway that led into the northern end of the city. A splotch of orange in the middle of the lump was using the road.

"I think three samurai should be able to take care of that without our help," Gomorrah said. "We should focus elsewhere, I think. There are two of us; we could go after some of the larger danger zones."

"I don't want to get swarmed in," I said. "Biting off more than we can chew wouldn't be nice, I don't think. I'd rather not have to call for help before the timer's even ticked down to zero."

"Not the greatest timer if the aliens are active already."

I chuckled. "It's an estimate, I guess."

I noticed a ping on the map, a small yellow-green circle that appeared over a spot some ways outside the city. It was pretty far out, near the outer edge of the map. The area was only just on the edge of one of the smaller yellow zones. Focusing on it opened a pop-up.

Crop Corp LLC—A subsidiary of Soil Is Green—Facility 658-NM
Facility currently being relocated. Low to mid priority.
Location holds several hundred tons of fertilizers and plant materials that could pose a risk if captured by xeno forces.
Samurai volunteers needed for guard duty during facility move.

"Did you see this one?" I asked Gomorrah. There was a handy share button to ping others about a location on the map. "Guard duty seems a bit easy right now, but we could fly over and check it out?"

"There's some orange near it; we might run into a few Antithesis on the way. We'll be far from the city, though."

"Close to some other samurai," I pointed out. There was another orange splotch next to a little town with a marker for . . . Buzz-Buzz? That wasn't one of the samurai who'd been at the meeting.

"I'm down for it," Gomorrah said. "By the way, I'm pulling into the hotel now."

I climbed to my feet, tugged my coat on straighter, then glanced around the room. A few folks were looking my way, but more of them were looking at their phones. A TV against the far wall of the lobby was presenting an emergency broadcast. Laserjack was there, nodding seriously while some reporter asked him questions. A bullet-point list was taking up screen space next to his head, telling people to keep on doing as they'd normally do.

Couldn't have people staying home from work just because the world was ending.

I headed out of the lobby. I didn't have time to stare at bad news or doomscroll with the rest of them.

The Fury slid into the hotel's parking tunnel and slowed to a gentle stop right in front of the doorway. A few other cars had to shift lanes to get out of its path. The driver's-side window lowered with an electric hum, and I saw Gomorrah looking out to me, maskless for once. "You getting in?"

"Yeah, yeah," I said as I jogged around the car. The window went up and the passenger-side door rose. I flopped into the seat and shifted around. Gomorrah had just removed her mask from the seat and was placing it onto the dash. "You're not all geared up?" I asked.

"I have my things," Gomorrah said. "Just had to get changed and I didn't bother equipping everything before I left the church. I like my suit, but it could use some more breathable materials. It gets hot in there."

"Really?" I asked. I tapped the chestpiece of my armor. "No problems here. Not that I've noticed, at least."

Gomorrah shrugged as she put the car into gear. "Mine's designed to be resistant to my own weaponry. I use a lot of burning liquids, so I can't really have the suit be porous or anything. My next upgrade will be a better undersuit, something with built-in cooling. I should have spent a few more points when I first bought it."

I nodded along. "Yeah. I've got to start shopping for gear too. I left my grenade launcher at home. It's too . . . clunky? Like, I like it as a weapon, it's versatile, but at the same time it feels like it's too niche. I don't know if that makes sense?"

"I think I know what you mean. We should be making some decent points soon; it should be enough for you to try a few things. Both of us are still really new to this; I think it's kind of expected that we'll try a few things before settling into a niche."

"Wait, does that mean you'll move away from lighting things on fire?" I asked.

"No. I meant that you can try different things to find the gimmick you like the most. I've found mine. It's got issues and downsides, but I can work around those."

I snorted. "All right, then. So, that Crop Corp place, or did you find somewhere more interesting to visit?"

Gomorrah tapped a few buttons, then let go of the wheel even as the view out the window was replaced by the Family's map interface. "It looks like most of those yellow spots are very low-risk places. There might not even be any Antithesis there, or if there are, it's likely only scouts and maybe workers. The orange spots are where there's proper movement."

I hadn't looked at the map in maybe three minutes, and already there were a few more swatches of yellow. "They're multiplying fast," I said.

"That's what they do," Gomorrah said. "I've been talking to Atyacus, and he says that most hive incursions like these will generally search for threats around the hive, and then if they find any, they start producing en masse with the goal of eliminating that threat. It kind of makes sense, if you're willing to think like a plant."

"Willing to think like a plant," I repeated.

She shot me a glare. "You know what I meant."

The city shot past, Gomorrah's autopilot taking the speed limit as more of a vague suggestion, and using the clearly marked roads was just not going to happen.

"Fine, fine," I said. "So . . . what, the xenos like murdering people? I think I noticed as much already."

"It's more that we can expect things to ramp up toward violence first, and growth second. If the Antithesis only has ten . . . units, I guess, it'll send six of them to attack the nearest town before using the rest to grow the hive."

"And if there's no threat around?" I asked.

"Then it'll only grow faster. But as soon as an unthreatened hive meets one that is threatened, it'll turn its attention to that threat too."

"So, we're going to have to deal with pitiful hives at first, then big, mean motherfuckers later?"

"That's how it's worked out, historically, at least," Gomorrah said. "I'm still of the opinion that we should just drop air-fuel bombs on any patch of greenery that looks at us funny."

"Isn't that a bit of a huge exaggeration?" I asked. "Plus it sounds like it wouldn't be great for the environment."

"We can plant new trees once the world stops being on fire," Gomorrah said.

I couldn't help but laugh.

The Fury flew lower and closer to the ground, following atop a wide stretch of highway that cut across the suburbs around the city like a plank over a ditch.

I leaned against the door, taking in the world outside New Montreal. I had seen all of this before, probably. On the days when the smog was thin and the sun warm, when Lucy and I snuck out to a mall or a rooftop shopping district. You could see the greenery and the fields all around the city, past the towns and suburbs that clung onto New Montreal's sides.

I'd never really been able to see it from this angle. Maybe on the flight to Black Bear, but I had been preoccupied then.

"That's the place," Gomorrah said some five minutes later.

I glanced up and took in the facility. "Well, shit," I said.

This was going to be more complicated than I'd hoped.

CHAPTER TWELVE

THOUSAND GARDENS

We're locking down sector B, rows 25 to 29, from further testing.

All plant life and plant matter in those sectors is to be disposed of by means of type 4 herbicides, followed by gardenwide ignitions. The ashes are to be collected for further analysis and proper disposal.

Note: I fucking told you that grafting Antithesis shit onto cabbages was a horrific fucking idea.

—Crop Corp internal memo, 2048

I tapped the door release, then set a foot on the cement ground just outside the Fury. A hand on the doorframe gave me the leverage I needed to pull myself out of the car.

The Crop Corp facility was huge in a way that made me feel small in comparison. It challenged my sense of scale.

The greenhouses weren't all that wide. Maybe thirty meters to a side. They were hexagonal, with glass walls all around lit up from within by faint lights. There were orange pillars, yellow ones, even a few that glowed purple. Their roofs were capped by blue solar panels, which were folded in on themselves like the petals of some high-tech flower.

Each rose up at least a hundred meters. Nothing compared to the skyscrapers back home. In fact, in terms of sheer size, at least the size of the greenhouses, the operation wasn't that impressive.

It was the scale that was terrifying. There had to be thousands of those pillars, all packed in tight with just enough room between them that a pair of smaller cars could dart past each other. "How big is this place?" I asked.

This is the third-largest growing operation feeding New Montreal. The facility covers six square kilometers.

"That's . . . a fuckload of plants," I said.

Yes. I should have just opened with that. This facility has the third-largest fuckload of plants in the New Montreal area.

I chuckled. "Yeah, all right." I dragged my attention down from the rows of pillars. It looked like some of them were moving. They had these big vehicles, large enough to wrap around a pillar and equipped with four wheels that were at least five meters tall. The middles of the machines looked like they could clamp onto a pillar, and there were workers crawling up and down them, securing the pillars that were about to be moved.

"Heads up," Gomorrah said. "We have guests coming."

I glanced her way in time to see her slipping her mask on, then followed the low hum of an electric vehicle to see a little golf-cart-looking thing zipping our way. It turned as it came to a stop, and a man in a shirt and slacks jumped out of it. "You can't be here," he said.

"Beg to differ," I said.

He glared, then reached up to adjust his half mask. He had a white hard hat on too; it was a bit incongruous over his business casual. "No, I mean this is where the gardens will be moved. Unless you want that pretty car crushed, it had better move."

Gomorrah shrugged, and half a second later the Fury shot up and into the air. In a blink it was out of sight.

The man stared for a moment, then turned his attention back to us. "I was hoping you'd be in the car when it left," he said.

"We're here to help," I said. "Got a warning that the region had some Antithesis presence?"

"You're samurai? Wait, no, of course you are. Fuck me, could have led with that."

"I thought it was pretty obvious," I said. Did he get a lot of visitors in nun getup and cat-themed power armor?

"Sorry, ma'am," he said. "Been a bit stressful. We have several thousand pillars left to move still. We've only moved twenty percent. At this rate we'll be here for another three days."

"That's . . . not ideal," I said.

He nodded. "You're telling me. I sent a request in for more movers three months back, but headquarters said it wasn't worth the expense. We'll see how much they like the expense of replacing lost gardens."

"Right," I said. "You might not have three days to move these things."

He shook his head. "We'll do what we can. Might be getting some movers from Facility 187NM; that'll cut down the workload. And if you can keep the bug bastards off our plants, that would be nice."

"Right," I said. "Where are our little alien friends? Oh, and got a name? I'm Stray Cat, this is Gomorrah."

He pointed through the rows of pillars. "Sectors H through J. I got reports from the boys who were there."

"Where?"

"Moved closer to this edge. Besides, need more help loading the pillars that can be moved. Caught sight of a few aliens on the security cameras." He reached into a breast pocket and tugged out a thin smartphone-looking thing that he unfolded to be larger. "These. I'm Jake, foreman, second class."

"Thanks, Jake," I said as I looked at the device. It was stuck on a still frame of a video. The lighting was crap, clearly coming from the pillars but still dark enough that it wasn't easy to make out the thing on the edge. Still, even out of focus, there was no doubt about it.

"That's an m-three," Gomorrah said.

"Big dog thing with a three-hinged jaw and green-black skin," I said. "Yeah, that's a model three. I guess they'll be pretty common while the hives are building up. Hey, Jake, what kind of crap is around those sectors? Anything in particular the aliens would want to munch on?"

"Sectors H to J? That's hyper wheat, trademark, super soy, trademark, and friendly broccoli, patent pending, trademark."

"Anything else?" I asked. "Fertilizers, big tanks full of biofuel?"

Jake stared at me for a moment. "Ma'am, this is a farm. We have several hundred tons of fertilizer."

"That's . . . fucking fantastic." I nodded. "Okay, I'm going to head over that way. If you could send me a map of the area, and maybe link us into your security, that would be nice." I figured that Myalis could break in, but hey, if they gave permission, that would make things nice and neat.

"I'll do what I can," Jake said. "I'll talk to the lead foreman and site director, but between you and me, I think they'll be happy enough to have a samurai on-site that they'd give you anything you ask for. We know we're in a high-risk location if the aliens find out what's here."

"You got it," I said. "Can we, uh, borrow that?"

Jake followed my finger toward the golf cart. "But that's my personal transportation vehicle."

"Yeah, it is."

"Come on, Cat, we can walk," Gomorrah said. "Leave the poor man's golf cart alone."

I rolled my eyes but didn't disagree. Gomorrah started to head toward the nearest pillars, so I jogged to catch up to her.

The world beneath all the garden pillars was strangely dark. I imagined that it was nicer at noon, but the sun had moved past that a while ago, so we were constantly in the shade as we moved along. At least the lights within the pillars helped, though they did cast everything in strange colors. It was also strangely bright whenever we reached a spot where the rows happened to line up to create a gap where the sun could shine through.

"So, what do you think we're going to run into?" I asked.

"Not much," Gomorrah said. "This early on, there probably isn't anything tougher than a model four. Maybe a few model threes that are stealing from the site. Unless the hive is really close; then the Antithesis doesn't have much business sniffing around here."

"Except that there are people here."

"And those people are a threat that it might try to wipe out before growing bigger," Gomorrah said. "If we can kill off the scouts, that might actually give us some time before the hive goes deep into producing combat models."

"Fewer points for us, but then we won't have to sit here all day. Or for the next couple of days."

"Exactly," Gomorrah said. She glanced up, and I followed her gaze to spot the Fury hovering overhead. "I think I've spotted something. How's your cardio?"

"What?" I asked.

Then she started jogging ahead of me, and I cursed as I ran to keep up.

Our faster pace meant that we were eating up the distance, but the size of the place still meant that it was taking forever to get anywhere. A few minutes in, and I was already a little lost. The pillars weren't all entirely identical, but the differences were just slight enough that I couldn't tell them apart at a glance.

There was no guessing how many rows deep we were, and a glance back only revealed more pillars.

This place was going to be a mess to fight in, I just knew it.

CHAPTER THIRTEEN

ON THE UP-AND-UP

These fucks! Do u know how much I sacrifice to keep this company rolling?

I only got a 29% pay increase last quarter, and these shits are complaining?

We're not getting enough for a house & food. Why did u cut medical? The company made big profits, why aren't we making more?

Selfish.

—Former Nimbletainment CEO's last tweet, 2028

"You got those security feeds?" I asked while looking around us. The garden pillars cut off my line of sight; I couldn't see as far as I wanted down any direction, not unless I happened to be in one of those spots where things lined up just right, and then I could see all the way across the facility.

Just connected to them. It looks like there was some hesitating from the head office as to whether to give you permission, but it was overridden.

"We might actually be working with someone clever," Gomorrah said.

"Well, you're used to working with me," I said.

She snorted. "Exactly. Working with someone clever will be a new and interesting opportunity."

I laughed while I continued to scan ahead of me. We were nearing the sections where Jake had said the Antithesis had been seen. At least, if I had figured out how the sections worked. We were in section G, according to the signs on the pillars we were passing.

Atyacus and I are poring over the feeds from the last few days. There are several thousand cameras all across the facility. It seems as though they're quite worried about employees stealing plants, or resting during nonbreak minutes. In any case, we've found three locations that are likely to be the places where the Antithesis are entering the facility.

"Three spots, huh?" I asked. "Can you mark them out for us?"

Done.

I blinked as an overlay popped up over my cybernetic eye's vision; it turned all the buildings ahead of us into wireframes, then highlighted three spots in a dull orange that I guessed could only mean one thing.

"The breaches are a couple of hundred meters apart," Gomorrah said. "Do you think we should split up?"

"There's three of them and two of us," I said.

"I can send the Fury to the middle one. It can shoot down any Antithesis trying to sneak in or out while we clean up the other two locations," Gomorrah said.

"All right, fair enough. I'll get the bigger breach, then, since you'll be covering the other two." I pointed to the southmost hole in the fence.

"That seems reasonable," Gomorrah said. "Stay on the line with me the entire time? If we bite off more than we can chew, we'll be able to run over to help each other." She raised her flamethrower and started to adjust a few little knobs hidden inside a panel on its side. "Are you ready for a fight?"

"In a minute," I said. I didn't have my crossbow or my grenade launcher. Both were back home. I liked them as weapons, but they both had a few disadvantages that . . . well, they weren't perfect weapons. What I did have on me was my trusty Trench Maker, currently loaded with high-explosive rounds.

I tugged the gun out of my right thigh holster and checked it real fast before putting it away.

My other holster had my Claw. The bulbous gun was loaded with tightly wound monofilament rounds that would shred anything. I aimed it ahead, making sure that the overlay worked before I tucked it away. It could teleport its payload into anything I aimed it at, which was pretty helpful against bigger enemies. I probably wasn't going to see anything big enough to be worth using the Claw on for a bit.

A shrug of my shoulders had both of my back-mounted railguns unfolding themselves and shifting so that they aimed over my shoulders. I checked their ammo counts, made sure they were topped up, then nodded to myself.

The only other weapon I had on me was my sword. I hadn't parted with that thing since I got it. Not that I'd had many opportunities to use it since. It was just too fucking cool to leave at home.

"I think I need a new main weapon," I said.

"You should probably work that out sooner rather than later," Gomorrah said. "What are you thinking about?"

"Uh, I don't know. The grenade launcher's versatility is nice, but it's too . . . clunky? The crossbow is fun too, but it's shit when it comes to crowd control. I need something silent that can still pack a punch."

Gomorrah hummed. "Ask Myalis about a shotgun, maybe. The shell type can change the range, and you'll have a lot of options. They can be pretty satisfying too."

"I thought you'd suggest a flamethrower," I said.

"No, that's my gimmick. Besides, having two of us so focused on close-range, wide-area-of-effect weapons might mean that we'll be leaving some huge gaps in our defenses."

"Aww, you're thinking of us as, like, a battle pair or something," I said.

Gomorrah shook her head. "We've been working together a lot, it's only normal. Besides, the average samurai who works solo can't specialize as much if they want to cover every possibility. Together we can afford to spend more points on specific parts of our kit if the other's covering the weaknesses that that would leave."

"Awfully clever," I said.

"One of us has to be."

I let out a long breath. "Okay, so your burns aren't just physical today. Damn."

"Ah, I'm sorry. I've been a little tense."

I waved it off. "It's fine, I know you're not being a capital-*B* bitch." I slowed to a stop at the next intersection between pillars. It was where I'd get the straightest path to where I wanted to go. "All right, I'm heading out here. Keep in touch."

"Likewise," Gomorrah said. She gave me a final nod, then stomped off to the left.

I flicked open my aug menus, then toggled on the invisibility on my suit and coat. My outfit wavered, then disappeared. All I saw looking down was the gray cement that covered every inch of the facility ground.

Reaching down, I tugged my Trench Maker out and held it by my side as I walked on. It was probably weird that I wanted my boots to make big clunks as I headed down toward my goal.

"So, you thinking about weapons?" I asked.

I'm thinking about many things, but yes, weapons are one of those. Are you in the mood to buy something now?

"Let's see how tough the aliens here are. I've got the impression that we're dealing with small fry."

That should be an accurate impression, yes. The hives that have just awoken likely haven't reached the point where they can produce anything that's a real threat yet.

"How long do we have? Until we start getting the scary aliens, I mean?" I asked.

If we rely on the general projections for hives that have lots of biomass and room to grow? Then one full day before the hives can start producing models above ten. Two days for models above twenty. Likely five to ten days for models above the thirties.

"Thirties," I repeated. A shiver ran down my spine. Gomorrah and I had

had a hell of a time against a model in the twenties. "Gonna need a big gun for those. Hopefully we'll make enough points in the next couple of days to be able to deal with them." If things scaled the way I thought they did, I'd be a snack for a model thirty if one showed up now.

I was a good fifty meters from the orange zone when I heard a scuffling.

I stopped, dropping into a crouch while holding my breath back. Something had moved. I focused on my hearing more, trying to pinpoint the exact location of . . . whatever it was that had scrambled like that.

There were plenty of things generating white noise around. Sprinklers hissing, ventilation shafts rattling inside the pillars, some fans humming along somewhere else. A lot of sounds that I hadn't paid any attention to until I had to listen past them.

Where had the . . .

I glanced up and to my right as I caught a shadow moving.

There was a pillar nearby, with the usual glass walls that allowed natural light in.

A model three was tearing apart the plants on the edge of the glass, little clawed paws digging away at everything like a street dog on meth. I stared for a moment until I noticed the large form of a worm moving up deeper in the pillar, its mouth wide open so that a few other model threes could toss in mouthfuls of plant matter and bags of what I guessed were fertilizer.

I opened a line to Gomorrah. "Hey. Found some alien buddies. They're going all Black Friday on the fertilizer over here."

A distant and familiar roar, like liquid fire being hosed around by a pyro-nun, echoed through the field of greenhouses. "I've found some too," Gomorrah said. "Just kill them all."

"All righty, then," I said as I started toward the pillar.

CHAPTER FOURTEEN

RESONATING

Enclosed vertical farming will be the only way to farm soon. Not only are land prices constantly on the rise, but things like environmental issues (flooding, droughts, acid rain, corporate warfare, fires) make traditional farming unviable in this half of the twentieth century.

Vertical farms allow full control of the enclosed environment to be achieved, ensuring optimal growth potential and protecting the profits of the company that operates the farm.

—Excerpt from the patent
for a fully enclosed agricultural control tower, 1981

I snuck up to the side of the garden pillar and waited.

Most of the aliens, it seemed, were held up on the floors above. I did notice some movement within, though. The tops of some of the plants were wiggling around, and I heard metallic crashing as a trolley rattled across the grated floor, the tools on it clattering about.

"Not exactly subtle," I muttered as I started to make my way around the pillar. "How many have they breached?"

In this area? This tower and the one currently to your right.

I glanced that way, noting that the next tower over was right next to the very edge of the facility. There was a fence there, just the sort of cheap chain-link fencing that was topped by a roll of barbed wire. A hole was torn into the side of it. "They didn't exactly go all-out with security here," I muttered.

In defense of the facility, this is a greenhouse. I think the fencing is mostly to keep wild animals away and perhaps deter industrial spies. It is far below the rating required to prevent any level of Antithesis entry.

"Yeah, fair enough," I muttered.

I glanced between the two towers before I made up my mind. "Myalis, I need two of those sonic melting grenades. You know the ones. With proximity detonators."

Myalis replied by having two boxes appear next to me.

New Purchase: Class I Resonator Mark I-D X2

Points Reduced from . . . 1,424 to . . . 1,414

I pulled the boxes open and tucked one of the grenades in the pocket of my coat while palming the other. I ran over to the hole in the gate, eyeing the world past the facility. There was a small bit of clearing, just scraggly grass that had obviously been trimmed once a season, then a thin forest. The sun was still bright above, but the woods were filled with shifting shadows.

Kneeling down next to the hole, I placed the grenade down, then fiddled with it for a moment. I set the distance to one meter, then set the timer for activation to thirty seconds. Plenty of time to move out of the way.

That done, I darted to the nearer of the two towers and found the way the aliens had used to move in.

They weren't exactly subtle. There was a pile of safety glass next to a broken window. I shifted closer, placed down the second resonator, then flicked it on as well.

That would fuck up any of the Antithesis trying to move around. Hopefully that would also lock them in place while I cleared out the other tower.

If I had to clear out more than two, then the entire thing would take far, far too long.

I glanced over in the direction Gomorrah had gone and couldn't help but notice the thick plumes of black smoke rising into the sky. I switched to the channel we still had open. "Hey, Gom, you okay?"

"Oh, I'm fine," she said with a pleased sort of purr that I decided not to question.

"Right, okay, just don't burn the whole place down."

"Noted."

Shaking my head, I moved back to the first tower where I'd spotted the Antithesis. I knew there were some model threes in there, and at least one worm. Not much of a threat, really, but I wasn't stupid enough not to take it seriously.

How was I going to clear this one?

I could go up floor by floor until I reached the top. It would work. I didn't have to worry too much about the low-level aliens here.

I could set up a killbox. Get two or three turrets around the base, maybe a cat mech, then attract the Antithesis inside the tower so that they'd run out.

But then they might hide.

So, a bit of both?

"Myalis, I'm going to need a lot more of those resonators. I need a bigger model. More range. And . . . do we have nanites that can eat plant matter without spreading too far? I don't want to destroy all the towers here."

Both can be arranged, yes. The nanites are by necessity not fast-acting, however.

I nodded as I counted the floors. The tower was a hundred meters tall but only had ten floors. It looked like each floor was filled with racks for the plants within.

The aliens hadn't smashed in a window on this one. It looked like they'd slipped in through the front door. There were scratch marks on the edge of the door, cutting into the thick rubber seals and the glass front. I pulled the door open, then let it shut behind me.

The carbon dioxide levels in this room are bordering on lethal.

I blinked. The air felt pretty humid, but I couldn't exactly smell anything, not with my helmet filtering everything. "Am I in trouble?" I asked.

No. Not unless you remain in this one room for over three days. Your helmet will filter out the worst of the contaminants.

"Good, good," I said. It was very warm, but some of that had to be the big lights spread out across the ceiling. The room was full of hanging racks filled with rows and rows of plants. "How many resonators will I need per floor?" I asked.

If you purchase a larger variety, only one, though it will need to be centralized.

I nodded. "Got it," I said. I darted to the middle of the room.

Then my heart leapt halfway out of my chest as I came to a sudden stop.

A model three stepped out ahead of me, its beady eyes scanning across the room while its three-hinged jaw dropped open. Its head turned, and for a moment I suspected it was looking right at me.

I swallowed, staying perfectly still for a moment.

Then I remembered that I wasn't some punk-ass little bitch, and I reached into my thigh pocket, pulled out my Trench Maker, and aimed down the barrel to the alien's head.

It saw the gun floating there, its eyes locking onto it.

Then I fired.

The model three flinched back, its ears twitching as I blew a hole through one of them.

I swore, lowered my aim a bit, then fired a second time.

This time the alien's head gained a fist-sized hole that splattered what passed for its brains on the wall of plants behind it.

Target Eliminated!

Reward: 10 points

New Total: 1,424 points

"Myalis, resonator," I said.

New Purchase: Class I Resonator Mark II-G

Points Reduced from . . . 1,424 to . . . 1,414

I picked up the new resonator. It was a chunkier thing, definitely heavier than the usual grenades I had.

Jogging over to the center of the room, I placed the bomb on a little counter space with tools and such behind it, then quickly activated it.

The sound it made was great, a grating, high-pitched whine that had my teeth feeling like they were about to wiggle out of my gums, and I wasn't even the target here.

A nearby plant, with some long trailing leaves, splattered to the floor as a section of it broke apart. So at least it was working.

"I need another," I said.

Coming.

I picked up the next, then ran up to the floor above. In the middle part of the tower, a staircase turned around a central shaft that had a sort of open elevator platform. I imagined it was there to bring the plantstock they gathered up and down, as well as whatever fertilizer or tools they needed to work the greenhouse.

I made it to the second floor, where a couple of model threes were already sniffing their way over to the stairs.

They couldn't see me, of course, but I ducked behind a counter anyway as I set up the second resonator.

The next floor up had more aliens, with one of those big model eight worms chowing down on heaps of plant matter with the help of a few model threes.

I placed another resonator down, then moved on.

I was getting a good workout by the time I reached the topmost floor. Even with my suit helping, it was good cardio climbing ninety meters' worth of stairs. The last five floors didn't have any aliens as far as I could tell, but I put some resonators on them, just in case. The tower was going to be a write-off regardless.

On the top floor, I called up the elevator, then stood in the middle of it before tapping the button to send it down.

"All right, I need some of those nanite grenades," I said. "Ten of them."

Myalis provided, and I got to one knee over the box before tossing one out onto the tenth floor.

Then I headed down, flicking a grenade out onto every floor.

By the time I reached the ground floor, I figured the aliens above were just starting to feel the sting of those nanites.

So, of course, that's when I activated the other nine resonators I'd left.

I was grinning to myself as I walked out of the tower, the entire thing screaming with the high-pitched whine of melting aliens.

CHAPTER FIFTEEN

PASSIONATE

I have a hard time looking down on them. You know, the people who tried really, really hard to find some good in the aliens.

I guess they're just empathetic people; they wanted there to be some redeeming quality in the aliens, they hoped that some of the first extraterrestrial life we've ever encountered wasn't . . . well, antithetical to human life.

Poor, kind souls.

—Garen Dispry, Secretary of Defense, 2028

Antithesis were quiet. It was one of those things that made them extra fucky. Normal animals were supposed to make noise, right? I hadn't seen too many, other than the occasional rat, but the videos and such of dogs always showed them moving and breathing and generally making a lot of noise.

The Antithesis in the second tower didn't make a noise as they melted. It was really disappointing.

"Gom? I think I'm done clearing this area. How are things going on your end?"

"I have an entire tower that looks like a pyre. It's beautiful. I can't tell if the crackle I hear is the building melting or the aliens, but I'm pleased either way."

"Uh," I said. "Right, that's . . . real nice, Gomorrah. Should we meet up by the third break in the fence? Myalis, spot any more aliens sneaking in?"

No, none so far. A small group of model threes escorted a model eight and tried to leave the area, but Gomorrah's vehicle annihilated the group.

"That's . . . not many aliens around here," I said. "We're talking what? A hundred?"

So far we have confirmed fifty-two kills in and around this facility.

Gomorrah hummed. "That's really not a lot. Barely a scouting force, especially not as spread out as they are. Did security really not see any others?"

We could trace back the approximate direction this group came from.

"That's an idea," I said. I started walking toward Gomorrah's position. It wasn't hard to notice, what with the pillar of smoke in the sky. "We might be able to take out a small nest."

"I think the Family might want to target those from orbit again."

"And destroy this whole facility while they're at it?" I asked. "I care for corpo property about as much as the next punk, but this place is making food. I like food. We could clear out the hive on our own, I'm sure."

"We'll see," Gomorrah said. "This early on, it's possible that the hive's barely worthy of notice. I'm not saying we ignore it, though; that would be irresponsible. Let's see if we can't destroy it in one go or at least prune it down and then mark its location for checkup later."

I nodded as I continued to walk along. A glance at the Family's map showed a few more growing spots of yellow, and even a couple of minuscule orange streaks. No red, though, and there was a growing green spot spreading out around the city. Secured locations? Places being patrolled? Areas that they could confirm had no aliens?

I'd have to play with the map some more later. In the meantime I found a filter option and toggled it open to select "Hive Locations." A few dots appeared on the map. Exactly five of them, all close to orange splotches. Three of the five had pins with the names of samurai attached to them.

"Looks like hives are getting a lot of focused attention."

More points to be earned for the moment, and since Antithesis hive growth is exponential, destroying one before it can grow large enough to defend itself is simply a wise course of action. There will be a couple of hives scattered around that remain undetected for each that is obvious.

"That's plainly terrifying," I muttered.

I paused a few minutes later as I found the last section where the Antithesis had broken through the gate. It was hard to miss, what with the injured model three slumping its way across the ground, its rearmost legs very clearly broken and a trail of whatever passed as blood following it across the cement ground.

I looked around to make sure there weren't any others around, then stepped closer to the alien. "Is this the only one alive out here?" I asked.

It seems to be. One of the towers was pillaged recently. The models tried to leave the area; those were the ones that Gomorrah's vehicle ambushed.

"And this little guy?" I asked with a gesture at the model three.

Perhaps a survivor. The Fury used explosives to eliminate the group; it's entirely possible that a model as light as this was tossed back some distance.

I walked around the little alien so that I was at its front. It was rather pitiful, dragging itself across the ground, breaths coming in deep chuffs and limbs trembling. "I feel kind of bad about shooting this guy," I said.

Technically it's genderless. Also, it is entirely incapable of seeing anything that isn't an Antithesis as anything but a threat. You won't find any compassion given reciprocated.

"Yeah, yeah," I said. I squatted down in front of it, still keeping a couple of meters between us. "Still, it doesn't look like it's doing so good, you know? This is like shooting a lame dog."

Perhaps toggle off your invisibility?

I raised an eyebrow at the suggestion, but there didn't seem to be any danger. I was fully armored and the model three looked like it was on its last legs, pun somewhat intended. I flicked off my invisibility, then stepped back as the model three immediately lunged toward me.

Its jaws snapped at the air, the only sound it made other than its labored breathing as it tried to cut the distance between us.

"Mean little fuck, aren't you?" I asked as I stepped back, then carefully drew my sword. "Well, fuck you too."

I stepped forward while keeping myself low. My blade hissed as air slipped into the portal that formed its edge. The sound shifted a little as Void Terminus cut right through the middle of the model three and came out the other side without any effort.

Standing up, I held the sword to the side and checked the body to make sure it was properly dead. I guess cutting the alien in half vertically was enough, because it wasn't moving anymore.

"Having fun?"

I glanced back to see Gomorrah coming over, her flamethrower hanging at her hip by a strap. She seemed to exude some sort of . . . pleased energy. Some real weird postcoital bliss going on.

"Yeah, I guess," I said. I flicked the sword off, then flipped it around before resheathing it.

She looked at the body, then back at me. One of her shoulder-mounted flamethrowers slipped out from beneath her habit and spat a line of fire at the corpse. "I was considering what to do next. I think we should torch the building the Antithesis visited here, then try to spot the hive. With the two of us together we should be able to bomb it from a distance without putting ourselves at any risk."

"That sounds fair, if a bit boring."

"I'm sure we'll have plenty of opportunities for close-quarters, high-risk combat in the next couple of days. Let's take the easy path on one of the few occasions where it's available."

I snorted. " All right, all right, that's fair enough. Want to torch the place, or should I?"

"Oh, I would be honored," she almost purred.

"Are you sure you're not a pyromaniac?" I asked.

She shrugged. "I was never diagnosed with anything."

"Did you burn the therapists?"

"Oh, shut up," Gomorrah said.

I laughed at my own joke as I followed her to the tower. Gomorrah was surprisingly gentle about setting the whole thing on fire. She went around, making sure the area was cleared, then bought a sort of canister with little holes all around it, which she placed in the central elevator in the middle of the tower.

We both stood back and watched the elevator—hacked by Atyacus—ride up and down at downright unsafe speeds as her little device poured fire across every floor.

"With the windows more or less intact, the only place for the super-heated air to go will be out through the ventilation," Gomorrah said. "It should burn out any spores or residue."

"Nice and easy, huh," I said.

"Exactly. Fire's simple that way." Gomorrah turned just as the familiar hum of her Fury sounded out. The car came in for a smooth landing between the pillars.

I got in after her and made myself comfortable. "I'm going to text Jake, and I guess Crop Corp in general. They'll want to know that we're done here."

"We can swing back once we've found and destroyed the hive. It's possible there are more Antithesis already on their way. They could hit the place while we're out."

I nodded. "Myalis, can you keep an ear open in case they spot any?"

Certainly.

"All right, then, let's go fuck up that hive, shall we?"

CHAPTER SIXTEEN

IT'S TECHNICALLY NOT A NUKE

Oh, for fuck's sake. No! You can't use a nuke on American soil, I don't care
who you think you are!
—Live open-broadcast message from US Army general to samurai near the
Oklahoma incursion, 2029

Gomorrah was probably frustrated at the speed we were moving at. It was
little more than a crawl.

In fact, I was pretty sure that I could run faster than we were moving, at
least for a couple dozen meters.

The Fury stayed just above the canopy of leaves that made up the patch
of woodland next to the Crop Corp facility. We weren't exactly brushing
past the topmost branches, but it was a near thing.

The screen before us was showing a detailed image of the ground,
taken from a few cameras on the car's underside and reconfigured so that
it looked as if there weren't any branches in the way. Some clever bit of
software pointed to tracks on the ground that looked obvious when outlined in yellow but that I was certain I would never in a million years spot
otherwise.

"Looks like this is where the groups split," I said. The tracks went off in a
few directions. We were maybe twenty or so meters into the forest.

"That seems probable, yes," Gomorrah said. "It's possible we'll run into
a number of tracks. We're going to need to be a little lucky to find a path
heading back to the hive."

"They all head back eventually, right?" I asked.

"They should, yes," Gomorrah said. "I'm worried that there are a good
number of Antithesis that aren't going to be at the hive itself. Scouts and
models sent out to gather biomass."

"They'll return to a crater," I said.

She shook her head. "Each one that returns is one more that can restart
a new hive."

"Ah, right," I said. "Well, we can at least set the big one here back a day or two. I think we're going to have to deal with a lot of rampant mini-hives in the coming days."

Gomorrah didn't comment, too focused on slowly steering the Fury along so that we continued to follow the tracks below.

I leaned back, idly watching as her software highlighted more tracks. I bet there were some samurai with better tech to track hives down, but . . . well, we didn't discuss it, but I had the impression that Gomorrah and I both wanted to take out this hive ourselves without outside help. It would mean more points for us, and with things ramping up, we were both greedy for those.

"Hey, Myalis," I muttered. "What's my point total looking like?"

Your current point total is 1,524 points.

"That's . . . not a lot," I said.

You spent a number of points purchasing disposable equipment to kill a relatively small number of Antithesis. To be entirely fair, I think you did the right thing. You could have saved points by manually killing all the Antithesis you ran across, but that would have been at the expense of more time spent killing them and a heightened risk of injury.

"Hmm." I shifted in my seat while I considered it. What was done was done, of course, but that didn't mean I couldn't think of better ways to handle things the next time. "I think I'm going to need some better tools. More cost-effective ones."

There are plenty. Though generally speaking, your propensity for using explosives and single-use items does allow you to punch significantly above your tier. Gomorrah is doing the same by specializing heavily in one field, but she lacks some of the versatility your catalogs afford you.

"That's fair, I guess. Still, I do need a new main weapon. Maybe we can look into shotguns or something. It's Gomorrah's idea, but I'd give it a try."

I think I have a few options that might interest you there. With specialized shells you can even deliver interesting payloads with little difficulty. Also, the larger spread of some shells could overcome your projectile dysfunction.

"Projectile . . . Myalis, are you mocking me because I can't aim again?"

Yes. The joke is old but I still find it amusing.

"Cat," Gomorrah said. I glanced up, then narrowed my eyes at what was on the screen. A single model three, sniffing at the ground and following the same tracks we were following.

"Should we blow it up?" I asked.

"We should, but it might alert any others in the area."

"Your Fury isn't exactly the stealthiest vehicle around," I pointed out.

Of course the model three chose that moment to look up right at us. Its jaws opened, and then it spun around and darted away.

"Christ's saving grace," Gomorrah . . . cursed? Was that a swear?

She turned the car and drove after the model three, keeping it more or less in the middle of the screen that took up the car's windshield. "You think it'll head back to the hive?" I asked.

"Model threes aren't all that smart," Gomorrah said. "I don't think it's wise enough to lead a threat away from the hive if it can't just run right at it."

We followed the model three for a good couple of minutes, the alien crashing through bushes, then bouncing over rocks as we arrived in a more clear patch of forest.

Something beeped, and Gomorrah spun us to the side. I saw something black dart by just as I was gripping the handle above the door to keep from being thrown out of my seat.

"What was that?" I asked as we gained speed and circled higher.

"Model ones, I think," Gomorrah said. "They came out of nowhere." Her hand twitched through the air, and the screens all around us returned to showing the world outside, though this time with large red circles all over the place where little black forms were flying around. A whole flock of model ones, the little birdlike aliens, were forming into a larger flock that seemed determined to head our way.

I glanced down, then pointed. "There, those rocks. There're model threes coming out from between them. I bet that's our hive."

"Give me a minute," Gomorrah said. She flicked a few switches on the dash, and a hole popped open on the Fury's hood so that a large gun could slide out of the front.

The gun twitched, fired, twitched, then fired again, a constant shuddering jerk that resulted in model ones falling from the sky in ones and twos.

"Think you can find a spot to land?" I asked.

"You want to get to the hive on foot?" Gomorrah asked.

"Well, I can't throw a bomb in there from the passenger seat," I said.

Gomorrah shook her head. "You can totally just bomb it from up here. It can't be that deep, can it? Atyacus, has anyone ever conducted a survey of the region? Are there any caves for a hive to hide in?"

A survey was conducted in 2034 at the behest of the same corporate entity that owns the nearby Crop Corp facility. The area is geologically stable. That is one of the requirements to build a greenhouse facility composed of hundreds of narrow, tall towers. There should be few naturally occurring caverns in the region.

It was weird hearing an AI that wasn't Myalis speak. Atyacus was a lot more posh sounding. "So not a natural cave. We could be dealing with just a big hole that the hive snuck into."

"There are normal trees nearby," Gomorrah said. "They're unaffected, which could mean that they're being tapped for resources. We'll have to burn this area down entirely."

"Fine," I said. "Fly us over the hive; I'm going to drop something special on top of it. Hopefully we can clear the whole thing out in one boom."

What sort of explosion are you looking for?

"Something that'll reach deep into those rocks or whatever. Would one of those thermobaric bombs work? Or is that too surface-level?"

"It could be pretty deep," Gomorrah said. "I have some missiles if it's only on the surface."

Might I suggest a bunker buster, then? It will appear as a small disk that, when activated, will teleport in a large bunker-buster bomb. The yield should be similar to the smaller nuclear devices humanity once built, though.

I glanced at Gomorrah, and she stared right back.

"So, we good on the nuke idea?" I asked.

It's not actually a nuclear device. With an artificial mass core, a relatively small projectile can weigh several tons. It will bury itself into the ground to a set depth, then detonate. As for the warhead, seeing as how the detonation will occur in an enclosed space, something like a low-yield fusion explosion should clear out a small hive. Five terajoules should create a crater approximately a hundred meters wide.

"I . . . yes," Gomorrah said.

"Neat," I said. "How much is that thing?"

Three hundred and twenty points.

I winced; that was kind of expensive. But then again, I was expecting a pretty spectacular boom. "Fuck it. Gomorrah, I want this on film, though."

"I loathe to imagine what you'll do with the video," she said.

"Very inappropriate things," I said.

New Purchase: 5 Terajoule Helium-Fusion Bomb with Mass-Altering Bunker-Buster Deployment System

Points Reduced from . . . 1,524 to . . . 1,204

The box that appeared on my lap was tiny. It had a small disk inside it, with a screen and a button labeled "Start Timer."

"Okay," I said. "Let's nuke shit."

CHAPTER SEVENTEEN

KABOOM

Samurai are a fine deterrent, and there's no denying that they'll kill more xenos than any properly organized army once they get going, but holy shit are they ever hard to work with.

Do you have any idea how many times I had to walk over to a samurai, hat in hand, and politely ask them not to commit war crimes at danger-close proximity to my troops?

—Live open-broadcast message from US Army general to samurai near the Oklahoma incursion, 2029

I inspected the disk for a moment. There was a timer on it with a couple of buttons to adjust it. "So, I press this, the timer counts down, and then the bomb appears?" I asked.

Essentially, yes.

"Why not just give me the bomb?"

Because while the core of the explosive is activated by a fusion detonator, the majority of the explosive power comes from the hyperdense explosives packed around the core. Those weigh in excess of one metric ton and would crush you and destroy Gomorrah's upholstery if you were to summon it inside the Fury.

"If your mangled body stains my seats I will be very disappointed," Gomorrah said.

"All right, all right, hold your tits." I scooted to the edge of the seat and grabbed the door handle. "I'm going to tap this and drop it; can you get us right on top of the hive?"

Gomorrah nodded and drove us around in a tight spiral, gaining height as we went.

"Myalis, how long should I set this for?"

The lower you are, the less time you'll want to have on the timer. The explosive needs a moment to angle itself in the air and to fire its downward thrusters to pierce into the ground.

"Got it," Gomorrah said. She slowed us to a full stop, then shoved her foot down on a pedal, which sent us shooting upward. I glanced at the dash, where I could see our height in meters rising; she slowed down when we were a kilometer or so over the hive. "Good enough?

Certainly.

I opened the door, glad for my helmet as a cool blast of wind buffeted the inside of the Fury. Leaning out over the side, I glanced way, way down. It wasn't too hard to spot the opening in the forest where we thought the hive was. It was one of only a few open spots in the forest.

I set the timer to three seconds, then held it out over the void.

"Hey, Gomorrah, you got anything witty to say?" I asked.

"Close the door, it's getting cold?" she tried.

"I meant as, like, a final fuck-off to the aliens."

"I'm not really keen on witticisms," she said.

I shrugged, tapped the timer with my thumb, then let it drop.

I watched the disk fall, somehow while keeping even in the air, and then with a loud pop it was replaced by what looked like a missile, a big bulbous lump of metal with a few thrusters on the back that immediately lit up and started to roar.

You might want to move; you are within the outer edges of the blast radius.

I blinked. "Oh fuck," I said as I slammed the door shut and pushed myself back into my seat.

Gomorrah didn't wait around; she put her foot down and the Fury shot forward. "Atyacus, can you put ground zero on the main screen?" Gomorrah asked.

Most of the screen before us switched from a view of the skies ahead to the forest behind and below us, the entire thing fading back as we sped off.

"We've got to be safe now," I said a few seconds later; we were a good four kilometers away.

"Probably," Gomorrah said without slowing us down.

Before I could come up with a rebuttal, there was a flash. A single, thin pillar of light shot out of the ground near the hive and into the sky, like a beam of sunlight through the clouds but exactly the opposite.

"Is that it—"

The ground wavered. It was as if the world were a still puddle and someone had just dropped a rock into it. The earth bucked down, and then the trees and rocks all around rippled.

The explosion itself followed a millionth of a second later, a huge uneven blast of expanding black smoke that was swallowed up by a growing wall of white smoke and angry fire.

I winced as the shock wave caught up with us. The Fury weathered the turbulence for a couple of seconds until Gomorrah seized control of it and leveled us off.

When I looked back, there was a growing misshapen mushroom of black smoke slowly crawling its way into the sky. The clouds above were parted from their endless rainy state, and a few white rings were still lingering above.

"Huh," I said.

"That was . . . beautiful," Gomorrah said.

I started to giggle. "I need that footage, Gomorrah."

"Don't worry, I'll save it," she said. She still sounded a little awed.

"Oh fuck, how close was the facility to the blast?" I asked.

Gomorrah gestured through the air, and the same map we'd been using opened up on screen. It was centered over our position, but it was easy enough to guess the distance to the facility. It was . . . maybe five kilometers away from the blast?

Would that be enough?

The projected likelihood of civilian injury was very low.

"Yeah, and I'm sure the shock wave was just a light breeze," I said.

The bomb used a directional warhead; it focused the vast majority of the explosive force upward.

I hummed to myself, then pointed to the dissipating mushroom. "We should do a flyby, check out the site before heading over to the facility. I want to see if we accidentally pulped anyone."

Gomorrah nodded, and we turned around to head back.

The pillar of smoke around the site of the explosion was still thick and heavy, with a few glowing twists of fire occasionally grasping out of it.

Still, the edge of the explosion was relatively clean. Every tree within two hundred or so meters was knocked down, and some were clearly on fire, but it looked like the fire was pretty weak.

As Gomorrah circled the edge of the crater, I could make out glimpses past the smoke. It was pretty clear that there was now a big conical hole under all that smoke. A few chunks of rock and other detritus had been ejected up and had come down sprinkled across the area too, adding to the fun.

The car's ventilation kicked itself up a notch, and yet it still felt warmer as we flew around.

"That's a job well done," I said.

"Let's just see if anyone got hurt from it before patting ourselves on the back," Gomorrah said as she pulled us out of our turn and headed toward the facility.

Incoming call. It's from Laserjack.

"Put him on," I said.

A screen opened in my augmented vision, with a smiling Laserjack staring at the camera from what looked like a nice minimalist office. "Hello, Stray Cat," he said.

"Hey, Laserjack," I said.

"Quick question. Did you just nuke Canada?"

"Technically no," I said.

He nodded. "Oh good. Could you explain that 'technically' part? Because a lot of sensors just went off, and the satellite imagery that I'm getting sure looks mushroomlike from here. No big burst of radiation, though, so I imagine that the bomb you used really wasn't nuclear."

"You'll be happy to learn that we took care of a hive," I said. "It was a small one, so we figured the easy thing to do would be to blow it up."

Laserjack leaned back a bit, thought, then gave in and nodded. "Fair enough. Usually we'd discourage that kind of methodology for destroying a hive. It might spread some biocontaminants far and wide, which might start new hives, but it's usually mostly effective. And right now, I don't think we have the luxury to look down on nontraditional methods."

"Thanks?" I tried.

"Well, keep up the good work! Though, in the future, maybe send us a text before not-nuking anything?"

"I can't send you a text for every bomb I use, that's just unreasonable."

He shrugged. "Every bomb over . . . say, a hundred tons of TNT in yield?"

"That's better," I said. "See you around, Laserjack. I think I'll be taking the evening off to get some other work done in the city."

"Sure. I imagine tomorrow will be a much busier day for all of us, so getting what you can get done now out of the way is only wise."

I nodded along. "See you around, bud." With that, I closed the line. "He didn't seem too annoyed," I said.

"I imagine it's generally unwise to be annoyed by people with lots of high-yield explosives," Gomorrah said.

"Ah, come on, he's a samurai too. I bet he's got a trick or two up his sleeve. So, facility next? Then I really do want to check up on some things in the city."

"Sure. I think I might slip around and help where I can for the rest of the day. I don't exactly have big plans."

"Oh, well in that case, wanna eat at my place tonight? Bring Franny, we'll make an evening of it!"

CHAPTER EIGHTEEN

THE LOWDOWN

There's something about the bleak. It just makes you want to wax on about it.

Dark and dark and grimness. Nothing but shit and lamentations.

But it's beautiful.

Fucking gorgeous.

—Bathroom stall poetry, 2057

Gomorrah parked the Fury next to the Crop Corp facility headquarters. It was one of the few non-pillar-like buildings around, with a wide parking lot next to it currently filled with go-carts and a few employee cars. I winced a bit at the number of cars with broken windshields.

There were also a lot more branches and little pebbles around than had probably been there pre-explosion.

I guessed that shit traveled a ways when propelled by mushroom clouds.

"You get your points yet?" Gomorrah asked. "I'm curious to know if we got the same amount."

"Uh," I said. I hadn't exactly been paying attention to that. "Myalis?"

Do you want a full breakdown of all your earnings or just the total at the end?

"You know what, give me the full breakdown; I don't think I've ever seen one before. Last hive, in Black Bear, you just gave me the big number at the end."

As you wish!

Targets Eliminated!

Model One . . . 179 Models

Reward . . . 179 points

Model Two . . . 7 Models

Reward . . . 70 points

Model Three . . . 19 Models

Reward . . . 190 points

Model Four . . . 2 Models
Reward . . . 30 points
Model Eight . . . 3 Models
Reward . . . 15 points
Model Ten . . . 17 Models
Reward . . . 17 points
Small Hive Destruction: 500 points
Total Points earned: 1,001
Points after partner share: 601
New Total: 2,205
"That's it?" I asked.

It wasn't a very large hive.

"Wait, I barely have more points than before we started," I complained. "That's bullshit."

"Come on, we hardly broke a sweat here," Gomorrah said. "Six hundred points isn't terrible for half a day's work. Translate it back into credits and it's more than what anyone but a point-one percenter would make in a week."

I didn't want to act like some spoiled brat, but . . . actually, that wasn't true at all. I definitely wanted to act like a spoiled brat. I was too mature to cross my arms and pout about it, though. "Well, fuck it. The hive's gone at least, so we did our part in all of this."

Gomorrah nodded along as she opened the Fury's door and stepped out. I scrambled after her a moment later.

There was a tall pillar of black smoke rising out into the sky above the spot we'd bombed, but it looked as though the smoke was getting thinner as time passed. I imagined it would dissipate to nothing in the coming minutes. There wasn't much to burn at ground zero except for some trees and the like. Rocks and dirt didn't burn well, at least as far as I knew.

Looking down from that, I took in the facility. It was still mostly intact. The crews working on moving the gardens were back at work. A few windows had cracked here or there, and it looked like falling bits of detritus had dented a solar panel or two, but otherwise things looked all right.

The greenhouses didn't all use glass. I imagined that they had some sort of plasticky shit that was cheaper to work with on some of them, and those were just fine.

Jake, the foreman, ran out of the headquarters, hard hat bobbing until he clamped a hand onto it. "Samurai," he said.

"Hey," I replied. "Anyone hurt around here?"

He paused, gulped a few breaths, then shook his head. "No, ma'am. A few cuts and bruises, and we had one worker trip and he might have broken his ankle, but he's part of a partial union, so a percentage of his medical bills will be covered."

"Uh, all right," I said. "I was worried things would be worse here."

"Did you cause that explosion?" he asked. "Should we be worried about radiation?"

"No radiation, don't worry. Uh, the hive's . . . evaporated, so no need to worry about aliens either."

"Thank you," he said, and he seemed genuinely relieved. "We'll be moving the gardens on that end of the facility tonight or tomorrow morning, and I've been dreading having to work so close to those aliens."

"You might want some security on-site nonetheless," Gomorrah said. "I imagine a few stray Antithesis might be skulking around. They could pose a threat."

Jake bobbed his head like some sort of nervous bird. "Will do, will do. Thank you both for your services. I'll relay that to upper management. Hopefully they'll consider the threat of your, ah, displeasure more important than the loss in profits from hiring security."

"For fuck's sake," I muttered. "How about you relay to them that if they don't, I'll fetch them by the scruff of their suits, give them a rifle, then put them on the front lines myself?"

"Uh," Jake said. His lips twitched as he tried not to smile. He looked pretty eager, actually. "I'll repeat that exact message, ma'am. Thank you."

I nodded along, then glanced back. The Family's map of the region was fading from orange to a less alarming sort of green. Not the same as the areas that were entirely safe, but close.

"Ready to head back?" Gomorrah asked.

"Yeah, I guess so. Hey, Jake, give us a call if shit hits the fans, all right?"

"Yes, ma'am," he said. "Thanks again. Crop Corp appreciates your timely intervention!"

"Yeah, okay, bud," I said as I backed off and returned to the Fury. Dude was a bit weird.

Gomorrah and I slipped back into the car and she started to lift us off the ground. "Where do you need to go now?"

"The museum," I said. "Or just home now, I guess. I haven't gotten any urgent texts from Lucy, so I imagine the move is going pretty well."

"That's nice to hear," Gomorrah said. "Are we still going to have dinner tonight?"

"Huh? Oh yeah. Probably won't be anything formal, though. I sure as shit can't cook fancy stuff, and Lucy's liable to set the building on fire if she tries. As much as you like a nice roast, I'd rather it not be my brand-new home that you get to watch burn."

"Cute," Gomorrah said, tone flat. "But yes, informal. I can manage that much. I'll have to see if Franny's up to it. I think she'd appreciate getting out, though."

"Cool," I said.

We rode on in relative silence. The skies were as overcast as usual, but a few tears in the cloud cover hinted at the bright blue of the sky above. Maybe things weren't going to be that bad. If every samurai in the region worked together to blow up every hive they could reach and the normal people out there worked together . . .

I sighed. I was being optimistic to the level of delusion.

The open fields and forests and decrepit little towns were replaced by cookie-cutter suburbs, then industrial and commercial complexes by apartments. New Montreal itself rose up and engulfed us in a warm embrace of smog and steel. We were the sword returning to its sheath.

"What are you thinking?" Gomorrah asked.

"Stupid poetic bullshit," I said.

She chuckled, and we flew on. Gomorrah didn't have much to say, at least until we reached the museum. We flew a circle around the building, Gomorrah paying no mind to the road ahead as she stared. "Are you serious?" she asked.

"What?"

"What do you mean, what?" she snipped. "It's a giant cat. It looks like a postmodern sphynx. I know you love your cat gimmick, but that's a bit much, don't you think?"

"Hey!" I said. "I think it'll be iconic."

"Yes, children everywhere will rejoice when they drive by the kitty building."

I glared. "Don't call it the kitty building. It's clearly modeled after an adult cat."

Gomorrah shook her head as we swung around for a landing. The big landing pad—conveniently placed between the cat's paws—wasn't as empty as I expected it to be. There were a couple of vans parked there, just boring but clean hovercars that had the logo of the hotel we'd been staying at emblazoned on their sides.

"Lucy must be here already," I said.

"Did you ever consider being Stray Dog instead of Cat?" Gomorrah asked. "The way you talk about Lucy, you remind me a bit of a puppy."

I held back a snort at that. "Did you ever consider fucking off?"

"As soon as you're out of my car," Gomorrah said. "Who knows, you might try to add cat ears and whiskers to it." She leaned toward me. "Just to be clear, you do that to my Fury and there's no god in this universe or the next that will keep you unburnt."

"Uh," I said. "Right, well, thanks for the ride, I'll text you the time for dinner in a bit?"

"Sure! Keep safe, Cat."

I waved Gomorrah off as she flew the Fury back out and into the city.

Now to see what sort of fresh trouble Lucy had gotten into.

CHAPTER NINETEEN

WHERE THE HEART MIGHT BE

With the world almost ending as often as it has in the last few decades, it's no wonder that the less robust parts of our society have failed. The economy went to shit sometime in the late 1990s; we didn't really see it collapsing in full until the 2020s, though. By the 2030s there were more new types of currency than you could shake a stick at.

Every corporation had its own currency. Primebucks, Steamdollars, various kinds of points, usually with some shorthand of the company's name at the start.

It all went to shit eventually.

Now we have the handy credit. A monetary unit that means nothing, that's tied to nothing, and that's accepted everywhere!

—*Ramblings off the Street*, episode 385,
"Interview with a Homeless Economist," 2041

"Lucy!"

"Cat!"

Lucy hugged me, and I hugged her right back. I didn't care much that some of the kittens were nearby and making disgusted sounds. They could fuck off for all I cared. "How's the moving coming along?" I asked as I pulled back a little—not so much that she could escape from the hug, but enough that I could see past her and into the lobby of our home.

The kittens seemed . . . a bit bored? A few of them were sitting around the large table in the center of the room, and the twins were hanging off the side of the staircases leading above. I heard some laughing from the sides and glanced over in time to see Nose running out of one of the bedrooms, soon chased by Tim.

"The kittens are all right so far," Lucy said. "They're a bit bored, but hey, the place has wifi so they'll live."

"Cool, cool. Did you figure anything out with the hotel?" I asked. The entire home was still barren. It worked, in a minimalist sort of way, but minimalist wasn't exactly my style.

"Yeah, I've figured something out. I met Rac; she's off somewhere right now. Anyway, she made, like, fifteen of these turrets?"

"Yeah, I gave her the blueprint for those. Or I gave it to the machine above, whatever," I said.

"I called up the hotel, got on the line with someone important, and we struck a deal. We give them fifty of those turrets and they'll furnish the entirety of our home at their cost."

"Fifty?" I asked. "That's a lot, isn't it?"

"Yeah, but they're providing the raw materials. I got Rac to give me a list of how much of every material each turret takes, and then I rounded that up generously. The hotel gives us materials, we give them turrets, and they furnish things for us."

I nodded along. Fifty laser turrets around the hotel would probably do a decent job of protecting it. Or they could put some inside, in lobbies or open spaces.

"They want you to do the delivery yourself. At least the first one. Uh, they'll probably turn it into a minor PR thing. Is that all right?"

"I guess so," I said. "We'll have to see how many turrets we can make in a short period. If Rac made over a dozen in half a day . . . yeah, maybe fifty won't keep the printer too busy. We still need some for around the house."

"I was thinking we set aside half of those we make," Lucy said. "Use the other half to arm the kitten house."

"We're not calling this place the kitten house," I said.

"The kitten place?" Lucy asked with a growing, shit-eating sort of grin. "The Cat Tree? Oh, the Cat Palace?"

"Cat Palace isn't too bad," I muttered.

"Does that make you the queen of the Cat Palace?" Lucy asked. "Oh, does that mean I'm the king?"

I sniffed. "You're the other, hotter queen," I said before giving her a peck. "Oh, right, speaking of gayness, I invited Gom and Franny over for dinner."

Lucy's eyebrows shot up. "You know we don't have cooking appliances. Or know how to cook."

"I figured we can order out," I said. "Maybe eat upstairs, away from all the brats."

Lucy nodded. "I'll see what I can do. We'll need to order for the kittens too. They'll start complaining soon. You know, it only took a couple of days for them to become complacent and used to eating as much as they want."

"I . . . don't think that's necessarily a bad thing."

Lucy shrugged. "It isn't. Well, maybe it's not too healthy to overeat, but whatever. We're all too thin anyway."

"Yeah," I agreed. "Right, I need to call Peter. You know, the nonprofit guy? We need to arrange things a bit better and I want to stay on top of things. Made a few points today, so I can afford to get some of the shit we'll need."

"Nice," Lucy said. "Did you fight a lot of aliens?"

"Eh, a couple. Mostly let some grenades melt them. Then Gomorrah and I dropped a bomb onto a hive. Oh, I need to show you that later. It was awesome. There was a mushroom cloud and everything."

Lucy giggled. "You sound enthusiastic."

"Lucy, it was one of the hottest things I've ever seen. Metaphorically and literally."

Lucy mock-gasped. "Should I be worried? Will you break up with me and try your luck with the mushroom cloud?"

"Hmm, I don't know," I said. "You're able to make me explode in much more interesting ways," I murmured as I tightened our hug.

"For fuck's sake, there's a crowd in here, you know."

I turned—still in Lucy's arms—and noted Daniel stumbling over. "Hey," I said.

"Yo," he replied. "Nice place. Decent internet too."

"You've got your priorities," I said. "Hey, Daniel, do you think you'd like doing volunteer work?"

Daniel shrugged. "I might. What's up?"

"Cool. So, I was thinking. We're going to start producing some prosthetics and shit soon. We'll probably be opening a sort of clinic in this building. I was thinking about our home at first, but, uh, that doesn't sound like a smart idea now that I'm thinking about it."

"Lots of injured people walking into our living room does sound a bit weird," Lucy said.

"Yeah, exactly. So, Daniel, can you find out who owns the floors below this one? Then bully them into letting us use them as a clinic. I'll get you in touch with Silverbloom. We can make the prosthetics here, then slap them onto people below."

"Sounds good," Daniel said. "And yeah, I can help. I've done my share of organizing before."

"You have?"

He shrugged. "Mostly getting raids together for a few MMOs. Same difference, really."

"Uh-huh, I'm sure," I said.

"Oh, come on, it's not like you have a degree in samurai-ness. We're all just muddling along here and doing what we can," he said. "Now, I couldn't help but overhear you mentioning that two babes will be coming over for dinner."

"Yeah, you should probably stay away from them," I said. "One's liable to burn you."

"Ohh, maybe he can help them, actually," Lucy said. "Make men look so cringey that they finally admit to their secret love for one another?"

"I'm pretty sure that's not how it works," Daniel said. "Also, ouch."

I shook my head, then glanced at the time. We were nearing five in the afternoon. It was getting dark outside, the overcast above shifting from gray-white to a burnt orange. "I'm gonna go give Silverbloom a call. Lucy, wanna order stuff for us so that it arrives on time? I bet a bunch of delivery drivers will be quitting today, what with the apocalypse happening."

"I got it," Lucy said. She gave me a peck on the cheek, then skipped off to the main room of our new home, where she bullied Nose off the table.

I nodded to Daniel before heading upstairs. I elected to send Silverbloom a long-winded text instead of calling him. I linked him over to Daniel's number at the same time; I was a little tired, and dealing with someone over the phone would just tire me out even more.

I found our bedroom, currently sans bed, and then with a sigh sat on the floor and laid myself down so that I could stare at the ceiling.

This day had been . . . a day.

Tomorrow, I figured, would be an even busier mess.

There are small cushions and mattresses available for just a few points. If you intend to lie there for a while you might want to consider something of the sort.

I hummed. "Nah, this is fine," I said. The hard surface felt good for my back, and it was nice to get some weight off my feet, armored boots or not.

I opened the map of the city and its surroundings.

There was a lot more orange. Huge smears of the color marked the countryside in every direction. I could imagine the hundreds and thousands of little Antithesis scouring the world for everything they considered a threat.

It was going to take a lot of work to make the area safe. More than I'd ever be able to do.

The likelihood of the city falling is relatively low.

"That's nice," I said. "I imagine it'll be even lower if we do our part?"

Every Vanguard lending their efforts to the protection of humanity helps.

"Good," I said. I'll help . . . tomorrow.

CHAPTER TWENTY

PIT BULLS AND TACOS

You're still worried about the gays?
Don't you think the Lord has given us bigger problems to deal with?
—Unknown cardinal during the Vatican incursion of 2037

"Cat!" Lucy screamed from the dining room upstairs. "They're here!"

"Got it!" I called back. I was in our bedroom, which was currently bed-less. We'd have to rough it for the night, but I figured we could manage one night without anything more comfortable than each other and a few blankets. My armor stood tall and imposing in the corner of the room, with most of my gear leaning up next to it.

We were going to be having dinner; I probably didn't need to be bullet-proof to endure some takeout.

I ran downstairs; swore as I almost tripped over Tim, who was using the bottom step as a seat; then eyed the main room, where the rest of the kittens were making a mess. We'd ordered enough junk food to feed a small army, and the kittens were doing their best to eat their way through it all.

To be fair, Lucy and I had never really ordered food with a full wallet before. We just kept adding more and more things to the order, half spurred on by our own hunger (I couldn't remember the last time I'd actually eaten) and half by the heady feeling of being rich enough to ignore the checkout price at the bottom.

"Y'all behave," I said over the noise of so many brats and one dog gathered in one room. My mecha-cats were lounging here and there, watching over the kittens or being used as mobile benches to sit on.

I got some affirmatives, but the kittens seemed too busy to give much of a shit.

Shaking my head, I ran past them and to the front lobby area. Gomorrah and Franny were waiting on the other side. I was relieved to see that they were in somewhat more casual clothes. I opened the door and grinned at the pair of them. "Hey! Welcome to the Cat Castle! Come on in!"

Gomorrah rolled her eyes, which was nice—I didn't often get to see her unmasked face—and then she gestured Franny in ahead of her. "Hello . . . Cat?"

"Yeah?"

Franny chuckled. "I think she's trying to figure out if she should call you Cat or . . . whatever your real name is," Franny said. "You know, is this business or fun?"

"My real name's Catherine, so Cat works either way. No one calls me Catherine, though; that's like two syllables too many." I shut the door behind them, leaving the colder air outside. "So, will it be Gomorrah tonight, or Delilah?"

"Delilah, please," Gom . . . Delilah said.

I nodded as I looked the two up and down. Franny was in skinny jeans and a band shirt for a group I didn't recognize. Her hair was up in a big red ponytail and she had a grungy army-surplus sort of coat on. Very casual-punk-looking.

Delilah, on the other hand, was done up in a black dress that stopped just below the knees and had a lace-covered cutout on the front. Black heels, dark makeup, some eyeliner. "I didn't know you were into the goth look," I said. I was feeling a little underdressed, maybe. Clean sweatpants and an oversized T-shirt were maybe too casual.

"She isn't," Franny replied. "She just doesn't know how to dress herself if it's not in a habit."

"Franny," Delilah said.

I laughed, then pointed deeper into the house. "Wanna come upstairs? Lucy's setting up the table now. I asked Rac and she found it somewhere downstairs. I decided not to ask too many questions."

"Because you're afraid of knowing too much about your little friend's questionably legal activities?" Delilah asked.

"More like I can admit to not knowing if one of our neighbors shows up asking about their table," I said.

We crossed the room with all the kittens, reaching the staircase surprisingly unscathed by the crowd of shitstains making a mess of the living room.

"This place sure is unique," Franny said as she looked around. "I thought the exterior would be a sort of one-off gimmick, but I guess the inside needs to be strange to fit everything."

"It's a bit weird, yeah," I said.

"How are your defenses?" Gomorrah asked.

"Not perfect," I said. "Still need to talk to Longbow about his AA gun above. Rac's made some little turrets that we're starting to place around, but we don't have full coverage yet. It's going to take a couple of days at this rate before the entire tower's a kill zone for any lower-level models. Longer before we can make it really dangerous. How's the church?"

"Better than here, I think. The nuns back home all have weapons training, and we have a decent armory. I set up a few towers with flamethrowers and some more traditional gun emplacements."

"Sounds nice. I might get someone to train the kittens in using guns; that might be a good skill to have."

"You could likely use the training yourself," Delilah said.

There's a skill package for that.

I huffed, but they weren't exactly wrong.

"Gomorrah, Franny!" Lucy cheered as we finally made it upstairs. She welcomed our friends with open arms, pulling Franny into a hug, then giving Delilah a squeeze too. "We have food! Come on, sit. We don't actually have chairs because Cat can't think that far ahead, but we do have some park benches. Just don't ask where they're from."

"What's for dinner?" Franny asked.

"Burgers! And fries, poutine, milkshakes, soda, uh, we have doughnuts and three kinds of pizza too. And hush puppies. Fried cheese bites. We have a whole box of coffee." Lucy frowned at the table. "I'm missing a couple of things."

"Like a doctor?" Delilah said. "This all sounds like a quick way to end up hospitalized."

"Oh right! Salads!" Lucy clapped. "We have those too. Proper American salads, with more meat bits and bread and cheese than lettuce."

Lucy pulled the two along, then gestured them toward a bench. It was a very small bench, with barely enough room for two people to fit onto it, and only if they didn't mind bumping hips while they sat.

I glanced at the bench, then up to Lucy, who gave me a knowing wink.

I nodded to her as I went around the other side and sat across from the girls. Lucy, it seemed, was keen on playing matchmaker some more. At least she seemed to be a bit subtle about it. It could all be excused away, and it wasn't like getting the two to sit close together was starting anything.

Grabbing a plastic plate, I started adding junk to it, which seemed to be the signal for the others to do the same. Delilah was the only one showing any sort of restraint. The rest of us were more like a pack of rabid animals tossed into an overfull dumpster.

"Oh, sweet potato fries!" Franny cheered as she grabbed a fistful, opened a burger, and smushed them in.

Delilah watched the rather disgusting display, but she just smiled fondly.

I glanced at Lucy. She'd seen it too, and we shared a nod.

"So, Franny," Lucy said as she chewed on a ketchup-dipped fry. "You're from the same church thing as Delilah, right? Is it, like, a fancy orphanage?"

"Huh? Oh, yeah, and no, it's not an orphanage. It's more of a boarding school, I guess. You stay there for, like, nine months of the year, with a few vacations and breaks here and there. The rest of the time you spend with your family."

Lucy nodded. "That's neat! Are your groups big? Or was it just, like, the two of you?"

"We're . . . thirty-ish in our year-group," Franny said. She glanced at Delilah for confirmation. "Delilah and I have been together for a while, though."

"Wait," Lucy said. "I thought you two were just friends . . . oh, did you break up? I'm sorry. Didn't mean to stick my foot in my mouth."

"Break? Uh, no, no, it's not like that," Franny said. She laughed, but it sounded forced.

"So, it's more of an open relationship kind of thing?" Lucy asked.

"No, we're not gay," Franny said.

She couldn't have convinced a kid that candy was good for them with that tone.

Delilah, next to her, shot me a glare that bounced right off the ablative layer made from my willingness to start shit.

"So, how long have you two known each other?" Franny asked. She took a bite out of her burger after firing her question off. It didn't disguise the bit of red on her cheeks.

I smiled and leaned over to Lucy, who turned my way. We kissed, just a quick, chaste thing that still left me licking my lips to taste the saltiness of what she'd been eating.

Delilah and Franny had both stopped midbite to stare, and both resumed eating with the same start when they noticed we were done. "Oh, it's been, uh, a while?" Lucy asked. "Do you mean when we started dating, or when we first met?"

"Uh," Franny said.

The poor girl, she'd gotten Lucy's attention. At this point Lucy wouldn't let go until the two were happily married. She was like a pit bull with a box full of tacos in her mouth.

CHAPTER TWENTY-ONE

THE CALM

Samurai tend to work alone. It's true that there are some larger organizations run by samurai that exist to assist samurai on and off the field, but even the members of these tend to be extremely self-reliant and want to work on their own.

It will happen, though, in rare moments, that two or more samurai will work together long enough to form a sort of bond. Lag and Dial-Up; DoubleDog and Electric Heart. There have been many iconic samurai teams that have lasted years.

Even the extremely powerful samurai accomplish more when working together.

In this teamwork seminar, we hope to use some of the tips and tricks learned by observing these to make your teamwork even greater!

—Obligatory Team-Building Seminar, 2056

Somehow, Lucy convinced Franny that she absolutely needed a tour of the house. She took the taller redhead by the wrist and dragged her off to see some of the neater rooms. She was pretty proud that she'd designed a lot of the house herself.

That left Delilah and me at the table, both of us more than a little stuffed and suffering from that pleasant haze that came from eating far too much of the worst kinds of food.

"It's a nice place," Delilah said. She made a vague, weak gesture at the room around us.

"Yeah, it's pretty nice," I said. "Not as safe as I want it to be yet, but we'll get there."

"I trust you," Delilah said. She picked at some fries, finding the most burnt, crispiest one before tossing it into her mouth. "Thanks for the supper, by the way."

"I hardly did much here," I said. "Mostly Lucy's work. I just tossed money at the problem."

"It's still a nice gesture. I needed to get out of the house."

"That bad?" I asked.

"I've complained about it at length already," she said. "Besides, it really isn't that bad. Just a lot of old, worried nuns who don't know what they can do to help. It weighs on you, you know? Not knowing, not being able to act. I think . . . maybe that's one of the requirements to become a Vanguard."

I tilted my head. "You mean you need to be pissed that you can't do anything?"

"Didn't you feel that, when you were offered the position?" Delilah asked.

I snorted. "If I recall, I was mostly thinking, 'Oh shit oh fuck I'm going to die.' There might have been some internal screaming too."

Delilah's shoulders shook with a single exhale of laughter. "I guess that's fair. We don't exactly have the most peaceful job there is."

"Yeah," I agreed. "I kinda like it, though."

She nodded along. "It's not bad work. Satisfying, in its own way. But it is dangerous. Hey, Cat?"

"Yeah?"

Gomorrah didn't say anything for a bit; it was clear she was thinking about something. "If I die, can you take care of Franny for me?"

"Uh," I said. "You know, I already have one girlfriend."

She jabbed her elbow into my ribs, and I coughed as I bent over from the blow. "Don't be a fool; you know what I meant."

I grinned. "I know, I know. Just messing with you. But okay, yeah. As long as you do the same with Lucy for me."

Gomorrah nodded. "It's a deal."

"Okay," I said before extending my hand to her. She looked at it for a moment before she took it, and we shook. "Deal. But only if you promise that you'll cork it first."

"Hah! Now that I think about it, I really picked the short stick with this one, didn't I? You're the one always in close proximity to things that are exploding."

"Damn right," I said. I leaned to the side, bumping her shoulder with mine. "So, you want me to take care of Franny, huh? That must mean you care about her a whole lot?" It was a statement, but I wasn't hiding any of the implication behind the words.

Delilah rolled her eyes and tore apart another fry before answering. "I do care a lot about her. She's my best . . . one of my best friends. I don't know if I care about her the way you're implying, though. So please keep your head firmly out of the gutter."

I couldn't help the grin. "One of . . . does that make me best friend number two?"

"In a far second place, maybe," Delilah said. "Also, while we're on the subject, can you tell Lucy to calm down a bit with her . . . romantic intentions? I think she's not nearly as subtle as she thinks she is."

"I can tell her. Don't know if that'll stop her. She's got this thing for hopeless people."

"Franny and I are hardly hopeless," Delilah said.

I made a so-so gesture with my hand. "You're both a little hopeless," I said. "Besides, you're our friends, and Lucy probably just wants the best for you. Or what she thinks is best."

"You know, you're rather sweet for a semiferal street orphan," Delilah said.

"Semiferal?" I asked. I grabbed a handful of chips and shoved them into my mouth, crumbs falling all over.

"Disgusting," Delilah said, but there was a hint of amusement under her haughtiness.

I perked up as I heard Lucy returning. She was followed by a red-faced Franny and a cat bot that had a few cheap bags balanced on its back. "Hey! The dessert arrived!"

"You ordered dessert?" Delilah asked. "After all of this?"

"What's wrong with dessert?" I asked.

She shook her head. "It's a good thing we lead such active lives; I can't imagine burning all of this off otherwise."

"Come on, there's ice cream for everyone," Lucy said. We had ordered those super-expensive little ice cream packs, the ones that had weird flavors that somehow sounded really good. Lucy passed them around and then handed out spoons, and soon we were pigging out on semi-melted sugary goodness.

"So," Franny asked as she licked her spoon, "are you two going to be doing more work tomorrow?"

I nodded. "Yeah. I don't know if we'll be together or not, though."

"I don't mind either way. But I intend to start early in the morning."

"I can get up early," I said.

"At around five," Delilah added.

"In the morning?" I asked. "That's not healthy."

"It's before the sun comes up. I'm certain the aliens won't sleep overnight. The earlier we hit them, the fewer we'll have to deal with."

"I guess, but for me to be up at that kind of hour I'd need to go to bed, like, before midnight." I shook my head. "That's just wrong. It'll take an hour or so to relax after we're done with dessert, then half an hour to say goodbye, and then we need to check on the kittens. Then after that Lucy and I need to take a shower together. By the time that's all done, it'll be tomorrow."

Delilah shook her head. "Degenerate," she said.

"Prude," I fired back.

We ate our ice cream, then argued over politics, all four of us clearly having no idea what we were talking about but with plenty of opinions to make up for our lack of knowledge.

Once everything was done, we lounged around for a bit; none of us had the energy to pick up the trash heaped before us.

"We should head out," Delilah said. She was a bit mournful-sounding about it, but she kept glancing up out of one thin window and at the cold, dark sky outside. It was getting to be pretty late.

"All right," I said. I stood up with a grunt of effort, then gave my hand to Delilah to get her to her feet. In turn she helped Franny, who seemed to almost be in pain from overeating.

We made our way downstairs; past the living room, where a few kittens were sleeping huddled up in piles of blankets here and there; and finally out to the lobby, where we all stared at the blustery rain washing across the landing pad outside.

"Drive safe," I said. "And give me a call tomorrow . . . maybe a few hours after five?"

Gomorrah chuckled. "I will, no worries. Taking on the aliens is always more fun when there's more of us on the scene. And more explosive too."

I grinned. "Damned right."

Lucy went around giving everyone goodbye hugs, and I got swept up in all of that too.

And then the two were off, running over to the Fury while covering their heads from the downpour.

"That was nice," I said.

"It was," Lucy agreed. "She's a good friend. Hot too."

"Uh-huh," I said. "Jealous?"

She laughed. "You wish. Unless getting cucked is a kink you haven't told me about?"

"I'm afraid not," I said. I leaned over and gave her forehead a careful peck. "Should we head back in? I think I saw some trash bags somewhere, and we can stuff the leftovers away for tomorrow."

"Mm-hmm, that sounds nice," Lucy said. "And then a nice long shower, which I deserve after doing all the work tonight."

"Ah yes, my hardworking Lucy, carrying all the boxes around and only stealing a bit of the food for herself."

That earned me a smack, followed by a chase through our new home.

CHAPTER TWENTY-TWO

JOLLY OLD DAY JOB

A lot of people, when they talk about the ideal samurai load-out or specialization, tend to suggest mass automation. Things like drone armies or reproducible nanoweapons.

It's strange that despite the number of samurai that do have some automated drones at their disposal, very few actually focus on using those.

—Spacefight Versus Forums, 2041

One of the first things I did on waking up was check the interactive map.

The Antithesis hadn't been sleeping much, it seemed. The orange blobs representing their positions had grown to cover almost twice the space they had the night before, and now there were a few red dots here and there.

If it doubled again, it was possible that they'd manage to encircle the entire city. As it was, the blobs were spread out into long tendrils, often poking out from one big area and reaching out in a dozen directions. I could almost see a pattern there.

Then, of course, I squeezed in closer to Lucy and opened a few media apps to doomscroll the night's news.

A few cities had been hit already. Some had had terrible problems with evacuations. Washington was taken over by protesters from some anti-doomsday cult who were chanting that the Antithesis were all made up. The forests around Los Angeles were on fire, because why not, and Mexico City's arcology had shattered.

Shit was hitting the fan all over.

I sighed.

And it was my job to stop that.

I got up, figured that I'd showered once in the last twelve hours and didn't need a second even if I'd been rather active last night, got my clothes on, then stepped into my armor.

Lucy was lying down on a heap of blankets, one bare leg uncovered while the rest of her hugged the spot I'd been on a moment before.

I took a picture before sneaking my way out of the room.

A few of the kittens were up and about downstairs, but they were mostly preoccupied with making a mess of the place. I told them off, maybe tossed a few threats around, then headed outside.

It was, of course, raining. Because we couldn't have a nice day of sunshine to go with the invasion. I called over my hoverbike while adjusting my coat against the constant weak drizzle. I bet a bunch of corporations were having a field day pumping the production on their factories while inspectors and the like were too busy preparing for the invasion.

My bike came to a stop before me, and I climbed on and shot up into the air.

It was just shy of noon, and the city below looked like it always did, as if the invasion were an afterthought. The banner ads on the sides of skyscrapers were warning people to stay home but only between ads for new hair gels and some celebrity porn sites.

Sighing, I opened the map and started looking for a place where I'd be useful.

Catherine, there's a mid-urgency call for assistance at this location.

Myalis highlighted a part of the city to the west: a long stretch of road where a smaller city was set up. It was almost big enough that its suburbs merged into New Montreal's. The priority alert was just on the outskirts of that, away from New Montreal.

"What's going on there?" I asked. There was a pin there, with an exclamation mark and a tag saying that one samurai was present.

In summary, a large convoy of supplies gathered from a collection of smaller settlements to the west is heading to New Montreal. The convoy has attracted a lot of attention from the Antithesis and is being followed. The Family suspect that this formation of Antithesis might be the first proper wave in this incursion, at least if it isn't stopped.

"What makes it a wave or whatever?" I asked as I turned my bike that way. That sounded like a good spot to make some points from.

A "wave" is a colloquial term for when a large body of Antithesis all start moving toward a singular objective or area. Often these will run into small groups who will join the larger formation.

"So this is, what, a pre-wave?"

Likely a large number of Antithesis all charging in the same direction. It's possible that other cells will join them in their charge and that any small hives in the path of the wave will start producing more models as the hive discovers that they are threatened.

So it was the start of an exponential shit show. "What does the Family want to do about it?" I asked. The pin on the map opened up a heap of documents, but I didn't have time to read those while racing over.

*Stop the wave before it grows large enough to overwhelm the defenses of
the satellite city. The datapack includes information about those defenses.
They are not exactly impressive.*

Myalis opened up an array of screens across the edges of my vision. A
map of the smaller city, with images of the defenses. Those consisted mostly
of chain-link fences that had been put up overnight, a few two-generation-
old tanks and armored cars, and a lot of local volunteers with guns older
than I was.

I tapped on the icon that indicated another samurai was around, then
blinked at the name. Jolly Monarch? He was the weird guy with the crown.
He seemed like he was decently experienced. Wouldn't he be enough on his
own?

Then again, the Family's request for more assistance hadn't been
removed despite him being there, so chances were that he didn't think he
would be enough on his own.

I searched the map for a moment before finding the spot where Gomorrah was. She was patrolling along the edges of another small settlement, in
an area that was orangey-green.

If she'd been at it since the morning, she was probably a little tired
already.

I revved up my bike and leaned down lower, cutting the wind resistance
and darting across the city a bit faster.

The moment I was out of the crowded skies of New Montreal, I pushed
the bike ever harder. Wind and rain whipped at me, but I couldn't feel
either within my armor. Dropping lower, I skimmed over the ground until I
neared the outskirts of the satellite city and started to circle around it.

I knew that the Family was working to build some sort of reinforcements around the main city, but it looked like this place had its own version
of that.

Like the cheap credit-or-less version of a wall. Secondhand fencing and
cement barriers cut across one of the bigger highways that went around
the edge of the city. It made sense that they'd put up their wall there. The
highway was a wide stretch of flat asphalt. The militia defending the city
could place their old tanks and gun nests right on the inner side of the road
without issue, and any Antithesis crossing over to them wouldn't benefit
from any cover.

The houses and businesses on the other side of that highway were shit
out of luck, though. It looked like a lot of the homes on that side had their
lights off. People had evacuated already, or they were too stubborn to leave
their cookie cutter for the safety of the city proper. Either way, it didn't look
like anyone gave much of a shit about them.

Jolly Monarch is at that major intersection.

Myalis highlighted a part of the highway where two eight-lane roads met.

The intersection was busy, with a police officer directing traffic holding a pair of batons and a roadblock set up on either side of the intersection, ready to close at a moment's notice.

Volunteers, onlookers, and a lot of local militia sorts were milling around behind the blockade while the last few cars drove back to the safety of the city.

One section of the road was closed off, and that was where I found Jolly Monarch.

The older samurai was parked next to what looked like a cross between a cartoonishly over-the-top throne and a parade float. He was standing next to the throne while drones moved all around him.

I brought my bike down nearby, put it in park, then swung off the back of it. I could feel all the eyes turning my way as I walked over to Jolly Monarch and his army of black-and-white drones.

He seemed to have a few models around him, most of them about the size of an adult. They looked like giant floating trash cans. Very postmodern trash cans. With little barrels sticking out of their sides.

"Hey," I said.

"Aha! Stray Cat, here to save the day!" Jolly Monarch said. "It's good to see you."

"Yeah, you too," I said. "So, what the hell is going on around here? And what are those?" I asked while pointing at the nearest drone.

"These are my pawns, and unfortunately, they won't be enough to keep us safe today."

CHAPTER TWENTY-THREE

GONNA BE

There's this pervasive idea, especially from those old-ass zoomer sorts, that one day things will return to normal. The samurai will disappear; the aliens will fuck off, back to whatever hellhole they're from; and everything will be right as rain.

It's not gonna happen.

Welcome to the new normal, motherfuckers!

—Award-winning high school essay, 2041

"So, what's the sitch?" I asked.

People ran around carrying sandbags, metal boxes, and other equipment. The only uniform they had was a distinct lack of uniform. They were normal folks, with that kind of desperate energy that said they were happy to be doing *something* but they weren't sure if it would be enough.

Jolly Monarch reached up and adjusted the oversized crown atop his head. His whole uniform took the theme thing to another level. He had a thick red cape and was wearing some sort of almost militaristic suit, with medals all over his chest and a scepter by his side. It didn't suit his face, though. He couldn't be older than thirty.

"The situation's looking a little bleak. I have twenty-four pawns here and four bishops." He pointed with his scepter to the nearest of the trash-can-looking drones. I guess they were meant to be shaped like the pawns in a chess set. That didn't give me much of a clue as to what kind of armament they had.

"And what'll we be fighting off with those?" I asked.

Jolly Monarch grinned. "A nice proto-wave of everyone's favorite man-eating plants." He gestured, and one of the pawns came closer. A small opening appeared on its side, and a projected hologram started to float between us: the city we were in and the long stretch of highway heading westward from there. "The wave is mostly following the highway. We're estimating between fifteen hundred and two thousand models. Mostly on the lower end of the spectrum. Threes, fours, maybe some model sixes."

"So a whole heap of them," I said. "Can you take care of the wave on your own?"

"My projections say . . . mostly?" Jolly Monarch said. His smile twisted a bit. "I have enough pawns here to blunt the front of the wave. I might even be able to stop its advance entirely. But that's only if I'm lucky. The more likely situation is that I'll be overrun if all I use are my current forces. Then the locals also defending this section will suffer for it."

"Can't you use the points to buy even more pawns or whatever?" I asked.

Jolly Monarch nodded. "Oh yes. But these pawns are about a thousand points each. They don't come cheap."

I frowned at the drone. It didn't look like a thousand-point investment to me.

"Right. How long do we have?"

"Forty-two minutes and change," Jolly Monarch said.

I glanced at the projection again. That was plenty of time. "Okay, then. I'll be back in forty minutes." I started out toward the road.

"What will you do?" Jolly Monarch asked.

"Does it matter if I blow up a few buildings on that side of the barricade?" I asked.

"Not really, no," he said.

"In that case, I'm going to turn this entire stretch of highway into a nightmare for those plant fucks."

"Oh, well, good luck!" Jolly Monarch said with a happy wave.

I had to wonder why someone who had clearly been a samurai for much longer than I had been felt like he wasn't able to take care of a wave all on his own. The cost of his drones didn't make sense either. My mecha-cats looked way cooler and were a fraction of the cost.

"Are those things really worth a thousand points?" I asked Myalis as I vaulted over the cement barrier and into the little no-plant-zone just beyond.

I see what you're thinking. And yes. The drones are. I suspect that Jolly Monarch's focus is not mainly a combat one. The cost of his drones mostly comes from their inherent versatility.

"Huh, all right," I said. I paused at the end of the intersection. The road stretched out ahead of me, almost entirely clear except for a couple of abandoned cars shoved to the edges. I nodded. It was a blank canvas, basically.

"Myalis, first things first. I need a new main weapon. Also, what's my current point total?"

Current Point Total: 2,205

Did you want to purchase a shotgun-like weapon? You've been mentioning something of the sort for a while.

"Something like that would be nice, yeah," I said.

In that case, I would suggest the Mark Two Bullcat. It's a fully automatic drum-fed shotgun, with aim assist systems and the capability to accept a wide range of ammunition, and it can be reloaded directly through the expenditure of a few points. It also has a decent stealth coating and comes with an adjustable sling!

That would be handy. No need to pause to reload seemed like it would be great on an automatic gun, as long as the point cost of each round wasn't too high. "Does it have, like, an underbarrel grenade launcher?"

You could just fire the grenades directly. As I said, it accepts a wide range of ammunition types.

"Oh, nice," I said. "How much?"

One hundred and fifty points.

Not bad. "I'll take it. If it doesn't work out, then I'll at least try to make more points than I spent with it."

New Purchase: Mark II Bullcat

Points Reduced from . . . 2,205 to . . . 2,055

A box appeared by my side. I kicked it open, then picked the Bullcat out from in it. The gun was matte black, about as long as my arm from fingertip to elbow, and had a large drum just before the shoulder pad. So it was a bullpup of sorts. The end of the barrel was shaped to look like the face of a hissing cat.

I picked it up, tucked it against my shoulder, then leaned my head down to look through the large reflex scope that unfolded on the top of it. "Neat," I said.

My free hand came up and rested on the slide on the front. Which raised a question. "Okay, so if it's fully automatic, why does it have a pump?"

It makes a satisfying and threatening sound when you pump it.

I frowned down at the sleek gun, and then, with a hand gripping around the fore end, I pumped the gun.

It made a crunchy *crack-chunk* noise. The sort of noise that says "I'm here to fuck shit up." Then the gun started to hum even as little lights on the sides and within the barrel glowed an ominous red.

"Oh, fuck yeah," I muttered.

I didn't have all day to cuddle my new gun, though, no matter how cool it was. I had something of a plan.

"All right, Myalis. I want to cover this street with things that will make the xenos' day worse. I was thinking we set things up with timers—let them get funneled in enough that when we set things off, it will be too late to pull the majority of the wave out. It should blunt the front of their assault. Maybe a mix of those resonators to begin with, then something with a bit more kick to it? Uh, maybe some of those fuel-air explosives."

You're in an open space; the fuel will spread farther, but its damage will be more limited. There are other nonconventional weapon choices that could slow down an advance. Perhaps zero-kelvin bombs? Those would freeze large areas. Garrote grenades could create pockets of unpassable space as well, perhaps slowing the Antithesis enough to allow your resonators to act.

"I like it," I said. "There's a lot of houses on the edges. We could break some windows, place turrets in there, and have an overlapping field of fire down the middle of the road."

That's a wonderful idea!

I grinned. "Damn right. Look, I'm not super clever; think you can figure out the ideal location for the bombs so that they overlap correctly?"

How many points do you intend to spend on this?

I shrugged. I didn't have many to work with. "All of them."

In that case, please move over to the drainage pipe to your left. Pull the cover off and place this within it.

I dropped to one knee next to a sewer pipe, pulled it open with surprising ease, then found a box appearing by my side, a resonator with a cord tied around its middle. I nodded as I figured it out. The cord I tied to the bars in the grate, and then I let the grenade fall down so that it hovered a foot into the pipe. "All right, next?"

Next, a zero-kelvin explosive under the wheel well of the vehicle abandoned to your right, followed by a diagonal row of garrote grenades across the street. We will also be placing a fuel-air explosive into the dirt next to the ditch on the left with the spray nozzle pointed downward.

Myalis's tone was fairly flat, but I couldn't help but get the impression that she was having a lot of fun with all of this.

To be fair, I was looking forward to blowing shit up too.

It was going to be a blast.

CHAPTER TWENTY-FOUR

SETTING THE TABLE

It is imperative that any agent collecting resources after the passage of a samurai ensure that they are up to date with company data regarding that particular samurai.

Samurai who are known for using disposable weaponry might be the most valuable members to follow, but they also frequently use disposable explosives and traps, which can be harmful to those collecting abandoned equipment.

—Coil Co. mercenary outfit agent policy, 2034

I struck at the window with my elbow, wincing a bit at the loud shattering crunch that came from the glass bursting apart. "That should do it," I muttered mostly to myself. I swiped my arm across a desk, tossing aside some loose documents and shit so that I had more room, and then I backed up half a step. "Drop it," I said.

A box plopped onto the table, then unfolded into a three-legged turret with a plasma gun on top that looked like little more than a barrel, some cooling pipes, and a small tank of whatever was used to make plasma.

There was also a cord sticking out of the bottom. I grabbed it, dropped to one knee, and plugged it into a wall socket.

This was the third home I'd broken into to install a turret. They were cheap, with no armor and only the most basic of firing and targeting systems, but as long as the power held out they'd be able to poke holes into passing Antithesis, and that was all I needed at the moment.

Install this next to the turret.

A box appeared next to me, and I caught it out of the air and broke it open. The explosive inside looked pretty simple. A stick of some sort of plastic with a detonator built into the end of it. I opened a drawer and tossed it in. Then the next explosive came, a resonator that I slapped onto the desk next to the turret.

"Time?"

Twelve minutes until the wave's estimated arrival.

I didn't have time to sit around and complain that I didn't have time.

I'd been running around both sides of the highway, ducking under cars to place bombs, tucking resonators between cement barriers, and putting little disks of more traditional explosives across the road with a certain precise distance between them.

An alarm was ringing nonstop across the deserted street. I'd busted through the front of a car dealership across the road, and that had set off the place's alarms. Myalis had encouraged me to place two fuel-air bombs inside the building, where the explosive gases would be contained by the glass walls.

Every pothole hid a bomb, turrets were placed under piles of trash with overlapping fields of fire, and I had punched some holes in the dry patches of grass on the roadsides and shoved even more explosives in those.

When everything went off, the entire highway would turn into a nightmare for anything plantlike.

"Next?" I asked as I scanned the road.

Garrote grenades, set four meters apart along both sides of the highway. If they're the first obstacle the wave runs into, they're likely to funnel in and avoid the edges of the road.

"Got it," I said. The road was empty from this point on, with nothing but a few lights between the two lanes and a thin cement barrier on the edges. A chill wind slid past, tossing around some balled-up burger wrappers and paper cups that scraped across the asphalt. It was too damned quiet.

I hopped over the fence on the edge of the road, then knelt down just as a box appeared by my side. I opened it and placed the grenade down. Then half a dozen more grenades appeared on the ground next to me, with long sticks poking out of their bottoms to make it easier to pin them to the ground.

I grabbed the bunch and ran over to what I guessed was about three meters off and planted the next one.

You're going to want to go to the other side of the road soon. Nine minutes until the wave arrives.

I cursed as I sprinted across the road, leapt the other barrier, then started planting more grenades while Myalis summoned even more of them for me to place. "All right," I said as I stood up. "Next?"

Too late. It seems as though the forward units of the wave have reached your position already.

My head snapped around, and I stared down the length of the highway.

A group of model threes were barreling down the road, claws scrambling for purchase on the asphalt and three-hinged jaws wide open to allow them to suck in more air. They were a good hundred meters away, but they were closing in.

I couldn't see the rest of the wave past them, not with the slight curve in the road and a few buildings in the way. "Shit," I muttered.

It might be time to return anyway. You're down to only a hundred and thirty-two points.

I nodded, spun on my heel, then started down the highway again. The space I'd mined was maybe two hundred meters long from start to finish, ending right at the intersection where Jolly Monarch and the militia had set themselves up.

"Any bombs to place on the way?" I asked.

A few. I would suggest using pheromone traps. They give off a scent that will attract the Antithesis into possible killbox locations. Additional explosives along the road might also distract or immobilize parts of the wave.

"Go for it," I said.

Myalis summoned some explosives and I tossed them into potholes or into the shadow of abandoned cars I hadn't already trapped.

I heard a scrambling behind me, getting closer and closer even as I continued to run.

"For fuck's sake," I muttered as I spun to the side and slid to a stop. The momentum of the stop tossed my new gun around, so I caught it by the grip and brought it up.

There were six model threes trailing after me in a nice, neat row.

I pumped my gun, then aimed down the barrel at the first before pulling the trigger.

The Bullcat barked, and I felt a satisfying kick back into my shoulder even as the first two Antithesis turned into a heap of bloody giblets that splattered past my feet. I aimed at the next and fired as it jumped.

"Oh, oh yeah," I muttered as the alien's trajectory changed in midair and it pirouetted into the ground with a hard splat.

The next two shots blew deep holes into the roadway before the third connected with the side of an Antithesis.

And then the last two aliens leapt right at me.

I raised my cybernetic arm even as I ducked to the side. One of them sailed past me while the other clamped onto my armor and chomped down for all it was worth.

My back shifted and my twin railguns unfolded from where they were hidden.

Two soft thumps later and the remaining Antithesis were dead.

I shook my arm to free it from the corpse still clamped on to me, then eyed the road. The main body of the wave was starting to show up. Contrary to what I was expecting, the horde of aliens weren't charging right out but were moving at a more cautious pace.

I wasn't going to wait around for them, though. I shouldered my gun and noticed one of the model threes wasn't quite dead yet, so I kicked it in the head, then started running back toward the intersection.

Just in case, I dropped a few more grenades here and there along the way.

You're effectively out of points now.

"Really?" I asked. "Even after killing those six?"

Yes, really. I wouldn't worry overly much. You are likely to see a large return in your investment in a few moments.

I grinned as I sprinted a bit harder. A bunch of civilians were poking their heads over the barricade; others were huddled behind stationary guns. Jolly Monarch was the only guy standing up straight and proud as if there were nothing to worry about.

I jumped, planted my foot on the top of one of the cement barriers, then hopped over the edge and landed in a crouch next to Jolly Monarch. "All done," I said.

"You've turned the entire road into a nightmare, haven't you?" he asked.

"Cost a few points, but I think it'll be worth it," I said. I slung my Bullcat off my shoulders and inspected the gun for any scratches. It seemed fine. Once I emptied it into some xenos, I'd ask Myalis about interesting new sorts of ammo. "The lot of them are going to show up soon enough, I think."

Jolly Monarch nodded. "Do you have the air covered?"

"Not really, no," I said.

"Then I'll have my pawns focus on that. Wouldn't want to lose our help because of some cheap model ones."

He gestured, and his robots shifted closer to the wall. Their sides unfolded, and a long cannon slid out from the middle of the drones and pointed into the air even as the bottom half of the drones broke apart into large landing-gear-like legs that planted themselves onto the road.

"That should do it. Now we wait for the fun to begin!"

CHAPTER TWENTY-FIVE

DINNER IS SERVED, AND IT'S YOU

Never underestimate the will of the common man. Certainly, they will lie back and take any small punishment you give them as long as the pain comes slowly like an ache in the back, but push too hard, push too fast, and they will be roused from their lazy state with great violence in their hearts.

—*Letters to My Son*, autobiography of a West African warlord, 2029

I dropped to one knee, Bullcat placed on the edge of the cement barricade with the stock pressed up into the crook of my shoulder. I closed my fleshy eye and zoomed in with the other.

I could see the wave coming. The Antithesis were clumped up, but those clumps were starting to spread out.

I didn't have the patience to count them, but there had to be a couple hundred of the bastards. Mostly it looked like we were dealing with model threes. I noticed a few of those tentacle-faced model fours and those really big model fives.

A flock of model ones was spinning around above the main body of the wave. They never moved too far from the central group. I was actually impressed by the quick switches in direction the model ones were pulling off, all in sync with each other too. It reminded me of some documentaries I'd seen about extinct birds that flew in large flocks. Things like starlings and such.

"You're sure you have enough AA to take care of the skies?" I asked.

I saw Jolly Monarch nod from the corner of my eye. "My pawns could likely take out this entire wave on their own. But I'd rather they not have to. I'll take care of the enemies above and any that get too close. Just do what you can to thin out the bulk of the wave."

"Right," I said. "Myalis, you got the timing down for all those bombs?"

Everything is set up. We only need to wait for the Antithesis to step into the right spots.

"So we just need to wait for the enemy to cooperate," I said. "I'm not any sort of tactician, but isn't that, you know, not a great idea?"

Incoming.

I refocused on the wave. It was obvious that the entire thing was starting to move hastily now. The aliens had our scent, I imagined. The civilians nearby started to mutter and curse as the entire formation of xenos started to run faster and faster.

Then the wave split down the middle, model threes scrambling aside to make room.

"Fuck," I said.

The Antithesis moving into the gap was a big motherfucker. A six-legged thing, about as tall as a hovercar. It had wings folded up against its sides and a long body like a grasshopper, though its head was all wrong, angular and with a large mouth that was a bit too vulva-ish for comfort.

"A model fifteen," Jolly Monarch said. "It's a little early to be seeing one of those."

"What's its gimmick?" I asked.

The model actually stopped, the rest of the wave continuing on past it without getting in its way.

"It's an artillery unit," Jolly Monarch said. "If you have any bombs near it, now would be a good time to set them off."

"I don't," I said. "Can you take out whatever it shoots?"

"I can," Jolly Monarch said. He gestured forward, and two of his pawn drones shifted to aim down toward the model fifteen. "Masks on, everyone!" he shouted.

All down the line, civilians scrambled to put masks on.

I didn't have time to ask why when the model fifteen fired.

I was expecting . . . something? A bomb, a bullet, maybe a large lump of acid.

What I wasn't expecting was for the model fifteen to spit out a spinning green wheel. It was about half as tall as I was, with a distended middle and furry sides. The wheel shot ahead, keeping balanced even as it bounced over potholes and raced past the front of the wave.

One of the pawns shot a burst toward the wheel and hit it dead-center.

The wheel exploded apart. I blinked as a cloud of pale dust filled the air before it. Then something rained down around me, a few plings sounding out as bits of the wheel made it all the way over to our position.

It wasn't until I heard one of the civilians screaming that I realized it wasn't just debris.

Model fifteens can produce a variety of projectiles, but for the most part they use a hybrid projectile. A wheel of tightly woven strips of flesh under incredible tension and lined with barbed hairs. That central wheel is wrapped in a cushion of soft spores, which are in turn wrapped in a thin layer of plant flesh. When the wheel collides with something hard enough to break the flesh, a signal passes through it that lets go of the core projectile. The rapid unwinding of the core sends the hairs within it flying forward and also releases all of the spores contained around it.

"Fuck," I said.

A few of those hairs were stuck in the barricade in front of me. Just one every handspan or so. Long, narrow, with a bit of a barb on the end.

I imagined it sucked to get one jammed into an eye or something.

"How often can that thing shoot?" I asked.

The alien answered by lobbing another wheel out.

"I'll take it out, no worries," Jolly Monarch said. He just stood there unconcerned while his drones shifted slightly. Then the air filled with criss-crossing lines of tracer fire and a cacophony of rattling machine guns. Brass clinked as it flew out of thin ports at the base of the drones.

The model fifteen was riddled through and through, its skin turning into a bleeding colander. Something burst apart inside the model fifteen, and its rearmost section basically just exploded.

The wave rushed around it, spreading out and speeding up. The drones widened their firing arc, taking out more of the models as they approached, but it was growing obvious that the weight of fire wasn't enough to stop the wave in its tracks.

Then two more wheels flew out above the wave and the pawns paused, shifted, then sniped them out of the air.

The swarm of model ones above twisted and darted ahead, a violent cloud rushing toward our position.

"Brace for impact, everyone," Jolly Monarch said. "Keep your wits about you. Aim for center mass. Kill them dead!"

Detonating the first row.

The garrote grenades I'd placed way out in the distance went off along the edges of the highway. The few models skirting the edge of the wave were instantly turned into purée by a twisting blending of angry monofilament.

I leaned forward, squinting to take it all in. I didn't know what the effective range of my gun was, but I was well outside it.

My railguns, though . . . I shifted my shoulders, allowing the two guns mounted to my back to unfold. They twitched, then fired. Two model threes collapsed near the front of the formation.

Then the aliens reached the next row of bombs.

Zero-kelvin bombs. There wasn't a big boom, but instead a wash of fog-like steam rolled across the ground. The Antithesis wave crashed into the freezing effect and died by the dozens.

When the mist cleared, I could see a solid sort of ovoid sphere pressed into the ground. The asphalt was riddled with cracks, the nearest cars were warped out of shape, and the model threes stuck within looked almost crushed.

It was an ice cube, but made of solid, frozen air.

The nearest Antithesis flopped as if someone had just dropped a plateful of half-cooked sausages on the ground. Those coming in behind them tried to jump over the effect, but it didn't do them any good.

I could feel it from where I was. A wash of cool air. The breath of some of the nearby civilians misted out of their masks.

The Antithesis were tough, though, and while that slowed them down, it didn't stop the wave.

Initiating next stage.

Windows burst on either side of the street. Quick flashes of blue light darted across the road from both sides as the laser turrets I'd hidden away opened up on the wave's flanks. They didn't rip the aliens apart. They didn't have the kick for that. They did burn into whichever aliens they hit, though, sizzling holes that took out one xeno at a time.

The pawns opened up with another loud burst of fire. Model ones poured out of the air, plummeting to the ground like so many sacks of meat to crash onto the road with dull thumps.

The wave continued, because there was no stopping it.

"Open fire!" Jolly Monarch shouted.

The civilians, already twitchy, didn't need to be told twice.

Old machine guns rattled and assault rifles barked. I tugged back the trigger on my Bullcat too. We greeted the front of the wave with a wave of our own. Lead met bone and flesh, and the Antithesis wave started to collapse.

Which was, of course, when everything went wrong.

CHAPTER TWENTY-SIX

BREACH, LOAD, CHARGE

Plans never survive first contact with the enemy.
If that's true, then the best trick is to have no plan at all.
—Longbow, about the Navajo Nation incursion, 2051

"Shit," Jolly Monarch said.

I don't like putting people into little boxes, but I'm human, so sue me. The little box I put Jolly Monarch in didn't include suddenly swearing aloud.

I snapped my head around toward the older samurai. "What?" I asked.

He glanced off to his right somewhere. "We have a breach. I've got two pawns working on it, but I think they might be outnumbered in the next few minutes."

"Did the wave split off?" I asked.

He shook his head. "I don't think so. Another smaller group, maybe. They're pouring out of a drainage ditch on the other side of our barricade. That's closer to the civilians than I'd like."

I stood up, glanced down the highway and at all the carnage there, then started heading back. "Gimme your video feed; I bet Myalis can set the bombs off without me here. I'll go kill the xenos and plug the hole."

"Thank you," he said. He snapped his fingers, and I flinched as a drone burst into existence next to him. It was either moving really fast or it had teleported in. Either way, a burst of air washed off it as it appeared. "My knight will escort you. Come back quickly if you can."

"Yeah, yeah," I said.

The knight drone buzzed out ahead of me, floating on three disks that hummed as they cut through the air. Other than the three disks, the drone looked like a teardrop, longer than I was tall and nearly as bulky on the big end. No visible guns, or anything else really, just a smooth white material with a marble-ish finish to it.

It looked expensive, though, and had lots of glowy bits, so I imagined it was a pretty good weapons platform.

I jogged after it with the occasional glance back to the road, where the bulk of the fighting was going down. "Myalis, will you be able to take care of the bombs?"

I've contacted Jolly Monarch's AI already. I am piggybacking over his pawn drone sensors. There won't be any issues when it comes to well-timed detonations.

"Cool," I said. "Those drones worth anything? They don't look that fancy."

They are versatile. More so than any drone you've purchased before. Destroying one would be a hassle, even for higher-tier Antithesis, and they can self-repair. Some of his pawn drones have been active for multiple years.

That was actually kind of impressive. I didn't know how long my own gear would last, not with the number of explosions going on in close proximity to me, or the number of monsters trying to eat me, or people shooting at me. I figured that most samurai switched gear out pretty regularly.

The knight drone sped down the highway leading deeper into the city, then around a curving off-ramp that dipped lower than the road and closer to the homes and businesses we were protecting.

There were plenty of vans and cars parked along the road here, with volunteers milling around them with the tense posture of people expecting to get swarmed by monsters at any moment. Three quarters of them were armed, but I wasn't sure how long they'd endure in front of a proper wave of Antithesis without cover.

I noticed a few of those same volunteers running just down the road, and the crack-pop of gunfire told me that we were getting closer to wherever the xenos had broken through.

I took in the scene as I rounded a curve.

The road turned to the left, leading deeper into the city. On one side was one of those sound-blocking walls; on the other, a small patch of scraggly greenery led up to the road with a pipe jutting out of the hillside over a muddy ditch.

The metal grating at the end of the pipe was torn off, and half a dozen Antithesis littered the ground around it.

Even as we arrived, another jumped out of the pipe, landed on the corpse of one of its pals, then got filled with lead as a pawn drone and a couple of civilians fired at it.

"What's the plan?" I asked as I got closer.

No one answered, and I realized that the person in charge of figuring out a plan in this case was me.

"Fuck."

This was going to be a problem. I could get Myalis to find a map of the pipe network. It was a storm drain; it wasn't going to be as complex as the sewers in New Montreal. Still, scouring the entire thing for aliens would take a while, and during that time, the Antithesis would be able to exit from anywhere in the city.

We were stopping one wave, sure, but this was going to get right past our little barricade, and it only took a dozen model threes to wreck someone's afternoon.

I nodded. "Myalis, I need to get in touch with someone from the Family. Can you send a ping to Laserjack?"

Sent.

"Cool, thanks," I said as I shouldered my Bullcat and walked over to the pipe. The interior was dark, but I had weird echolocation ears, and they did some bullshit that let me "see" into the dark by listening to it. My cybernetic eye had low-light vision, but that wasn't as cool.

It was enough that I knew to pull the trigger a moment before a model four reached out for me with a pair of tentacles.

I stepped to the side as one of those tentacles flopped to the ground, then fired into the pipe twice more to make a point.

"I need to fuck up all the aliens in there," I muttered. "Without destroying the entire damned thing . . . Myalis, can I get an extra-large nanite bomb? Something a bit faster-acting?"

Certainly. You're gaining points at a decent rate at the moment; you should be able to afford many such explosives.

"Nice," I said. "We'll need something to seal the tunnel too."

An expanding foam? It's nonlethal to the Antithesis, but it will prevent them from breaking out.

I nodded. "That'll do it," I said.

Myalis summoned a large cylindrical bomb with some eighties-movie glowing liquid inside it and a large display on one side with a timer. The nanite bomb, I figured.

The knight drone hovered behind me, and parts of its surface slid open to disgorge some spotlights, which lit up the inside of the pipe.

Then my shoulder-mounted railguns fired and took out the aliens lurking in the dark.

I climbed up into the pipe and walked in, bomb in one hand, shotgun in the other, with the strap acting as a third point of contact. Walking in a ways, I paused next to the first intersection, kicked aside a model three's corpse, then placed the bomb down and set the timer to a minute-thirty.

"Easy as operating a microwave, these things," I said. I pressed start, then waddled my way out of the pipe.

Myalis summoned a small, round grenade. I pulled the pin and rolled it in until it bumped against the body of the tentacle monster bleeding a few meters in.

Laserjack called me just as the grenade went off and the pipe started to fill with off-white goop that expanded up and out. "Stray Cat?" he asked.

"Hey, Laserjack," I said as I started back to the road. The muddy ground made it kind of tricky, and I didn't want to face-plant in front of a bunch of strangers. A few of them had to be filming, because if you weren't filming something that could kill you, then were you even human? "I'm over next to Jolly Monarch; we're defending some shit-hole little city, but we've got Antithesis pouring around our blockade through the storm drains."

"I see. That sounds unfortunately plausible. They can be like rats," he said.

"Yeah, that tracks. Look, I just dropped a nanite bomb into the storm drain, and I'm going to bully some volunteers into plugging all the exits with these goop grenades, but that probably won't stop all of the xenos. There's a fuckload of houses here, and they look occupied."

"You want the area evacuated?" he asked.

"Don't know if I have the authority to tell normal folks to leave their homes," I said.

"You're still new. You'll discover that no one has more authority than a samurai running away from something."

I frowned. "Don't like the implication that I'm running from something, but I get what you mean. Look, can the Family or whatever get this area evacuated before the locals get turned into fertilizer?"

"We're on it already. Can you keep the Antithesis out of the city for another few hours?"

I paused as an incursion siren went off, a loud, undulating wail that was impossible to ignore. "Yeah," I said. "I'll do what I can. I got a lot of points to make up for, and there doesn't seem to be a lack of willing targets around here."

CHAPTER TWENTY-SEVEN

ONWARD

Yeah, they can be pretty weird.
—Professor Besters, after-class interview, 2048

I pinched the tip of my tongue between my teeth. Lucy always mocked me when I did that while concentrating, but I had a full-face helmet on; no one could tell.

I pinched an eye shut, lined up the end of the barrel over the model three, then squeezed the trigger.

My Bullcat thumped back into my shoulder, and the shot I took flew off into the distance.

I shifted my grip on the front of the gun a little. Maybe if I leaned into the gun a bit more? I aligned the hovering red dot over the alien and kept my breathing calm. I was more careful as I tugged the trigger this time.

The shot tore apart a chunk of asphalt in front of the alien, spraying it with a ricochet of gravelly chunks that had it flinching back.

It, of course, started to run at a bit of a zigzag after that. "Fucker," I muttered.

I was losing patience a little. My finger stretched out and flicked the Bullcat from semi- to full-auto.

I hovered the sight over the alien, then tugged the trigger back. "Dodge this," I swore.

A torrent of buckshot roared out of the Bullcat, ripping apart the road and flying off into the distance, and by the time the gun clicked empty, a few of those had winged the model three.

It flopped onto the ground, injured enough that it couldn't keep running at me.

I nodded as I stood up and checked the highway for more aliens. Other than the piles of unmoving corpses, there wasn't much to see. Nothing running at us. It had been maybe an hour since the wave ended, and since then only stragglers had come down the road.

The first wave of aliens had been decimated.

The second ran into the next row of bombs and traps and the crossfire from the civilians behind our barricade.

The third made it past those and into the blender that Jolly Monarch's drones created.

It was rather nice seeing all those aliens get mulched. All in a day's work, though.

"It's still alive," Jolly Monarch said as he walked over.

He was the last person, myself excluded, left near the barricade.

I looked at the model three. It was struggling toward us still, gripping the ground and pulling itself along with scraping tugs that left a smear of its blood behind. "It'll bleed out," I said.

"You wasted more points in ammo than you earned there."

I shrugged a shoulder. "It's aiming practice."

"I suppose practice doesn't hurt," he said. "Did you intend to stay here for much longer?"

"I don't know. How's the evacuation going?" I asked. I'd been sticking around the barricade for a while, only occasionally running off to patch a hole or to fuck up some cleverer aliens. The militia volunteers had packed up an hour ago and driven off, leaving just me and Jolly Monarch's pawns at the front line. Not that there had been much to worry about.

"Well enough. We started with the streets nearest this edge of the city, and we're about halfway down. Another six to twelve hours and it'll be clear," he said. "Volunteers are going door-to-door to help people, and we have patrols moving all over to keep things safe."

"All right," I said. "You going to stick around here?"

He nodded. "I will. I'm not much of a frontline fighter. Defensive battles are more to my liking. And I never planned on moving even this far from the city center. If you want, you can head over to where the action's a bit hotter."

"Yeah, this has been a bit anemic after the initial bombing," I said. I still glanced over at my point total.

Current Point Total: 6,874

Much better than what I had upon arrival, and pretty decent considering the number of points I'd spent on bombs and the like.

"Yeah, I think I wouldn't mind heading out. Still plenty of daylight to burn. You sure you're good with staying here?"

"I'm certain," Jolly Monarch said. He grinned. "Head on out; I'll keep the area safe. Besides, as long as you're killing xenos, you'll make the job lighter for me."

"All right," I said. "Keep safe, old guy." I shouldered my gun and started off toward my hovercycle while Jolly Monarch had what looked like an existential crisis at being called old.

I hopped onto my hoverbike, then turned it on with a flick of my eye across the right menu. The bike hummed beneath me before it gently rose up into the air. I didn't point myself in any one direction. I had to know where I was going first.

The Family's map came back up, and I winced at the huge washes of orange splashed across it.

The Antithesis had been busy, and it looked as though they were starting to converge. The bigger blobs were running into each other now, so the map wasn't just dots of Antithesis presence but larger coils of it. There were more red spots too, and a lot more pins on the map looking for attention.

"I don't even know where to start," I said.

By the looks of it, the small wave we'd stopped here today was barely a drop in the bucket. The incursion was growing nearly exponentially, and so far we'd just been plugging the smaller holes it left.

This one seems interesting.

One of the pins glowed for a moment. A moving pin. Focusing on it brought up a menu with some more context. A large supply shipment was moving across an orange zone. The only road it could take had spots of red on its edges. A single samurai was already on the scene, but they had asked for more assistance. Grasshopper? The chick with the weird armor who liked hanging off the ceiling?

I searched for Gomorrah's pin and found her on the edge of the city, doing a patrol with some mercenaries along the path of a future wall to clear out any possible Antithesis in the area. The space was orange-green at best.

She was probably fine, then.

"Yeah, why not," I said. I aligned the front of my hoverbike with the distant convoy, then shot off in that direction.

The world slipping by under me was strangely empty. Little towns were abandoned; streets were devoid of cars. A few places were burning down, with firefighters and mercs congregating around the fires with flying tankers and gunships to protect them.

I imagined that it was only going to get worse if the Antithesis claimed all of this land for itself.

I flew up a ways to make it easier to spot the convoy. According to the map, it was still a bit away from the next dangerous zone. This would be a good time to catch up to it.

For some reason I was expecting a row of semi-trailers, maybe with a couple of buses or something.

Instead, the convoy was taking up both sides of the highway and was hundreds of vehicles long, mostly wider self-driving trucks, but there were a few old-school human-piloted trucks in there as well. The front and sides of the convoy were being escorted by some mercs in light armored vehicles, manned turrets on the back scanning the environment for trouble.

I shot over the convoy and started to turn, going wide so that I could take the whole thing in. It had to be four, maybe five kilometers long. How much shit were they carrying? Apparently, a crapton.

You received a ping from below. No message, just a radar tap. Highlighting the location now.

The very front of the convoy was dominated by a large mobile base: a truck on eight huge wheels, with a cannon on the front and gun nests on the sides. It was tall too, high enough off the ground that the lower-tier models wouldn't be able to jump up onto it without assistance.

A single figure was standing on the roof, head tilted up to see me coming.

I slowed over the mobile base, matched speed with it, then hopped off the side of my bike and landed without a thump on the roof. "Hey," I said with a wave. I flicked through my hoverbike's menus and set it into a hold-ing pattern far above, where it would be out of the way.

"Hello, Stray Cat," Grasshopper said. "Are you looking for a place to take a catnap?"

I chuckled. "Not quite. Figured you might need a hand, so here I am. I can run off to the next fire, if you don't need the help."

The woman tilted her head to the side, a strangely insectile gesture, especially with her beige and brown armor with its chitinous design.

"I could use the help," Grasshopper said. She turned and stared out toward the road ahead. I noticed a large gun lying on the roof to the side—though calling it large was a bit of an understatement. It was longer than I was tall and looked like it could belong on a tank. "You like cats?" she asked.

"Uh, yeah," I said. "So, what's the plan?"

"Do you know how humans think that babies are ugly?"

I had no fucking clue how to reply to that. "I guess? They're a bit ugly. Never really saw them as cute, but I, uh, don't consider babies a problem, I guess."

"Oh, okay," she said. "The plan is to shoot the aliens." She flopped for-ward, falling down flat onto the roof and cradling the back of her gun. Little parts of her armor clicked and shifted, moving her over closer to the front of the vehicle.

"Right," I said.

"I like cats," she said. "But I wonder. Do cats think that kittens are ugly the same way we think babies are?"

I worked my jaw for a bit while I considered if it was too late to go work with someone more sane.

CHAPTER TWENTY-EIGHT

WHAT NEWTON'S GOOD FOR

It's only been twenty-four hours since the start of the world's first global incursion, and already the signs that we were not as prepared as we could have been are showing. I'd like to take a moment to remember Buenos Aires. Those poor souls didn't deserve to have a kaiju walk up to their shores this morning.

—Family-wide communication, 2057

I knelt down on one knee as a chill wind whipped around me and hooked onto my jacket to throw it open. The area around the highway was cleared of any obstacles, with no trees or forests or even much of a hillside to cut the wind. That wasn't always going to be the case. There was a forest out ahead, with big old pines turning the sides of the roads into a dark pit where I couldn't see anything mean lurking.

"Why are we moving so slowly?" I asked.

The mobile base truck we were on was moving at a zippy ten, maybe fifteen kilometers an hour. I was pretty sure I could outrun it with little difficulty.

Grasshopper turned her head around so that she could stare up at me. There was no way her neck was normal if she could turn her head that much. Her face mask split apart, the big globes over her eyes sliding back so that I could see her staring right into my eyes.

She didn't say anything for a moment. Then, right when I was about to break the silence, she spoke up. "Baby elephants," she said before her head spun back around and her mask reset itself.

"What?"

Grasshopper sighed. "Baby *elephants*." She waited for another moment, then shook her head as if I were the dumb one here. "Herds with weaker members must move at the fastest pace of the slowest and weakest member so that the combined force of the entire herd can be brought to bear upon any aggressor."

"Oh, right," I said. We were moving slowly because some of the trucks behind us couldn't keep up otherwise. That made sense. "Baby fucking elephants," I muttered.

"I see one," Grasshopper said. Then she started to dance.

It was one of the weirdest fucking things I'd ever seen, someone wearing armor that had far too many limbs on it, swaying from side to side like an excited puppy while lying flat on her stomach.

"So . . . shoot it?"

"Oh, yes, I will," Grasshopper said. "Do you want to see? I like seeing the aliens die. It makes me happy."

I looked out ahead. The forest was still a good kilometer away, maybe a bit more. I wasn't a great judge of range. I couldn't see anything alive over there, but then the scope on her rifle was longer than my forearm. "Sure?"

A ping to my augs later, I had a small screen open in the edge of my vision. I made it grow larger.

It was the forest but zoomed in. A single model four was climbing up a tree with some difficulty; the smaller branches were not entirely strong enough to hold its weight, but it was making its way up the tree nonetheless.

Then the screen flickered and a dozen red outlines appeared, then a dozen more. Antithesis, a few hundred of them, if I had to guess, all scurrying about in the underbrush.

"Want me to leave some for you?" Grasshopper asked. She sounded almost shy about it.

"Nah, you go ahead," I said. "I'm more of a spray-and-pray kind of gal; at this range I'm useless."

"Okay, then," she said.

All along the length of her gun, the little tripods holding it up hissed, and the barrel shifted around with tiny, minute motions.

"There are many ways to kill," Grasshopper said.

I was about to ask if that was a question when her gun barked. The sound made my teeth rattle, and I swore the mobile base shook a bit with the recoil.

In the screen occupying my vision, three of the Antithesis that happened to be lined up disappeared.

"The most ancient and most effective," Grasshopper continued, "is the meeting of two opposing objects. Upon meeting, these two opposing objects will exert a force against each other. Newton's second law."

She fired again, and this time two aliens were wiped out. The Antithesis were starting to catch on that they were under attack and were moving around in what almost looked like panic.

A large model five shifted, then started charging out of the forest in our direction. All the little model threes started to group up behind it.

"Newton's second law states that force is required to change the velocity of an object. When sufficient force is exerted onto an object, and then that object is allowed to impact another, the force can, in part, be translated to the second object. This object is what I designate as the target."

She fired again and the model five's upper half was turned into a gaping hole big enough that I could have crawled through it. The bits of its body flying out the back brained a few of the model threes behind it too.

"Time for a pop quiz!" Grasshopper said. She flicked something on the side of her gun, then shifted left and right almost mechanically. "Pop, pop, pop!"

Every "pop" came with a much weaker bark from her gun, and in the distance a pair of aliens died with a bang each. She never fired unless there were at least two of them lined up.

"Do you like math?"

"What?" I asked. "Uh, math? Not really, no."

"Oh," Grasshopper said. I couldn't hear any judgment there. She fired a few more times, thinning out the herd. "I like math. Numbers are non-judgmental. I like violence too, but there's a certain level of societal stigma around the application of great and sudden violence. But math? No one minds if you like math. Oh! I like animals too."

"Bugs too, I bet," I said.

She stopped firing. "How did you know that?" she asked.

"Your . . . name is Grasshopper?"

"That tracks," she replied before she continued to kill off the aliens. "At this current rate, this group will be dead two hundred meters before reaching the front of the caravan. Problem. There's a second group coming in from the south, and a third moving in from the forest to the west. My specialty will allow me to remove any of the larger threats with little issue, but I'm not good at swarms."

I glanced to our left, then squinted. There was definitely something moving in the field that way; the grass was shifting a lot as what looked like a small wave spread out to hit the entire caravan. They were a good way out still, though.

The other forest she was talking about was across the street from the one she'd been sniping Antithesis from.

I stood up, careful to compensate for the wind and the slight rocking motion of the mobile base underfoot. Glancing back, I took in the convoy as a whole. It was too damned big to cover from one place. Sure, there were some trucks with guns on them, and the mobile base itself was bristling with guns, but I couldn't imagine the convoy holding out once the aliens were waving through it.

"Okay, here's the plan. It's a shit plan, so feel free to interject with better ideas, all right?"

Grasshopper stopped firing, moved back and up onto her knees, then knelt there with her hands on her lap and her head tilted up to look at me. "I'm listening."

"Uh. Yeah, I'm going to drop a few cat bots around here. They're mecha-cats, they have guns, so . . . yeah. Then I'm gonna place some cheap laser turrets on the roofs of a few of the trucks back there. And once that's done, I'm going to fly over the bigger pockets of the wave and drop bombs on it."

"Are the mecha-cats warm and huggable?"

"No," I said.

"That seems like a terrible waste of points. But I won't tell you how to live. I can work around your plan. I'll keep removing the greatest threats as they appear."

"Cool, you do that. Keep your coms open. You can ping me if something comes up." I glanced at my map while my hoverbike lowered itself down to my level. We were still a long way from the city, and at the speed we were moving, it would take us a while to get to the outskirts.

The area around the city was still mostly green, though. We were only going to have to defend the convoy for most of the way there, which was brilliant.

We were about to dip into an entire zone that was nothing but orange and red, though: a few kilometers of Antithesis-infested hell that we'd need to cross with nothing but two samurai and a few bottom-of-the-barrel defenses.

The more I looked at the situation, the uglier it looked.

My hoverbike came down, and I leapt up onto it. "Okay, see you around, Grasshopper. Call me if you need me."

"Good luck, Stray Cat" was her reply. "Show these aliens what Newton's good for."

CHAPTER TWENTY-NINE

TRENCH RUN

Operator: Why is the city on fire?
    Lord Burninator: There were aliens in it.
    Operator: That can't be your response to everything.
    Lord Burninator: You clearly haven't thought this through.
    —Excerpt from official transcript between Family operations center and samurai field command, 2038 Venezuela incursion

The turrets I was setting down on the edges of the tallest trucks were the same cheap crap I'd been using for a while: a laser gun, a small battery pack, a little strip of solar cells, and three legs that ended in suction-cup grippers that had no difficulty attaching to the stainless steel roofs of the trailers I was passing.

From earlier observation, the turrets took about three, maybe four seconds of continuous fire on a single model three to take it down. Way less time to take out model ones, though; the little birds were easy to knock out of the air.

By the time I was at the back of the convoy, I'd set down nearly fifty of the things. They had pretty decent range, and some of those near the front were zapping the quickest of the aliens already.

I'd dipped down four times between slower trucks and bought a few mecha-cats. They were more than capable of keeping up with the convoy, and I figured the extra bit of mobile firepower might give us an edge if . . . or when the aliens reached us.

I placed the last turret on the roof of the last vehicle in the convoy. I probably didn't need to bother; it was another of those oversized mobile bases, with guns bristling out of its sides and a few turrets on the top already, but the turrets would give me and Myalis an idea of the convoy's status as it moved ahead, and I figured I could retrieve them after, maybe hand them off to the Family to place them along the length of the defenses around the city. It was that much more firepower, and the self-sustaining sort.

"Hey, Grasshopper," I said.

"That's me," Grasshopper said. "Is something wrong?"

"Nah, not yet," I said. "I'm about to start my bombing runs. I've set down some turrets here and there, should keep the convoy . . . safe-ish. Honestly, it's not much, but it'll put a dent in their numbers, I hope."

"I understand," Grasshopper said. "Do your best!"

"Right," I said. I kicked my bike into gear and shot up a ways. From above I could see the vague formation the Antithesis were taking. A large group of them were spread out to the left and rushing in toward the convoy. More were out by the front, where a few patches of forest made it hard to tell where they were hidden.

There was actually some sort of facility in the middle of those woods. Probably abandoned by now. Still . . . "Myalis, can you check to make sure there's no one alive around here? I don't want to bomb some poor sap hiding in that building over there."

Searching now . . . no signs of life. The facility is an older slaughterhouse; it has been out of operation for a decade.

"Got it," I said.

I turned my bike over to the large group heading into the side of the convoy.

The Antithesis at the front were more numerous, but they were starting to enter the effective range of the guns on the mobile base, and a few of those armored cars with machine guns on their roofs were near the front, spraying down lines of fire into the approaching mass.

The group to the side didn't have as many obstacles, and if they reached the convoy, they'd spread out, and rooting them out would be a mess. Some of the trucks were driven by flesh-and-blood people; we didn't want to deal with dead drivers causing blockages on the road.

So I was going to teach the fuckers about the beauty of high explosives.

"Myalis, I need lots of grenades with the pins already pulled," I said. "Maybe one every two meters or so?"

Noted. What are you thinking about for the payload?

"Can't have anything that might damage the convoy. Just a big boom?"

Concussion grenades will release a large burst of kinetic force without launching any shrapnel from the explosive itself. Pieces of Antithesis might reach the convoy, but not at speeds that would endanger the vehicles. Also, the explosives are relatively inexpensive.

"Works for me," I said.

I lined the front of my bike up with the far end of the row of aliens, guesstimated how far ahead I needed to be for the grenades to drop on the formation, then took off.

"Now!" I called out as I leaned into my bike.

Grenades started to appear next to me in midair, matching my velocity for just a moment before trailing down and toward the ground. I'd miss the very start of the formation, but then, I kinda figured I would need to make another pass at it.

Loud *whumps* sounded out behind me, louder than a gun going off, but much bassier, the kind of sound that was felt as much as it was heard.

"All right," I said as I reached the front of the formation and pulled back on my bike so that I flew up and around.

Glancing down, I saw the horde of spread-out model threes rushing toward the convoy and occasionally right into an explosion.

The concussion grenades were going off in a roughly straight line a half-dozen meters ahead of the Antithesis line, big blasts that tossed up dirt and flung away any alien unfortunate enough to be within the radius.

The bombs went off like a metronome, a bang every tick.

I grinned as part of the explosive line went off right on top of the meatiest part of the horde and dozens of aliens were ripped apart. The last bit went off behind the horde, which was a bit unfortunate.

I'd thinned it, though, and a good chunk of the remaining Antithesis were limping or were too injured to keep on going.

"Myalis, I think we need to switch it up," I said. "Concussions are nice, but they're too . . . binary. They either kill the fuckers or miss outright. Maybe something a bit more . . . fire-y?"

Something that will last longer, then. A liquid that combusts with contact to oxygen might suffice. With a dispersal system to spread it. Perhaps a napalm-based explosive? It would create a temporary barrier between the Antithesis and the convoy.

I nodded. "That sounds perfect. Same rate, on my mark?"

Ready.

I dropped down, much closer to the ground than I had been on my last run. A bit more dangerous, sure, but I also wanted to be more accurate with my fire.

"Now," I said as I took off.

The first grenade appeared next to me, a small canister the size of a bigger soda can. It flopped down and out of sight. I couldn't afford to look back, not when I was so low to the ground that the taller stalks from roadside weeds were whipped back with the air from my passage and the nearest Antithesis to my right were so close I could see the saliva clinging to their teeth.

The first grenade went off with a sound like a fart in a tin can. It made up for that with a wash of heat that I felt on my back as I raced ahead.

Each burst increased the burning crackle until I pulled up and away at the end of the Antithesis formation. When I glanced back, it was to see a sight that would make Gomorrah proud: a wall of flames, thicker by the middle but still a good couple of meters wide. Some aliens were caught in the flames, writhing around as they burned.

The rest, smart enough not to run into a puddle of napalm, were bunching up and hesitating. A few started to run around the flames, but they'd have a long way to go.

A long way while staying entirely within the range of the turrets and manned guns in the convoy.

Flickering laser beams caught aliens in their sides and followed them long enough to put them down, and the few trucks with turrets protecting the convoy opened up, firing past the napalm and into the enemy's flanks.

"That's a lot of fire," Grasshopper said over the coms. "It's actually good for the environment to clear out some surface brush on occasion. I don't think you're supposed to use napalm for that, though."

"It'll go out eventually," I said. "How are things by the front?"

"Well enough, so far," Grasshopper said. "But the numbers are increasing. I think the forest will be a problem."

"Well, I have plenty more napalm," I said.

"I think passing through the forest while it's on fire would also be a problem. Maybe we can come up with another solution. One that doesn't harm the nice trees as much?"

I sighed. "We'll see."

CHAPTER THIRTY

WHEN THE TREES START SPEAKING PLANT

We're not eco-terrorists. That word leaves a sour taste in my mouth. Terrorism is the unlawful use of force to coerce action.

We don't submit to the laws of humanity, but rather to the laws of Earth itself. We can hardly be labeled as villains for wanting to protect our own world!

You too can help our crusade for a cleaner, greener world by buying our exclusive Mother Earth NFTs!

—Eco-friends website, 2025

"Spare the fucking trees," I muttered as I hovered over the forest. The convoy was just about to slip into it, and it wasn't going to be pretty.

Thick, older woods, with only the road splitting it apart. We had maybe a kilometer and a bit of woodland to pass through, some of it pretty thin in places, but a few chunks were pretty thick. It looked like the fields before and after the tree line didn't line up. Maybe this area was some missed spot on a bureaucrat's map of the region, left alone so that it could grow peacefully.

Didn't matter.

I didn't need to clear out the forest of aliens. That was too much of an ask. All I had to do was stop the little fuckers from hitting the convoy.

And Grasshopper added to the fucking challenge by asking that I not hurt the nice trees. For fuck's sake.

Resonators might do it. Place enough of them down along the main path and it would melt the aliens. I could ask Myalis to tune them so they didn't melt the greenery too. Resonators weren't fast-acting, though; they took a good dozen seconds to start liquefying an Antithesis, and it had to be relatively close to the grenade for it to work.

Good area denial, shit at alpha-damage.

It was going to be like using one of those sound-guns on a crowd to disperse it.

"Oh, that's an idea," I said.

Something came to mind?

"Myalis, is there a kind of . . . tear-gas bomb?"

Yes. Up to and including some that have been outlawed by international treaty!

"Anything like that that works on the Antithesis. I don't need them dead, I need them to fuck off away from the convoy."

I think I see your reasoning. Yes, there are some gaseous chemicals that can irritate and ward off Antithesis. Unfortunately their impact is greatly diminished when used in open areas. Laying some down along the convoy's route is possible, but the amount of gas necessary to secure the path would be prohibitive. There is currently a strong wind blowing opposite the direction the convoy is traveling in. I have another solution that works on a similar idea.

"I'm all ears," I said.

I would propose using a Biodegradable Enforcement and Extermination Swarm grenade.

"A . . . B.E.E.S.?" I said, working out the obvious acronym. "What is that, a jarful of bees?"

Small mechanical flying drones, entirely made of biodegradable materials, able to bore and cut their way into the softer flesh of organic adversaries. A singular unit is mostly harmless—their time to kill is too great—but a swarm of several hundred or thousand can slow down, injure, and eventually kill a great number of Antithesis within a designated area. Their operation time and range is limited, though.

"Coupled with resonators, though," I muttered. "Yeah, fuck it, let's try it. I'll zip down the road. You drop resonators every couple of meters. We'll have the entire road be lethal to the xenos so they won't linger there. Then we drop your B.E.E.S. all over."

You will only need to deploy them at the head of the convoy; they can travel alongside the convoy and relocate themselves along its length. Dropping a canister every fifty meters as the convoy moves should be sufficient.

"That sounds perfect," I said. I started to fly lower, the road zipping by beneath me. I noticed Grasshopper waving to me as I shot past. The bike self-corrected and pulled up a notch, which was probably good because otherwise I was going to really test my armor's capability when it came to road rash resistance.

"Start dropping them," I said.

Resonators appeared by my side and fell, same as the bombing run a few minutes ago, but without the big booms or the satisfying whoosh of fire.

Instead . . . not much, really. Myalis wasn't setting the bombs off already, not when there weren't any aliens around for them to work on. It made more sense to wait until the Antithesis were in a compromising position.

The road curved a few hundred meters in, then turned around in the opposite direction for a little while. The forest thinned out, and I pulled up as I exited the woods and flew out across open fields of . . . some sort of farmable stuff. Corn, maybe?

I flew in a wide circle, turning to head back to the convoy. "Grasshopper, I'm heading back to the convoy. I think we'll be defending the convoy from close up from now on."

"I'm ready to be the danger in danger-close," Grasshopper reported.

I had no idea what that meant. "Yeah, cool," I said.

Motion below had me slowing down and searching the forest until I could spot what had caught my eye. Model fives, with a few model threes zipping past them in the underbrush. The smaller models were hard to spot; their skin was mottled and dark enough that they were just plain hard to see.

The model fives had their own camouflage of sorts going on, but they were big enough and clumsy enough that it didn't help them all that much.

I gave my bike a bit of throttle and shot out ahead. "We're going to have some bigger company," I said to Grasshopper.

When I finally arrived at the convoy, I found Grasshopper standing atop the same mobile base, her gun folded up next to her. She had a pair of hand-guns out instead: long, curvy ones with covered grips and what looked like a blade going from beneath the barrel all the way down to the underside of the grip.

I hopped off my bike and landed in a crouch not too far from her. "Hey," I said.

"Hello," Grasshopper replied. "I was thinking."

"Were you?"

She nodded. "I think the convoy will slow down a little."

"That seems counterintuitive," I said.

"Sometimes things are like that," Grasshopper said. "Did you ever do arts and crafts?"

"What?"

"Making pretty things from paper and cardboard, and even wood and fun things like sprinkles and glue."

I shook my head. "No, sorry. I never really went to, uh, a proper school. Kinda missed out on all of that. I'm guessing you're going to make a point that's tangentially related to arts and crafts now?"

"It's too bad you never went to school," Grasshopper said. "I think you would have been a very good student. You seem very smart. Anyway, when doing arts and crafts, if you try to go too fast, you'll make lots of little mistakes that going slowly will help you avoid. Art takes time. It's an important lesson."

"And what's that got to do with slowing the convoy down?" I asked as I glanced out ahead; we were entering the forest already. I could see the aliens in the woods. "If we slow down any more, we're going to have a hard time with the xenos."

"Only a little. If we're slower, they will have an easier time reaching the area where they perceive the greatest threat to be. That will, of course, be right in front where we're walking."

Grasshopper's mask folded back so that I could see her entire face. She was . . . a rather plain-looking thirtysomething woman, with clever brown eyes and a few freckles on her cheeks.

She grinned. "Come on, let's kill them up close and personal. It's good cardio."

I shook my head as Grasshopper's mask closed back up and she ran off the front of the mobile base, leaping into the air and disappearing over the edge. "Insane," I muttered. The convoy started to slow down, and I noticed the Antithesis on the sidelines starting to rush in.

"Myalis, that B.E.E.S. thing. Now would probably be a good time to deploy those."

Understood.

I was expecting a little grenade, but instead Myalis had a large canister appear next to me. It was about the size of one of those three-gallon water bottles used above water coolers, but all stainless steel with a big plastic-like cylinder filled with glowing motes.

Unleashing the B.E.E.S.

The top popped off and a swarm of buzzing machines flitted out of the top. They left yellow streams through the air as they passed and spread out below.

"Neat," I said as they rushed down the front of the convoy. They were already lining up toward the nearest Antithesis. I pulled my Bullcat off my back and pumped it for good measure as I started walking to the front of the mobile base.

I couldn't just leave Grasshopper alone down there.

CHAPTER THIRTY-ONE

GOLD STAR

Ah, hello there, everyone!
Old friends and new!
Today I'm presenting to you, something that's quite the view!
A new book I've written, that'll have you quite smitten.
It's called *A Is for Ants*, and it will knock off your pants!
—Ad for *A Is for Ants*, by Grasshopper, 2056

I wasn't sure if I could drop the three or four meters to the ground in front of the mobile base without breaking something.

I probably could; my armor was pretty good. The problem was that I had a mental image of nailing a cool landing only for the mobile base to drive into me, and I didn't feel like getting run over.

So I did the smart thing and climbed down the side, where a ladder hung down to a few feet off the ground. I jumped off halfway down, landed in a crouch, then took off sprinting to the front. The convoy was slowing down, just as Grasshopper said, which made it easy enough to catch up to the front.

I found Grasshopper ducking to the side as a model three leapt through where she was a moment ago. She pointed a gun into the alien's side and emptied three rounds into its chest before it flopped on by.

More aliens were pouring out of the forest in ones and twos, but they were being intercepted by my B.E.E.S. If they slowed down any, then Grasshopper casually planted a round into their heads.

"Good so far?" I asked as I ran up next to her and shouldered my Bullcat. My shoulder-mounted guns deployed and I checked my gear real quick, just in case. My bike was hovering just over the mobile base; if I was needed somewhere farther back, I could hop on it and race over.

"So far, so good," Grasshopper said. "Big group, four o'clock."

I glanced to the right, then tensed up. A couple dozen model threes were rushing out of the woods, a model five trampling after them on huge, bulky legs. The entire group sailed over the ditch on the roadside, then scurried toward us. At some point they slid into the range of the nearest resonator, but that didn't slow them down any, nor did the B.E.E.S. that flew over to the group and coated them.

"Shit," I muttered before shifting to the side and aiming down at the group. I opened fire, and for a moment all I could do was work to keep the recoil down as I sprayed them with pellets.

Skin was shredded, and one model three's head burst like a melon being dropped onto a speedway, bits of the alien's face flying all over.

My gun clicked empty, and I stepped back. "Myalis, reload."

The Bullcat could reload automatically, the magazine in the gun dropping down and a fresh one teleporting into place. It still took a couple seconds.

Grasshopper hummed to herself as she ran toward the group. I almost screamed at her to stay back, but then she was a samurai as much as I was.

The woman ran low to the ground. Halfway to the first model three she leaned way, way down, then twisted around in midair so that she fell onto her back. The dozens of limbs on her suit clattered against the ground as she slipped under the first leaping model three.

She shot up and into its torso before her legs kicked up and she flipped back onto her feet. The entire time, her arms swung around, almost like she was dancing, and with every swing, she fired.

I blinked as a dozen aliens fell around her, pierced through their heads and the middle of their chests, all clearly dead. Then she spun and ran up toward the model five.

Grasshopper dropped both of her handguns, the two of them swiped out of the air by the arms on her gear. Reaching over her shoulders with both arms, she grabbed on to a pair of hilts pushed up by her equipment.

Two bright knives flicked out of the handles, each one longer than her forearm, and in one smooth motion, she stabbed down with both in an ice-pick grip and impaled either side of the model five's head.

Grasshopper kicked off the alien, then retracted her knives. She placed the hilts at the base of her back and retrieved her guns. "I like that sentence."

"What?" I asked.

I was impressed. Not even reluctantly impressed, just impressed.

"So far, so good," Grasshopper said. "It's an interesting sentence. It's not particularly unique, but it's still a fun expression."

"Yeah, sure," I said. "Why did you run over to them? You have guns."

Grasshopper looked away from me. "It looks cooler when you kill them from up close. I've been practicing my gun-fu for months now."

"Oh," I said. "Well, yeah, that looked really cool."

Grasshopper glanced up and clapped her hands together once. "Thank you. I appreciate it. Sometimes, just a few kind words can serve as enough justification for a lot of work. Humans are creatures of praise."

"Hey, no problem," I said.

More aliens started to pour out of the woods, and I fired into the head of the group. There were so many of them that even I would be hard-pressed not to hit at least a few of them with every shot I took.

Grasshopper continued to prove that she was the better markswoman, each shot from her handguns punching a hole through the head of a new alien and sending their body flopping onto the ground, very much dead.

The convoy was moving at maybe four or five kilometers an hour, about normal walking speed. It was about a kilometer long, and we had to cross a kilometer of ground, which meant that it would take us . . .

I tried to work it out in my head—find x where x was the duration of time the convoy would be staying in the forest, but I couldn't figure it out. Maybe if I had pen and paper and a shit to give.

"How long is this going to take?" I asked.

"Do you need help with the math?" Grasshopper asked.

"I just need an answer," I said.

She shook her head. "Come on, Stray Cat, it's not too difficult. I'm sure someone as clever as you can work it out. Oh, look, a model four!" She spun around and fired full-auto into a model four tentacling its way over the ditch.

I muttered to myself as I worked it out. This was now a matter of pride. "Okay, one kilometer of woods, at about five kilometers an hour, that's . . . sixty minutes divided by five? What's sixty divided by five?"

"You can work it out by making the question a bit easier. How many times does ten fit in sixty?"

I swore under my breath. "Six."

"Good! And how many times does five fit in ten?"

"Twice, so twelve. It'll take twelve minutes to reach the end. At least, for the front of the convoy."

"The convoy is a bit longer than a kilometer, but we can round it down to make it easy," she said.

"So, twice that? Twenty-four minutes to cross the forest?"

"More or less! Good job!" She lowered her arms, stored her guns away, then walked over to me while bringing her hand out. A small box fell into her outstretched palm. She'd bought something from her AI?

Grasshopper opened the box, then pulled out something from within: a piece of folded paper of some sort? She peeled something off it, then before I could react, pressed it against my chest.

I stared. There was now a golden star on my armor, just below my collarbone. It said "Math whizz!" on it.

"Good work. I'm proud of you."

I felt some warmth climbing onto my cheeks and was thankful for my helmet hiding my face. "Seriously?" I asked.

"Yes," she said without any hesitation or even a hint that she was joking. "You did well. I know that math isn't easy for everybody, but I'm proud that you tried—and succeeded—out in the real world."

"You are so fucking weird," I muttered as I turned around and refocused on killing the nearest xenos. I didn't pull the sticker off. It was probably some weird alien tech that would make it hard to remove.

"Being weird isn't bad," Grasshopper said. "It doesn't stop you from being a good person. If you ever need more help with learning math, I give classes. My students would love to meet you."

"You give math classes?"

"Pre-K to sixth grade, yes."

"That explains so much," I said.

Still, even if Grasshopper was more than a little strange, she seemed nice enough, and for the next . . . twenty-three minutes or so, I was going to need her help, because the number of monsters rushing our way wasn't stalling any.

CHAPTER THIRTY-TWO

MEAT THINKING

They're like rats. Don't corner them.

Hmm? Oh, you want to know if I mean the aliens or the samurai?

Both.

—Mayor Laplace, 2028

"Reloading," Grasshopper said.

"Got it." I stepped up around her and shouldered my Bullcat. My rail-guns were smoking already, but they didn't let up the fire, picking off stray Antithesis on the edges. My own fire was more of a covering spray of lead that had some of the more skittish of the aliens backing off.

B.E.E.S. buzzed around in large swarms, falling onto any Antithesis that didn't look quite dead enough or piling onto the faces of the higher-ranked models to take them out of the fight for a moment.

All that racket played over the incessant drone of the resonators I'd left behind. The mobile base behind us occasionally joined in with a burst of machine-gun fire or a shot from its big gun that kicked up dirt and threw a few of the smaller Antithesis around.

"I'm set," Grasshopper said.

I stepped to the side and stopped walking long enough for Grasshopper to take my place at the front and in the center of attention. She was a better shot and a better fighter than I was. She twirled around and nailed every bastard in sight.

"Area's clear," she said. "We have a few seconds."

"Got it," I said.

So far our tactic, if we could call it that, was to have Grasshopper move up, kill everything, then keep moving. I'd replace her at the head when she needed to reload or breathe a bit. Judging by the number of corpses we were leaving behind, the tactic was working.

"I'm going to set up another B.E.E.S. container," I said. "Can you watch my back?"

"I will, no worries," Grasshopper said.

I nodded, then sprinted out ahead and past the latest pile of dead xenos, who were all merrily melting away.

Dropping to one knee, I picked up a B.E.E.S. container just as it dropped and set it off in a quick, practiced motion. A fresh swarm rose up and joined the remnants of the last.

"Cat, model fours," Grasshopper warned.

I spun, taking in a trio of those creepy tentacle fucks crawling out of the woods with their long appendages reaching out toward me. "God damn it," I swore as I fired into the nearest. How hadn't I heard it?

The swarm above fell on them, and I saw holes punched through them in time with Grasshopper's shooting. The three fell.

"Probably an ambush," she said. "They were waiting for us to reach them, but you ran out ahead. We're going to have another wave coming . . . yup, right there."

A dozen or so model threes shot out of the other side of the woods, shoving bushes aside and slipping through the tall grass before they sailed out toward us.

The mobile base opened fire while Grasshopper did the same, and the ground melted as it was caught between two deadly streams.

"Nice work," I said as I stood in the middle of the road and waited for the convoy to reach me.

"Thank you," Grasshopper said.

"This is weird; they're just streaming in, but we've pretty much proven that they can't reach us."

Grasshopper tsked and shook her head. "You're thinking like an animal, Cat."

"Pardon?"

"You're thinking like a person who can think, like a mammal. When you see someone like you fail at something, you learn from their mistake and try something different. If someone tells you not to do something, you'll consider it if they mention a sufficiently grand risk. We are animals."

"All right," I said. I scanned the woods for more aliens but couldn't see anything. Then again, I usually only saw them when they were already charging.

Grasshopper gestured ahead toward the woods and the Antithesis in general. "They are plants. They have plant thoughts. If something doesn't work, just push harder. Roots can crack stone if they push enough. Sometimes they'll find a route around a problem, but only by pushing at the problem from every angle."

"Yeah, I get what you're saying. They're still pretty stupid."

"Let's hope they remain that way. Stupid as they are, they're still winning, aren't they?"

That was sobering.

Something crunching through the foliage ahead had me looking up. We were at the bend in the road, or at least we were nearly there. The curve did make it harder to see out ahead. Still, I couldn't see what was making all the racket.

"The next one's going to be big," Grasshopper said. She lowered her guns to her back and let her gear reload them for her. "This will be fun!"

"You say fun, but I'm not sure we have the same definitions for it," I said. I was smiling all the same.

As we reached the curve in the road, the Antithesis waiting in ambush for us rushed out: a few model fours on either side, a couple of dozen model threes rushing ahead of them, and two massive model sixes. The big bastards trampled toward us, not quite as fast as the model threes, but not much slower either. "Shit," I muttered as I opened fire.

The mobile base joined in, spraying down the xenos on our flanks. They'd be hitting us first.

Something grabbed me by the scruff and tugged me back. I almost shouted before I realized that it was Grasshopper pulling me back. I glanced where I stood and found a model four's tentacles reaching toward me.

Grasshopper shoved a gun forward and into the mass of tendrils and opened fire. "Eyes all around," she said.

"Right." I half turned, targeting the nearest model threes. They were dying in droves, but each shot one of them took was a round another wouldn't have to deal with, and they were making up ground.

I dropped my Bullcat, as it needed to be reloaded, and fished out my Trench Maker from my thigh pocket. I held it two-handed and fired into the crowd as fast as I could tug the trigger back.

My railguns whumped constantly, and I noticed that they were firing upward.

I looked up, but all I saw were branches, some of which were falling . . .

"Fuck!"

"Language," Grasshopper gasped.

"No, stealth units, above."

Model nines, the stealthy fucks that can make themselves look different. In this case, they were nearly indistinguishable from the branches they were hanging from. One of them leapt down, limbs spreading to reveal nasty claws tucked into what looked like a pile of leaves on the end of its branchy arms.

I ducked to the side as one hit the ground next to me. It spun around, long limbs reaching out to try to swipe at me.

I punted it, armored boot digging into the little shit's side and sending it flying off into some of the other aliens coming at us.

Firing forward, I nailed a couple of model threes with my next seven shots, then clicked on empty. "Dammit," I swore as I shoved my gun away. Was my Bullcat loaded yet?

Would it be enough to stop the model sixes almost on us? Grasshopper was doing well but . . .

My hand reached down and wrapped around the hilt by my hip. Screw it, I was going to kill everything and it was going to be nasty.

I slid my sword out of its sheath with a whisper of steel on steel, then charged toward the massive xenos running toward us.

A swarm of B.E.E.S. zipped around me, then latched on to the aliens turning to track me.

"Fuck . . . you!" I shouted as I swung.

I didn't know how to use a sword. There was all this shit about edges and proper form and all that. But I was cheating already, so I didn't see why any of that would matter.

My sword made a loud snapping noise, like a piece of glass cracking, and the blade sprang to life, hissing and spitting as it tugged at the air around it.

With a single large swing I took off the nearest model six's forelimb. Then I grabbed the hilt with both hands, brought it up, and swung down even as I stopped my forward momentum by planting a boot down firmly on the asphalt.

The model six slipped down the middle, its insides slurping into the hungry sword even as its forward momentum continued to carry its remains past me.

I shook my head to clear out some of the blood splatter on my visor, then turned with another swing into the side of the next model six.

Smaller aliens leapt at me from the side, so I met them in midair blade first.

For the next dozen seconds, seconds that felt like entire minutes, I swung around me as though I had the world's most dangerous baseball bat, smacking and slicing through anything that got within a few meters of me.

Then it was over.

"That," Grasshopper said. She was covered in Antithesis remains, but looked uninjured otherwise. "Is a very cool sword."

I nodded, breath coming in too heavy for me to trust my voice. I looked around, but all I saw were heaps of aliens and chopped-up bodies.

Out ahead, the road continued on, the exit just a couple of hundred meters down.

CHAPTER THIRTY-THREE

LONG ROAD AHEAD

There have been proposals over the years for a comprehensive defensive strategy. Something that would keep Earth entirely secure, no matter the size or scope of an invasion.

The issue is always the same, though: Who would foot the bill?

—Quote from *Ongoing Threat*, 2051

I kicked a model three's corpse in the head and, with the added boost from my armor, sent it flopping back to the edge of the road. "Think we'll have to deal with more of them?" I asked.

The convoy was rolling on behind us, surprisingly quiet, actually.

"Maybe," Grasshopper said. "But there's always more xenos out there. Even in this forest . . . I don't envy those who will eventually clear it out."

I winced. Yeah, someone would have to go tree by tree, checking every inch of the place for any missing chunks of Antithesis stuff, just on the off chance that the fuckers rooted themselves down and started a fresh hive here.

"We're going to need to do that everywhere, aren't we?" I asked. If the incursion was worldwide, then even after clearing all the current hives, we'd have to canvass the entire damned planet.

"Seems like it, yes," Grasshopper said. "I don't know what that will mean for the future, but maybe it will be for the best. We'll have a chance to root out every last foothold they have on our world."

"Yeah," I said. I wasn't quite as optimistic as she was.

I kept an eye out on the trees and brush around us, but nothing showed up to try to eat our faces. Even as we reached the very end of the forest, I could feel my heart thundering away, as I fully expected something to jump out at me.

It never happened, though.

"Want to pick a side, or should we both stand on the same one?" Grasshopper asked.

"Huh? Oh, of the convoy? Uh, splitting up is probably safer," I said.

Grasshopper nodded, then moved to the side. "See you in twelve minutes," she said.

I snorted and found a spot of my own on the edge of the road. We both stopped just a few meters from the edge of the woods, where the trees grew a little more sparsely. I raised my gun to my shoulder but left it pointing at the ground.

"That was something," I said.

It was a good experience, I think.

"I guess," I said. "Hard to say how often I'm going to have to do something like this. Doing a lot of new things lately."

A Vanguard's life is rarely stagnant.

I snorted. "Yeah, tell me about it. So, how many points have I made?"

Current Point Total: 19,874

Tokens Earned: One

I whistled. "That many?" I asked. Had I really killed enough aliens to make my point count climb so high? Token was nice too. Harder to get and all.

Since you were working with another Vanguard, the total number of kills was divided between the two of you; in turn, you both received slightly more than half the total points. It means that you shared in the kills that you didn't make as well.

"Huh," I said. That was a good deal.

It encourages Vanguards to work together. The difference in points earned is negligible to us, especially when you consider the increased survival rate among Vanguards who work together as a group.

"I thought samurai were picked from people who like working alone," I said.

They are, yes.

I frowned. "Then doesn't that, uh, contradict the other bit?" I asked.

No, not if you see the wider picture. For one point you could purchase a crayon drawing of said wider picture. It might be helpful.

I laughed. "You're such a pain in the ass," I said.

I relaxed a bit as the convoy moved on. All the trucks were accounted for, and other than a few smoking turrets, it didn't look like it had been damaged all that much. A few trucks had splatters of Antithesis gore on their bumpers, but that wasn't a big deal.

The few drivers I saw waved at me, and one even honked his horn as a friendly greeting. I waved back, because why not.

Finally, the last truck in the formation rumbled by, and it wasn't followed by a trail of salivating monsters.

"That wasn't too bad," I said as I joined Grasshopper in the middle of the road.

She nodded. "I imagine we killed a good number of the aliens here. Now we need to catch up to the front of the caravan. Though I imagine letting it get a little farther down wouldn't be a bad idea before asking it to stop."

"If you don't mind riding in the back, you can hop onto my bike," I said. The hoverbike was already flying back, a distant black speck growing nearer and nearer.

Grasshopper stared up at my ride. "Did you know that a full quarter of all motor vehicle deaths in the last decade have involved a hoverbike? They only account for one-tenth of all personally owned vehicles."

"Is that a no?" I asked.

She shook her head. "I don't mind, though I have to admit I'm not too comfortable with close physical contact."

"Oh," I said. "Uh, we can buy some blankets or something, if you want?"

She giggled. "No, it's fine. 'Uncomfortable' doesn't mean 'allergic to.'"

"Right."

My bike spun around and came to a gentle landing right next to me, so I hopped onto it, then scooted forward so that Grasshopper could get on. She did, though I immediately realized that she was going to make flying awkward. Her gear had to weigh a lot, despite being all spindly and weird.

I moved just a bit faster than the convoy, mostly so that Grasshopper wouldn't be nervous, and because it gave us a good opportunity to see what kind of shape the convoy was in from above.

"We did pretty well there," Grasshopper said.

"Yeah, I think so," I replied. "Any obstacles between here and the city?" I started to lower us down with a press of a pedal, then winced when the bike's autopilot kicked on and stopped me from dropping too fast. Hopefully Grasshopper didn't notice that, or she'd get to point out that her accident statistics were spot-on.

"Only the strange boredom."

"The what?" My hoverbike's legs deployed as I landed us on the roof of the mobile base with a solid thump. I wondered what the guys inside the base were thinking about all of this. Probably some pretty horrific shit if they saw us wiping out a wave right in front of them.

Grasshopper climbed off my bike, then stretched as though it had taken us an hour to get there. "The strange boredom, where there's nothing to do but plenty to look out for. We should be in light orange to green from here until the outskirts, but we still need to be on the lookout for trouble."

I nodded along, then moved to the front of the base. I sat myself down next to an antenna thing and just let my legs dangle off the front. "No reason to be bored and uncomfortable," I said.

Grasshopper hummed in agreement as she moved over to that huge gun she'd been using earlier. "I suppose not." She laid herself down behind it and pressed one of the big eyes of her helmet right up against the scope. "Nothing but clear skies ahead."

She was right. The mobile base and the entire convoy moved on toward New Montreal with barely a hitch. We had to squeeze past a few cars that had been abandoned on the road, but Grasshopper was able to connect to the car's systems, boot them up, and drive them into the ditch. Turns out they'd just stopped working because the local internet network glitched out.

A little ways closer to the city, and I could see why. A small town was on fire. Or had been, at least.

It was one of those stopover places. Just a few hundred homes and a big four-way intersection with a couple of fast-food chains and some gas stations. Smoke still rose out of the shell of homes, and one of the stations was covered in whitish fire suppressant foam, likely dropped on it from above.

Not one person was out and about, and some of the homes we passed had boarded-up windows and doors. Freshly done, if I were to guess. Didn't know if that would even slow looters down. If I were looking to loot someone's place, I'd go for the homes with lots of security. They probably had more shit worth the trouble.

And then, maybe an hour after we left the edge of the forest, the convoy was rolling into New Montreal, or at least the suburbs.

Cranes were lifting massive slabs of cement, and I noticed entire rows of buildings being torn down. Thousands of folks in bright hard hats and vests were crawling around the city like maddened ants, and the proof of their labor was impossible to miss.

A wall was going up around the entire city, topped with guard towers where crews were installing AA guns, and larger cannons were being mounted on swivels.

It seemed like the city was preparing for a long war.

CHAPTER THIRTY-FOUR

THE NEXT MOVE

As cities grow, so do their energy requirements.

If you were to use coal fire as a source of energy, for example, then a single megacity the size of N-Three York or the Texan Mega Slum would burn more coal in one month than the industrial revolution did in a decade.

That's why we are so dependent on more reliable and consistent sources of power, and why nuclear, both fusion and fission based, is the main source of power that many cities depend on.

—Excerpt from *The Nuclear Future*, 2038

It was approaching late afternoon and I was sitting atop the newly built wall around part of New Montreal, legs dangling over the edge, helmet placed on the ground next to me, and wind whipping my hair around so hard I was considering what Lucy would think if I went short.

I had a plastic container in my mechanical hand, filled with some sort of meaty paste that looked absolutely vile but tasted like how an orgasm felt, and a cheap plastic spoon in the other hand.

All said and done, it was a nice spot for a break.

Grasshopper pushed herself up, standing on the very edge without any concern at all. "I'm off," she said.

"Hmm?" I asked. I looked up to her, then back down. The convoy we'd escorted was parked down below. The trucks were being looked over and hosed down before being allowed inside the walls. No one wanted any Antithesis meat to be brought into the city. You needed a critical mass of the stuff to start growing a hive—at least, that was what I understood—but still. Better safe than sorry. "Where are you heading off to?" I asked.

"I have evening lessons," Grasshopper said. "I don't want to miss them. What will you be doing?"

"Skulking about and stuff," I said. "Maybe find another samurai who needs help, or check up on Lucy and the kittens."

"Kittens?" Grasshopper asked.

"The orphans I look after. You should see them; they'd like you." I smiled up at her.

"So, you're a mommy cat." She chuckled. "I might visit. That sounds very cute. But not tonight, I don't think. Goodbye, Stray Cat."

"See ya, Grasshopper," I said.

I waved her off with my spoon hand, then scooped up another bite.

She left the area a bit later, and I stayed perched up on the wall, looking over the outskirts of the city. Smoke rose in the distance. I hoped that was a good sign.

No massive armies of skittering plants were visible, not yet.

I almost jumped when Myalis spoke up.

You have an incoming message from Laserjack.

"Yeah? What's it about?" I asked.

It seems as though he sent over a summary report of the last twenty-four hours. Personnel and Vanguard losses. Areas highly affected. Potential action plans and calls for assistance in certain areas.

"Vanguard losses?" I repeated. "Some samurai have died?" I asked.

It wasn't Gomorrah, I didn't think. Sam-o Ray? Jolly Monarch? Cause Player? I didn't really know any of the others well enough to remember their names off the top of my head.

The Vanguard known as Nomad is the only confirmed casualty.

Nomad . . . that had been the chick who talked about cars and such. She didn't seem like a fighting type, but still. "Fuck," I muttered. I set my meal aside. As good as it tasted, my hunger wasn't there anymore.

A call came in just as I was standing up, from Gomorrah. I answered it while picking up my helmet.

"Cat? How are you?" Gomorrah asked.

"Good enough," I said. "What's up?"

"Did you look over Laserjack's report?" she asked.

I looked around for a garbage can but didn't spot any. I did see some construction guys loitering around farther up on the wall. I started their way. "Nah, but Myalis skimmed it. Why, what's up?"

"The Family spotted a few hives. They're looking for volunteers to take them out. I thought you might be interested in helping me. One's maybe twenty minutes outside of the city. No one else has claimed it."

"You can claim hives now?" I asked. "You're going to head over and become the bug nun? Maybe start spawning fire-breathing critters?"

"If you claimed it that way, all that would come out of your hive would be horny cats," Gomorrah shot back.

I grinned, then pushed my half-finished meal into the hands of some construction guy. "Here, eat this, the fate of the world depends on it," I said before moving on. My bike was stationed a bit above, next to one of the bigger cannon emplacements. "Yeah, if you need a plus-one to take on a hive, I'm all in."

"Great. I don't think we'll be able to bomb this one from near orbit, though."

"That's not fun to hear; why not?"

Gomorrah sighed over the line. "The hive is about two kilometers away from a micro-nuclear plant. It's next to a river. The plant should be fine, in theory, but the Family specifically says that we shouldn't blow up the area around it. Just in case."

"All right, fair. Where do you want to meet up?" I asked.

"I'm with the ground crew guarding the outer edge of the wall, where it's still being added to. They've stalled here for a bit. Lots of people here, lots of guns too; I don't think we need to worry about anyone being killed by an Antithesis."

I climbed onto my bike, and Myalis helpfully punched in Gomorrah's location. "What's the issue?"

"The Family and a few companies secured the right to build the wall through a section of a native reserve. But they want to cut a straight line through, and that means demolishing a lot of stuff. The tribe isn't pleased with the idea. The other option is to go around the reserve, but that would lengthen the entire wall by a considerable amount, and it would mean more wall to defend."

"Huh," I said. I wasn't too sure who was in the right there. "Sounds like a bitch to deal with."

"Which is why I've excused myself from the entire thing. It went from a civil disagreement to a screaming match in far too little time for my comfort. I think tempers are running rather high all over the place right now."

That was normal, probably. "More than enough stress to go around."

"I suppose. Every minute they spend arguing is another where things aren't moving forward, though. It's frustrating."

It took all of two minutes of flying along the length of the wall, avoiding heavy lifting vehicles and the cranes pulling up the massive slabs that became the foundations for the wall. Gomorrah was next to the Fury, arms crossed and a wafting aura of frustration coming off her to ward off anyone who would dare test her.

"Hey," I said as I jumped off my bike. "You ready to go? We can take my bike. Ride together."

"We're taking my car," she said. No negotiating there.

I shrugged and went around to the other side while my bike parked itself. Gomorrah wasn't lying when she said there were plenty of people arguing with each other, though it mostly seemed to center on one group.

"Laserjack's on his way to smooth things over," Gomorrah said.

"Huh, all right. So, the current mission," I asked as I sat down.

Gomorrah started the Fury up, and we took off into the skies, heading northward, if I wasn't mistaken.

"A hive was spotted thanks to some seismographs next to a micro-nuclear unit fabrication plant."

I raised my hand. "Question. What's a micro-nuclear plant?"

Gomorrah took a moment to reply. "You know what a nuclear power plant is, right?"

"Yeah. Are you going to say that it's that, but small?"

"That would be a little reductive, but not entirely inaccurate," she said. "I think someone just sat down and figured out the exact minimum amount of machinery you need to boil water with radioactive products and then build a reactor out of that. They're meant to be more efficient than the older, bigger reactors. You can fit a few hundred in the footprint of an old facility."

"That's neat," I said. "And now there's a bunch of aliens next to one of these plants?"

"The plant makes those reactors. It's not a power plant. Though I imagine they produce their own power. The hive should be relatively small. It's taken over an old factory complex. I think it was a brick-making place, actually."

"How old are we talking here?" I asked.

Gomorrah shrugged. "I didn't bother checking. The hive's fully active, though. I don't think we'll be able to land right on top of it."

"Just to be clear. No big bombs, but little ones are fine, right?"

"I suppose."

"And no one has any problems with us using B.E.E.S., right?"

"I have no idea what you're talking about," Gomorrah said.

I grinned. "Well, then, you're going to love these."

I wondered if Myalis would give me some B.E.E.S. that lit on fire if I paid her a little extra. Just as something to show Gomorrah how much I appreciated her.

CHAPTER THIRTY-FIVE

A TERRIBLE MISTAKE

There are two kinds of survivalists: the enthusiasts, who only wish to participate in a hobby that could well save their lives later, and the true survivalists, those who wish to abandon the shackles that society has placed around their necks.

This forum is for the true survivors.

—Opening page of a dark web forum, 2025

Gomorrah flew a wide circle around the top of the brick factory. It was pretty much what I imagined when she described the place to me: big, made of red bricks, with a tin roof that had seen better days and three big chimneys poking out above. A large channel in the dirt ran up and through the building, and I had the impression that it was once meant to pass water through.

Maybe this was one of those super old mill-like places, using hydroelectricity or something to keep working.

Right now, the nearest river forked away from the factory, and the channel leading up to it was partially filled in. Plenty of stagnant water in the bottom, though. I couldn't wait to smell it.

The complex itself went on for a while, with a dozen smaller buildings and warehouses, and even what looked like a small town filled with mobile homes nearby.

"Are you sure we're the only ones for this job?" I asked.

"What do you mean?"

"No explosives kinda cuts me off at the knees, and this place looks like it's going to be nothing but close-quarters fighting. It's not exactly my forte."

"There were a few other hives spotted, but this one seemed like the easiest to take on. It's still small. The others have started spawning Antithesis past the single digits already. The Family's planning on hitting most of them from orbit later."

"Oh, shit," I said. It was basically going to be raining god-rods in a few hours, then. "Not this one?"

"Not this one, and not any that are in very sensitive areas," Gomorrah said. "They needed someone a little more delicate to take care of this hive in particular."

I nodded. "And you instantly thought of me when the word 'delicate' crossed your mind. Makes perfect sense."

Gomorrah chuckled. "Yes, that is a word I would use while describing you. I'd perhaps add 'in-' before it, but that's up for debate." She gestured out ahead. "I'm going to land on that rooftop there. The flat one. The Fury can hover while we jump out."

"Got it," I said.

We flew lower, the Fury surprisingly quiet as we coasted to a gentle stop atop one of the smaller buildings next to the main factory. I guessed that it was some sort of admin building, next to the parking lot.

I opened the door, glanced down to make sure Gomorrah didn't want me to drop too far, then shifted out to the side.

The roof clanged as I landed, and then it rattled even louder as Gomorrah touched down next to me. She reached around and adjusted the pack of her heavy flamethrower. "Is the area clear?" she asked.

I got my head into the game, flicked on the invisibility on my coat and armor, then brought my Bullcat around to scan the area. "Seems like it," I said.

There was a roof access hatch nearby, but I didn't know if we'd be able to pull it open, rusted as it was.

Then Gomorrah pointed her flamethrower down, pulled the trigger, and spat out a foot-long jet of blue flame that melted right through the hinges of the door. "Want to pull it off? I'll cover you."

"So, this is the amount of subtlety we're going for," I said as I reached down and yanked the cover off. "Good to know. I was worried I'd have to be careful."

There was a ladder inside the darkened room below, but the floor wasn't too far down, so I grabbed on to the edge of the roof and dropped myself down. The moment my knees absorbed the impact, I checked the room for trouble. All I found were cleaning supplies that had been unusably old two decades ago.

Gomorrah came down with a bit more trouble. She ended up tossing down her flamethrower, pack and all, before dropping herself. "I am not fit for this kind of activity," she muttered.

"Hey, no big deal," I said. I opened the door into a corridor, Bullcat sweeping the room for any nasty surprises. Nothing, just an ancient office space with some old desks, their panel wood peeling apart. No computers under the desks, though I did spot a couple of those big boxy screens piled up in one corner, their fronts blown right off.

"Someone's been here," Gomorrah said.

I followed her gaze and noticed the cans off to one side of the room. There was a couch there, probably for people who were waiting, and all around it was all sorts of shitty junk, wrappers, and a few boxes.

I moved over, boots making my tread basically noiseless, then knelt next to the couch. "Unless they had Deus Ex–branded Prepsi back before I was born." The can didn't just have Deus Ex on it; there were about five or six samurai, but she was the one I recognized immediately.

"Could just be people coming over here to hang out," Gomorrah said.

"Or to fuck," I said with a gesture to the couch. "I wouldn't sit in the middle of this thing."

"Disgusting," Gomorrah said.

"I actually agree. You're just asking to catch something if you're rubbing your fun bits against something like this. I think this thing is corduroy? It's nasty," I said.

I could feel Gomorrah giving me the stink eye, even through her mask. "We should move on. The Antithesis clearly aren't in this room. Probably not even in this entire building."

"Was the hive supposed to be somewhere specific?"

"The Family only suspects that it's around here," Gomorrah said. "There might not even be a hive. Though if they spotted Antithesis around the area . . ."

"Then they'll have started a hive," I finished for her. It was probably even a good spot for one. Walls all around, some natural stuff to chow down on, and no one to interfere with their growth for a while.

Well, no one but the two of us. I suspected we were about to do a whole lot of interfering.

Heading out, we found the exit, an old glass door, so dirty it was almost impossible to see out of. It wasn't locked, and someone had helpfully jammed a brick at the foot of the door. I rubbed my hand against the glass to see outside, then checked for aliens.

I wasn't actually expecting to find any.

"Huh," I said. "Model three."

Gomorrah tensed up behind me. "Where?"

"Dead," I said. "Right up next to the factory. It's in the shadows, next to this little entrance spot that's sticking out." The entrance was a boxy protrusion on the side of the factory, with a peaked tin roof and a few windows that I couldn't quite see into. "Can't see what killed it. Want to wait here?"

"Certainly. Leave the door entirely open, in case I need to join you."

I nodded, then slid the door open. It creaked a bit, and the brick I jammed in place to keep it open wasn't exactly quiet either.

After listening in for a moment—the only sounds I could hear were the faint pitter-patter of a very weak drizzle of rain and the creak of an old building moving—I ran out and across the parking lot of the factory. I kept my eyes on a swivel until I slowed to a stop next to the model three.

The thing was very dead, its face blasted right off so that all that remained were fleshy giblets hanging on with sinew and skin. "Looks like someone shot our alien pal here," I said over the coms to Gomorrah.

"Can you date it?"

"Uh." I touched the body. "Do model threes give off much heat? This thing is room temp."

While most Antithesis will give off some heat, it is usually much cooler than the average earthly mammal. More comparable to the temperature seen in cold-blooded creatures. Exceptions exist, of course. Models bred to resist colder climates will actually be significantly warmer.

That was good to know.

"I'm going into the lobby," I said.

"Careful," Gomorrah warned. "I imagine whoever shot the model three might still be around."

I nodded, even if Gomorrah couldn't see, and moved over to the doorway into the factory. Turns out her warning was warranted. "Oh hey, a booby trap," I said.

"What sort?" Gomorrah asked. "Remember, no explosives. Not even if they're not yours."

"Not a bomb. This is a bit more low-tech than that." Above the door was a long piece of string, wedged between the doorway and the doorframe. Peeking through the glass on the door, I could make out the string going above, and holding on to a trio of tin cans with holes punched into them for the cord.

If my guess was right . . .

I reached up, grabbed hold of the string, then carefully opened the door.

The string loosened, and would have fallen if I hadn't been holding it.

Once the door was open a crack, I checked around for more traps and, finding none, slid inside, still holding on to the cord. I gently, gently gave it more slack until the strung-together cans touched the floor.

"Looks like someone rigged some cans to clatter around if you opened the door," I said.

"Interesting," Gomorrah said. "I'm running over to your position now."

I watched as Gomorrah darted across to where I was.

She was only halfway over when someone opened fire on her.

CHAPTER THIRTY-SIX

THE SURVIVALISTS WHO PROBABLY WON'T

Life in a megacity isn't for everyone. There's a constant hustle and bustle, millions of people crowding in around you, and you never know which one of them might want to harm you.

If you're looking for a retreat to a better life, then check out Comtown-dot-com! Your one-stop shop to find the company town that's right for you!

—Comtown.com ad, 2047

I swore, or at least screamed something that might have been a swear. I wasn't entirely coherent for a moment as I heard the rattle of gunfire and saw the asphalt around Gomorrah spark and crack with missed shots.

She stumbled, and I froze, expecting her to fall.

Then Gomorrah raised her flamethrower up above and ahead of her and pulled the trigger.

A massive burst of fire, spread wide like a flaming umbrella, burned the air above her and created a barrier between her and whoever was shooting down at her.

She ran faster, and I jumped to open the door. The fire stopped, but not before licking at the roof of the entrance.

"Shit, shit, are you okay?" I asked. "Myalis, I need shit for bullet wounds. Fuck, okay, sit down, sit down here, and it'll be okay, we can fix this." I pulled her to the side and started fretting over her, looking for the blood, for the wounds. I could fix this, just shove the wound full of magic healing goop. She'd be fine.

"Cat."

"Oh, fuck, fuck. Okay, which one hurts more? Shit, we need to—"

Gomorrah poked me in the belly, then looked up to me with her expressionless mask. "Catherine."

I paused, breathing still a bit ragged. "Yeah?"

"My equipment's bulletproof. All of it. I wouldn't go out to fight without decent armor on. Not like some people."

"Oh," I said. That explained the lack of holes in her gear. Though I did notice a few wrinkles in her habit, and some bronze smears on the metal bits of her pauldrons. Was that where she was struck? "Okay."

"I appreciate the concern, though," she said. "But you can let go of me now."

I let go of her, then grabbed my gun from where I'd dropped it next to the entrance. I couldn't remember letting it go, but everything had happened so quickly that I wasn't too surprised that I'd dropped it.

"So, that wasn't an alien," I said.

"Not unless they've started carrying fully automatic guns, no," Gomorrah said. "That came from the right side of the factory, on the second floor, I think. I just saw a flash before I started to burn the air."

"That was clever," I said. "The fire, I mean."

Gomorrah chuckled darkly. "I thought of the move as something of a deterrent against model ones. I suppose it works well enough against people shooting at me."

I nodded, then moved back over to the door. My head was entirely invisible, so I wasn't too worried when I poked out of the building and looked around. No sign of the shooter, but I didn't have a good angle from the doorway. The fire that washed over the roof seemed to have burned itself out without catching the bricks or tin on fire. That was good.

"Okay," I said. "We're not dealing with aliens here. We're dealing with armed people. Which might be worse. Should we call this one in?"

"There might still be a hive around," Gomorrah said.

Sure, there might be a hive, but there was also at least one punk with a gun and poor eyesight. That, or he didn't mind opening fire on someone who didn't look anything like an Antithesis. "I'm going to run ahead, check out the rest of the factory. Keep your coms open; I'll shout if I meet anyone."

"I don't like staying idle," Gomorrah said.

"You're not exactly equipped for dealing with people," I said. "Not unless you intend to cook them."

"That . . . is a fair point." Gomorrah swung her backpack off, then set her flamethrower down on the ground next to the entrance.

"What are you doing?" I asked.

She glanced up. "Buying something to deal with people. I can spare the points, and I can store it in the Fury once I'm done with it. In case something like this comes up again. What would you suggest, weaponwise?"

I sighed. "Something that won't burn people? You had that glue stuff in the sewers. That was nonlethal, right?"

"True, but the range wasn't ideal. Ah." Gomorrah dropped to one knee and a box appeared next to her. She flicked it open to reveal a grenade-launcher-looking gun. "This should do it. It fires Taser nets."

"Cool," I said. I pulled the magazine out of the back of my Bullcat. "Myalis, got nonlethals for me too? Taser-y stuff should do it."

There are Taser slugs available. Though I'd suggest Taser flechettes. They'll pierce through a bit of armor and will auto-modulate so as to avoid being lethal while also ensuring that anything hit that has an electrical nervous system will be unable to function.

"Neat," I said. A fresh magazine appeared inside the gun and loaded itself in.

I worked my shoulders to loosen them up, then pushed on the door leading into the factory.

If there were any doubts about people living here, they vanished as soon as I was on the main factory floor. Lights hung from the ceiling, like those old Christmas lights, but without the colored bulbs. Couches were pushed up against walls, and partitions had been created to split the room apart.

Some girders and brackets stuck out of the floor where I imagine the machinery used to make bricks or whatever had been long ago. The factory was split into two sections. One with a tall ceiling, the windows on the upper section allowing dusty light through. The second half was much lower, with a second floor taking up the upper section, which could be reached via some catwalk stairs.

A corner of the factory had been turned into a kitchen, and I noticed that someone had dragged in a dozen solar panels of different makes and models and left them piled up in the middle of the room.

What the hell was going on here?

A drug op, maybe? With self-sustaining power stuff, they could grow all sorts of shit without anyone noticing.

I passed by a partition that was made of smoothed wood. There were toys within, and an older TV. A playpen?

I wasn't sure what to think anymore.

Gomorrah was moving along behind me, much slower than I was. She was taking a bit more time and watching out for trouble. "I think this was some sort of commune," she said.

"You mean a bunch of hippies hid in here?"

"Something like that. Could be a cult too. Stuck far away from the city, cut off from the rest of the world. They might not even be aware that there's a mass incursion occurring."

"Fuck," I muttered. I glanced around, but other than a few posters for some bands and brands in one of the partitions that had a little living space, I couldn't see anything overtly religious around. One partition had a cross, but the one next to it had a Star of David. I didn't think we were dealing with a cult of that sort.

I reached the catwalks first, then hesitated. "Above or below?" I asked.

"We could split up," Gomorrah said.

"I'd rather not," I replied. "All right, I'm going to summon up a mecha-cat. We might need one later anyway if we'll be hitting a hive. It can keep an eye on the lower floor while we go above."

Gomorrah nodded, then slipped to the side where she could stand behind a cement pillar that was chipped away on the edges.

Just the usual sort of mechanized cat drone?

I nodded. "Something quiet and fast-firing, yeah."

Noted.

New Purchase: Stealth and Reconnaissance M.E.O.W.

Points Reduced from . . . 19,874 to . . . 19,674

"You really worked hard on that acronym, didn't you?" I asked.

It stands for Mechanized Environmental Obliteration Weapon.

A box appeared next to me with the barest *click* as it touched down. The top slid to the side, and an all-black pantherlike mecha-cat jumped out of it. It was a bit smaller than the usual cat drone, with proportionally bigger paws and some slits on its back where I imagined its guns were tucked away for the moment.

"Right, let it scan around; I'm heading up." I took the catwalk two steps at a time. My boots didn't make any noise on hitting the steps, but the entire thing shifted with my weight, and there was no hiding the creak of rusty metal and the occasional clink.

On racing to the top, I shuffled closer to the only doorway up there and pressed myself close to it. Now that I was closer, my bullshit alien-tech ears could pick out sounds from within. People breathing, a kid trying hard not to be heard while crying, metal things shifting around.

There had to be a dozen people in that room.

"W-we know you're there," someone said. "Come on out, and we won't blast you!"

Well, so much for stealth.

CHAPTER THIRTY-SEVEN

TRIGGER HAPPY

Manufacturing trends started to shift after the first incursion. Domestic production returned as international supply lines were cut, and it suddenly became cheaper once more to build everything a local economy needed next to that local economy, rather than on the literal other side of the planet.

—Excerpt from *Economy of Scale: Wartime Manufacturing*, 2034

I wasn't sure what to do for a moment.

On the one hand, some guy was talking to me. That meant that unless the Antithesis had learned speech and how to use guns, then I was probably just dealing with a nutjob or three. I could hear kids back there as well.

On the other hand . . . someone did shoot Gomorrah, and I was a little bit miffed about it. Shooting things had thus far proven to be an excellent way to work out my anger.

"I didn't quite hear what he said." Gomorrah shifted lower on the catwalk steps. "Can you hear him properly?"

"Yeah," I said. "He wants us to—"

"Come on out! With your hands up!" the guy screamed. He was closer to the door this time.

"He wants us to do that," I said.

Gomorrah sniffed. "I'll admit I'm a little . . . what's the word . . . salty, that I was shot. I'm tempted to burst in and spray everything down."

"Bit rude, no?" I asked.

"I know you're out there!" our pal called out.

I sighed, then flicked my coms off so that when I spoke he could hear me. "Then why don't you come out and say hi, huh, asshole?"

"It's not aliens," someone muttered on the other side of the door.

I rolled my eyes. This was just stupid. Moving up to the door, I reached up, turned the handle, then threw the door open while standing well to the side.

A roaring blast blew through the opening, and some buckshot ripped apart the edge of the doorway, sending a spray of wood flying down into the factory's main floor.

"Nice shot," I said, entirely aware of the hypocrisy.

I heard someone shifting, and I could make out three figures behind a desk; two of them had shotguns. They both started reloading at the same time.

I bounced to the side, slipped through the entrance, then ran and leapt over the table before they could figure out that anything was amiss. Being invisible probably helped to confuse them.

I grabbed the two men who had guns by their shirts, then yanked them back and onto the floor with hard thumps.

Standing, I spun and brought my Bullcat up and pointed its barrel between the eyes of the third guy.

The moment held for a bit; one of the guys on the ground started to shift back to his feet, but I pushed him back down with a boot on his chest. "Let's not," I said.

Once I was sure I wasn't about to be shot, I flicked off my invisibility. The guy behind me shifted toward his gun. I lit the tip of my tail on fire and shifted it around so that the sparking, burning head was between his hand and the stock of his gun.

"I said," I repeated myself very carefully. "Let's not."

"You're a samurai," the guy on the business end of my gun said.

"Yup," I said. "So's the girl you shot."

"She was trespassing," the idiot under my boot said.

"Paul," the guy I had at gunpoint said. "Shut the fuck up."

"Listen to your friend, Paul," I said. I pulled my foot off his chest and retracted my tail, then carefully lowered my tail. "I can hear a couple of dozen people up here. What the hell is this?"

"This is none of your business, you corporate dog," Paul said.

I glared down at Paul. "I'm a cat, you dumbass. Didn't I tell you to shut up? You—" I wiggled my gun in the direction of the guy who still stood. "You seem halfway sensible. What's your name?"

"Charles," he said. "I'm, uh, one of the leaders of this community. Paul is too."

"Well, half your leadership seems a bit trigger-friendly," I said. "What are you people still doing here? You don't have any connections to the net? TV . . . radio, even?"

Charles sighed. "We know about the incursion," he said. "But we elected not to head back to the city, not if it might mean losing our home."

"Right." I said. "How many people are here?"

"We're fifty-nine members," Charles said. "Not including children and those too young to vote. Maybe ninety people, total?"

Gomorrah peeked into the room, saw that it was clear, then stepped in while sweeping for trouble. "What's going on?" she asked.

I gestured to Charles. "We have ninety people here. More or less. Don't know what they were thinking."

"We voted," Charles said. "We just want to stay home."

"The aliens want to stay in your home too," I said.

"We're fine," Paul said. He glared as he stood up. He wisely left his gun on the ground. "We took out a few of the things already."

I frowned. "What about the hive?" I asked.

"What hive?" Paul and Charles asked at the same time.

I turned toward Gomorrah. "Think the reports could be wrong? Might have been this bunch doing something that the Family misread as there being a hive nearby."

Gomorrah shook her head. "There are aliens here. We both saw the body, and they just admitted to killing others. If the Antithesis are around, then there's a hive nearby. We know it's not closer to the nuclear reactor facility; they have enough sensors and security that we'd know. It has to be around this area. Though I suppose it doesn't need to be within this factory."

"Huh," I said. "Hey, Charles, are there any places that a nice alien hive could hole itself up in? Caves nearby? Maybe a really thick forest?"

Charles glanced at Paul, and Paul spoke up. "It can't be a hive. We'd all be dead already."

"Oh boy," I muttered. "Come on, out with it. We're not the feds; we don't give a shit about your . . . weird cult thing going on here."

"We're not a cult," Charles said.

"That's what people in cults say," I pointed out.

He shook his head. "We're just office workers, factory workers. People who were tired of the rat race. We all live here. It's peaceful, it's quiet, it's less cutthroat than living in the city. Simpler. We garden for some of our food, buy the rest. Lots of us work online."

"Cool," I said. "Aliens, where?"

Charles gestured to the side. "We've seen a few of the smaller ones coming from that way. The far end of the factory; there was a large generator complex, with a big basement. It connects to most of the other buildings."

"So, a tight series of corridors, dug under the earth?" I asked.

"Essentially?" he replied, turning it into a question.

Gomorrah shifted from side to side. "That does sound like the kind of place the Antithesis would enjoy. Is there access to it from around here?"

"There's an entrance below, yes," Charles said. "We used to use it for storage; it's rather cool, but it's also very humid, and in spring it floods a little. We even had to run some pumps to keep it dry a few times when the river ran higher."

"Ah, a wet dark tunnel, I imagine with no lighting, dug into the ground and covered in . . . I'm guessing cement?" I asked.

"I suppose."

"Cool, so it's like a free bunker for the aliens. Are you sure I can't use explosives on this one?" I asked Gomorrah.

"Very," she said. "Besides, you might cave the entire facility in. Seeing as how it's humid, though, using fire won't pose too much of a risk. Atyacus can check to see if there are any natural gases in the area that are flammable."

"You get to have all the fun today," I complained.

She sniffed. "You got to drop that large bomb yesterday. I think this is only fair."

I nodded. "All right, Paul, you seem like the most expendable one here. Guide us down to that entrance. We'll see if there really is a hive down there. The rest of you should really consider voting on leaving again. It's a long way to New Montreal, but it's safer there than it is here."

"We can't just leave," Charles said.

I shrugged. "I can talk to the Family. At least get the kids to someplace that's safer than here. The rest of you are all adults; if you want to last-stand against the aliens in here, then that's on you. Hope you have a lot of ammo, though, because I've already seen and fought swarms of aliens hundreds strong, and it's only going to get worse."

Charles rubbed his eyes. "I'll talk to the others, thank you. And . . . I apologize for shooting you."

Gomorrah nodded. "You're forgiven. Thank you for apologizing."

I pointed my thumb back out the door. "Okay, we're off. We'll stop by after, hear what you guys choose to do. Hopefully it's not something real stupid. Come on, Paul."

Paul didn't seem happy to be our guide, but he tramped down the catwalk after picking up his gun all the same.

Now to find that hive and burn it up.

Maybe I could use a small bomb? Just a little one?

CHAPTER THIRTY-EIGHT

BASEMENT

There's a whole new category of entertainment called simply Samurai Entertainment. Sometimes it's shortened to SE, or "See," as in the verb "to see."

The genre mostly consists of following samurai the way that paparazzi of the past followed celebrities. The big difference is that most samurai don't care for the attention, and most celebrities don't saunter onto battlefields on the regular.

—Modern Stream Entertainment, *Genre Guide*, 2031

Paul clambered down the stairs with all of the attitude and ill mood of a five-year-old who had just been told off. If I weren't such a bastion of moral integrity and good spirit, I would have mocked him for it.

Wait . . .

"Who shat in your shorts, Pauly boy?" I asked as I followed him down the steps.

He paused so that he could level a glare at me. "I don't like you," he said.

"Well, shit, there goes my mood for the next week," I said.

"Cat, maybe less quipping and more walking would be in order?" Gomorrah asked.

I shook my head. "Sarcasm and snark are the only things I had for a long time, you know? When you don't own anything, you cling to whatever you have," I explained.

"Yes, but you're a samurai now. You can hardly be said to have nothing. You have your equipment, plenty of resources, a girlfriend. Even a home," she said. "Perhaps you can finally do away with the snark?"

"Huh," I said. "Does having a home make me a part of the bourgeois?"

"You don't actually know what that is, do you?" Gomorrah asked.

"I don't, but something deep inside me still makes me want to blame them for all of my woes."

Paul tsked. "You're exactly the kind of thing we left the city to avoid," he said.

Did he just literally objectify me? "Just get us to the basement so that we can do our jobs," I snapped.

"And then what? You'll leave us all alone?" he asked.

"Yeah, that's the idea. We have other hives to break, and other people to save. I still think you'd be clever to move back to the city. There's more of us bougie types to keep you nice and safe. If you want to use that boomstick of yours, I'm sure there's some militia out there that's desperate enough that they'll hire even you."

"Fuck off; I want to defend me and mine right here. This is my home. I worked hard for it. Did you ever work hard for anything in your life?" he growled.

I was very close to pumping a few rounds into Paul's legs, then leaving him behind for the Antithesis to take care of. But they'd probably use his meat to grow some sort of terrifying boss-tier monster that no one wanted to deal with, so I refrained from doing that for the moment.

Paul stomped across the factory floor and swept right into the kitchen area at the back. He stopped there before bending down to pull at a strap sticking out of the ground. It opened a large trapdoor, with cement steps leading down and to a metal door.

"That's the basement," Paul said.

"You know your way around in there?" I asked.

"I'm not guiding you through," he said.

"We just need some directions," Gomorrah said.

Paul rubbed at his nose. "There's a large boiler room one building over. The basement opens into it. If you follow the big steam pipes you'll always find your way back to that one. It's more or less central to the whole factory. There's a loading dock on the far end that's barricaded up; that's a pretty wide room. And then there's the big old building by the waterfront. That one's nearly always flooded."

"Thank you," Gomorrah said.

She stepped down first, then fiddled with her launcher. Judging by the switched tanks, she just went from nonlethal to burn-everything fuel.

"You can run back, Paul," I said.

He sniffed, shouldered his gun, then stomped back across the factory floor without so much as a how-do-you-do. I heard him clambering up the stairs a minute later and put him out of my mind for the moment.

"So, what's the plan in there?" I asked.

"Do you have something that allows you to breathe in a low-oxygen environment?" Gomorrah asked.

"That's a terrifying question to be asked. Can I know why?" My helmet did have a rebreather. I'd used it plenty in the sewers.

"Because if there is any oxygen in the tunnels, then there's a good chance I'll be using it as fuel."

I crossed my arms. "And I can't use explosives?"

"You have other tricks up your sleeves, and fire doesn't create as much of a problem as your bombs would," Gomorrah said.

The door at the bottom of the little stairway was a thick metal thing, with big steel bars holding it in place. It took some effort to twist the handle around to unlock it. Then Gomorrah put her shoulder into opening the door, and it swung open onto a tight corridor: cement walls with ducts above and a large pipe fixed to the wall by rusty brackets. It had once been covered by some sort of cloth wrapping, but age had made it sag and rot off.

"Nice place," I muttered as I stepped in behind Gomorrah. I swept my gun over the space behind us, just in case, then turned back around toward where Gomorrah was facing.

"Not very flammable," Gomorrah said.

"Is that a good thing, or not?"

"It's good in this case," she said. "Come on, I'll take point for once."

We started down the tunnel until we came to an intersection. Paul had failed to mention that the basement was basically a rat's nest of narrow passages. I had expected it to be more like . . . a few rooms connected together by some corridors. But it seemed as though the basement was more of an accessway for machines and stuff that wasn't around anymore.

A little ways in we arrived at a large room. There were old crates up against the wall and a loading area at the far end.

I glanced around and dismissed all of that in favor of staring into the floor. We had to go down a couple of steps to get to the ground, steps that disappeared under a layer of black, motionless water.

"Bet it smells wonderful down here," I muttered.

"Movement," Gomorrah said.

I snapped my head up and looked. I couldn't see anything at first, not until I noticed the ripples in the water.

They came from a stack of crates in the middle of the room. Old wooden boxes with mold growing up their sides. And right there on top of them was what looked like a pile of rags.

"That's a model nine," I said. I could see its little beady eyes between two folds. The little shit was waiting for us.

"It is," Gomorrah said. "This isn't a stealth mission, though." She raised her flamethrower, and I winced back as a jet of high-pressure liquid fire roared out of the gun and onto the model nine and the crates beneath.

The rotting old wood might have been damp, but that didn't save it from Gomorrah's wrath.

The entire room, as big as it was, turned into an oven in the time it took to blink. The water on the surface bubbled and hissed; steam rose into the air, pulled into the gushing flames, then disappeared with a squeal.

The crate and the alien on it didn't exist three seconds after Gomorrah opened up on them. She pulled her finger off the trigger, and a single burning corner of the wooden box—still on fire—flopped into the water with a hissing splash.

"Do you see any others?" she asked.

"Are you going to do that to all of them?" I asked. Next time I got a suit, I was getting one with better temperature controls. It was beyond uncomfortable in here. "Might as well dry off the floor while you're here."

Gomorrah took that suggestion to heart, and soon the flamethrower was being swept left to right across the floor. The water in the room rushed back from the flames, but whenever Gomorrah moved, the water would pour right back into the void. The air was filled with a foggy steam by the time Gomorrah gave up.

"I think the entire basement is filled," she said. "I might run out of fuel before it runs out of water."

"Then we'll be getting our ankles wet," I said. "We'll live. Though I'm worried that the Antithesis will have invented some sort of ankle-biting fish-thing just to fuck with me."

"Aren't cats supposed to like fish?" Gomorrah asked.

"Now who's being snarky?" I muttered.

We started splashing our way across the room, on the lookout for the next alien to burn.

CHAPTER THIRTY-NINE

INTERRUPT

We are the Sisters of the Holy Extermination.

Our creed and duty is to remove that which is impure from the cities in which we live. Foul xenos, rats, insects, and squatters, all will be judged by fire.

It is the only way to be certain.

—The Sisters of the Holy Extermination Manifesto, 2045

"This way," Gomorrah muttered as she started down another tunnel. This, at least, was a bit wider than the last.

The water sloshing by our feet made it hard to move forward, but we were pushing through it. I was just glad that my boots were waterproof; otherwise the trek was going to get real unpleasant real fast.

The worse thing was that my armor let me feel just how lukewarm the water was, which was just . . . super unpleasant.

As we started down the tunnel, the water grew cooler, and it was clear that it was flowing back into the big room we'd come from. Had Gomorrah burned that much water out?

"Can you hear anything?" Gomorrah asked.

"Hmm? Oh, let me listen," I said. I focused on my hearing for a bit, then snapped my fingers a few times. It created something like an echo, and I could "see" ahead of us for a little ways, though the water was making it weird. "Uh, right up ahead, then left. No beasties that I can see."

We approached a corner that turned right, and then it immediately turned right again.

"Okay, so right-right, not right-left," I muttered.

"Maybe I shouldn't have bothered asking," Gomorrah said. She raised her flamethrower, the pilot light at the very tip of it providing most of the light we had, that and my glowing shotgun.

I rolled my eyes but continued to listen ahead. "Wait," I muttered.

Gomorrah and I both stopped as the water around us wavered and bobbed. Still, I could hear something ahead: sloshing and the *tip-tap* of something clicking against tin. "What is it?" Gomorrah whispered.

"Aliens, I think," I said. "There's a room ahead, right? I think our friends are waiting for us."

"All right. Do we move in, or do we toss them a surprise?"

"What are you thinking?" I asked.

Gomorrah gestured ahead with a little thrust of her flamethrower. "You toss in something to flush them out. I burn any that come this way. Then we sweep the room."

I thought for a second. Resonators would act weird with the water. Anything explosive was out. Nano stuff might have trouble with the water too . . . I grinned. "I have just the thing." Stepping up next to Gomorrah, I shut off our coms to speak with Myalis. "Need some B.E.E.S. Can you make any that are on fire?"

Of course. Though that will make the manufacturing process somewhat more complex. Expect fewer B.E.E.S. and for them to have a much shorter life span overall. Only one to two minutes. Their lethality also won't be significantly greater.

"Yeah, that makes sense. But they'll be on fire, right?"

Yes.

"Perfect. Get me a jarful, Myalis!"

A container of B.E.E.S. appeared by my side and splashed down into the water. I could feel Gomorrah's interest, especially as the little bugs within blurred around their transparent enclosure. "What is that?" she asked.

"You'll love it," I said. I opened the top cover, then grinned as the tiny robots swarmed out of the container and lit up with a hundred little hisses. A shower of burning sparks raced around us, then shot off down the passage and into the room ahead. "Let's move," I said.

Gomorrah jogged up to the entrance, and for a moment both of us stared as the B.E.E.S. slammed into every alien in the room. They were clearly not hurting them much, but what they were doing, and very well, was showing us where the aliens were hidden.

"Burning," Gomorrah announced a moment before she stepped into the room with a splash. She hosed the aliens down. I saw the burning forms of model fours writhing as they melted and model threes darted out from cover, hounded by burning motes until Gomorrah's fire swept over them.

The water steamed, the aliens cooked, and Gomorrah started to chuckle in a way that had every hair on the back of my neck standing on end. She was having a bit too much fun, I think.

When she stopped, there were only husks of fleshy, charred meat left. The water in the room swirled around our legs, and steam flirted around us until the air cleared.

"That should do it," Gomorrah said. She sounded satisfied with herself, like someone congratulating themself on a job well done.

"You're scary, you know that?" I said.

"Why thank you," she said. "Onward?"

I gestured ahead, and she took the invitation by stepping into the room. It was hard to see the entirety of it. There was a large machine in the center, made of thick old steel and (until very recently) covered in ancient grease and oil. The metal was a bit glowy in some places, but for the most part it had weathered Gomorrah's affections better than most things would. I wouldn't touch it for a few hours, though.

Gomorrah checked the next corridor, and the few remaining flaming B.E.E.S. darted into it to look for trouble.

I wasn't expecting it when something grabbed my ankle. For the first half second, I thought I'd gotten caught on some old scrap, unseen under the brackish water. Then the thing tightened its grip.

"Oh shit-fuck," I screeched before I was ripped sideways and into the water.

I splashed, arms flailing for a bit before I realized two things.

First, I couldn't drown. Not in water this shallow, and not without anything grabbing my upper body and holding me down.

Second, some fuck was still grabbing my leg and pulling me under the big metal boiler.

I half turned, the motion made awkward by the constant pull, and then I aimed down the length of my body before hesitating. Could my own rounds go through my armor? How badly did I want a prosthetic foot?

A short jet of flame burst out from above me and burned through the grasping tentacle. It flopped through the air, pissing black-green gunk from its seared end before it retreated back under the boiler.

"Oh no you don't," I swore as I spun myself around. I aimed my Bullcat into the recess below the machine and fired. The muzzle flash lit up the squeezed-in form of a model four. I fired into it three more times, just to be sure. Then a fourth and fifth time as a final fuck-you.

"You okay?" Gomorrah asked.

"Yeah, I'm fine," I said. My heart was trying to beat out of my throat, but I'd live. I accepted Gomorrah's hand to get me back onto my feet. "Damned thing caught me off guard."

"We should have done a better job of scouting the room," Gomorrah said. "Imagine if we destroyed the hive and that one remained. It might be enough to start a whole new hive."

I felt myself blanching. "Damn. We're going to need to go over the area with a comb."

"I don't know if we have the time for that."

"I really hope those idiots upstairs are packing their shit, then," I said. "Or if not, then I hope they're a lot braver than they look. Maybe they can clear the area out themselves."

"Until the next wave sweeps by," Gomorrah said.

We didn't speak on it anymore. I brushed off some of the gunk from my jacket, which fortunately was made of something slick enough that crap didn't stick to it, and then we continued on at a slower, more deliberate pace.

I jumped when an alert popped up before me, and judging by the way Gomorrah froze, she got the same thing too.

There's an urgent, high-priority message from the Family to all Vanguards in the New Montreal area.

"What is it?" I asked. I wasn't too worried. The aliens hadn't gathered enough momentum to hit the city itself yet.

Wave incoming. The Family suspects that the risk level of the next wave will be high enough that they want to recall all Vanguards outside the city.

"What?" Gomorrah muttered.

"You got the same message?" I asked.

"Laserjack wants us to head back," she said. "He's making it sound urgent."

"Myalis, can you show me the message itself?"

The message, as it turned out, was a short video. Laserjack, obviously standing on one of those bunkers atop the newly built wall, was talking into some sort of camera. "Pardon the intrusion, everyone, but we have a situation developing and we need assistance for it right now. The xenos have caught us with our guard down. We have a medium-large wave, maybe sixty thousand models, moving in toward the northeastern end of the city. The walls there aren't completed and won't be for another twelve to sixteen hours. We don't have the defenses in place to keep the wave at bay. We need you."

The message ended, but there was a lot of information attached to it. Movement plots, predicted numbers, satellite images. The works.

"What do we do?" I asked.

"We go," Gomorrah said. She turned and started heading back.

I stared at her, then the darkness beyond, entirely uncertain about what to do next.

CHAPTER FORTY

ONCOMING

The battle is only lost when there are no more humans left to save. That is when we can finally allow ourselves to despair. They might come in their thousands or millions, but as long as we are here to meet them, then there is hope.

Today, there is no hope.

Despair for all these aliens. Hell. And may none of them escape satisfied!

—Major General Dimitri Strugatsky, moments before detonating a fail-safe nuclear device near the city of Mogocha, 2050

I hated it when I had to make hard choices without the time to think them through or any ways to weasel my way out of the problem in the first place.

"We're not leaving until we warn the idiots upstairs," I said.

Gomorrah paused and half turned to face me. "What?"

"Look, we've barely dented this hive. The least we can do is warn the people living here that the hive is still active and that we're leaving. They think that they're relatively safe, you know?"

"It'll take more time than we have," Gomorrah said. "Laserjack's request sounded urgent."

"I don't care," I decided. I wasn't going to run off and leave these people without at least a warning. I stared at Gomorrah, and her emotionless mask stared back.

"Fine," she said. "We're losing more time arguing. I'm going to park the Fury out front. Once we're out of this damnable basement, you can warn them all you want."

"Thank you," I said.

We walked our way back out of the basement, retracing our steps as we went. Neither of us seemed patient enough to walk with the same care as we used to enter the basement, so we made good time on our way out.

This time I took the lead, sloshing through the water with frustrated energy. The faster we made it out, the faster we could warn folks, and the less Gomorrah would be irate. And we'd get back to the city faster too.

Once back in the drier section of the basement, I jogged over to the door and pushed it open.

I wasn't expecting to find Charles and Paul and a few others all grouped up in the factory's main living space, but there they were. One of them was even lounging on the couch. "Hey!" I said.

They jumped. Not hearing my footfalls I could forgive, but the big iron door? That thing squealed when it opened.

Charles jogged over, and it seemed that he was something of a spokesman. "We voted again," he said.

"So, you're getting ready to pack up?" I asked. "That's good, because I've got bad news and worse news, and you don't get to pick the order."

"No, actually. We're going to stay. Enough of us want to stay that . . . we can't justify abandoning them. In either case, the vote was clear."

I shook my head. "Well, fuck."

"The news?" he asked.

"Bad news, the hive's still down there. We didn't kill it. Didn't even reach it, really. Burned out a few aliens in your basement, but my bet is that there's a lot more where they came from."

Charles winced. "And the worse news?" he asked. It didn't feel like he wanted to ask at all.

"We're leaving," I said. "Gomorrah and I. New Montreal's about to get hit, the walls aren't done, and no one's ready to take the brunt of it. So we need to go do our thing. You'll be all alone for a bit. I'll make sure the ping's still up, so maybe someone else will pop around. Or maybe Gomorrah and I can swing by once things calm down, but . . . yeah, I don't know when that'll be."

Charles nodded along. "It's fine. We'll manage."

I looked at him, with his old rig over a sweater, then at the others. A couple of them had bulletproof vests: ill-fitting things that looked like they were police surplus from three decades ago. Their guns weren't much better.

"Right," I said. I heard Gomorrah stepping out of the basement. She didn't waste any time here and headed outside to get the Fury. "I'm going to leave you some things. Otherwise you'll all be dead in no time."

I moved over to the side, to an open space on the floor.

"Myalis? What do we need to keep these idiots safe?"

Ideally, to relocate them. The factory isn't a defensible location. Too many windows that are accessible to the average Antithesis model, and the area isn't well hidden. But if they cannot or will not leave, then automated turrets, some basic guns, and a few thrown explosives could give the locals a fighting chance.

I nodded. I didn't have much time for shopping, though. "Get me five of those turrets, the laser ones with the solar panels. No, make it eight." They'd be able to place them around the factory and create a kill zone. "And . . . hummingbirds. Those little flechette guns that auto-target aliens. I don't trust these guys with proper guns. Get me some resonators too. I don't know . . . a dozen? No, make it two. If they're smart they can create choke points and fuck the aliens up when they slip into them."

Understood. For one additional point, I can provide a technical manual. A simple one.

"That's not a terrible idea," I said.

I have been known to have nonterrible ideas on occasion.

Myalis got me everything I asked for in a set of big plastic boxes. They appeared with satisfying thunks onto the floor. "Charles!" I called out while opening one of them. I found the manual. Its first dozen pages had simple instructions, tailored for the factory, even, with blueprints and firing lines. "Hey, take this. I'm leaving that cat drone here too; it can take one or two of them out. Just . . . hold tight, okay? I'll check in on you tomorrow, promise."

Charles took the manual, then looked at the pile of gear. "This is too much," he said.

"That's not a tenth of the points I'd spend taking out a hive," I said. That might have been a lie. I'd stopped paying attention to my points a while ago. "It's worth it to keep most of you alive. Start a guard rotation, set up choke points, and take the aliens seriously, for the love of God."

"Right," he said.

I patted him on the shoulder, then ran off. I didn't have time for drawn-out goodbyes. Whether they lived or died would be very much up to them now.

Gomorrah was waiting for me in her car. It was idling a foot off the ground, growling and eager to move. I jumped in, then let out a long breath.

"You all right?" she asked.

"Stressed, I think," I admitted. "What does stress feel like, anyway?"

"I think it varies from person to person," she said. "I just feel nervous, I suppose. Franny complains about a pain in her chest, though she's not stressed often."

I hummed, then put it out of my mind for now. If it got bad, I could get something for it.

"What are you buying?" Gomorrah asked.

"What?"

"Gear," she said. "You've been out all day. You must have a few points to spend. If we're going to be facing off against a large horde, then now's the time to start looking into whatever gear you need."

"Oh, yeah," I said. That made sense. "I don't know what I need, though. My current setup is working just fine, you know?"

"Then get better prosthetics, better augs, and better armor," Gomorrah said. "They'll pay themselves off quickly enough."

I shrugged. It wasn't a terrible idea. "What are you getting?"

"A jetpack."

I blinked. "You're getting a jetpack?" I asked.

"Yes. They let you fly."

"I know what a jetpack does. That's . . . okay, that's kind of awesome, honestly." I imagined myself with a jetpack. I then imagined myself with a jetpack giving Lucy a princess carry. Yeah, I was getting one of those. Maybe not right now, though. I didn't see how it would be helpful with the current wave.

Gomorrah really put the pedal down, accelerating us until the pressure was uncomfortable, even with the comfortable seats the Fury had.

We'd be on top of the city in a few minutes.

Already I could see smoke on the horizon, pooling under the overcast sky. A lot of stuff was burning. Out of curiosity, I checked the Family's map, then just stared at it for a while. When had it turned so red?

There were huge blurs of red across the countryside, and anything that wasn't red was yellow fading into orange.

We had a few hours until the sun set. When it rose, would everything be crimson?

I sent a text to Lucy, just to be able to interact with her a little. She replied immediately, and so for a moment I ignored the world and all the shit about to go down and focused on trying to make my girl laugh by being an idiot. It was better than thinking.

CHAPTER FORTY-ONE

RAPID RETURN

We're not so different from the Antithesis, in some ways.
   Back either of us into a corner, and that's where you'll see us fighting the hardest.

—Nomad, 2056

Gomorrah flew the Fury over the gap.

I didn't know what else to call the long stretch of space where the wall just stopped. Cranes were set up on either edge, and there were huge cement slabs ready to be pulled up onto the foundation that was even now being poured, but there was no missing the fact that a three-kilometer stretch of the city was entirely unprotected.

It wasn't an empty spot either. Suburbs were set up on what was going to be the outside of the wall. A satellite city sat on the southernmost part of the gap. It looked like the wall was going to bulge out a little to accommodate it.

"Atyacus, did Laserjack give us a spot where we'd be needed?" Gomorrah asked.

"The Family has suggested some locations that require reinforcements," a smooth, posh-sounding voice said. "The entire stretch of space without a wall needs to be defended. Anywhere along or around that area could use Vanguard-tier reinforcements."

I glanced out the window and noticed that several armored vehicles were forming a barricade just outside the area where the wall would be. More vehicles were moving into the space behind the wall: mobile bases, semi-trailers with mobile offices on their backs, and a whole heap of supply vehicles.

"Looks like every other PMC in the city is coming over," I said.

"This location is the most likely to lead to the Antithesis breaching the city," Atyacus said.

I nodded. "Makes sense. Get everyone over the spot that's weakest. The plants will definitely be pushing that spot hardest. Least resistance, and all that."

"Indeed," the AI said.

"I'm going to station myself a bit out in the open," Gomorrah said.

"Isn't your range pretty short?" I asked.

"Yes, but I expect that there will be enough of them that it won't matter," Gomorrah said. "Besides, I do best when I have a lot of space with no one friendly inside it."

I considered that for a moment—not so much Gomorrah's fighting style as my own. How did I fit into all of this?

"Can you drop me out at the far end of that city?" I asked, pointing to the suburban sprawl: lots of apartment buildings and a few dozen condo-enclaves. "My gimmick's not going to be useful in the open, not if there's going to be thousands of the fuckers. I'm going to head in toward the walls, leave a few hundred traps behind."

"We don't have a lot of time for traps," Gomorrah said.

I shrugged. "I can run pretty fast. Maybe I'll get a jetpack of my own?"

Gomorrah chuckled. "Go ahead. I won't need to taxi you around quite as much."

I grinned as we swung around. A glance at the map wiped that smile away, at least a little. The wave was way too close for comfort. I could see plumes of dust in the distance, getting closer.

"Go," Gomorrah said. "And remember to stay alive."

I nodded, then reached out a fist to her. She bumped it.

My boots hit the ground with the softest of thumps, and the Fury whined as it rose out above and shot out across the city. Gomorrah had left me on a once-busy street. Ten-story buildings on either side, their first floors nothing but colorful shop fronts with screaming-bright advertisements.

"Not much time," I muttered. "Myalis, you ready to buy some shit?"

Catherine, you should know that I am always prepared. What are you thinking of?

"I need . . . fuck it, I need a better suit. More mobility, better guns. Stealth too. And I want to be able to fly."

Do you mind sacrificing your back-mounted guns for flight?

I winced.

Understood. Your current armor is modular. I wouldn't be surprised that you forgot that. Let me suggest a cheaper alternative to a whole new set. Boots with deployable jump-jets; a jetpack that will fit in the center of your back and over your lower back. You will have to remove your coat unless you wish to find a different solution?

"No, no that sounds good," I said. I was already shucking the coat. It was cool, and I'd be sad to see it go, but . . . yeah. Needs must and all that.

New Purchase: The Leaping Lion's Paw

Points Reduced from . . . 20,764 to . . . 20,514

New boots appeared before me at the same time that mine hissed and basically fell off, the armor panels clunking aside until my feet were covered in nothing but a skeletal frame and some sort of padding.

The new boots were in a box, with little clamps holding all the parts separate. I put my foot in, and as soon as it was on the sole, all the parts pressed in and fit together like a demented engineer's idea of a jigsaw puzzle.

I did the same for my other foot, then noticed the third item in the box: a sort of rounded scoop thing that trailed down to a point with nozzles on the bottom. It was obviously designed to affix to my back.

I grabbed it and felt things shift behind me.

Press the wider part to the small of your back.

As I did just that, the arms for my railguns deployed and helped the upper section of the jetpack together.

I shifted my shoulders, feeling a slight difference in weight. The boots were definitely a bit lighter, despite being bulkier.

Ideally, the entire suit would be lightened to make flight more efficient, but such is the sacrifice of a modular system.

"Right," I said as I shouldered my Bullcat. "I need . . . shit, what else do I need . . . I wish I could send all of this back home.

A small mechanized cat drone could carry your coat and older boots back to your house.

That wasn't a terrible idea. "Okay, yeah, do that."

New Purchase: Stylized Servitor—CAT Mech

Points Reduced from . . . 20,514 to . . . 20,364

A box appeared, and then immediately opened up as a cat mech jumped out of it. It was smaller than the mecha I had for fighting, with a whole set of thin mechanical arms sticking out of its back. It used those to quickly pick up my boots, then folded my coat with its forepaws and grabbed it in its jaws. The cat looked up at me with glowing cat eyes before slinking away.

"Right, what else," I muttered.

Catherine, the wave is incoming. You have under one minute before the forwardmost section is upon you.

I swore, then looked up at the nearest building. "How much fuel does the pack have?"

Each container should last you long enough for half a minute of flight. They can be replaced automatically, same as the ammunition in your current gun. The tanks cost ten points each.

That would probably add up.

"Okay . . . uh, how do I fly?"

I think it would be safest if I flew for now. Keep your legs together, please.

I tensed up a half second before I took off into the air. The worst part was the lack of sound. Except for my screaming, of course, but that didn't escape my helmet. At least, I hoped it didn't.

Myalis landed me on the edge of a flat rooftop, and I paused there for a moment while my heart considered whether it would leap out of my chest. "Okay," I said. That was all I could think to say.

A rumble to my right had me looking that way.

The dust cloud was getting closer, much closer. My augs drew a square at the base of the cloud, and a small screen opened up with a zoomed-in view of that square.

Model threes. Packed in so tight they were bouncing off each other's shoulders. More behind them, and through the faint dust, I could make out bigger models. There had to be thousands. How were they kicking up dust when it had to have rained in the last day or so?

"Fuck me," I muttered.

Any path in particular you wish to take?

That many would be hard to kill. Impossible, even. Not by me alone, at least.

Unless . . .

"Okay," I said. "I'm going to need a few mecha-cats, and . . . some sort of bomb that will create a barrier. I want walls to cut off their path. Funnel them in a little. Maybe those expanding foam things? With resonators? We'll push the entire swarm into a few corridors, and then we'll fuck them up from above."

All I had at my disposal was an infinite armory of exotic explosives and the high ground.

It would have to do.

CHAPTER FORTY-TWO

EARNING THE TIER

At lower tiers, the effectiveness of a single samurai on the field is actually questionable.

That might lead some to wonder: If a samurai is little better than a small battalion of trained troops, then why not replace them with just that?

The answer is that while a low-tier samurai might only be that powerful, they won't be low-tier forever.

—A discussion on the value of samurai on large-scale battlefronts, 2028

I was just planning my route, a map open in the corner of my vision, when some clever asshole decided that a large mass of bunched-together aliens would make for a great target for some artillery.

Something screamed above, and I raised my head and tracked a tiny black speck through the air. Its parabolic arc ended with it smashing into the ground a good fifty meters ahead of the wave.

A loud boom echoed out while dust and smoke rose out of the impact crater as a massive column. "Nice," I muttered. "Myalis, can you get in touch with whoever fired that? Tell them they missed."

On it.

The wave was undaunted by the blast. I think most human armies would start running faster to get to cover or something, but the sea of bugs charging toward the city didn't change their breakneck pace at all.

I looked at my map again. There were lots of streets to cover. "Okay. We're going to push them down . . . Mapleway. I need . . . these six bigger roads blocked off, and all the alleys along them before the blockage."

The city was laid out as a grid, with some concessions made for the underlying terrain. This wasn't New Montreal, built on a massive platform raised above the ground, but a more normal cityscape like they used to build before.

I couldn't funnel the entire wave. There were too many of them. But maybe I could funnel in a fraction, a good chunk of those heading in toward the city. It would concentrate them, sure, and that would be fucking awful if they ever reached the defenders covering the gap, but I didn't intend to let that happen.

Funnel them into a big group, then bomb them back to whatever hell they'd crawled out of.

"I need mecha," I said. "Six . . . no, eight. See these roads. I want them blocked off. Foam, maybe pepper in some resonators for if they try to climb over."

I quickly drew some lines across the map. In the end, my design looked a bit like a square-stepped pyramid, with the tip pointing toward New Montreal itself. Every blocked road would be next to an alleyway or a side street that would let the wave move closer inward. If we blocked off enough alleys and the previous side roads, then they'd have no choice but to be pulled in. At least, if they didn't stop to sniff around.

Fuck, I was treating the entire wave as if it were made of water or something, not living things.

"What are the chances this works?" I asked Myalis.

Relatively high, actually. Otherwise I would have cautioned you against it. Though it will act more to crowd the wave in than to kill the members of the wave.

Right, that made sense. "Other plans?"

Use the height afforded you by the rooftops to drop proximity charges and other explosives onto the largest mass of aliens. A little dull, but no less effective. In fact, you might want to consider doing that all the same. The numbers in the current wave would overwhelm more barricades, and some will instead find themselves breaking into the buildings around them.

I glanced down at the street. Most of the bigger buildings had shops on their first floor, and most shops had a lot of glass in front of them. Big display windows and shit. I didn't doubt that a few were designed to be bulletproof, but that wouldn't stop the aliens for long.

"All right, let's get to it. Mecha with 'nades. Whatever you think is best for creating a barrier. Maybe a few guns on them to keep them safe. And can you ping me the location of any particularly big motherfuckers? We don't want anything in the twenties to reach the gap."

Understood.

Eight mecha-cats appeared on the rooftop. They were a bit slimmer than those I had guarding the house: longer legs, with a few little limbs tucked into their sides, and what looked like a laser array similar to my turrets on their backs.

"Nice," I said. "Payloads?"

As you suggested. Expanding foam bombs, resonators. You will likely want something with more direct stopping power to remove bigger threats and thin out the bigger knots of opposition. If your intent is to crush the enemy, then perhaps a literal application of that? Gravity grenades, with a limited range to avoid collateral damage, can destroy most things they hit.

I shrugged. "All right."

I'd see if they were as impressive as Myalis claimed.

Budget?

"Doesn't matter, as long as we come out on top pointwise, and I don't think that'll be a problem."

Another shell screamed across the sky above. This one exploded right above the forward edge of the wave. Then another exploded, then another. There was a constant booming from the city, like heavy rain on tin as a whole army's worth of artillery opened up. Looked like they wanted to thin the herd before it reached the more urban parts.

Boxes appeared next to the mecha-cats, and the robotic cats opened them up to reveal a selection of grenades in neat rows, held in place by plastic molding. The mecha-cats picked up the grenades in a long strip, then clamped them onto their sides with the little arms sticking out of their backs. Everything folded neatly back in, and I was left with a pride of Rambo-looking mechanized cats.

"All right," I said. "Let's go."

The cats darted off in two directions, to the left and right of the oncoming wave.

I wasn't going to sit back and let them do all the work, though.

While artillery rained down on the aliens I ran toward New Montreal. I stopped by the first alley I had to clog up. "Sticky," I said.

Myalis obliged, and I caught a grenade out of the air as it appeared next to me. The pin flew off to one side, and the bomb dropped down into the unlit alley. It clanged against the ground before bursting. In the space of a couple of seconds, off-white foam was pouring out of the passage, and more of it was expanding upward to create a wall that I hoped would slow the aliens down.

But in case it wasn't enough . . . "Resonator."

That one dropped down into the foam with a dull splat. It managed to stay afloat as the foam expanded, a tiny screaming present for the first fucks to try to claw their way over the wall.

I jumped over the alley, legs bunching up so that I'd clear the gap. Kinda forgot I had a jetpack for a moment. "Next one," I said.

The artillery fire started to grow less coordinated and precise. I could tell that some shots were flying much farther out, and I winced as a shell crashed into a building that immediately exploded, fire and cement siding flying everywhere.

At least some of the shrapnel would probably brain a few of the xenos.

A glance over my shoulder revealed that the wave was hitting the city proper. They slipped around abandoned cars and over guardrails. It was hard to tell the individual models apart, they were jammed so close together.

Then I noticed something in the dust behind them. Wings, beating fast.

A swarm of flying models swooped out of the dust. Little models, no bigger than pigeons, but also huge fuckers with wingspans like private jets.

"Ah, fuck," I muttered as I whipped my gun around. I didn't fire. There was still a ways between them and me, and the chances that I'd do more than take out a few of the smaller ones with some stray pellets weren't great.

The wave hadn't even hit my barriers and already my plan had gone to shit.

"We need AA," I said.

Something screamed through the air. Not a shell, something bigger and faster, accompanied by a loud buzz. A glance above and I found a squadron of prop-planes shooting forward. The guns fixed under their wings opened fire with a mechanical hum, and lines of bright-green tracers flitted through the air and into the swarm.

Maybe I didn't need AA just yet.

Large hovering vehicles were rising above the gap, with guns affixed to their sides. They started firing, and the air exploded with black-gray bursts of shrapnel ahead of the flying aliens.

I turned and continued running across the rooftops.

This wasn't a one-person effort, I realized. There was an entire army here.

For a moment, I wondered what I could do alone. But then, maybe my job was just going to be picking up the slack.

I flung another pair of grenades down a maintenance passage between two buildings, then kept moving.

Soon the swarm would be on me, and then I'd have other shit to worry about than how useful I could be.

CHAPTER FORTY-THREE

DANGER-CLOSE

All locations in proximity to a samurai in action are to be considered danger-close.

—US Armed Forces NCO Basics manual, 2027

When I thought the swarm would be on me "soon," I meant in a few minutes.

I severely underestimated the speed that a few thousand aliens could pick up when they were hungry for human. The tip of the swarm poured down the streets below me. Teeth glistened, eyes narrowed, and they started their mad search for threats. No growling or mad howls, though. The creeps were as silent as ever.

So I decided to make up for their silence all on my own.

"Thanks," I muttered as I caught a grenade out of the air. I tugged the pin off, then underhanded it down the street.

Dropping to one knee, I watched the explosive disappear in the swarm.

Then it detonated.

A loud *whomp* filled the air while a circle a couple of meters wide appeared in the swarm. Every alien in the circle was flattened to the ground, as if they'd just been stuffed into the world's biggest hydraulic press.

Body parts flipped along the edges of the effect, entirely detached from the rest of their bodies.

"Not bad," I muttered.

The hole filled itself up a half second later. There were just too many of the bastards for it to make a difference.

"Not bad, but not enough," I said. I glanced around the city. Lots of apartments, plenty of shop fronts. All fucked now. "Yeah, we're giving up on the no-collateral thing. We can rebuild, but only if every last one of these fucks is dead. Myalis, I need something that'll wipe the street."

There are hundreds of options.

"Not fire," I said. "Don't want to step on Gomorrah's toes. How about . . . hey, do you think we could melt them all?"

An acid? There are grenades that can spread acids around them. There are even some that will hover over the ground and mist the air with highly corrosive chemicals, some of which are tailored to melting Antithesis flesh.

That wasn't what I had in mind, but it sounded really cool. "Yeah, I like that idea. Gimme something to drop; I want to see how it works."

Myalis summoned a box next to me. It had a container with a sloshing liquid within, and three little propellers on stalks around it. It looked a bit like a cheap toy drone.

Toss it ahead of you after pressing the activation button. It will move to hover over the street. It has cameras with which to find the best location.

I pressed start, then tossed it out ahead of me. The drone flipped twice, then fired up with a high-pitched hum. It bobbed in the air for a second before a nozzle opened beneath it and it started to spray a mist of glowing green liquid.

"Is the acid glowing?" I asked.

Yes. Humans are more cautious around dangerous chemicals when they glow.

The mist hit the monsters below, and I could see fur falling off in great tufts and skin blackening and peeling off. A few of them got some in their eyes and they went rabid, shaking their heads.

That worked.

I stood up, checked the sky for trouble, then started running again. Every time I jumped to another rooftop I'd drop another grenade down to block the alleyway, at least those I'd marked out on my map. Myalis provided me with a constant supply of acid drones. They hovered over the street, and soon the entire road glowed a faint green as the mist was carried over everything.

The shit was eating through the paint on abandoned cars and peeling ads off bus stops, but it was doing a number on the model threes too.

The bigger models, not so much. Model fours were hit hard. They had a lot of tentacles and all that, but I think something about their skin might have made them more resistant, though not by much. The model fives were just tanking the damage. They were big and thick enough that even my latest war crime of a grenade wasn't killing them quickly or efficiently. Maybe it would weaken them, injure a few even, but unless they chose to stand under the acid shower, they'd still be a threat.

"Need some gravity 'nades," I muttered as I leapt onto another rooftop. Myalis obliged, and I underhanded a couple of them over the crowd of aliens.

Increasing the gravity in an area or whatever messed up the bigger, tougher bastards.

The mecha-cats on the other side have completed your project. The swarm has started to funnel into one road, though the Antithesis have found some ways through via the interior of various buildings.

"Got it," I said.

I ran faster, pushing myself so that I'd be out ahead of the swarm.

If they were being pushed onto one road, then that meant that the ideal place to kill them would be . . . I scraped to a stop and glanced down. The last open alleyway to join the swarm was one building away from a large intersection. That was where my funnel ended. A glance behind showed that it was working. Aliens were pouring out of the side roads and pressing into each other on a straight path to this one passage.

A few dozen had sprinted by already. A concern for someone else. I'd be doing a lot more good by killing the tide here.

"Let's turn this place into a killing field," I said.

Myalis provided me with a pile of those acid bombs, and I tossed them out so that they'd cover the entire road. A thump or two behind me announced the arrival of my mecha-cats, their missions accomplished.

The cats on either side of the road shifted to the edge of the roof, the guns on their backs deployed, and then they started to fire their lasers down into the crowded aliens. It would take a couple of seconds to kill one, but with eight lasers spearing out into the street . . .

"Myalis, need a way to kill them all," I said as I watched a chunk of the swarm sprint by. They were injured, painted green by acid, but still alive enough to be trouble. The main mass of the swarm would slip right on by. "Give me some resonators."

Certainly. Though while you toss those down, I should warn you that at the speed the swarm is moving, neither the resonators nor the acid will be sufficient to kill even the smaller models.

"Right," I muttered.

What else could I do?

"Ideas?" I asked.

You essentially need weapons that can kill the Antithesis in a sustained way. Turrets placed above, combined with area-denial explosives such as your garrote grenades. Though both would eventually be overrun.

"Yeah, maybe, but it'll blunt the edge of the swarm, and I think that's what we need right now. Push the worst of it back so that they can get on with building the wall. 'Nades first."

Myalis dropped a box full of grenades next to me, and I kicked it open, picked up a few, then flicked them down and onto the road. My aim wasn't perfect, but I didn't exactly need accuracy for the oncoming horde. When the garrote grenades went off, it created pockets where everything was shredded.

The swarm pushed into them as if trying to blunt the edge of the grenades with sheer force of meat.

The grenades won out, though one of them did spark and break apart as a model five charged through it. The tougher hide was able to blunt and eventually break the explosive, though not without killing the model five first.

"Give the cats a few of these," I said. "They can toss them in, keep the area deadly.

Fewer aliens were making it past, and those that did often flopped over dead a few dozen meters past the intersection. Too many cuts and acid and melting internals.

Still, the wave came, and I knew there would be more big fuckers to come.

I set down a few turrets: one near the middle of the roof, just to ward off any fliers, and another near the roof-access doorway, for when some halfway clever alien inevitably snuck onto the roof.

In the meantime, I kicked the door open and ran down myself. Just offices and break rooms and a sea of cubicles. I ran to the nearest window and started setting up more automated turrets, the cheap laser ones that could recharge themselves over time with a bit of sunlight. Cheap, weak, but dependable.

I left proximity charges next to each, for the first lucky alien that came around and tried to grab a bite out of them.

I glanced down onto the street and grinned.

The pile of melting bodies was already hip-high in places, and it was only growing bigger as the wave pushed against itself, like meat through a strainer.

"This is going pretty well," I said.

Which was about when the artillery started to hit my position.

CHAPTER FORTY-FOUR

DIRTY BREAK

Mental health services are, like healthcare, one of those things that just aren't profitable for a society whose main concern is monetary.

In fact, it's worse than healthcare. With that, you can at least extort people for money. Someone with a gaping wound will be willing to pay much for treatment and to live. Someone hearing voices, though? Someone going through a depressive period? Well, they're just not great clients.

I think that's why all of the help and assistance we had just . . . disappeared one day.

—Jacob Washington, last member of the all-volunteer Suicide Watch group, 2023

I'd seen buildings collapse before. I mean, on my media feeds.

Happened all the time. Usually it was buildings that needed to be demolished, but every couple of weeks some mega-complex would fall apart all on its own. Shitty construction, too many cut corners, maybe the place was only designed to last thirty years and that was before you counted the years shaved off by subpar materials.

So yeah, I'd seen plenty of buildings fall apart.

Never seen it happen from the inside in first person, though.

"Fuck fuck fuck," I swore as the floor started to tilt.

Office shit went flying, desks crashed down, and chairs with those little wheels at the bottom went sailing across the room.

I half turned and planted a foot onto an exterior wall. The building was tipping toward the street below. The chairs and desks crashing around me eventually lost their momentum or hooked onto something, so the din in the room stilled.

The cacophony outside, though, didn't. A glance out the window showed blackened marks and craters punched into the road where a liberal application of heavy ordnance had rained down.

The aliens had been pushed back a bit, but then so had some of my defenses. Most of the garrote grenades were destroyed, and I didn't see any of my acid sprayers left.

The aliens regrouped and resumed their charge, this time meeting a lot less resistance.

"Dammit! Myalis, can you tell whoever aimed that last volley that I'm going to kick their ass? We need to reset the defenses."

Message sent.

"Right, thanks," I said. I paused as the building creaked. A building this big *tilting* wasn't good, but maybe whoever had built the place knew what they were doing because it seemed to be holding.

Catherine! Incoming volley!

"Are you seri—"

Explosions rained down across the street; shells rammed into some of the buildings across from us, shrapnel and glass raining down in a cascade atop the aliens below. Then I heard something punch through the ceiling.

I spun and saw a hole the size of my head in the middle of the office.

Whatever had punched that hole went off and a gout of dust poured out into the office. I was blind, dust and smoke robbing me of sight.

The floor fell out from under me, and I swore as I tumbled. Everything was moving in different directions, and for a panicked moment, all I could do was be rag-dolled around. Even with my armor, the breath was blown out of me as I was thrown about.

Metal screamed and glass shattered. I think the building just decided to give up and crashed down onto the street.

I hit something hard and it shifted beneath me. Then all my fighting and rolling around was stopped. A pressure grabbed on to my mechanical arm and didn't let go.

Everything ended in a single, final boom that rattled my head.

I blinked as the dust cleared a little.

I was on my back, with a cement barrier about a handspan away from my face. I wiggled my toes, then shifted on the spot. Still had all of my meat limbs. There was no burning. I was fine. Peachy, even. Never better.

Armor integrity is at seventy-four percent. I'm afraid you'll need a new suit. The back component of your jump-jet is damaged as well.

"Okay," I said. "Okay. Uh . . . where the fuck am I?"

Pinned under the building you were on. The topmost floor hit the building across the street, then collapsed on top of your position. Here.

A screen opened up in my augs and I got to see . . . a lot of wreckage through a thick film of dust. Some shit was on fire too. "What am I seeing this from?"

One of your mecha-cats survived.

"Tough little shits," I murmured. She was distracting me, wasn't she? "Uh . . . Myalis, I think I'm stuck."

You do have a building on top of you at the moment, yes.

I swallowed. "Okay. Yeah. That would do it." My breathing came in a little faster, chest heaving. I didn't know why, but I almost felt like laughing. "I can't get out."

Catherine, you have a multitude of methods to remove yourself from this location. I can guide you through them. You are safe.

"Right. My arm?"

Your cybernetic arm is pinned. Please do not activate the rocket within it. That would be irresponsible.

This time I did laugh. "Yeah, yeah, okay." I tugged at my arm, but it didn't do much. The space I was in was . . . not very big. I'd used public toilets with more room. A pocket that was maybe a meter wide, half that tall. I'd lost my Bullcat somewhere along the way. Still had my sword buckled to my hip, though. Too bad, I liked that gun.

I tugged on the arm again, but it didn't move at all.

"I need to get this unstuck," I said.

I can release the arm. You'll be able to purchase another. It was beginning to be outdated compared to your other equipment anyway.

"Huh? Oh, yeah, okay."

There is one issue. The armor is nonfunctional in that section. It is likely that some of its internals were damaged. I cannot disengage it.

"Okay, okay," I said.

Well, when all you had was a sword that could cut through anything, everything started to look like a nail. Or something like that. I tugged the sword out of its sheath, then brought it up and around, blade part hovering over my biceps.

I paused.

What the fuck was I doing?

There are more delicate tools for that sort of operation, if you wish. Or I could contact other Vanguards for assistance.

I swallowed. "No, it's fine." Myalis had to know that I'd put my own pride before any nervousness about self-mutilation. I took a deep breath. "Fuck you," I said.

The sword activated with a snapping hiss and I closed my eyes as I sliced down.

I didn't realize it, but the place where I was resting was uneven. I shut the sword off quickly as I slid down deeper into my little nook, suddenly free from the arm holding me in place.

"Oh shit," I said. I looked at the stump by my side. I'd lived most of my life with only a stump there; it would probably be a lot more dramatic for someone losing their arm for the first time. But hey, practice made perfect and all that.

I shifted, then sat up. There was barely enough room for that.

"Myalis, I want to get out of this hole."

Are you certain? It's actually relatively safe.

"Are you kidding me?"

If you're going to purchase new limbs and new armor, then it makes sense to do so from a place of relative safety.

"Just get me out of this hole!"

I closed my eyes and leaned back, head clunking against the cement behind me.

"Sorry," I muttered.

No apology is necessary.

The ground shook a little, and I almost screamed, but the building held.

Just artillery hitting nearby. Now, as for options to remove yourself from this location, might I suggest a short-range wormhole bomb? There are several other options, but this seems like the cheapest and most expedient. It is also relatively safe.

"I don't know, the words 'wormhole' and 'bomb' put together don't sound . . . safe. At all."

I can guarantee its safety, if that helps.

"And if you're wrong?" I asked.

Then you'll be too dead to make a complaint.

I felt like that deserved a laugh, but what escaped wasn't quite that. I sniffed. "Okay, okay, let's do that."

New Purchase: M.I.C.E. Bomb

Points Reduced from . . . 36,042 to . . . 35,742

"M.I.C.E. bomb, really? What's that one mean?" I asked as a box landed on my chest.

Micro-scale Intralocation Cat Extractor.

I paused. "You really dove deep for that one," I said. The box had a cylinder in it with a switch. That was it. Not even a pin to pull, or options to toggle. I shrugged, suppressed the weird feeling from my right side at the motion, then flicked the switch.

I was in midair.

That didn't last long.

I crashed down, fortunately only a couple of centimeters, and winced as cement and rebar rained down around me. I was back on the street, or above it and the building I had been on. Did that teleport me a few meters straight up?

"Okay," I said. It was immensely easier to breathe without the metaphorical weight of a building atop me.

Unfortunately, being up here meant that I didn't have a building between me and the beasties.

"Ah, fuck," I muttered.

CHAPTER FORTY-FIVE

GEAR ON

Deus Ex: And then they said that I couldn't just talk the talk.

Hyper Cutie Zoom Ranger Sparkle Girl Bubble-chan: Makes sense, yeah.

Deus Ex: They said I had to walk the talk too. How . . . how do you walk a talk? What's that even mean?!

Hyper Cutie Zoom Ranger Sparkle Girl Bubble-chan: . . . Oh, Deus, sweetie, no.

—r/GapMoeSamukawaii, top post of 2053

Myalis had landed me above the wreck of the building that had toppled over. Which meant that I had appeared atop what was essentially a huge barrier blocking off an entire street. The horde couldn't pass here, not unless they were willing to climb the wreckage.

I groped for a gun, then slid my arm into my thigh holster and pulled out my Claw. I took a calming breath, then carefully planted a round in the middle of the chest of a model five that was busy scrambling over the ruined building.

The wave had likely split off to run around the wreckage, but I had been busy before redirecting them this way. Now there were a lot of the fuckers waiting below to attempt their own climb over the wreckage.

I spun, then started to climb up the wreckage as well.

The aliens didn't fail to notice me, of course. I was crawling right past a bunch of them, and more had already made it to the other side and were resuming their charge toward New Montreal.

I flicked up my back-mounted rails, but only one of them responded. It was enough for the moment; the railgun fired, poking a hole through the nearest model three.

"Myalis, need to get out of here," I said.

We could replace the back section of your jetpack. You could fly out of danger.

I glanced back down. The wave was shifting, more aliens heading my way as if they intended to gobble me up on the way over. "Sounds good," I said.

Something clunked on my back and the broken jetpack module fell. A box appeared on a flattish piece of concrete nearby, and I tore it open while my railgun worked hard to keep the area around me clear.

I slapped the jetpack on, then picked my Claw up again to fire a few rounds into the biggest aliens trying to catch up.

The jets on my legs spurted, and the one on my back whined. "Ready?"

Indeed. Where to?

I glanced up. "Got to be a spot around here that's safe-ish," I said.

Checking . . . some security systems are still online. Here.

The jets fired, nearly silent, and I was flung up and into the air. From above I could see the rubble of the fallen building and some wreckage from other buildings too. The shelling hadn't been kind, and having one building ram into another created a huge fucking mess.

The jets flew me sideways and then across the blockage created by the rubble.

This location is somewhat safe for the moment. Firing your railgun.

The gun over my shoulder swiveled around and fired three times in quick succession into the side of what looked like an office. A window burst apart from the impact, and then I folded my legs up and ducked my head as Myalis tossed me through the hole that had left.

I had to jog a bit to keep from falling over. A glance around revealed . . . a spa? Fancy place, lots of wooden paneling. Big windows overlooking the city and little semi-open rooms to the sides with massage tables.

This is a luxury relaxation location for what seems to be a criminal syndicate. The location is currently abandoned.

"Okay," I said. I could deal with that weirdness later. "ETA for the next alien hungry for me?"

I would estimate at least three hours. Likely more. The Antithesis seem to be focused on reaching New Montreal first. They will push forward before they start to scour the entire area for food and threats. Though the opening in the wall might let some flying models slip in.

I nodded. "Turrets, please."

Myalis gladly complied, and I casually tossed a couple of turrets down facing the window.

"Right, I need new armor, and an arm. Let's buy everything, and then I'll start changing, in case some fuckwit shells this place too."

The mortar companies have been warned not to hit the immediate location.

"Fat load of good that did me last time," I muttered. I looked around, then noticed a sign that read "Sauna" hanging from the ceiling. I followed that into a large room with a domed ceiling and a ring of wooden seats. There was a big fire pit in the center, with jugs filled with water next to it that had ladles hanging from the side.

Big fancy sauna. Perfect for what I needed.

"Arm first," I said.

Certainly. Can you assist in removing the armor over your shoulder?

The armor shifted, plates moving up and away, but some of them looked jammed in place. I shoved my hand under those and tugged. Something snapped, and the plates over my shoulder and back fell apart.

That left my shoulder exposed. I still had a meat shoulder, but it was covered by the mechanism for my prosthetic. That hissed, and I felt something like . . . like someone licking my brain. Then the prosthetic just fell off.

"Oh, hey," I said. I wiggled my stump around. It was a bit pale, with some indentations where the prosthetic pushed into the skin. It actually felt good to free it, like taking off too-tight boots after a long day of walking. "Been a while since I've seen you."

What are you looking for in a new arm?

I was going to be dismissive and brush the question off, just get something temporary. But I knew myself. My temporary was the next person's permanent.

"Uh . . . I want something with better tactile than my last one. Tougher would be nice. I didn't use the internal rocket much either, so maybe we skip that this time."

We could get an arm with a built-in grenade launcher. Something that would let you place explosives exactly where you want them. Or an arm with an aiming assistance module.

"No. I'm going to learn how to aim all on my own. I'm not useless. I'm figuring it out. My aim is improving." I took a deep breath. "Can we do a grenade launcher that you can reload via teleportation?"

That is easily done, yes.

"Cool," I said. "Also, I've been thinking about this for a while, in terms of arm upgrades."

Yes?

"Can we have a vibrating function?" I asked.

. . . Yes. I imagine this is for Lucy?

"And for myself," I added.

Duly noted. What's your budget here? That will help determine the quality of the arm. I don't believe I can get anything that will fit all of your requirements for below one hundred and forty points.

"Call it a thousand points? It's going to be semipermanent, I think. At least until the next time a building falls on me."

In that case . . . From your Sun Watcher Technologies tree, I'd suggest the Lynx Nine. It's a modular design, which means it can come configured with the additions you want. A grenade launcher with an internal magazine, tactile receptors, and a vibration system with seventeen vibration modes. It's significantly more durable than your previous arm, though it is a little heavier. No more so than your own flesh-and-blood limb.

"Sounds perfect," I said. I glanced out of the room as I heard a distant boom. More artillery? "We should speed this up."

New Purchase: Lynx Nine Modular Arm

Points Reduced from . . . 36,559 to . . . 35,559

A box appeared on one of the wooden benches next to me. I didn't open it just yet. "Armor next?"

Certainly. Did you like your previous suit?

"Yeah, it was great, still kind of is," I said. I tightened my fist, then let it open. "Something similar?

A slightly upgraded model, perhaps? You won't be doing as many stealth-based activities in this active war zone, I don't believe. We can get you something a little heavier. More armor, with more hardpoints. Built-in jump-jets and more power. Next time artillery strikes your position, you won't notice it as much.

I laughed. "Sounds good. I do like my stealth, though."

We can switch out the servos for higher-end, quieter models, the boots can have silent-running treads, and the jump-jets can be designed to be whisper-quiet. The armor panels can also have adaptive camouflage, though it won't be as good as a suit entirely designed for stealth.

"Get it," I said. "Price isn't much of an issue.

New Purchase: The Tiger's Mane, Mark XXI

Points Reduced from . . . 35,559 to . . . 34,159

The armor that appeared before me wasn't too different from what I had on. It was bigger, though, a least half a head taller than what I had on, and a lot bulkier.

I also purchased some back-mounted guns, as you like them.

"Nice," I said.

I pulled the release on my own armor and stepped out of it. It was time to gear up.

Then, back to killing xenos.

CHAPTER FORTY-SIX

NEW PLAN: KILL EVERYTHING

Are you worried about the incoming horde of hungry man-eating aliens invading your city?

Coming to the realization that while money is great, it doesn't mean much when there's an alien munching on your face?

Then invest in Protecto-Tech today! The world's leading provider of VIP vaults and high-end protective services! Live a life of temporary luxury in one of our hyper-fortified bases!

No human experimentation, guaranteed!

—Protecto-Tech, prototype ad, 2050

The moment I was completely out of my old armor, the entire thing closed itself back up and stepped to the side.

It actually freaked me out a little. But the armor just walked itself to the room's entrance and stood there, one back-mounted gun pointing out into the hallway beyond.

"All right," I muttered.

Just a safety precaution. What do you want to do with your old armor?

"I don't know," I admitted. "Think Lucy would like it?"

It would need to be modified slightly to fit her proportions. She's a few centimeters shorter and wider at the hips. It would be uncomfortable. She also lacks the augmentations or AI support to fully utilize the armor.

"Eh, fair enough. Can it stick around in here and defend itself? We'll see about picking it up once things have calmed down a bit."

Noted.

I walked over to the box with my new arm. It had a single clasp on the front, which was handy because I only had one hand now. The case hissed as it opened, and a bit of antiseptic-smelling steam escaped the edges.

The arm wasn't too dissimilar to my old one: sleek gray metal with a few plates that were edged in glowing neon. It was a bit less bulky. Likely the lack of a missile launcher worked into it. "So how do I equip this one? Just jam it on to stubby here?" I wiggled my stub.

More or less. You can expect something similar to having a "sleeping" limb awaken.

I raised the arm and turned it around. There was a hole for my stump, and some sections that would reach all the way up to my collarbone and over my shoulder bone thing . . . what was that called? The scapula or something.

You will have to remove your suit for it to make contact with your skin.

Lowering the arm back into its box, I unzipped the front of my armored suit and tugged it off my right side. I hadn't realized how chilly it was here. Then I grabbed the arm again and slid it on. There was a warm pressure over my side, and a feeling of suction, like I was getting the world's biggest hickey.

Then I suddenly had feeling in my new hand and arm. I gasped as I felt a million tingles running up and down the arm. It really was like waking up after Lucy used me as a pillow and cut off my circulation. "Oh, that's annoying," I said. Moving the new hand around seemed to help, the pins and needles feeling fading gently.

Connection established. Everything should be functional now.

"Nice," I said. Then I used my new arm to remove the rest of my under-suit. "Need a new one of these." I slipped my feet out of my old suit, then flicked it aside like so much dirty laundry. I glanced around. I was entirely naked, aside from the new arm, in the middle of enemy territory. "Actually, give me a minute, I'm gonna use the washroom while I'm here."

How wonderfully pragmatic. Do you want an improved version of your under armor too?

"Sure," I said as I started looking for the bathroom. It couldn't be far from the sauna, could it? I found it behind a faux-wood wall. It was the men's washroom, but no one was around to tell me no.

New Purchase: Armored Stealth-Capable Undersuit
Points Reduced from . . . 34,159 to . . . 34,009

My new suit appeared in a little box, and I unwrapped it—after washing my hands—then slid into it. It was about as comfortable as the last one, which is to say it felt like I was slipping into something made of the fur of a hundred newborn kittens. The design wasn't changed too much. Still mostly black with a few neon highlights and some armored plates over important bits.

"Okay," I said as I fiddled with the neck. It was a bit tight. Not uncomfortable, but nearly. "Let's armor up."

The new armor's back unfolded, revealing a space that looked about me-shaped. I placed a foot in the opening meant for it, then climbed in properly, the armor closing up around me and pulling me in tighter against the armor's front.

My vision was entirely darkened for a moment before everything ahead of me lit up, the screens within the helmet part of the armor turning the world into a more vibrant version of reality, where shadows were only a suggestion.

I wiggled my shoulders and felt the armor responding without any noticeable delay. It was a bit weird to bring my hand up and see the armor's hand move at the same time. It wasn't quite in the right spot. My meat hand was somewhere in the armor's forearm.

I'd get used to it in a minute, I suspected.

"What's this armed with?" I asked.

Only two shoulder-mounted guns. They are a significant upgrade over your previous models.

I nodded, then stopped. It was still weird moving my head.

Heading out of the room, I was stopped by my old armor. It grabbed my Void Terminus by the hilt and raised it up before me, holding the sword in my path.

"Oh, right," I said. I grabbed the sword just under its guard, then leaned forward to see my waist. A small armor segment unfolded by my hip, and when I pressed the sheath against it, the armor grabbed on to it. Handy.

There was a mirror just outside the sauna, and I glanced at myself as I walked by.

The armor gave me a good boost to my height. I wouldn't be taller than the tallest man, but I'd be meeting him eye-to-eye. I was also a lot stockier. My old armor had curves. This one had armored plates. That was sexy in its own way, I supposed.

Also, a tail, with a very sharp-looking thagomizer.

"All right, get me one of those Bullcats, and I think I'm ready to go," I said.

A gun appeared in the air next to me, and I caught it before it had time to fall.

If you don't have a current plan, then might I suggest some actions?

"Uh, sure?" I said as I started to look for an elevator or stairwell up.

The Family has an updating feed of the wave and its movements, as well as feeds from Vanguards on the front lines and from the various PMC commands. The current most urgent call for assistance is relatively close to your position.

"What is it?" I asked.

Vanguard Grasshopper has been injured and is requesting assistance.

I froze. "Why the fuck didn't you tell me earlier?"

The request is only seconds old. She is one point two kilometers northwest of your position. Your suit can fly short distances. Once you're out in the open it should be easy to make your way there.

"Which way's north?" I asked.

An arrow appeared, pointing me in the right direction, and I took off running in that direction. There was a wall in the way, of course, with a big window that opened up onto the busy city below. So I raised my new Bullcat and opened fire with full-auto into the glass.

My new armor was sturdy enough that I didn't even feel any recoil. The glass felt it, though. It might have been that tough sort designed to withstand some damage and prevent office suicides, but it wasn't rated for dealing with anxious samurai.

I shot out into the open air, trailing a cascade of tinkling glass. The streets below were teeming with aliens, some of whom took a moment to look up toward me.

Then my jump-jets kicked on and my downward fall turned into an arc that led me up and over to the next building. "Myalis, acid bombs. Let's give those fuckers down there something to think about. Actually, fuck it, let's mix it up with some normal bombs too."

Certainly.

"And while we're at it, can we unlock the next tier on my bomb catalog? I want more fun toys to play with."

New Purchase: Esoteric Single-Use Explosive Devices Tier II

Points Reduced from . . . 34,009 to . . . 32,409

Expensive, but probably worth it. And honestly, not doing much to put a dent into my current savings. "Thanks, Myalis."

Anything to lessen the Antithesis threat.

I sprinted across the rooftop, then jumped once I got to the other side. While I was in the air, Myalis summoned a heap of bombs for me, which I dropped with glee atop the alien horde. They'd be able to track my progress with the bodies I left behind.

CHAPTER FORTY-SEVEN

SAFE, NOT SOUND

We are here today to lay a good person to rest.

It's . . . it's something I've heard before. They always say that the person who died was a good person. It's usually a load of bullshit. Not today, though.

Sprocket Rocket was a good person. A real fucking hero. Sure, he was . . . he was a bit nuts, and he was a reckless kind of guy. But fuck if he wasn't spectacular. So many people owe their lives to him. I . . . I might too.

I'm sorry, big bro. Your dream's not going to die with you, all right? I promise.

—Longbow, at the funeral of the samurai Sprocket Rocket, 2048

I ran to a stop on the edge of a rooftop. Some boring rectangle of a building, with nothing to make it stand out except an odd number of AC units on the rooftop. Behind me, on the road I'd just jumped over, were a couple hundred aliens currently enjoying some acid rain coupled with a sprinkling of more traditional explosives.

The property damage I was leaving was going to cost billions, I suspected. Grasshopper's tally probably wasn't going to be far behind.

Looking down at the street below, I could make out entire chunks of concrete missing, some looking like they'd been punched right off the walls. Other areas had a sprinkling of bullet holes poking into the buildings and roads and through the corpses of dozens and dozens of Antithesis.

It was a charnel house down there. Aliens lying in heaps, having fallen where they ran. Not as much blood as I might have expected. Each alien that was dead had a hole poking right through their skull, usually between the eyes.

I imagined that all of those holes in the walls were created after a round went through some alien's brain.

"Which way?" I asked.

Myalis's reply was to create a red circle that hovered over everything off to my left. There were more bodies that way, not that the bodies would remain there forever. The Antithesis were starting to poke into the road from the sides, some of them moving with a bit more caution, others running in while their skin sizzled under the effects of my acid.

I tossed a pair of acid bombs up and over the road. They'd dissolve the bodies, maybe keep some of the aliens from following.

Running along the rooftops, I traced the path that Grasshopper had left. At some point she ran into an apartment building. Judging by the semicircle of bodies piled up by the entrance, she had stayed there for a while.

Some of the bodies were shoved aside on one side. I squinted, then zoomed in with my cybernetic eye. Lots of footprints in that spot. Easy to make out since they'd stepped through a puddle of Antithesis blood-stuff.

"Was she with a group of civvies?" I asked.

Unknown. It's possible, though. Let me verify . . . yes. Grasshopper received a report that a civilian safe house was in this area and wasn't going to be able to withstand an artillery assault.

"Oh," I said. I listened for a bit. There was a nonstop thumping in the background, with the occasional whistle to punctuate it. The constant bombardment was mostly on the farther edges of the city, though, and it was easy to dismiss it as a sort of horrific background noise. "Are they going to bomb this position?"

Eventually, yes. Currently the area is marked as a do-not-fire zone. You should be safe.

That was nice. I didn't feel like getting crushed twice in one day.

I picked up the pace. Grasshopper wasn't far. She wasn't moving either, not according to Myalis, and I was growing increasingly worried that whatever injury she had, it wasn't just a bruise and a paper cut.

I came around a corner, then slowed to a stop as I took in the scene. Half a dozen model fives, all splattered around and very dead. Next to them, with half of its body shoved into the back of some office, was a bigger, nastier-looking alien. "What's that?" I asked.

That's a model fourteen. It's a transportation unit. Fast-moving and well-armored. Not necessarily effective at being offensive, but it is capable of carrying other models across the ground fairly rapidly. It never stops growing, adding new segments whenever it has consumed enough biomass.

The alien was about the length of a bus, its entire body made of segments of greenish flesh covered in thick carapace and filled with sharp legs beneath. A few holes the size of my torso were missing from some of its segments, but it looked like it took quite a few of those to kill it.

I launched off the edge of the building, jump-jets activating to slow down my fall before I hit the ground with a heavy thump and bent knees.

I ran around the model fourteen, just in case it wasn't as dead as it looked. "Resonator," I asked.

Myalis delivered, and I flicked the grenade on and tossed it underhand beneath the model fourteen's corpse. If it wasn't entirely dead, then that might melt off the rest of it. I didn't envy Grasshopper having to deal with that thing.

"I didn't think we'd see models that big so soon," I said.

It has been long enough that models above ten should be appearing, though in limited numbers.

Limited numbers was good. Now if we could just limit those numbers to zero or below, then everything would be just fine. The model fourteen looked armored enough that I wasn't sure the average artillery shell would take it out.

I squeezed past the centipede's head—an ugly thing, with a tiny mouth and far too many eyes that looked like they were squeezed out of the big armored plates on its "face"—and into the office proper.

More dead aliens. Model threes and fours, most of them with those perfect holes between their eyes, but a few were just blasted full of holes pretty much at random. It was the kind of shooting I'd do, which worried me even more.

I walked a bit faster. Grasshopper was close.

I came around a corner and found her pressed up against the fallen wall of a cubicle. She was sitting on the ground, arms lying by her side, her green suit covered in black-red blood. A rifle was discarded off to the right, and the arms of her suit held a few handguns that pointed at me for a moment before lowering themselves.

She wasn't moving.

"Oh, fuck," I said. I ran over to her, jumped over the body of some unimportant alien, then landed at a crouch by her side. "Myalis, tell me she's alive," I said.

I'm registering a heartbeat from her suit. Her AI is still active. Her brain is still oxygenated and functional, though her vitals are decreasing. Blood loss, as well as shock. She has some internal modifications that are compensating for the biological organs that aren't functioning.

"Med kit, now," I said.

A box appeared by my side. The same kit that I'd used on Raccoon a while ago, though this one seemed a bit bigger. I tore it open, found the right tubes, and pulled them over to Grasshopper. I hesitated. Where was I going to stick them?

I'll ask her AI to open parts of her armor.

Grasshopper's armor unfolded around her face and upper chest. It jammed around the middle, where it was obvious something had struck her.

I didn't waste any more time, pressing the tubes in close before backing off as the machine got to work. "I need mecha-cats. Give me, like, six of them. Secure the area around here."

Six boxes appeared and robotic cats unfolded themselves from inside them and immediately started to patrol the room; some of them moved outside and out of the range of my hearing. That'd keep any of the smaller aliens at bay for a bit.

"How is she?" I asked. I pulled Grasshopper back so that she was lying down flat instead of up against the wall. The arms sticking out of the back of her armor helped a little, repositioning themselves to make it easier.

She's unlikely to die at the moment, though her injuries will make combat difficult. Do you want me to call for additional assistance?

I considered it for just a moment. "Yeah, do so. We need to get her out of the front lines. She can recover better without having to worry about some alien popping out of nowhere to eat her. Probably somewhere a little less dirty too."

Myalis brought up a scan of Grasshopper's body. It looked like all of her veins and muscles and bones, with more and more details being filled in as the nanomachines I was pumping into her traveled across her body and cataloged her injuries. It looked like one leg was broken at the shin, and her knee on that same leg was fucked. There were a few ribs that weren't in the right spot too. Lots of internal fuckery around her abdomen.

"What hit her?" I asked.

The model fourteen. A moment of inattention or hesitation and she was struck hard enough to be injured. Her armor fortunately took the worst of the damage.

I looked around. There were a few little healing-pack things on the ground that weren't mine. Had she been trying to heal herself while laid out here? "She's tough," I said. "She'll make it."

"Yeah," Grasshopper agreed.

"Hey!" I gasped before leaning in closer. "You're awake?"

"A little," she said. "That was unpleasant. Is that you, Stray Cat?"

I nodded, then realized her eyes were screwed shut. "Yeah, it's me. Lemme get you some painkillers. Something to get you back on your feet."

"I'll be peachy," she said. "I like that word. It's tasty." She gasped. "Cat! The people. Go check on the people. They're behind me. I sent them away. Had to keep them safe. Please!"

Her eyes opened, and she locked onto me, pleading.

I nodded. "All right," I said. "Myalis, turrets. I don't want anything nasty interrupting her healing."

Then I ran off, because helping people was something I could do better than waiting around for a friend to get better.

CHAPTER FORTY-EIGHT

IT'S NEVER EASY

And so I thought to myself . . . these games, their gacha mechanics and rewards, they addict our clients, the players.

What if I ran a business the same way? Competitive WvW, where the *W* means "Worker."

It was genius!

—Extract from the biography of Nimbletainment's owner, 2039

"Who am I looking for?" I asked Myalis.

The group that Grasshopper was escorting was thirty-six members strong. I'm afraid that I can confirm that some of them have died. There are some cameras still active throughout the building.

"Fuck," I said. Knowing Grasshopper, with all of her . . . Grasshopper-iness, she wouldn't take that all that well. "Let's find at least some of them alive."

The first floor of the building was all offices and cubicles and that sort of horrific shit. I counted no less than three water coolers as I ran deeper into the building.

The center was a wide-open space sporting balconies on the floors above with glass sides, a large staircase, and in the very center, a glass-walled elevator. It probably made the poor fucks tied to one of the cubicles feel great when they could crane their neck back and see the people a few levels above them.

Right now, the steps leading up had a lot of blood on them.

I swore as I ran through the lobby and skipped over some woman's corpse. "Was she one of Grasshopper's?" I asked.

She was. The group moved up.

Made sense. They wanted distance. Didn't look like it worked out too well, though. I counted four more bodies on the staircase. Three dead aliens too, model threes with their faces caved in or with mangled bones.

So the group were fighting back. Probably for the best. Model threes weren't too hard to kill, overall. I'd done it with one arm and a pipe. I crouched, then jumped up. Myalis caught on to my intentions and fired off the jets on my legs, sending me rocketing up the space around the stairs.

I twisted a bit and landed unsteadily on the third floor. Another body, this one next to three dead model threes. A fourth was chewing the corpse's face.

The alien paused midchew and turned its too-many-eyed face my way.

I stomped over to it and swung a boot into the side of its face. I don't know if it was the anger, the armor, or some combination of the two, but the kick smashed it hard enough that it crumpled to the side, very much dead.

Leaning down, I checked on the faceless guy, then shook my head. Very dead. It looked like he was still holding on to a big knife that was stained green with alien goop. Those around him had clearly been stabbed a few times.

Good man. In other circumstances, he'd be hailed a hero.

I walked past him. There was a trail of blood leading deeper in to follow. As good an indication of where I had to go as any.

Bullcat raised, I started to follow the blood trail. The group must have moved pretty quickly. How long had Grasshopper been out of the fight for? A few minutes?

There are Antithesis entering the building from a sky bridge linked to the next building over.

"All right," I said. "Which floor?"

The third.

"Which floor are we on now?" I asked.

The third.

That was just brilliant. Folks had run up here for safety, and then they'd run to the one floor that had more aliens coming onto it.

I entered a large cafeteria space. Lots of tables with seating for two spread out across the room, with a couple of franchise food-dispensers up against one wall with some vending machines next to them.

Someone had died pressed up against an anime figure, some company mascot, with a speech bubble above her head. *"Don't forget! Only company-approved meals in the official rest and restoration cafeteria!"*

Not the nicest place to die. I leaned down, one hand dropping from my gun to shift the body aside. She'd been bitten in the back of the neck. Claw marks cut through her pseudo-leather coat.

I continued moving, eyes sweeping around.

More bodies near the room's exit. It looked like the room's exit was one of those barricades that dropped from the ceiling. It had been pried open, the long pole used for leverage discarded to one side.

The small opening meant that everyone had to get to all fours to squeeze through. That had probably taken some time. A fat guy was currently wedged in the gap, a few more bodies mangled behind him.

I looked around for another way through, then lowered my gun so that it hung on by its strap, and I grabbed the metal grating in both hands and pulled in opposite directions. The entire thing ripped apart above and tipped to the side. Not what I wanted, but it worked. I pulled at it again, and the barricade came crashing down with a jangle of metal on metal.

I walked on through.

More offices, these much bigger, with glass walls between them and big desks with chairs to receive clients. The front-facing part of the business, then.

A helpful body pointed me in the right direction. Some guy bent over weirdly, a couple of dead model threes next to him. It was only as I was walking past that I noticed he was bent over a second body, clutching it close to keep it . . . her, safe. I checked for a pulse on both.

I moved on.

Screaming up ahead had me refocusing on what was at hand. I started running down the corridors until I rounded a corner and found Grasshopper's people. They were using a couple of desks as a barricade. One was wielding an office chair like a battering ram.

They were stuck in a corner office, the entrance hounded by half a dozen model threes and a model four. It felt strangely familiar.

I slowed my sprint to a more careful walk, then raised my Bullcat. I made sure there wasn't anyone behind where I'd be shooting, then flicked the gun to full-auto.

It was like pressing a chain saw into a steel drum filled with loose pans. A screeching scream filled the corridor as pellets rained across the passage.

The aliens were shredded in a blink, the wall behind them filled with a thousand pinpricks. The screaming from the office intensified for one brief moment, and then calm settled.

I walked over, then eyed the other length of corridor. I could see the sky bridge from out of a window, but not the entrance onto this floor, which was past a few walls. There were some aliens running in through the passageway. I mowed them down with a quick burst, and then my gun clicked empty.

"Reload," I said before turning to the barricade. "Any injured?" I asked.

There was a sudden cacophony of thanks and demands. "Save me!" "Thank you!" "Oh God, oh God."

I pumped the Bullcat. The heavy *ker-chunk* silenced everyone. "I asked if there were any injuries," I repeated myself. "We'll tend to those, then move back downstairs. Grasshopper's down there. She'll be wanting to see you."

The barricade came down in quick order. I got two more mecha-cats, just to keep an eye on the group, and then I handed out healing packs like they were candy. They were basically smaller, cheaper versions of the nanomachine healing suite that I'd used on Grasshopper. Small enough that someone could just stick it against their own side and hold it there while it did its thing. Probably nowhere near as effective, but the worst injury I saw was a bad cut on one guy's leg.

"Myalis, I need a way back down that won't pass through the same corridors," I said. There were some kids in the group. They'd probably seen worse on TV, but . . . yeah.

Myalis outlined a map for me, and with a nod, I started off in that direction.

They followed, though some of them protested. I think the idea of not having a samurai around to keep them safe did wonders to quell the protests of those who were in that kind of mood.

Our path back down was done mostly through more discreet stairwells on the edges of the building. No one complained about having to go down a couple of floors. The mecha-cats I'd bought watched the group's back while I took the front.

On arriving at the first floor, I was greeted by one of the mecha I'd left with Grasshopper. The cat nodded, then turned and strutted off in the way only a cat could. We crossed some dead aliens a bit later, which might have explained all of that.

All that was left was getting back to Grasshopper, then figuring a way to get her and the civilians out of the area safely.

Easy.

CHAPTER FORTY-NINE

THOSE WHO LOVE CANNONS

You saw something scary? You were a little afraid?

Aww, poor baby. Have you tried Manning the Fuck Up?

Manning the Fuck Up is a vitamin and protein supplement for REAL MEN. It is packed full of protein, essential vitamins, and serotonin reuptake inhibitors that'll have you feeling like a killer again! PTSD is a myth. There's no such thing.

What's that? You're some crybaby woman? Then try Woman the Fuck Up! It's the pink bottles, bitch.

—Force-Viral ad for Doctor Fist's Real Medicine, 2026

The first thing I did once I was back on the ground floor was to check on the mecha-cats. I had a handy app-like bit of software I could tap into that basically gave me a shitty map of the area and showed me where the cat drones were in relation to me. They were all green, which I figured meant we were safe for the moment.

Then I checked on Grasshopper.

My friend was leaning up against a wall, legs sprawled out and the nano-machine healing kit sitting on her lap. She had a granola bar in one hand and was chewing it slowly as I approached.

"Hey," I said. "Feeling better?"

She chewed a few more times, then swallowed. "Yes," she said. "I suspect I'm dosed with enough painkillers that attempting to operate anything wouldn't be a wise choice."

"Yeah, I bet," I said.

The civilians filed into the area behind me. They were sticking close to each other, like a frightened herd of deer that had just been startled. Their eyes were open the same way, as if the first loud noise they heard would be enough to spook them. Honestly, I couldn't blame them.

Still, if they were a bit more calm, I'd consider arming them up for their own safety. As it was . . . that didn't seem wise.

Grasshopper leaned up so that she could see the civilians better. "There's . . . less of them," she said.

"Yeah," I agreed.

"Oh."

It was just one little sound, but the way she said it carried a lot of baggage. I half turned and gestured the civilians away. They were reluctant to move until a few of the mecha-cats in the area herded them away.

I knelt down next to Grasshopper. "Are you okay?" I asked.

She considered it, then took a bite of her granola bar and nodded. That was the most I'd get out of her, I figured.

"We need to find a way to get everyone out of here," I said. "I don't think we can escort the civvies out to the edge of the city. Not with the wave already on top of us." I pulled up the Family's map and winced. They had a separate, more zoomed-in and detailed map of the current area. It was being updated a lot more frequently than their regional map. The wave was already *at* the space where the wall should have been.

A glance revealed it to be made of hundreds of red pinpricks, some of which winked out. I imagined that the defenders were pretty busy. We were maybe seven hundred meters away from the edge, if we could go in a straight line.

That wouldn't be possible.

"I'm going to call the Family for backup," I said. "Bet we can get some mercs to fly a tank over. Then we can load everyone on and send them off to safety."

"I imagine you'll want me to go as well?" Grasshopper asked.

"If you think you need it," I said. "Personally . . . I don't know what I'd do. But I'm both stupid and hardheaded, which I've been told is about as attractive as it is annoying. You always struck me as being pretty smart, smarter than I am, so I'm not gonna tell you what to do."

Grasshopper chuckled. "Thank you, Stray Cat."

"Just Cat," I said.

She nodded, plopped the last of her bar into her mouth, then made a shooing gesture at me. "Make that call, Cat," she said.

I did as she asked, climbing to my feet and walking over to the edge of the room, where I pulled up Laserjack's number. I dialed and hoped he wasn't so busy that he'd just ignore the call. It rang twice before he picked up.

"Are you going to die in the next ten seconds?" Laserjack said, his voice gruff and not ready to take anyone's shit.

"No," I said.

"Give me half a minute," Laserjack said. I waited as the line clicked off and went mute. I crossed my arms but made an effort not to get irritated.

The dude was taking care of a whole lot of shit all at once. He was a samurai, just like me; I could afford him a bit of respect.

"All right," he said a minute later. "What's on fire?"

"Nothing. I need evac at my location for a bunch of civilians."

"That'll be hard to swing," he said. "You're in the middle of it."

"Civilians and Grasshopper. She's injured. I gave her some shit, she won't die here, but seeing a doc wouldn't hurt. Might need stitches or whatever you give to someone that got chewed up."

"Ah," he said. "How many civilians?"

"Maybe twenty, twenty-five? I didn't count," I said.

"Is there a cleared landing space nearby?"

I shook my head. "No. Roads are quiet, but they're a mess." I could hear the familiar thump that my railguns made from nearby. My mecha-cats were working hard to keep any curious aliens down. That wouldn't last forever. The moment the wave shifted, or a bigger group passed by . . .

"Clear a space on the road for a transport," he said. "You have . . . about three minutes. Prep the civilians too. Laserjack out."

The line went dead.

I stood there for a moment, then swore. "Okay, fuck. Grasshopper! Your evac's coming in a bit. I need to make room for it. Can you help the civilians get to it once it touches down?" I asked.

Grasshopper blinked a few times, then rolled to her side and climbed to her feet. It didn't look easy, but she made it. "I'll do my very best," she said.

I nodded, then hesitated. Front or back? The back was a mess; the front probably had a lot more aliens to deal with. But then the front would be easier for the civilians.

"Myalis, pull the cats back. Keep them close to Grasshopper. We don't need to secure the entire damned building, I don't think."

Understood. How do you intend to secure the street?

"With a lot of bombs," I said as I crossed the offices on a straight path to the front of the building. "How many accessways are there on the street? I mean . . . there's both ends, plus how many alleys and how many compromised buildings?"

One moment . . . I count thirty-two ways for an Antithesis ground unit to reach the road within one hundred meters of this building's exit.

"I need thirty-two of those acid-rain bombs. I want every passage in to cost the fuckers. As many resonators too. We'll enclose the area."

There was a model four at the entrance, prying the doors open with a pair of tentacles. It was strong enough that the glass door was starting to open.

I pulled up my Bullcat and fired through the glass and into the alien. Then I stepped out onto the street.

I may have been a little hasty, I realized as I took in the number of aliens running across. They noticed me at about the same time.

My back-mounted guns snapped out of their housing and immediately started to fire. I expected them to fire single shots, but instead both of them purred, a constant wave of superheated air pouring out of them while aliens all across the street were ripped apart.

Not to be outdone, I leaned into my shotgun, flicked it back to full-auto, then swept across the horde, raining buckshot into every alien I could see.

"'Nades," I said.

Myalis caught on, and a large box appeared by my side. I kicked it open and the acid-rain grenades within zipped up into the air above. They darted over the alleys and to the end of the road a moment before a glowing mist started to come down over those entrances.

The immediate area around me was clear, so I dropped to a knee next to the box and started to pick out resonators from within it. I turned them on with a flick of my thumb, then tossed them out across the road. My throwing aim wasn't perfect, but the fun thing with explosives was that accuracy was optional.

"We're going to need something for the air," I said.

Turrets? A bit uncreative, but they kinda worked. I had a lot of points to work with, though, and it would feel kind of lame to just face a few cheapo laser arrays on the edge of the street, plucking the smaller alien birds out of the air.

"Myalis, got any ideas for keeping the skies safe?" I asked. "Not something dinky."

I imagine you need a solution that doesn't require your direct attention? In that case, how about a Flak Cat Cannon?

CHAPTER FIFTY

EMOSCYTHE

Things have gone to shit, as expected, but New Montreal's not doing too bad.

The Corporate State of Ontario's fucked. Québec City has started full-on drafting, and Manitoba is . . . actually, nothing's changed there. It's still a hellscape.

—Real Canadian News, 2057 live broadcast

When Myalis suggested a Flak Cat Cannon, I had a mental image of what would appear when I bought it.

That mental image was all wrong.

The Flak Cat Cannon was a biggish device, maybe the size of my hover-bike, with a large base that had four legs and a barrel that stretched out above it. It looked pretty normal. Sleek and futuristic, but normal. The "CATS R Cool" decals on the side were a given, of course. What really threw me off were the three mecha-cats that came with the cannon.

They were wearing little camo army helmets (I realized that the camo was just cat silhouettes in different shades of green that overlapped each other) and hi-vis vests. The cats climbed onto the cannon and started to man it right away. Two of them worked the controls while a third fit a shell into the gun's breech.

"Myalis, is this some sort of joke?" I asked.

I find it funny.

"You're the worst," I said.

The cannon is entirely functional. I even managed to reduce the price so that it packs more of a punch than it should for its point cost. And the mechanized cats operating it can defend themselves as well, giving it some much needed point-defense.

I was going to argue some more when the cannon fired.

Some of the nearest windows burst apart, glass raining down from on high as a ball of gray dust appeared a hundred meters above. A few seconds later the tinkle of glass was joined by metallic clinks as shrapnel tumbled out of the sky along with some Antithesis chunks.

The cats scrambled to move the gun around a few degrees, and it fired a second time, the shell exploding in the middle of a flock of aliens, which were shredded by the expanding cloud of shrapnel.

"Well, at least it's working," I said.

With the acid grenades and resonators occupying every entrance into this stretch of road, the only aliens making it close looked like shit. Their skin was burned and their bones half melted. It only took a few railgun rounds pumped through them to take them down for good.

"ETA on that transport?" I asked.

One minute, twelve seconds. It's a Vanguard's vessel. You won't have to worry about the safety of the passengers, not against lower-tier threats.

That was a relief.

I pulled up the regional map and scanned it while I waited. The wave wasn't broken. Far from it. It looked like it had met a few pockets of resistance here and there and had flowed around those. On meeting the main defenses where the wall was meant to be, the horde couldn't continue. So instead it was spreading out and back, a few small tendrils sneaking back into the city.

Those would be trouble. They'd probably start looking for survivors and those too slow to evacuate, or they'd set up hives right on the edge of New Montreal. We didn't need aliens growing right on our doorstep.

I searched for the pin that marked Gomorrah's position and found it somewhere to the north of me, closer in toward the wall. The area surrounding her was orange and green, with fewer aliens around.

The area I was in was mostly orange too.

I zoomed back out, then took in the city as a whole. The blockage bridging the gap in the wall kept New Montreal safe. The other side of it was entirely green. Orange and red tendrils reached out to that border, but it looked as though they were holding firm.

The city beyond the wall was a mess of oranges with an equal number of green swatches and red ones.

"Is it just me or are they moving slower?" I asked.

It's likely that the Antithesis, or at least those capable of thinking that well, have realized that they don't have the strength to reach what they consider to be the biggest threat.

"That's good, right?"

They'll likely either regroup for a more concerted effort against their threat or root themselves down and try to outproduce the threat. In all likelihood, the Antithesis will try to do both.

I swore under my breath, then refocused on the task at hand. I couldn't save everyone or do that much about the larger situation. So I'd do what I could then and there and let someone smarter than me worry about the bigger picture.

A noise from above had my ears perking up, and I half turned as a shadow slid overhead and spun around.

A hovercar, a big one.

The hovercraft spun around as it lowered itself toward the road, so I got a good look at it. It was stubby and square, painted in all-black with silver highlights over the many skulls and spikes that decorated it. Landing gear hissed out of the bottom of the craft, even as a few turrets mounted on the ends of its stubby wings turned and blasted a few of the aliens still on the street.

The ship landed with a heavy thump, engines still humming. A door on the side slid open and a figure stepped out, even if they were still a meter off the ground.

Black skirts shifted around the armored form of a thin girl with pale skin. She blinked and glanced around, her braided twintails slipping off her shoulders as she took in the street. Then her attention locked onto my flak cannon and she just stared, confused, as the cats loaded a new shell.

"Emoscythe," I said. "Didn't think you'd be the one to show up," I said.

She turned and looked right at me. I wasn't sure what she was thinking. "It's Emoscythe Mordeath Noir," she said.

Ah. I was thinking that she'd be a stuck-up pain in the ass. I grinned. "Sure thing," I said. "Is there enough room in there for twenty or so scared civilians?"

She nodded. "There's room. I was told that Grasshopper was hurt?"

I detected some actual concern there. "Yeah, she's injured. Alive and stable, but I'd rather see her on a bed than on the front lines right now. She needs a doctor or two. You know her?"

"Most people don't deserve the gift they've been given," she drawled. "Grasshopper . . . might not be one of those people. Even if she's bizarre."

She had enough makeup on to black out every window on a skyscraper; I wasn't sure if she could start casting stones about people's bizarreness.

"I'll get Grasshopper and the civvies out," I said. "Can your ship keep the road cleared?"

"I'll manage," she said. She reached back to the ship even as a staircase unfolded itself from the side, leading to the doorway she'd jumped out of. Emoscythe grabbed a pair of long black sticks that I guessed were some sort of weapon.

Good enough. I wasn't sure how much of her outfit was armor, but I imagined that if she could afford a ship that big, she could kill a few aliens.

I ran in and met one of my mecha-cats just inside, sitting in the middle of the floor with its tail twitching impatiently. "How are the civilians?" I asked.

No major changes.

I nodded along and continued past the cat guarding the passage. I found Grasshopper with the civilians, patting one of them on the shoulder even as she continued to look like death warmed over. "Transport's here," I said. "With Emoscythe along for the ride too."

"Emoscythe Mordeath Noir is nice," Grasshopper said. "I'll be happy to see her. She's a very kind young woman with a bit of a prickly exterior. Just like you, Cat."

"Yeah, no," I said.

She smiled at me, but I wasn't going to deal with that. Grasshopper hobbled forward for a step before one of the civilians stepped up next to her and swung her arm over his shoulder. "I'm sure you'll make more friends, Cat," Grasshopper said. "It's important to make friends while you're still young and have a reason to spend time with your peers. It'll become increasingly difficult to do as you age."

"I'm not a kindergartner," I said.

We exited the front of the building, the mecha-cats forming a cordon around the civilians in case some clever alien tried to grab one from behind. Emoscythe was waiting by her ship when we came out; those bars she'd picked up earlier had turned into a pair of mini-scythes, which she held by her side.

"Emoscythe Mordeath Noir!" Grasshopper said. She took her arm back and stumbled toward the smaller goth. The girl stood still as Grasshopper approached, but the older woman didn't hug her or anything. "I'm glad you came. I think you'll make a great friend with Stray Cat here."

"Ah, right," Emoscythe said. "Just get in the hovertank; you look like you need some rest."

"Rest is important, yes," Grasshopper agreed.

It was only after the civilians and Grasshopper were done loading up and the ship took off that I realized that Emoscythe was staying on the ground with me.

CHAPTER FIFTY-ONE

GOTHIC PUBLIC RELATIONS

It's all about the memes.

—Emoscythe Mordeath Noir,
seventh annual PR Specialist Conference, 2049

"So, what're you doing here?" I asked.

Emoscythe stared at me. For some reason her lack of armor was bothering me. I mean, she was her own girl, and if that big ship was anything to go by, she could afford some pretty nice shit if she wanted to.

I couldn't even toss that many stones from my glass house; I had been reluctant to get armor for myself for a while. I'd learned better since, especially after my gear had likely saved my ass a few times.

"I'm here to kill aliens," Emoscythe said. "And to keep an eye on you."

"Me?" I asked.

She nodded. "I have access to the records. You're the third-newest samurai in the city. The newest who didn't become a Vanguard in the last forty-eight hours."

"All right," I said. "But I think I'm doing okay for myself."

"You think that?" she asked.

"Yeah," I said.

She looked me up and down. "I suppose it could be worse."

"Thanks," I said flatly. "Look, I don't mind keeping someone company, but I don't do babysitting and I don't need to be babysat. I'm guessing you can pull your weight, if you're acting so self-confident."

Her eyes narrowed, but she nodded. "I can handle myself, Stray Cat."

"You sure do have a stick," I said with a gesture to the staff she held next to her.

Emoscythe's thumb ran along the shaft. "It's my preferred weapon. Maybe you'll get to see it in use. But . . . that can wait. What are your objectives now?"

"I don't know," I said honestly. "I got sidetracked when I heard that

Grasshopper needed help. Wasn't doing much before that. Well, that's not true. I was setting up choke points and ambushes to take out as many aliens as possible before they reached the front."

She nodded. "Invisibility and explosives. I remember. You have both of those and the cat gimmick going on. You're spreading yourself a little thin, I think, but you're new enough that some experimentation's normal."

"Uh, yeah, sure," I said. "Anyway, the building I was in collapsed and I got pinned at the bottom. Had to get a new arm." I wiggled my hand around.

I was expecting some sort of reaction from that. What I'd just described had been kind of metal, but Emoscythe didn't seem either surprised or impressed. "We should probably head back to the wall. We can plug any gaps in the formation there, and it's possible that they need the assistance we could provide. Two samurai not assisting is a huge loss in firepower."

"You're a bit more . . . no-nonsense than I was expecting," I said.

She stared at me. She had a good stare going on, what with the eyeliner. "I'm a goth, not an idiot. Sure, I accept and understand that every action I take, no matter how hard I work, will likely amount to very little in the end, but I'm not a coward. I'll fight against the void until the very end."

That would have sounded a lot cooler if it hadn't been delivered in a monotone. "Okay, then," I said. "Front lines?"

She nodded. "Front lines. We can discuss personal style and how one's attitude and appearance play a role in shaping others' perception of you."

I raised a hand in a "wait a moment" sort of gesture. "What?"

"Would you rather talk about something else?" Emoscythe asked. "You have my attention, might as well use it."

"I got that part, but why would I . . . how do I politely say that I don't know what you're on about without sounding like an ass?"

"Grasshopper didn't explain," Emoscythe said. She looked away from me and took a deep breath. "I should have known. Yes, that's very much like her. Grasshopper's a good woman, but her communication skills some-times . . . well, it doesn't matter, I suppose." She bowed in my direction. "I'm Emoscythe Mordeath Noir. I cut things."

"Yeah, uh, Stray Cat. I . . . blow shit up and kiss cute girls. Pleased to meetcha."

Emoscythe rolled her eyes. "Your introduction could use some work."

"Yours was fantastic. Never expected the bowing. Ten outta ten."

She didn't seem amused. "At least the sarcasm fits your cat persona." My what? "My job, more often than not, is to help new samurai find their place. Not so much in combat but within society. To make them recognizable, so that when they inevitably die we have something to remember them by."

"Wait, you're a samurai PR person? Who's also a goth?"

"Yes."

"Okay," I said. I thought about it for a moment, then decided not to anymore. "Can you at least fight?"

"Obviously. I'm a samurai. We can talk while we move."

"I haven't agreed to getting my image or whatever poked at," I pointed out.

She shrugged. "Consultations are free and compulsory."

"What?"

"You don't have the strength to stop me," she said. "Not that I'd push to that extent. I'm depressive, not a bitch."

I chuckled. "All right, fine. If it'll make you happy. Can you fly at all? I don't plan on staying on ground level for any longer than I need to."

Emoscythe looked up the nearest building. Seven, maybe eight floors of concrete and glass. "I can't fly, but I can make it up there with no problem," she said. With a flick, she spun her long staff, and it somehow split apart into two shorter sticks. She stopped their spinning motion, then tightened her grip on their handles.

The ends of the sticks unfolded and a pair of foot-long blades snicked out at ninety degrees from the handles.

"Mini-scythes?" I asked.

"These are kama," she said before she stepped right past me and up to the wall of the building. She tensed, then took off sprinting toward the wall before launching herself into the air. Emoscythe ran three steps vertically with heavy crunches as her knee-high boots dug into the concrete, and then she stabbed into the wall with one of her kama and pulled herself up to the ledge a floor above.

I watched as she easily climbed up the vertical surface, using her mini-scythes as handholds whenever she needed one.

There was no way her body wasn't modified. Especially not when her knees shifted and more blades slipped out from her legs to turn her climb into a skitter.

"She's pretty fucking weird," I muttered.

Her record as a Vanguard is impressive. Several years of constant effort, though it seems that she has discovered what she wanted to accomplish and has turned her focus on that rather than improving overall or becoming more powerful.

"Is that a bad thing?" I asked.

No. A Vanguard is free to choose how they will develop. If they find a level where they are comfortable, there's nothing stopping them from staying there.

I jumped up and fired my jetpack thrusters, propelling me into the air and past Emoscythe just as she reached the top of the building and rolled onto her feet on the rooftop. I landed next to her and glanced around for any trouble that might be waiting for us.

"Straight to the wall?" I asked.

"We don't need to rush back. Not if a detour might mean more dead xenos or living civilians." Emoscythe pointed toward New Montreal proper, the city acting as a landmark that was impossible to miss.

I glanced at the map again. We weren't too far from a few spots that were darker orange. A few blocks at most. "Myalis, can you plot a course over the worst areas while heading back to the gap? I can drop some ordnance from above to thin out the worst of the wave while we pass."

"Not a bad idea," Emoscythe said. "Artillery won't strike so close to the city and the wall. The tremors from it and the shrapnel from any big explosion could damage the parts of the city we're trying to safeguard."

Myalis drew a line across the map that zigzagged a bit on its way back to the gap. "Thanks," I said. "You got a copy of that?" I asked Emoscythe. At her nod, I gestured ahead. "Well, then, let's go."

"While we're going, we'll continue that talk about your image."

"Really?" I asked. "In the middle of a war zone?"

"You don't seem the type who sits on her laurels and has long discussions about style and public perception," she said. She wasn't wrong, but it still felt like this wasn't the place for it. "So, why the cat theme?"

"I'm not the one who named herself Stray Cat," I said. "Longbow gave me that name."

"Oh. I named him, actually."

I paused. "Wait, really?"

"That was several years ago," she explained.

"How long have you been a samurai for?" I asked.

"Ten years in a few months," she said. "So, you seem to have really leaned into the theme. I've seen some examples of your armors. It does seem to fit in with your stealth specialization, which is handy. People think of cats as quiet, nocturnal hunters, so the association is easy to make there."

I had a hard time keeping up with what she was saying, mostly because I couldn't stop thinking about how long she'd been a samurai. That made her something of a veteran. Which also made her scary.

And here she was, talking about cat memes while jogging next to me on a rooftop.

CHAPTER FIFTY-TWO

CONTACT

The first samurai—or the one who was the first reported, at least—was forty-two-year-old Alfred Prickleback.

He assisted in a local incursion when the governments of the world were still utterly confused as to what was occurring, and he successfully repelled what we now know to be one of the weakest incursions on record.

He turned himself in to the authorities afterward, claiming to have suffered a psychotic break because he kept hearing voices in his head.

—Vanguards, A History, 2034

"Contact," Emoscythe drawled.

Usually, when someone spotted a massive group of aliens they put a bit of oomph into their words, maybe a bit of excitement. Emoscythe said "Contact" with all of the enthusiasm that I'd expect from a secretary saying "Next."

The street below was filled to the brim with aliens. Surprisingly, though, they weren't charging around like mad dogs in a kibble factory. I moved closer to the edge of the roof, stealth systems on so that I'd be just a little harder to notice. Emoscythe was still a few steps back, but I guessed she had some way of seeing over the edge.

"That's a lot of them," I said. I squinted at the crowded street. Lots of model threes; some model ones resting here and there; the usual mix of fours and fives, because everyone needed tentacles and tanks in their lives.

What concerned me more was what I couldn't see. The aliens were crowding around the opening to a parking garage. This wasn't so much a street as it was a cul-de-sac with access to a couple of parking spaces for landbound vehicles. One of the buildings across from us was a twenty-floor parking lot, for hovercars and normal cars.

"Why aren't they moving?" I asked.

"They're protecting something," she said. "You'll see this kind of behavior sometimes, next to a hive."

"You think they have a hive down there?" I asked.

"Right now? No, it's a little too early for that. I think we'd have noticed a hive if it were here before this wave started up. The buildings around here are pretty tall, few street-facing stores, so not many cameras, and the road is narrow. I think this might be a spot where the Antithesis are setting up a fresh hive."

"Oh, great," I said. "So, bomb the entire street until there's nothing left but ashes, and then salt the earth behind us?"

"That's an option," she said. "I have the impression that there might be something else going on here. They're too docile for being so close to so much action. At the very least they should be scavenging for biomass."

I pulled back from the edge. "Then what?" I asked.

"I'll go down and check," she said. "We can continue talking after that."

"I'm not letting you go down there on your own," I said. "That'd be irresponsible."

She shrugged. "It's fine either way. I mostly fight close to whatever I'm killing. Can you do overwatch? Snipe them from afar?"

"I . . . can't, no," I admitted. "My aim's kind of trash."

"You know, there are things you can do to fix that. Practice, for one. But there are brain mods and body mods to help with your accuracy." She grabbed her two kama, the blades snapping back into the sticks, and pressed the bases of them together to form a longer stick. Something clicked within, and a three-foot-long blade snicked out of the end. It now looked like she had a sword with a really long handle.

"I know," I said. "I'm not sure if I really want more shit jammed into my head."

Emoscythe shrugged. "That's fair. And entirely up to you. Your meat-sack, your choice. But if you can't do something well, then I'd suggest working hard to find a way around that. I imagine that's why you use bombs over bullets?"

"Bombs don't need to be aimed," I said.

She nodded. Then she walked off the side of the roof.

I gasped and threw myself forward to catch her, but she was long gone by the time my hand reached out and caught air.

I saw her falling, arms out and legs together. Her clothes flapped in the wind in the three or so long seconds it took for her to reach the ground.

Then she landed goth-boots first on the head of a model five.

The big tanky alien exploded as both feet rammed its skull into the ground. Boots and ground proved tougher than skull, and bits of alien brain goop poured out across the ground.

The other aliens, of course, noticed.

Emoscythe stepped forward as if she hadn't just gone from terminal velocity to no velocity in a blink. One hand swiped to the side with her long-handled sword, a couple of model threes slumping back with bisected spines, while her other hand reached to the small of her back and pulled out an object that writhed and snapped, reconfiguring itself into a handgun. Or maybe it would have been more appropriate to call it a hand cannon; it was nearly as big as my Bullcat but clearly meant to be held in one hand.

The gun fired, and with that, Emoscythe was sent flying through the air by the recoil.

I blinked. That didn't seem physically possible. No matter how little she weighed, there was no way a gunshot could send her flying.

Emoscythe didn't seem to give a shit about my interpretation of physics. She just flipped through the air, sword reaching out to almost delicately separate the heads of a few aliens from their torsos.

"Well, shit," I said. Emoscythe fired again, a loud booming report that echoed off the tight walls, and again, she flew off in another direction while the aliens in the direction of the blast were ripped apart.

I shouldered my gun, then hopped off the rooftop.

Halfway down, just as my stomach was considering relocating to my throat, my jump-jets fired and my fall turned into a slightly gentler tumble. I landed with a heavy thump, asphalt cracking underfoot even as my armor absorbed the impact.

A model three turned my way, obviously confused.

I put the confusion out of its mind with some buckshot.

"Need help?" I asked.

"No. I'm used to death," Emoscythe said. She kicked a model five into the air, and then while it was at the apex of its arc, she cut it in half with a swipe of her sword so fast even my cybernetic eye only caught a blur.

I was a bit more conservative with my attacks, only hitting the aliens farthest from Emoscythe and letting my back-mounted guns do a lot of the work. I did summon a few resonators that I flicked around. They started melting up the dead left in Emoscythe's wake.

I felt a little useless as Emoscythe chased down the last alien—an unlucky model four whose tentacles wiggled in a panic before she sliced each one apart with a quick, precise cut from her sword.

"We're done here," Emoscythe said. She flicked her sword to the side, and a spray of blood flew off it and coated the ground. Somehow, she was entirely spotless.

"I guess so," I said. My ears twitched toward the opening to the underground parking lot. "There's more down there."

Emoscythe glanced at the entrance. "Do you want to look into it? We have the time to spare, and it might make everyone's lives easier later to have one fewer hive to deal with."

"I could bring the building down on top of whatever's in there," I said.

"Could be something valuable that's keeping the Antithesis's attention. I'm sorry, I like more precise attacks. Indiscriminate bombing makes me somewhat uncomfortable and goes against my style."

"Nah, it's all good," I said. "Not everything's for everyone."

She nodded. "So, have you considered implementing your stylistic choice with your weaponry? It wouldn't be difficult to do for melee-type weaponry. Claws are a cat's natural weapon, and I imagine that fangs could be arranged."

"Uh, yeah, I had claws. Never really used them, though," I said.

She nodded. "That's interesting. What about the sword?"

I glanced at Void Terminus, hanging off my hip. "What of it?"

"It has a cat charm, which is cute, but it's not really on theme, is it?"

"Why does that matter?" I asked. "Not like my bombs meow before going off."

She frowned. "I suppose it doesn't matter in the short term. My goal is to ensure that every samurai leaves a legacy behind. It's much easier to do that when they have a clear image and style that they adhere to. It can be done for everyman-type samurai too, but then it becomes more about . . . public relations and great accomplishments. Not that you should avoid either one of those. You have the potential to do great things, I think."

"Thanks," I deadpanned.

She sniffed. "Longbow's an example of a samurai with no clear gimmick. He's done well for himself, I think."

"He one of your projects?" I asked.

Emoscythe rolled her eyes. "I don't have projects. I have friends, and a subject I'm passionate about. That's all."

"So you're not going to force me to get fur-covered armor and go 'nya' whenever I speak?"

"No," she said. "I advise and help where I can. I don't push things on people. Like I said, I'm not a bitch."

I do like the idea of making you go "nya," though.

CHAPTER FIFTY-THREE

MOP UP

No no, there's nothing to worry about, Mr. Mayor. We have a dozen samurai guarding the city. I'm certain we'll be able to prevail against any threat against New Montreal.

—Laserjack to the mayor of New Montreal, 2057

"Who goes in first?" I asked with a gesture to the parking garage entrance. It wasn't anything special: a cement ramp leading down to a hip-high barricade that could sink into the ground when someone paid the entrance fee. The lights were off inside, which wasn't surprising; none of the lights I could see outside were on.

Either the area had been cut off or some of that earlier shelling had done a number on the power grid. There were probably hundreds of generators around, but who would install one in a glorified parking lot?

"I'll take point," Emoscythe said. "I'm used to closer-range engagements than you are, I think."

"Fair enough," I said with a sweeping gesture to the hole. She nodded to me and stepped ahead. "Myalis, get me a couple of cats. Maybe with spotlights or something. I'm sure Emoscythe can see in the dark, but I like light more."

Understood.

Emoscythe glanced over her shoulder as two cases thumped lightly onto the ground and a pair of mecha-cats slid out from within. "Drones?" she asked.

"Yeah. They're handy."

She nodded. "They can be, yes. Don't rely on them overly much. They eventually become a point sink when dealing with higher-tier adversaries."

"How's that?" I asked.

"You risk spreading your points out too much. Ten ten-thousand-point drones is impressive. But a single samurai with a hundred thousand points' worth of gear would be a lot more effective. And there's a point falloff with drones. Not when you're right next to them, but when they're operating independently. They're like giving normal people weapons. You'll only receive a fraction of the points. Good for plugging holes in defenses, though, especially if you find a way to keep the drones on theme."

She reached down and patted one of the drones on the head. It was, in most respects, a normal cat mech, but this one had really big eyes that glowed like headlights, and the gun on its back had a light attached to the side of it that turned on with a thump and acted as though a very narrow sun had just risen in the room.

I squinted at a sea of cars and aliens.

Emoscythe and I paused near the base of the ramp and kind of just stared as more and more glowing eyes opened up in the shadows.

The two lights from my drones scanned across the lot, making the many, many aliens they swept across flinch back. I loosened my shoulder, expecting a charge at any moment.

Instead, the aliens started to shift and move around the edges of the room.

"They're going to try to pinch us in," Emoscythe said. "This isn't normal behavior. There's something important to them here."

"Let's take it from them," I said. "They're trampling on our shit, aren't they? It's only fair." It was like an eye for an eye, but I was a vindictive bitch and I'd be taking a lot more than that. "Where do you think they're hiding whatever's so important here?" I asked.

The floor trembled.

It was a subtle thing. Just a slight rumble that I might not have noticed if I hadn't been paying attention to it. If the place had power and the vents were on, then I probably would have missed it entirely. A few puddles of spilled oil, water, and soft drinks shivered as another thump made the floor shift.

I prepared for trouble: gun up, eyes searching the room for whatever was making that noise. It wasn't any of the Antithesis looking at us. The biggest there were a few of the chunkier model fives hanging out in the back.

Then I saw it. One of my mecha-cats turned, its spotlight splashing onto a black wall. The wall moved, and I realized that it was flesh and fur. As the alien turned, I could make out some more details. It was partially hidden behind a delivery van, but the van wasn't nearly big enough to hide all of its bulk. The model turned, six legs bigger around than I was in all of my armor, working in tandem.

Its face was . . . disconcertingly human-looking, with a fixed neck that kept the face tilted toward the ground. Two long mandibles came down from over its shoulders, big and sleek, but with a pair of three-fingered hands at the end and a joint in the middle so that they could flex.

The monster was holding on to a person's body in one hand. It brought it up to its mouth and chomped down with flat, cowlike teeth that nonetheless crunched through bones the same way I might chomp into a chicken nugget.

"What in the fuck is that?" I asked.

"Model twenty-two," Emoscythe said. "That explains why they're all acting as if there's a hive around. There is one."

"That thing's a hive?" I asked, taking in the obvious implication.

She nodded. "Mobile hive. Slower to make fresh aliens than a normal hive, of course, and it can't make anything too large, but it'll be trouble nonetheless. I'm certain there's plenty of biomass around here to keep that thing going. And it could supply a new hive with worker drones and pre-processed biomass."

"So we kill it," I said.

"Obviously, we're here, aren't we? I'll report this to the Family, though. That thing wasn't made here. It snuck in and I can't see any reports of any models in the twenties spotted in the current wave."

Some disturbing possibilities there, but I liked the solution to all of our problems. "Do I bring the whole building down on it, or do I just burn it out?" I asked.

"Let's not crush ourselves," Emoscythe said. She flicked her sword around in a tight circle. "I'll take out the model twenty-two; can you cover me?"

She didn't wait for a reply before she started moving in toward the big alien. That was like the gunshot that set off the race for all the other xenos. They saw her approaching and rushed across the parking lot. I brought my Bullcat up and snapped a shot or two into the nearest, but that wasn't going to be enough.

The mecha-cats I'd deployed opened fire as well even as they backed up toward me, headlight eyes focusing on the nearest of the aliens.

"Myalis, I need B.E.E.S.," I said. "A whole lot of them."

Myalis obliged, and a crateful of B.E.E.S. grenades appeared next to me. I grabbed the first, flicked it on with the same hand, then flung it to the side while glowing micro-drones poured out of the grenade and started to hum through the air.

By the time I'd deployed my sixth grenade, the entire parking garage hummed with the incessant drone of a whole lot of very angry robots.

I ran to catch up to Emoscythe, who was slicing her way through any obstructions on her way to the model twenty-two. The big mobile hive stared placidly as she approached, still chewing on some unfortunate nobody. Then, when she got closer, it started to move.

Emoscythe slipped to the side while pirouetting on one foot as one of the model twenty-two's legs struck out where she'd been.

Her sword casually flicked up, and the model twenty-two blinked dumbly as its foreleg crashed to the ground, gushing green blood.

I picked a few resonators out of the air and tossed them around the room. Their high-pitched whine added to the chaos. I wasn't an expert, but I think the room's enclosed acoustics might have helped the grenades' range.

A model three made it past the circling barrier of B.E.E.S. and leapt at my face. I grabbed it out of the air out of sheer reflex and was surprised that I wasn't bowed over by its weight shoving up against me. I held on to its head with my mechanical hand for a moment, before I squeezed my fingers shut.

Brains splashed all over, as if I'd crushed a fruit, and I made a mental note to be careful if Lucy ever tried to hug me while I was in this suit.

Emoscythe danced under the big alien, sword slicing across its underbelly so that guts and innards spilled out of it. There were long strands in there, like a weird colon, but filled with what were unmistakably model threes the size of large chickens.

Another leg was cut off, and the model twenty-two finally started to panic, legs kicking out and body spinning. It even threw its lunch at Emoscythe, who ducked out of the way.

And then she held her sword by her side, set her feet apart, and glared.

A moment later her stance had changed and her sword was now on her other side, a long blur fading out of the air before her.

The model twenty-two groaned as it split apart down the middle. Behind it, a few of the pillars holding up the parking garage crumbled.

"Let's mop this up," she said. "We should report this too, while we're at it."

CHAPTER FIFTY-FOUR

ESSENTIALLY DOOMED

The entire generation born after the year 2000 was made aware, from a very young age, that they were essentially doomed, and that no one was going to do anything about it.

Climate change continued to be ignored, because fixing that would require too big a change. The government continued to print money to bail out corporations. Inflation jumped to an all-time high while interest plummeted.

That generation saw a tightening of the cycle wherein the middle class got a little poorer and the rich got a little richer.

So for a lot of them, the alien invasion was just a cherry on top.

—Extract from *Memoirs of a Zoomer*, 2047

I glanced around the parking garage, helped by the spotlights from the two mecha-cats that were still lingering by the entrance. "I can't see anything left alive down here," I said. "Except for us, I mean."

Emoscythe nodded, flipped her sword around, then slid it into a loop on her belt. Somehow that loop coated the sword in something that looked like a sheath. "We're done here, I think," she said.

I asked Myalis for a few of those nanomachine grenades that ate Antithesis flesh, and after activating them, I tossed the 'nades to the far ends of the room. The few resonators left were winding down and going quiet at last.

"That should make the area a little less hospitable for them."

"But only here," Emoscythe said. "Ideally we'd go floor-by-floor to ensure that there aren't any more xenos left, but I don't think that would be wise right now. Securing one building that is likely surrounded already isn't going to help anyone. We're going to have to push back the entire wave, then secure this part of the city building by building."

"We're going to have to do that everywhere," I said. "The entire country-side, every little shit-hole town, every cave and forest . . . we're kinda fucked, you know."

"You don't sound depressed about it," Emoscythe said.

I shrugged, but I wasn't sure how well that gesture came across with my bigger armor on. "My entire life I have been acutely aware of just how fucked I am. And I don't mean just the big-picture shit. I've always had bigger, closer problems to worry about than climate change or the economy."

Emoscythe started toward the exit. "You know, I'm the one who's supposed to be all doom and gloom."

"Hey now, there's enough gloom for everyone to share a bit of it." We walked up the exit ramp and I raised my gun and fired point-blank into the side of a model three that was sniffing around. "Back to the wall?"

Emoscythe checked our surroundings, then started walking that way. "Might as well. Something tells me the defenders are going to need all the help they can get."

"Is that 'something' the presence of a model twenty-something? Because I'm pretty sure we aren't supposed to see those for a while."

"It's too early for them. And if a model twenty did show up, then we should have spotted it."

"But we didn't," I pointed out.

Her eyes narrowed. "We didn't. I can think of a few reasons why we might have missed one, and I don't like any of them."

"Sabotage?" I asked.

"Possibly. Or carelessness. Let's not attribute malicious intent to what could simply be idiocy."

Emoscythe bent down into a runner's stance, then took off in a sprint that would put the average doped-up super Olympian to shame. She hit the wall of a building, ran straight up for a bit before gravity took a hold of her, then jumped off and flipped to the next building over. She ping-ponged her way up onto the rooftops while I watched. It was pretty impressive, the kind of shit I'd expect to see in one of those exaggeratedly over-the-top Japanese games.

I shook my head and jetted my way up to the rooftop. "Myalis, can you have all the cats in the region head over to the blockade?"

Certainly. Though a number of them have since been destroyed.

That was unfortunate, but not too surprising. The city was still being shelled; there were loud explosions in the distance, and as I looked back east and toward the outer edges, I could hardly make out the horizon from all the smoke climbing into the air from some two dozen or more fires.

The other direction wasn't so dire.

The wall had continued to expand even as the wave approached. I counted two more segments on the nearest section. Those were maybe ten meters wide, quite a bit taller, though not much. The gap in the wall was still massive, but there were people there.

"Let's move out," Emoscythe said. "I think the Family's about to ask that everyone out here head back to the barricade."

"So there's no point in being out here?"

"It's more likely that we can do more good over there," she said. "We're force multipliers. Out here, we're only multiplying ourselves. Over there, where the wave needs to break, that's where we can be the most useful. If that barrier doesn't hold, we'll have aliens inside New Montreal. It'll be hard to defend the city while hives are growing inside it."

I swallowed. I had plenty of reasons not to want the alien fucks inside my home.

We ran across the rooftops on our way to the gap. Every so often I'd glance down to the street. There were even odds of there being nothing at all or an entire mass of aliens down there. I dropped some acid bombs as a gift to any alien we crossed.

There was a massive split between the outer city and New Montreal. An entire area, maybe a hundred meters wide, where every building had been demolished. I didn't know who was going to shoulder the cost for that. The heaps of crushed concrete, rebar, and furniture were pushed back, some of it filling in the holes where basements would have been, but the rest of the debris had been built into a wall.

Past that was a second temporary wall, or rather, a dozen of them pressed up against each other. Sandbags in one spot, large metal barricades a few meters down, then farther off, movable cement barriers.

The reason for the mishmash of different styles was pretty obvious. Behind those walls were the people responsible for taking care of them. I counted seven PMC groups and what might have been an all-volunteer group of militia.

The gear was wildly different. One group had exo-suits and heavy machine guns. They had tanks parked behind purpose-built barriers with forward-facing spikes. Next to them, civilians with cheap headphones and rifles were shoring up a wall of sandbags.

It was a fucking mess.

I took note of the heaps of dead aliens around the first wall of debris. It was an effective mess . . . maybe.

Emoscythe took a running jump off the top of the building we were on and rolled to a landing below. I respected gravity a bit more and took my time descending with my jump-jets, landing with a crunch a few steps behind her.

"You think the Family will be telling us where to deploy?" I asked.

"Likely," she said. "It won't be hard to see which area needs the most assistance regardless."

That made an uncomfortable amount of sense.

I noticed a lot of guns from a lot of groups turning our way, but most were clever enough to aim elsewhere as soon as they noticed that we were human. It wouldn't be hard to guess that we were samurai, I imagined.

Emoscythe looked like a pretty plain tech-goth kind of girl, the sort of person who had no business walking out of a section of city entirely overrun by aliens without so much as a blemish on her black lipstick, and I was wearing power armor with cat ears.

We ran across the no-man's-land, around the corpses of the few aliens who had made it deeper in, and over craters left behind in the dirt and mud. Someone had been using explosives all across the area. I couldn't really blame them either.

Emoscythe jumped over one of the cement barriers, then slowed to a stop on the other side. I climbed over it with a bit less grace. Almost as soon as she stopped, a man in full combat dress ran up to us. "Ma'am," he said with a sharp salute. "Glad to see you here. We could really use the help."

"How bad is it?" I asked.

He turned toward me and snapped the same crisp salute. I didn't know which PMC he was part of; the symbol on his chest read *Bear*, but I wasn't sure if that was the company or his group. "Things have been positive so far, ma'am. We pushed back the last wave, but they broke through in four places. We had to relocate some of the rear lines to prevent the breach from going in too deep."

I looked past him and to the rear line he was talking about. The front had barricades of one sort or another, with the few odd tank or machine gun emplacements here and there. Then there was the space where the wall would be. Workers were pouring cement and machines were digging out holes even as we spoke.

Past that was a second line of barricades. That one had a lot more armor: tanks, properly big ones, with temporary towers that had gun emplacements on them. A few AA trucks were parked here and there, guns aiming skyward.

"You getting paid more to be up here?" I asked.

"Combat pay and a half," he said.

"Right." Well, I wasn't going to get paid like that, so I might as well make the best of it. "Tell me where the breaches happened. I'll try to shore up those spots."

CHAPTER FIFTY-FIVE

THE CALM BEFORE

Rural living has become a thing of the distant past, but you can recapture some of that essence today by joining one of our Stabiloos Prime Trailer Parks!

Find comfort and easy living next to like-minded and like-classed people in one of our permanent temporary housing units!

—Stabiloos housing ad, 2034

"I'm going to split off for a moment," Emoscythe said. She extended a hand my way for a shake. "It was nice meeting you properly. If you ever need image help, give me a call. If you're looking for a reason to live, then maybe call someone else."

"Uh, yeah, sure," I said. I took her hand in mine and shook, careful not to squish her with my armor. My gauntlets basically eclipsed her hands in armored steel, and I worried I'd hear a crunch. Nothing of the sort happened, though.

She was a more experienced samurai. Maybe her arms were all cybernetic. Or maybe she was a remote-controlled meat puppet the entire time. It was impossible to tell without asking, and asking felt like a faux pas. It was like asking a girl if she was wearing a wig.

"Keep an ear open for updates from the Family. Knowing Laserjack, he's going to want everyone in particular spots until the wall's entirely closed up. Your choice whether you listen or not," Emoscythe said. She waved me goodbye, then headed out. A couple of PMCs jogged over to her and started trailing after her like dogs after someone with a bagful of treats.

I watched her go for a moment before turning around and facing the suburbs the aliens were gleefully taking over. "How long until the next wave?" I asked.

It was meant for Myalis, but the Bear-PMC next to me took it to mean I was asking him. "We predict that the next wave will be ready within the hour. We're expecting a much bigger one tonight."

"Right, they'll have all day to replenish themselves, especially if we're here defending the city and not fucking over their hives." I looked up and down the length of the defenses. The edges were going to pinch in eventually.

The crews working on the wall were laying down another section of it. Ten fewer meters of space that the aliens could easily cross. I imagined that they were doing the same on the far end.

"How quickly are they adding wall segments in?" I asked.

"About one every twenty to thirty minutes," he said. "They have to slow down whenever enough xenos approach the wall."

I nodded along. "How long do we have left, then? Assuming that no aliens bother us?"

"One point two kilometers left, ma'am," he said. "Segments are ten meters each."

I cursed silently. More math. I worked it out, though. Sixty hours if they only did one side. Half that if they came in from both sides. "How's it going to take so damned long? We've covered the rest of the city in a day and a half."

"Ah, I think for the rest of the city they had a lot more than two crews working at once."

That made a heap of sense. I checked on the Family's map thing to see how things were going. The city map was predictably a red mess of alien sightings and confirmed locations. The pins for other samurai were all either behind the fortifications or moving back already. Gomorrah was about three hundred meters north of my position. I glanced up but couldn't see her past the tanks and temporary towers and moving troops. I couldn't even use the smoke in the air to tell where she was, there was so much of it.

I got a text the moment I closed the map. From Laserjack, of all people.

Laserjack: *To: all Samurai currently defending New Montreal—RE: city defense. We are assembling a defensive position within the gap on the eastern side of the city. For best results, please move to the following locations at your earliest convenience. See attached.*

Jolly Monarch: *Moving to position.*

Emoscythe Mordeath Noir: *Very well.*

Gomorrah: *Understood.*

Sam-o Ray: *No problem, bro.*

I paused for a moment, then with a roll of my eyes I sent my own reply.

Stray Cat: *I guess.*

I opened the map again and noticed a few squarish sections added to the gap; each one had a samurai's name over it, and if I lingered my attention on any one of them, more information would pop up: which PMC or militia group was located there, who to contact to get in touch with them.

I wasn't too far from where I was supposed to be. A bit farther north. Maybe two hundred meters from the wall. Gomorrah was stationed to my north, and there was a small slice just below mine. It was maybe half the size of either my or Gomorrah's chunks.

Hovering over it didn't tell me much. *New Samurai, Temp Designation: Farm Boy.*

"All right," I said to the PMC officer. "I've got a place to be. Keep safe."

"Yes, ma'am, glad to serve," he said with another salute.

I walked on past him, then looked at the path I'd have to walk. It was filled with people moving back and forth and a lot of vehicles and barricades.

Sighing, I moved to the side and out past the barricades. No one was using the no-man's-land to move around, so there wasn't anyone in my way. "Are there mines around here?" I asked.

There aren't any, no. The Family's policy is to avoid that kind of ordnance next to an actively defended area. The reasoning seems to be that other explosives might launch a mine over the barricade and toward the defenders.

I chuckled. "That's horrific. Bet the policy was only updated after some poor unlucky fuck got to meet his maker early."

It happened three times over the course of six years before the policy was changed. The report I'm finding indicates that a remote-detonated claymore was launched from an area-denial zone and into the turret hatch of an anti-air vehicle, killing the entire crew.

"Well, fuck," I said.

I walked over to my spot of the gap, then continued on to the far end to get an idea of how big a spot they wanted me to cover. It wasn't a small gap. I had maybe fifty meters to cover. Three groups were gathered up, with barricades pushing up against the edge of the no-man's-land.

Two were unfamiliar mercenary groups; the third, in the middle of the other two, was a group of militia. The District Ninety-Two Gunners. They were stacking sandbags still, with a few guys plopped down behind a pair of big machine guns.

All of the civilians were wearing leather jackets with cheap bulletproof vests under. Half of them were ruining their Mohawks with ear protection, which clashed with all of the neon cyberware they had.

Were they a militia or a street gang that had mobilized?

I decided that I didn't care.

I planted a boot on the edge of a barricade, then pulled myself up and over. While I was up there, I glanced at the city where the aliens would be coming from. We had a bit of room between us and the wall of rubble. It wasn't piled so high that I couldn't see past it, standing as I was atop the barricade.

Turning, I noted that both PMC outfits had set up some towers to get a better view. Dull green things that looked like those scaffolds construction workers set up next to homes sometimes, only with more armor plating on the upper half and a proper roof and mounts for guns.

"All right," I muttered. "Myalis, I think we're going to mine the shit out of no-man's-land. I'm thinking stuff that won't be lethal if it flies back in our faces. Resonators are my go-to option here. Maybe we can get some of those acid bombs up in the air? Spray down anything that tries to run at us."

Did you want to place the mines yourself?

I considered it. That would be time-consuming. I could probably order some of the PMCs or militia types to do it, but . . . "No, too risky. Can I get a couple of mecha-cats to do it?"

Certainly. Adding that kind of mechanism to your drones is entirely possible.

"Right, let's do that, then. I'm sure you can figure out a good grid system for the mines. Maybe we can mix in a few others. I'm thinking garrotes right after the rubble wall over there. Turn any fucks that get past the wall into mincemeat the moment they're over. Some of those zero-kelvin bombs too, in case something big bursts past the wall."

Noted. Do you want me to preload the mine-layer drones with that kind of ordnance?

"Please and thank you," I said.

Myalis summoned a trio of cat drones for me. They were a bit smaller than usual, with a back-mounted arm and backpacks that were clearly full of explosive goodies.

The cats ran off into the no-man's-land and, as one, started digging with their front paws like giant kitties in a litter box.

"Right, I'm going to go meet this unnamed samurai. Maybe say hi to Gomorrah before the fun starts. Don't need her burning my mines out by accident."

CHAPTER FIFTY-SIX

WAIT FOR IT

One of the more interesting facets of modern class stratification is a person's relationship with advertising.

Lowbrow advertising, designed to appeal to the poorer masses, is loud, brash, in-your-face, and not afraid of using gore and sex to draw attention to a product.

Highbrow advertising is quiet and discreet and can often be missed entirely.

The reason for this distinction is simple, and it has little to do with class and taste.

The richer you become, the less advertising you will see. Ads will be swept away by subscriptions and expensive ad-blockers. Which means that any ads that don't want to offend those people unused to seeing any ads at all must be discreet and careful enough to slip by those expensive filters.

—Marketing Con, streamed online conference, 2031

"Yo," I said, one hand rising lazily to wave.

Gomorrah nodded. "Hello," she said.

We were on two sides of a hip-high fence one of the PMC groups had put up between their section of the defenses and another group's. It just so happened that the fence split off the section I was responsible for from Gomorrah's.

"New armor?" she asked.

I nodded. "Yeah, a building fell on me. New arm, new armor. You know how it is."

I couldn't see her face, but I could tell she was concerned. Something about the way she shifted just a little. "Are you all right?"

"Oh, yeah, no, the arm I lost was my cybernetic one, so it didn't actually hurt. My flesh-arm's still there. At least for now. The new one can vibrate, so maybe Lucy will insist that I replace all of my limbs, you know?"

Gomorrah sighed. "If you're making crude jokes, then you can't be that badly hurt."

I grinned right back. "What about you? Have fun burning the xenos?"

She nodded once. "Yes. Yes, I did. I never really went all-out with a flamethrower in such a crowded city before. I . . . I didn't know how satisfying it would be to see entire blocks light up, with little aliens running out of the fire already near death. It was . . . beautiful, in a way. Purifying."

My grin became a little fixed, and I'm pretty sure I noticed some of the PMCs who had been sticking around backing off. I'd overheard some of them boasting between each other that they were lucky that they had the pyro-nun on their side while the competition had to deal with me. I think they were reconsidering.

"So, how are we going to fry the fucks who come over here?" I asked. "I've been deploying mines. Or those mecha-cats over there have."

"I think that as long as we put enough pressure on it, the wave will buckle around the points with more resistance and focus in on any spot where there's less," Gomorrah said. "I'll be out on the front, cooking anything that gets too close. You won't have to worry about this flank."

I nodded along, then glanced to the other side. Gomorrah was on my left, if I was facing the now-ruined city. Which left the unnamed samurai to my right. Their sliver was relatively thin, which probably meant that the Family didn't expect them to be able to take on a bigger burden.

"I'll go see the new kid, talk to them a little and find out what they can do."

"You're not so old yourself," Gomorrah said.

"You're not wrong, but then look me in the eyes and tell me I can't handle myself."

She nodded. "You can handle yourself," she said. "You watch my flank and I'll watch yours. Same as usual?"

I nodded right back, then extended a fist to her. She stared at it for a moment before bumping hers against mine. "You got it. By the way, want my cats to dig a few surprises ahead of your chunk of the wall?"

"I wouldn't mind, as long as whatever bomb you bury there won't impact my own abilities."

"They shouldn't," I said, thinking over what my mine-layer cats were setting down. "If you feel like burning some aliens that get past the mines on my side, don't hold yourself back on my account. I've got more points than I know what to do with right now."

"Thank you," Gomorrah said.

"Oh, by the way, how'd the jetpack work out?" I asked before I turned away.

"Fun. Very fun, actually. Terrible as a weapon. It's hard to aim at something below and behind you. But the additional mobility is a godsend."

"Cool!" I said. "See you in a bit, gonna bother the new kid."

She nodded. "I'll whip the PMCs on my side into shape. They don't seem overly keen on working together, and that's bothering me."

I crossed the area I was designated to defend. Walking across it on foot gave me a good idea of how much room I was dealing with, which was . . . more than I'd like, actually. I figured I wasn't a terrible fighter. A shit shot, sure, but I could blow up xenos along with the best of them.

That worked best when I had the drop on the aliens and when I could prepare the area before they arrived. This would be different in a way that I wasn't really suited to.

I had a few ideas in mind, though. "Hey, Myalis, I was thinking. My gimmick is blowing shit up, but I think I'm going to need to be in the thick of it this time. Do you think we could get some mortars going? Like that AA gun but for bombs?"

Yes. Something of the sort could very easily be arranged.

The two PMC companies and the District Ninety-Two Gunners were set up to deliver a lot of lead downrange. We had a few light tanks parked behind sandbag walls and some trucks with big guns at the rear too for AA duty. I don't think we were lacking in forward and direct firepower.

So maybe I could help to thin out the wave before it hit. I'd bet any artillery that Myalis set up would be far more accurate than the fuckwits who bombed the building I was in earlier. Mortars would work for the short-medium range just over the debris wall. We could even support other parts of the gap if they needed it.

I reached the far right end of my section and hopped up and onto a cement barricade. A pair of PMCs on the other side jumped. They were some of the better-equipped PMCs I'd seen so far: lots of fancy armor that covered everything and high-tech guns that looked almost samurai-tier. "Yo," I said.

"Ma'am," one of the two replied with a quick salute. "Can we help you?"

"Yeah, heard there was a new kid around here. I'm guarding everything on this side of this wall here. Wanted to make sure my flank was safe, you know?" I lightly kicked the edge of the wall I was standing on.

"Thank you, ma'am, we'd appreciate the help," he said.

That was telling.

"Mr. Davis is by the CO's tent," the PMC said with a gesture toward the back. "I can escort you."

"I know how to walk on my own, but thanks," I said. I jumped down, landing with a slight bend of my knees. After shutting off my helmet mic, I spoke to Myalis. "What can you dig up on Davis?"

It's considered a faux pas to assist a Vanguard in spying on another. Though the line between basic information and spying is rather clear. Jimothy Davis is a twenty-two-year-old New Montreal native.

Jimothy.

Holy shit, did his momma not love him? I shook my head. "Thanks. That actually helps a bit."

The CO's tent was less a tent and more a prefab building with tin walls and sandbags all around. The interior had a few desks with techs at them and a pair of people who stood out like sore thumbs. One had to be the commander. A short, older woman who had more wrinkles on her face than shits to give. She eyed me, but didn't protest me coming in.

Next to her was who I assumed to be Jimothy Davis, the new samurai kid (who was a few years older than me, but that didn't matter). Tall, bean-pole of a guy, with dirty jeans and a flannel button-up under a vest that looked bulletproof. He had a cowboy hat on, one that was glowing with RGB, and of course the spurs on his boots glowed too.

He had a rifle slung over a shoulder, but it didn't look like anything special. Just Grandpa's peashooter.

"Yo," I said while extending a hand to him. "You're Temporary Designation Farm Boy?"

Jimothy smiled ruefully and shook my hand. "Ah, that's what they're callin' me?" he asked. "Didn't think that'd be my, ah, samurai name, ya know? Sorry, I don't know yours."

"I'm Stray Cat," I said. "Just Cat between friends. As for the name, I think usually what happens is that one samurai will name another."

"That means my name's now Temporary Designation Farm Boy?" he asked with a chuckle.

I shook my head. "We can think of something better than that, I'm sure."

He adjusted his hat, raising it up to sweep his hair back before putting the hat back on. "Yeah, I know, Enyries, I'm making nice."

I blinked. Did he just talk to his AI?

Wow . . . so I did look crazy when I did it.

"So, want to talk shop before we get overrun by flesh-eating nasties?"

CHAPTER FIFTY-SEVEN

BEFORE THE STORM

Times change, weapons change, but the fundamentals don't.

You have no idea how hard it is to armor someone up so that a piece of metal moving really fast can't kill them. In the eternal arms race between projectile and armor, the projectile has one hell of a lead.

We keep that race going. This year we introduce civilian-grade Class Seven armor. Able to stop even a DMR round dead in its tracks. We also introduced a new nine-point-five-oh-millimeter AP round that can brush through Class Seven like it's tissue paper.

—Mestle Arms and Childcare Division head, 2039

"You know, I'd appreciate any advice you can give," Jimothy said. He rubbed at his chin, where there was a bit of stubble. Not enough to be like . . . hot-guy-on-a-poster stubble. He looked more like someone who needed to shave. Then again, I wasn't really keen on facial hair.

"How long have you been a samurai?" I asked. It couldn't be too long if he didn't have a name. Then again, Gomorrah had gone around without one for a bit.

Jimothy shrugged. "About . . . four hours now? Five? I don't know, the day's been pretty busy."

"Huh," I said.

"Yup. Was back home, minding my own, when some monsters roamed over. I lived by Hitchen's Brooke, out to the east of here. Nice little community. Anyway, I thought we were right done for when the aliens started showing up in the morning."

"You decided to stay there?" I asked.

"We were packing still. We decided to move as a big group. Smart thing to do, you know? More people means more protection, but also more chances of getting help if something goes wrong. But it also means that we were slow. Couple of retirees over there, you know? Not the fastest tools in the shed."

I wasn't sure if that was how the expression went, but I didn't have the credentials to second-guess him. "Yeah, fair. So you took a stand or something?"

"Mm-hmm, with my great-grandpa's Mosin. Took out a few beasties. Then this nasty tentacled fuck, pardon my French, showed up. Ate nearly every round I had. Grabbed me by the leg, and I only got out of there because I got a knife in my pocket. It did let the others get to safety."

"You're a brave one," I said.

He chuckled. "Didn't you have to do the same?"

"Well, no, I only had to kill two of them."

"Just two? You got off easy."

"I only had one arm at the time, and a piece of pipe," I said, defending myself.

He grinned. "Now that makes for a better story."

I patted him on the shoulder. "It's not all about the story. Just getting the job done, keeping your folks safe."

"I don't know about that. This pretty samurai lady showed up a bit after. She . . . gosh, she was something else." Jimothy was blushing a bit, which was . . . something, all right. "We got to talking. Well, she talked and I shut my trap and listened. She said that having a good and proper image is one of the most important things you can do as a samurai, to get recognized easily. She didn't wanna name me, though."

I frowned. "Wait, was that Emoscythe?"

"Miss Emoscythe Mordeath Noir, yes," he said. The way he spoke her name made it sound like something fancier than it was.

"Right, yeah, she'd say something like that. Anyway, my advice isn't about image, all right? Just shoot the enemy dead, then kill the next one. Keep yourself safe too, I guess. Maybe buy a helmet so that people don't think you're insane when you're talking to your AI."

"Ah, that's a good idea, I guess," he said. "Don't know how I'll incorporate a helmet into my look, though."

"Life finds a way," I said. "Or your AI can, at any rate. If you want to play into the gimmick . . . I guess big guns and woodcraft stuff. Knowing how to track and find hives will be damned important in the next bit."

He nodded. "I've gone hunting before. I'm a fair shot too."

We both paused as the ground shook. One of the nearby buildings decided to give up the ghost and collapsed. Fortunately there were a few buildings between it and us, so the dust cloud went up instead of out.

"We're going to need to get into position. So, you shoot things well?"

"I try," he said. "Might get a thing or two to help my aim."

That sounded like a waste of points to me. "Get a bigger gun too," I said, thinking of the rifle Grasshopper had.

"I'm rather keen on keeping this one. Do you think that's all right?"

I blinked. "I guess? Maybe you can get your AI to modify it a bit? Adding sights doesn't make it a new gun, right?"

"I guess not."

"And switching out a part or two can't hurt either. It can be one of those . . . ship-of-Theseus things. Besides, bullets are half the reason guns are good at killing things, right? The gun's only the delivery method. Try firing black-hole grenades or something out of that thing."

Jimothy blinked. "I hadn't thought of that. Enyries is saying that it's a workable idea. Don't have many points yet, though."

"You'll earn plenty," I said. I glanced toward the city. Something was happening. There was a distant rumble, and I noticed most of the PMCs around us starting to move with a bit more alacrity. Whatever break we had was over. "Get to somewhere you can shoot from. And stay alive. You can't try to date the cute goth girl if you've been eaten."

Jimothy grinned sheepishly. "Sure thing. Maybe once we're done here you can give me advice on how to talk to girls, yeah?" He waved, then ran off to join some PMCs while gesturing to one of their lookout towers.

Did . . . I not count as a cute girl? What, just because I was wearing a metric ton of armor? It had boob-plates!

Grumbling to myself, and deciding that I'd commiserate with Lucy later—because she'd think it was funny, if nothing else—I returned to the center of the area I was meant to protect. "All right, Myalis, we need mortars. I'm thinking six or so of them? In a rough line. We can load them up with something that goes boom in a big way. Oh, maybe some sort of frag rounds? Really punch holes into the bastards."

There are a multitude of flavors of fragmentation rounds. Though, seeing as how you'll likely want to avoid collateral, perhaps proximity-detonated macro-fragmentation shells?

"Sounds hot. And we have plenty of points to spend," I said. More explosions sounded out, from behind and before the gap. I glanced back and spotted a few artillery barrages starting to open up. The arcs they were firing in were landing shells only a few hundred meters deeper into the outer city.

How close was the wave?

Six mortar systems, coming right up.

Six light thumps sounded around me, and I jumped back as six boxes, as big as I was—armor and all—appeared next to me. Then twelve more thumps sounded and a gaggle of mecha-cats unfolded themselves and ran around so that there were two per box.

The cats grabbed on to little handles and lifted the boxes up, then started to move across the area.

They'll set up the mortars. Each team has twenty rounds already, though you'll want to replenish those eventually.

"Can we auto-buy new rounds as they're depleted?" I asked.

That is certainly an option. Do you wish to?

"As long as it doesn't break the bank."

The nearest cats opened up their case, which unfolded into hydraulic legs and a long tube with a case next to it and a bunch of measuring doo-dads and what I suspected were recoil tubes to absorb any impact when they fired. These were less mortars and more small artillery pieces, I realized.

A bunch of PMCs and militia folks were staring as one of the cats opened the breach, loaded in a shell, then hopped onto two legs and started to turn a little adjustment wheel to point the barrel skyward.

"Nothing to see here, folks," I said. "Just some robotic cats about to do some weird shit." That was mostly aimed at the one guy who was very clearly filming with the augmentation covering an eye.

Cat, you might want to direct your attention to the Family's map.

I frowned and did just that.

There was a lot of red. More than even the initial wave had. "What the fuck."

It seems as though this second attempt will be somewhat more numerous than the first. More diffused too. Expect to see an increase in higher-ranked Antithesis.

"Shit," I said. Suddenly, I felt like maybe a few mines and some mortars wasn't going to be enough.

I saw Gomorrah running to the front, and within a half second, I was doing the same. We needed to break this wave, or else the streets of New Montreal, of my home, would be flooded with alien filth. Again.

CHAPTER FIFTY-EIGHT

CRACKSHOT COWBOY

A silent movement began over the turn of the century. It fought back against the increasingly extreme nature of religious belief.

The movement suffered from one glaring flaw, though. It assumed that the religious cared about the tenets of their own religion when acting.

Nothing could be further from the truth.

—Atheists Anonymous, 2029

"You guys had better be ready," I shouted. "Shit's about to hit the fan!"

Shit wasn't so much about to hit the fan as it was about to grab the fan, drag it into an alley, then beat it black and blue.

Or something like that. I wasn't an expert on analogies, and honestly, my mind was on other things.

I moved up to the front of the line and looked out across the no-alien's-land between us and the incoming wave. It was a decently sized field, but it wasn't nearly as big as I would have wished. A model three could really scramble when they wanted to. It would take one . . . maybe ten seconds to cross the space at a dead sprint. Plenty of time for a single one to be gunned down, but what if there were hundreds of them?

My grip tightened on my Bullcat. Behind me, the mortars clunked as shells were loaded into them. The militia folks and PMCs were breathing harder, as if they'd already started running around even though nothing had happened yet. I heard leather creaking around handles and the clinking of loose ammo in boxes as they were repositioned for easier access. A few soldiers pulled their mags out and checked them before resetting.

"Safeties off!" someone called from behind me.

The not-yet-a-battlefield became surprisingly silent.

A ping from my augs almost made me jump out of my skin. "Fuck," I muttered as I checked who was calling. Gomorrah. "Hey?"

"Cat. I was thinking we should keep in contact. This might not be easy," she said.

"All right, makes sense. Want to bring our local farm boy in on the call? He seems a nice enough sort. New, though. Might be good to keep an eye out on him."

"That's not a bad idea," Gomorrah agreed.

I nodded. "Myalis, think you can find his aug number? Or can you ping right off his AI?"

I think I can manage that much. One moment . . . adding him to the call.

"Um, hello?" Jimothy's voice asked over the line.

"Hey," I said. "Jimothy, Gomorrah the pyromaniacal nun. Gomorrah, Jimothy the cowboy with a big rifle and a thing for cute girls with attitude."

"Hello," Gomorrah said. "It's a pleasure. We're going to stay in contact with each other, in case we need assistance. I'd love to speak some more, but I think our time is running short."

"That's all right. Pleasure to meet you too, Miss Gomorrah. You just holler if there's anything at all I can do for you. Not that I suspect you'll be the one needing help here."

I grinned. It was nice when everyone was getting along so well. Maybe all the world needed to put aside their differences was the threat of impending and immediate doom. Not that that had worked well before.

I was about to try to make some small talk when I caught motion in the corner of my eye. Something was moving into the no-alien's-zone, but from our side. Something big.

Way off on the other side of Gomorrah's section of the defenses, a large machine thumped into the divide. It was taller than a semi-trailer from front to rear and nearly as bulky: a huge four-legged machine made of white plates over a core of armored steel. The machine stomped into the middle of the gap, then stood there, huge and imposing.

My head whipped around as a second, this one black, moved into the gap farther down.

The horse's sides opened up and barrels poked out of the gaps. It was a mobile gun platform, of sorts.

"Is that one of Jolly Monarch's?" I asked.

"The map says so," Gomorrah said. "They're his Rook drones."

"Fucking hell," I muttered. "How much does one of those cost?"

"More than either of us can afford right now," Gomorrah said.

I shook my head. Maybe things weren't going to go that poorly after all.

I heard a sharp intake of breath over the coms. "I see one. Big, ugly bastard, coming in from above," Jimothy said. I turned to the front and squinted into the sky. There was a big flock coming, but at the center of it was one big motherfucker whose wingspan dwarfed all the others.

"Got a shot?" I asked.

"Let's see," he said.

A loud crack sounded. A faint gray blur was left painted across the air. It met the head of what was probably a model eleven and splattered it. The huge flying alien flipped through the air before crashing onto the roof of a distant building.

"Nice shot," I said. "Maybe we should name you the Crackshot Cowboy."

"Crackshot Cowboy," he repeats. "Yeah, I like that. Going to need to live up to it, but I think I can manage that."

"I think the time for chatter's just about over," Gomorrah said. The dust of the incoming wave was growing closer. I could feel a faint rumble beneath my feet. The people around me, those who were so inclined, started to pray. It was a faint murmur in the background. These were the same people who repelled a wave earlier today; I imagined that the cowards had been weeded out already.

Then, between one blink and the next, the wave crested over the wall of debris.

I froze. Not for a long time, but for a moment I was almost entirely overwhelmed.

There were so many of them. They came pouring over the edge like an angry tsunami of plant flesh and teeth and claws. Stones and cement were rammed aside as bigger aliens shoved their way over, the smaller aliens slipping around their legs and over their backs. The air filled with more and more fliers, darting ahead of the wave on a straight path to our barricades.

And then some poor alien fuck stepped on one of my mines.

Aliens were flung into the air in shredded hunks of meat. Mortars thumped, and a half second later they detonated over the barricade, sending clouds of zipping shrapnel down onto the horde.

"Fire!" someone ordered.

The air filled with the roaring scream of a thousand guns. Muzzle flashes lit up the gap ahead of us with a constant yellow-white strobe, each flash marking the death of another alien.

The wave turned into a deadly tumble, bodies flopping over each other on the downslope of the debris barrier. Still, they kept coming.

I brought my gun up and started to fire too. I wasn't even aiming. It didn't matter. Sure, there were a few dozen meters between us and the aliens, but there were so many of the fucks that it was impossible to miss.

Acid rained down on their ranks. Bigger artillery pieces boomed behind us. Tanks fired salvos of high-explosive shells into the aliens' ranks.

I flinched as something's leg splattered against the side of my head, blown clean across the area.

Gomorrah joined the carnage with a wave of fire to counter the wave of flesh rushing at her. Even with my armor I could feel the warmth as a long blue line of liquid fire screamed over to the aliens and started to melt them.

It wasn't enough.

They kept coming. Teeth and claws and angry eyes but never, never any sounds. Lasers lanced out from somewhere behind the line, swatting model ones out of the air so that they crashed around us as smoking corpses.

I saw the first casualty on our side of the wall.

A PMC woman ran to one of the machine-gun nests with a big box of ammo. A piece of some alien flipped through the air. A forelimb. Its clawed arm brained her in the side of the head and she went down, just like that.

"Fuck this," I said. "Myalis, I need something to kill lots of shit, really fast."

Before Myalis could reply, I flinched down and half hid behind one of the cement walls as debris was tossed into the air ahead. A big lumbering fuck stumbled through the new gap, and then it started to run across the empty space, faster than anything that had come before.

Everyone in the area turned their focus to the monster. No matter how tough it might have been, there was only so much it could do against the amount of armor-penetrating rounds being flung at it.

That moment of distraction, though, was all the wave needed to get over the barrier in droves. Now they were spreading out, slipping behind cover and rushing out; we couldn't just focus on those on the very top of the wall anymore.

"Oh shit," I muttered.

CHAPTER FIFTY-NINE

NYANPALM

The most annoying thing to deal with is people who come around and call you an idiot, they say that you're stupid, sometimes even to your face.

Some might even be right. The actions you took in the moment were wrong, or less than optimal. But oftentimes, they themselves aren't any smarter. They're just critical without self-reflection behind the criticism.

Is it any wonder that so many of us just plain refuse to deal with any sort of fan?

—Sprocket Rocket, livestreamed interview, 2043

I fired until my gun clicked empty, then lowered it while Myalis reloaded. My back-mounted railguns were spitting at any of the bigger aliens to pop their heads over the edge. It wasn't going to be enough.

The wave of aliens was acting like a real wave. It would push out, Antithesis racing to us, almost running over each other to reach the barricade. Then we'd mow them all down and the wave would be shoved back, dead falling down to the ground until nothing was alive from where we stood to the crest of the wall of debris. The next wave would surge right after, so many bodies coming over the hillside that even our collective firepower wasn't enough to push them back.

Gomorrah was actually having a better time of it. Some of her fire stuck to the ground after she sprayed it. A glance to the side and I got to see a model three rush across burning soil, its flesh melted, and by the time it was halfway to Gomorrah's position the alien had fallen, limbs unable to work and body alight.

"Gomorrah," I said.

"Yes?" came her terse reply. She was under about as much stress as the rest of us. It didn't lead to much chattiness.

"I'm borrowing your gimmick," I said. "Fire's working where bullets aren't." Our goal wasn't to kill as many aliens as possible. It was to hold.

You can work together with another Vanguard, combining known catalogs to purchase something new. It's not done too frequently, though, as there's little overlap. In this case, there might be some.

"That would have been nice to know earlier," I muttered. "You hear that, Gom?"

"Yes? What's your idea? Firebombs?"

"I was thinking of something more maneuverable," I said. I paused as my mortars fired again, the booms drowning out all else. The shells went off and sprayed the next wave with enough shrapnel that the wave crumbled early and only needed to be mopped up. "I think I can equip some cat drones with flame throwers. We could spread them out, maybe. Push in?"

Gomorrah took a second to reply. "Atyacus says it's doable. I'm not sure about the name of them, though. Sounds like another one of your stupid puns."

I balked. I didn't make stupid puns, ever. That was . . . "Myalis, what did you call these things?"

Seeing as they're basically an upgraded version of a Lynx-type mechanized cat drone, I suggested that we call them Flamethrower Equipped Lynx Intelligent Nyanpalm Edition, or F.E.L.I.N.E. for short.

"What the fuck is nyanpalm?" I asked.

I need to give credit to Atyacus for the composition of that one. It's essentially a viscous kerosene mixture with small capsules mixed into it. Those contain white phosphorus and thermite. The capsules will stick to any surface, and then as the coating around them melts, they'll activate the chemicals within.

"That sounds horrific," I said.

Inventing new war crimes is one of Atyacus's favorite hobbies. I personally prefer wordplay.

I shook my head, but I didn't have time to mess around. "You okay with this, Gomorrah?" I asked.

"It's fine," she said. "We can send them in waves. There are plenty of points to reap here, so go nuts."

I nodded. This entire thing would actually be a lot easier if we could use really powerful explosives. But that wouldn't work in this situation. "Myalis, let's get a dozen of those F.E.L.I.N.E.s out here."

Understood. A dozen F.E.L.I.N.E.s incoming.

I didn't have time to stare at the boxes appearing around me as another wave started to rush us down. I planted my feet in place and opened up at the front of the line. Buckshot tore through the ranks of model threes, and then I turned my focus to the sky, where a swarm of smaller model ones were flocking.

A glance to the side revealed one of the F.E.L.I.N.E.s jumping up onto the barricade. It was a big, sleek cat, with an armored body that opened up at the shoulders where a pair of nozzles were poking out. The cat hissed, and then twin beams of fire roared out ahead of it and sprayed the nearest edge of the wave.

The flames couldn't quite reach the top of the debris wall, but that was fine. The splatter at the end was going everywhere and lighting up the corpses the previous waves had left behind.

The other cats joined in, a few of them jumping on to the barricade, then over to the other side.

"Right, I'm going to push," I said. I stepped onto the barricade, then over it. "Can you get those mortar teams firing faster?"

Certainly.

"Cat, why are you pushing?" Gomorrah asked.

I paused. "I don't know. Feels like the right thing to do?" I said.

"At least let me come with you. You'll just get yourself killed," Gomorrah said.

"I think I'll stay back here. Not one to cower much, but I'm not equipped for that kinda fighting yet," Jimothy said.

I checked back to the tower where he was holding up, then gave him a thumbs-up. "No problem. Watch the skies for us, would you?"

"Will do, ma'am."

Gomorrah vaulted over the hip-high wall covering her section, then casually walked through the flames, only pausing when an alien jumped out from under a corpse. She met it boot-first, shoved it into the ground, then leveled her flamethrower at it and cooked it.

"You ready?" I asked as I joined her more or less between our two sections. I pumped my shotgun, the satisfying *krack-clung* and humming glow making me feel a bit better about . . . I wasn't sure if this counted as a plan or not.

"Let's just peek over the wall, light some of them on fire, then back off if things get too hot for us to handle," Gomorrah suggested.

I nodded once. "Sure," I agreed.

As we started to stomp our way to the front, another wave crested the barricade. My new F.E.L.I.N.E. units met it with hissing flames. Even with my armor on, I could feel the temperature rising. Sweat was matting my hair down against my forehead.

I stepped up the wall of debris, finding purchase carefully between mangled corpses. Behind us, the PMCs and volunteer defenders were stuttering their fire, only taking out the aliens that weren't too close to us. Those that came close to Gomorrah and me didn't stay a problem for long.

With my free hand gripping the edge of the wall, I pulled myself up, then looked over.

"Mother of fuck," I swore.

The city was full. Every street was crammed with aliens. Most of the space was taken up by smaller ones, but larger models stood out everywhere I cared to look, a lot of them in their tens. I swore again when I saw some of those big artillery models near the back, and a few of those mobile hive units were shoving their way into the sides of buildings.

They'd have the entire place infested in a matter of hours. How long before they started making fresh aliens right here?

There was some breathing room just on the other side of the wall, space where the aliens gathered up for another charge.

"We're going to need bigger guns," I said. "And a lot more fire."

I winced as shells came raining out of the sky. Explosions burst apart against the sides of buildings, and some went off right on top of the Antithesis. Huge balls of fire and churned-up alien chunks.

The gaps they left were filled long before the dust cleared.

I glanced back. Our barrier in the gap didn't look so strong compared to what was coming. What were a few thousand people and a hundred-odd tanks going to do against so goddamn many warm aliens?

"Myalis, you know that second tier with the exotic explosives? I think we're going to need it pretty bad right about now."

"We're going to need more than a few bombs and some fire," Gomorrah said.

We both ducked as one of those big artillery models flung a spinning wheel our way. It rumbled past, used the edge of the debris wall as a ramp, then exploded a few meters from the edge of the barricade.

"We'll figure something out," I said. I think I might have sounded more confident than I felt. "That, or we'll die trying."

CHAPTER SIXTY

THE ENEMY WON'T DO AS YOU WISH

Vanguard have got something of a knack for things. Look, I ain't saying they're magic or anything, they're not Jedi or wizards or whatever. They just . . . you know, they've got a little something that makes them stand out.

You think them brain-AI just picks any git off the street?

—Curbside interview, 2034

"Myalis," I said.

Yes, Catherine?

Myalis's voice was, as ever, calm, which was reassuring when I was so very close to having my ass eaten by a whole heap of aliens, and not in the fun way. "I need a way to kill all these fucks real fast-like," I said.

How much collateral damage are you willing to accept responsibility for?

I bit my lip at the question. That was terrifying to hear. "However much would result in the most dead aliens," I said.

That's easily arrangeable. Your main issue isn't killing the Antithesis. You've proven quite capable at that. Your problem is getting your explosive payload delivered to the Antithesis. Honestly, you might be best served with a slight change in tactics. I have some options for short- to midrange weapons that can weaken or outright kill most weaker Antithesis.

"What kind of weapon?" I asked.

The High Intermittency Sound Scrambler is a device you can fit onto your armor that would act as your resonators do, though with greatly increased efficiency.

"You just want to give me something called a H.I.S.S. while I'm distracted, don't you?"

That may play a role in my proposal. Though it would be effective in keeping you alive.

"Fine, but I want to kill things more than I want to stay alive. Not that I don't want to . . . fuck, you know what I meant."

A box appeared by my feet, and I popped it open. It was relatively small, with a badgelike device within it that was round, maybe the size of my palm, and with a few concentric circles within a metal case.

Just apply that to your armor. It will stick on and mesh with your stealth systems. The system will activate on its own when an Antithesis is near. The sound might interrupt any attempts at stealth, though.

I smacked the H.I.S.S. against my upper chest, and it stayed on with a clunk. Then I poked my head back up and over the debris wall.

The renewed shelling had pushed the nearest part of the swarm back, but they were starting to run up toward us again, gaining speed as they covered more ground, leapt over craters, and slipped around the roasting bodies of other dead aliens.

Gomorrah found a chunk of cement to stand on, then raised herself up so that her torso poked out above the debris. She shifted her flamethrower around so that it clunked onto a broken piece of fallen masonry, and then she started to spray.

The liquid fire splashed out ahead of her, and Gomorrah slowly swept her flamethrower from left to right.

The horde didn't stop just because the ground had turned into a flaming mess. They charged through the smoke and paid for it an instant later as they cooked alive. The bigger models pushed into the fires as well, just as heedless as the smaller, though the more clever among them used the bodies of the fallen as stepping-stones.

"Keep it up!" I shouted. "Myalis, 'nades."

A grenade appeared in the air next to me and I caught it, recognizing it as one of those black-hole bombs. I pulled the pin, then tossed it forward and in an arc that had the bomb going off just as it slipped past the edge of Gomorrah's fire.

We had a slight choke point ahead of us, what with the buildings serving as funnels toward the rest of the city. The roads created long, narrow strips that the Antithesis had to use, and there was little cover for them there.

"Cat," Gomorrah said.

"Yeah?" I asked. I brought my Bullcat up and laid into a model five that was trampling its way through the fire.

"I don't think we're doing any more good here than we would back behind the barricades," Gomorrah said. She flinched back as one of those artillery balls exploded above us and sent pins scattering against the debris.

I glanced ahead, then back across the no-man's-land.

"Fuck," I muttered. "You're right. Can we hold for a minute? Myalis, reload the mine-layer cats and get them back out here. We'll keep the aliens back long enough to have the area trapped for when the next wave arrives, all right?"

"Fine," Gomorrah said.

My favorite nun peeked out over the edge of the wall we were using for cover, then reached to the small of her back and came out with a pistol of all things.

I was about to question why she was about to use that instead of her flamethrower when she whipped around our cover and fired.

I followed the arcing trajectory of the projectile she fired. It glowed, like a flare, and descended right atop the model fifteen that had likely been the bastard flinging spike balls at us. The flare exploded, sending burning motes of something down across the street and onto the model fifteen.

Even from afar, I could tell that whatever those motes were, they were hot as hell. The model fifteen writhed as it burned.

"Nice shot!" I said before slipping out of cover. I fired until my gun clicked empty, then dove back down while it reloaded.

"This doesn't make sense," Gomorrah said.

"What part?"

She gestured ahead of us. "The constant waves. They're wasting bio-mass for nothing. I know the Antithesis aren't too smart sometimes, but this seems wasteful."

I almost dismissed what she said. It was easy and nice to assume that your enemy was a dumbass.

The problem with that was, as a dumbass myself, I knew that underestimating idiots was sometimes a bad idea. "You think they're up to something else?" I asked.

"They might be stalling," Gomorrah proposed.

I shook my head. If they wanted to stall, all they had to do was nothing, and we'd be sitting pretty behind our walls for a bit longer.

Were they going to hit another area and this was a distraction? But no, we'd see them coming. Above? The wall had pretty good AA. And the Family would have noticed huge flocks moving around if they were planning to attack all-out from above.

Which left below.

"Myalis, I've got a hunch," I said.

I'm listening.

"Do we have any sort of ground sensors in the area?"

There are several. Though currently their readings are complicated by the presence of so many heavy vehicles and drones by the walls. Not to mention the combat and explosive use.

"I . . . would it be stupid to ask the Family to check? It's just a hunch."

You are a Vanguard. You were chosen for a multitude of reasons, including your instincts. Your hunches are worth more than others.

"Thanks," I said.

It doesn't mean you're not wrong. Frequently. And humorously.

I chuckled. "You're the kindest," I said.

"Sorry for interrupting," Jimothy said. "But I've got an ounce of experience with ground-related things. If you two are busy I can get something and check on your hunch, Miss Stray Cat."

"That would be appreciated," Gomorrah said. "Go ahead, Crackshot."

"Oh, I think I'm liking the name. Not sure I've earned it yet, though," he said. "Give me just a minute."

Gomorrah glanced my way. "You think they're under us?"

"Has the Family shut down all the connections between New Montreal and this part of the city?" I asked.

According to the Family's reports, yes. Though it is possible some unmarked infrastructure remains.

"Are there any sorts of Antithesis that can dig, then?" I asked.

The Antithesis model eight and eighteen can both dig.

Model eights were those big worm ones that carried food back to the hives. It figured that they could dig; they were worms. I figured a model eighteen was just more of the same.

I heard a shift from behind me: a few screams and a pause in some of the gunfire, though the shooting had died down a little around our section ever since Gomorrah and I moved to the front.

"Oh, hells," Crackshot said.

I spun around. "What is it?" I asked.

Then I saw one of those big tanks sitting by the back tip over onto its side. Then, much to my surprise and everyone else's, the tank was thrown back. Several hundred tons of metal bounced up, flew a dozen paces back, then crashed down.

A moment later, long black limbs started to press out of the ground.

"Misses," Crackshot said. "I think we might be needing you back here."

CHAPTER SIXTY-ONE

GO KILL THE THING

All students at Bartholomew G. Wordstum Elementary School must follow the dress code. That includes:

Dress shirt/blouse (white, logo on breast)

Fitted slacks/skirt no shorter than the knees (black)

Class II bulletproof vest (black)

Lounge jacket (school standard, winter or summer variant)

All students will be provided with new school software for their augmentations at the beginning of the semester.

—Letter to parents of students of
Bartholomew G. Wordstum Elementary School, 2039

I had about a second to come up with an idea of what to do.

That second passed.

"Cat!" Gomorrah shouted. "Go kill that thing."

"Got it!" I said. Then I ran.

The earth shifted and rent, and from the growing hole came a beast whose appearance alone was enough to clutch my heart.

I wasn't a coward or anything, and there were few things that made me nervous or that scared me, but that Antithesis . . . fuck me if it wasn't terrifying.

The Antithesis clambered out of the hole it had made, slabs of cement falling into the growing pit even as dozens of model threes came pouring out of the hole after it.

Its legs were tree trunks; its body was long and covered in thick bones with leathery segments between them. Four legs, and a face like a lamprey-fucked cthulhu. As I ran, eyes on the monster, two long tusks ripped out of the sides of its head. They were bigger than I was, with serrated edges and sharp points.

One of the tanks nearby started to back up, turret turning toward the Antithesis while the big beast was still pulling itself out of the ground.

The tank fired, and I slowed my run down. Was that it? Had I been freaking out for nothing?

The dust cleared, revealing the Antithesis, which was shaking its head to clear out the smoke left behind by the exploding shell. It was injured, a crack in the off-white bone over its sternum and skin ripped through, but it wasn't dead.

"Myalis, what is that?" I asked.

A model twenty-eight, though that is a small specimen of the model.

A small specimen? It was the size of a tanker! The PMCs and militia around the hole turned around. Some opened fire immediately. The smarter ones ran for cover first. I saw two of them get gunned down as a nasty cross-fire started near the back lines.

The model threes were going to be a problem.

"We need to patch that hole," I said.

The model twenty-eight turned, then started to charge with its head lowered. It rammed its tusks into a parked van and lifted it clear off the ground before swinging its head around. The tusks retracted and the van went flying.

"We need to kill that thing," I said. I must have had fire on my mind. "Myalis, need a fire grenade, something long-lasting."

A bomb appeared in the air before me, just at the right height for me to catch it without having to slow down at all. I pulled the pin, then vaulted over the barricades.

Militia people were scurrying around in barely contained panic. Officers were screaming orders out, and I could tell that the other sections were looking our way, wondering what to do.

I flung the grenade Myalis had given me out and ahead as hard as I could. It sailed through the air in a nearly perfect arc, bounced off the head of a model three, then disappeared into the hole. A heartbeat later a dozen red beams flashed out of the opening, some of them spearing into and through the model threes still on the edge of the hole.

That will last for approximately one minute.

Good enough for the moment. I refocused on the model twenty-eight. A lot of others were doing the same, firing into its sides and flanks. The big alien seemed almost confused for a moment before it spotted a group of power-armored PMCs running by. It ran after them, like a hyperactive dog who'd just spotted a juicy squirrel.

I winced as the monster swung its head down and picked one of the men off the ground and into the air, its lamprey mouth crunching down on the soldier.

Now that I was closer, I raised my gun to fire at it, then paused. Plenty of others were doing the same. It wasn't working. The damned thing had tanked a shell to the torso with barely more than a scratch to show for it.

If I couldn't do anything from the outside, then . . . the inside?

My Claw wouldn't go deep enough. For that matter, I'd bet the bastard was nearly as tough inside as it was on the outside. I needed something with more oomph. "Myalis, get me the Claw's bigger, meaner brother," I asked.

Certainly.

New Purchase: Mark VI Claw

Points Reduced from . . . 54,379 to . . . 54,129

Myalis didn't bother with a box. That would have taken seconds I didn't have. Instead a big gun appeared in the air before me. It was squat, with a wide front with a handhold beneath and a curved grip and handguard. No barrel, which in hindsight made sense.

I let my Bullcat drop, the strap hooked to it allowing the gun to dangle by my side as I raised the Claw. A crosshair appeared in my augmented vision, and I placed it atop the big alien. Then I took in a deep breath and pulled the trigger.

There was a faint *clack* and some of the lights on the gun glowed for a moment. A timer circle appeared around the crosshair and filled up until it disappeared.

I moved the crosshair down toward the middle of the alien's body, then fired again.

A moment later, the alien's side where I'd put the first round exploded. Skin and bone and blood gushed out of a hole large enough that I could have crawled into it. Soldiers and PMCs cheered, but I ignored those in favor of firing into the alien again.

A little flesh wound like that wouldn't kill it.

The smarter soldiers opened fire again, this time aiming for the opening in the alien's side, where its tough skin wouldn't be able to absorb as much of the damage we were laying into it.

A second explosion occurred, this one partially swallowed by the alien's side. Then a third, near the flank, which ripped apart enough of the model twenty-eight's hip that the alien stumbled to the side, one of its rear legs only hanging on by a few tatters of skin.

The tanks stationed at the back had turned their attention inward. Fortunately, they weren't firing desperately at the monster. Instead they were taking their time. When one of them fired, the others waited to line up their shot properly.

The model twenty-eight groaned as armor-piercing shells punched holes into its sides.

Coupled with the explosions I was setting off within it, it was only a matter of time before the alien collapsed onto its side. There was enough weight crashing down all at once that I felt it in the soles of my feet.

Well done. That was a difficult opponent.

"Yeah, well, it wasn't just me," I said. I glanced at the hole where the lasers had stopped and more model threes were starting to poke their heads out.

The hole was partially encircled by PMCs now, some of them dragging barricades over, others on overwatch to shoot anything that stood out.

"Can I get a boxful of whatever grenade that was last time?" I asked.

Certainly. They're area-denial explosives that fire lasers. They're called HAIRBALLS.

I shook my head, then grabbed a passing PMC. Myalis's box of HAIR-BALLS appeared by my feet, and I pointed to it. "Bring this to the troops defending that hole. Toss one into the hole every minute."

The man nodded his head, grabbed the case, then ran off toward the hole.

He'd probably follow my instructions. There was the risk that he was greedy, but . . . well, running off with a boxful of explosives was stupid when you didn't know if the person who'd given them to you could detonate them from afar.

"Cat!" Gomorrah called back.

I spun around.

No one was paying attention to the front. At least, no one in our part of the defenses.

The Antithesis knew it. And they abused the fact.

Gomorrah was walking backward across the no-man's-land. Her flame-thrower was spitting fire over what was left of the wall before her.

The tide was pouring over the debris, hundreds of them pushing over each other's flaming corpses to try to reach Gomorrah. When she lit up one group, another would slip into the gap. She was going to be overrun.

"Fuck. Attention to the front!" I shouted. A few people were paying enough attention that the fire ahead redoubled for a moment.

I didn't wait. I fired my new gun, hit a model five that was moving with a limp, then discarded the gun a moment later. It was too slow.

Just as the tide reached Gomorrah, she bent her knees and jumped backward. Fire bloomed out beneath her and she rocketed into the air on a plume of burning thrust.

I let out a relieved sigh. I wouldn't be seeing my friend chewed up just yet.

Still, I didn't think our troubles were over.

CHAPTER SIXTY-TWO

GETTING OUT OF HAND

You can never be too prepared when dealing with an incursion. When on defensive duty, it behooves a commanding officer to spend their entire budget on good equipment. Yes, cutting corners is tempting, but history and statistics have proven that more money is saved by having better equipment than by purchasing and equipping soldiers with poorer equipment.

—The Awe Strikers, CO manual, page 257, 2044 edition

"This is getting out of hand," I shouted over the din of constant gunfire.

The debris barrier had served its purpose; it had slowed down the alien swarm for a good long while.

Now, the wall of crumbled cement was riddled with holes as artillery shots from the Antithesis exploded against the far side and bigger models rammed their way through the debris. The smaller, more nimble aliens just continued to flow over the wall without much issue.

We were burning them. We were shooting them full of holes. We were even outright melting them with acid and resonators. The occasional bomb set off in their midst was chewing through their numbers too. I was tossing everything over to the wall to slow the tide down.

Black-hole bombs could only take so much before they stopped. Zero-kelvin grenades would slow the advance down, but only in pockets. Garrote grenades were great at mulching the smaller Antithesis, but against the more armored ones they would break apart after a few seconds of sustained use.

Gomorrah's flames grew hotter as she switched over to a new gun. Soon the PMCs on her side were inching closer to mine, away from the scorching heat. I think Crackshot Cowboy to my right got some sort of infinite-ammo thing for his gun because he was firing a whole lot faster. He'd need to replace the barrel soon; it was glowing orange, and not from any RGB.

"Christ," Gomorrah said. "This isn't working. We're not going to hold them back forever."

Eventually bigger, stronger models would show up. The barricade we had would fail. Or maybe we'd just run out of bullets. There were vans driving over to the backlines with entire pallets of ammo boxes, but I didn't think that would be enough, even with teams of volunteers reloading magazines that were being run back and forth.

"Myalis, one of those fire-lasers, please," I said. She dropped the grenade into my open palm, and I flung it forward with a grunt. It flew a good long ways before bursting and sniping a dozen aliens with fiery beams of reddish light.

That poked a hole in the alien carpet.

The hole was filled a moment later.

"Fuck me," I swore.

"Yeah, I feel ya," Jimothy said over our shared coms.

I had points to spare. Thousands of them. What I didn't have was time. I was really tempted to start chucking nukes or their equivalents onto the aliens, but I had to worry about collateral damage, which meant using more precise weaponry.

"Go wider," Gomorrah said. "Bigger effects, everyone."

Bigger effects . . . I could do that. "Myalis, I need the mother of all acid bombs. I want to carpet the entire area in alien-melting goop."

That can be arranged. Might I suggest bombs that have highly pressurized compressed space within them? If filled with sufficiently dangerous chemicals you could quite literally flood a large space with your chemical of choice!

"Sounds perfect," I said. "And give me something to shoot it with. I don't want something too dangerous to go off at our feet."

Understood. Delivering.

"Heads up!" I shouted aloud. "Switching guns. Keep up the fire!"

The amount of gunfire redoubled for a moment while I ducked back. A pair of boxes appeared next to me. One long and big enough that I could have stuffed Lucy into it, the other the size of a fat briefcase.

I opened the smaller of the two, revealing two big, egg-shaped objects that were very obviously bombs. They had little fins on the back and black-and-yellow warning stripes around their middle. Each had a cap with a different color. Green and blue.

The green one should be fired first. It's an aerosolized acid-dispersal bomb. Despite its size, the bomb contains point-five tons of hypercompressed gas. The blue bomb contains a connection to what is essentially a massive off-planet vat of liquid acid. It's technically a sulfuric acid, though the exact chemical makeup is somewhat dissimilar to the frequently used acid, and there are several additives.

"Green first, got it," I said. I popped open the second box to reveal a long tube with pads for it to hang on my shoulder and a trigger mechanism at the front. There was a big opening on the side, very conspicuously bomb-shaped. "All right," I said. "I think I've figured this one out already."

Very well done. Place the bomb into the slot, business end pointing forward, then aim and fire. The launch device has no safety, so please be careful.

I picked up the launcher, grabbed the handle, then reached down for the green-topped bomb.

Damn thing was heavier than it looked, by a lot. Still, I managed to load it into its slot. As soon as it was in, the opening closed with a clunk and a few lights on the side of the barrel went green.

I dropped to one knee and aimed down a holographic sight on the side of the barrel. It very conveniently showed me the arc the bomb would take. Tipping the entire thing back, I aimed skyward, then pulled the trigger.

The bomb flew forward with a dull *thwump*, and I felt a slight kickback against my shoulder.

I followed its pretty arc across the sky. Just as it was about to disappear over the debris wall, the bomb whooshed and the air filled with a growing cloud of bright green smoke.

"What's that?" Crackshot asked.

"Acid," I said. "Might want to warn the folks around here to avoid it. I'm going to fire something else at them."

"I'll take care of that," he replied. "Need to let my gun cool down anyway."

"Thank you," I replied. The opening on the launcher's side reappeared, and I picked up the second bomb. The damned thing was heavier than the first.

This time, I aimed a little higher. Another loud thump, a hard shove against my shoulder, and I got to see the bomb fly over and smack a model five atop the head with enough force that I was pretty sure it wasn't going to make it.

No bang this time, though maybe the bomb's noise was swallowed up by the still-growing green cloud.

"Acid! Acid! Masks on!" some sergeant shouted. The PMCs took turns pulling on full-face masks. The militia folks too, though I questioned the quality of the masks I saw them putting on.

The shift meant that for a good few seconds, we weren't firing into the mass of aliens anymore. The Antithesis didn't slow down, but when they came pouring closer, it was clear that the acid was working.

A model three with its eyes leaking down the side of its face jumped onto the barricade, jaws wide open to reveal a mouth with gums that had turned to liquid. A militiaman jammed the butt of his gun into the alien's jaw, and its many teeth tinkled onto the ground before it flopped back onto the other side of the barricade.

More aliens came pouring out of the smoke with their skin melting off. Eyes and lungs seemed to be impacted first. The Antithesis were usually rather quiet, but now they were gasping for breath with liquid rasps.

Having no eyes meant that they weren't as coordinated as usual. Plenty of them were running parallel to the barricade now, and a number of them charged up and rammed the cement walls headfirst, some hard enough that they died then and there.

I noticed some sort of gel-like substance sticking to a lot of them, usually around their legs and on the smaller models, their stomachs and tails and torsos. It was eating through their flesh at an alarming rate.

The gas was slowly dissipating. Or rather, it was spreading itself thin.

"Nice work," Gomorrah said. "It doesn't seem flammable either, which is nice, I suppose."

"I mean, if you want to go all thermobaric on them, go nuts," I said.

"Don't tempt me," Gomorrah said.

Our banter was cut off by a ringing. The Family was calling, and it seemed urgent. I answered, of course, while bringing my Bullcat up to spray at what aliens were making it through the acid cloud.

"Everyone," Laserjack's voice said over the line. "We're almost in the clear. Almost. We have a large number of higher-numbered models coming. Brace yourselves. This is about to get a lot harder. For those of you at the very front . . . thank you. If you would rather back out now, we'll understand."

I think the PMCs and militia got similar messages. A lot of them were clearly listening to something.

And then, just like that, there was a sudden exodus.

I stared as entire squads grabbed their gear and ran back.

"What the hell?" I asked.

"They're retreating," Gomorrah said simply.

"Why? We're winning, aren't we? We can take on a few of the bigger bastards, no problem."

That wasn't quite true. "No problem" was a lie. It would be hard. It would be much harder without the help of nonsamurai.

"Ladies," Jimothy said. "I don't rightly think I'm ready for this part. Going to back up a ways and lay down fire from afar. Good luck, all right?"

I cursed under my breath. Why now, of all times?

"I think I need to make a call," Gomorrah said solemnly.

CHAPTER SIXTY-THREE

BURNING

I miss the good old days. You know, when one game in ten was still single-player, without live-service microtransactions and gacha mechanics. What's the last time a good game came out that wasn't made for mobile?

—4channel forums, 2032

I thought that maybe knowing I was going to die would depress me a bit more than it did.

In reality, all I felt was a little cold.

Lucy would be sad. The kittens too. Some of them, at least.

The acid cloud was slowly dissipating. The wind, fortunately, was pushing it back and away from us. The acidic goop covering the ground wasn't moving, though. A few fallen aliens were sinking into it. Or maybe melting into it would be more appropriate.

The front was quiet for the moment. There was still shooting way off to the side, but it was less active than it had been before.

I glanced over and took note of Jolly Monarch's Rooks, the big mecha still standing guard over the majority of the gap. "I need me one of those," I said as I stared at the bristling array of firepower sticking out of the tower.

You can almost afford one now.

I snorted. "Maybe later." A big walking mech would be pretty fucking cool. I couldn't see any use for it beyond defending this kind of place, but it would be undeniably cool. Myalis—and Lucy—would insist that it look like a giant cat. I could live with that.

I shook my head, clearing my mind a bit. I was supposed to be thinking of my impending demise, not giant robots.

Glancing around, I searched for Gomorrah, then froze up when I couldn't see her. My blood chilled. Had she retreated? A few PMCs were still running back. Others were defying orders and staying by the front. Had Gomorrah decided that she had enough?

Then I spotted her a little ways to the back, standing next to a tank and seemingly unaware that she was in its path.

She was bent over, hunched. Had she been hurt or was she changing out her gear? I jogged toward her, skipping over a barricade that stopped at hip height. I slowed down from a jog to a calmer walk as I came closer.

Gomorrah's mask was off, which was unusual. She had placed her mask atop the tracks of the tank and was looking off in another direction. "I know . . . yes, I know that too," she said. She was frustrated, obviously, and talking to someone. "I don't know, Franny, it's not looking too great down here . . . no, I can't go back. It's my duty, to God and the people behind me. I won't *retreat*. But— Franny, shut up!"

I stopped a ways away. I'd never heard Gomorrah quite so raw before.

She took a deep breath. "I think I love you," she said. "Maybe. I don't . . . I'll talk to you later. No. Bye." She swallowed, then in a lower tone, addressed someone else. "Atyacus, send her to voice mail when she calls, please? Or, no, tell her that I'm busy. Please?"

Gomorrah turned, then froze on seeing me.

I raised my hands in surrender and pretended not to see any wetness or confusion in her eyes.

She slipped her mask on, then cleared her throat. "Ready?" she asked.

"Yeah," I said. "What's the plan?" I wasn't going to push. She sounded conflicted and, yeah, I'd been there once. Confessing was hard. Though, well, maybe I had it easy with Lucy.

Gomorrah stared ahead of us, toward the ruins of the city. "I have a plan. It's a bad one."

"Those are the only plans I take part in," I said.

"Good. Want to toss out more of those acid bombs? We could create a sort of barrier to prevent the horde from reaching the wall, retreating PMCs or no. Then we fly over the acid and nuke the plants back into their constituent atoms."

"That sounds great to me, but I'm pretty sure I'm not allowed to use nukes within . . ." I glanced over my shoulder toward New Montreal. The city towered above and behind me. "About two kilometers from the edge of the city."

"Not nukes, then," Gomorrah said.

I hummed, then flicked through my contacts until I landed on Laser-jack. He replied nearly as soon as I tapped send. "Stray Cat? What's wrong?"

"What's wrong is that it feels like we've been told to sit tight and wait to die. Do I sound like the type of girl who dies? So fuck that. Going to blow shit up, drop some literal acid on the aliens, and generally make myself a nuisance with Gomorrah. We've got stacks of points to burn over here, you know."

There was a second-long pause. "Okay. Try to avoid any attacks that might damage the protected part of the city, or at least the defenses that remain."

"You're real nonchalant about this," I said, pulling out one of my fancy words.

"You're samurai; there's no such thing as hopeless as long as one of us is drawing breath. The horde's been thinned considerably already, and we've moved more heavy equipment around; we could be able to close up the wall within the next two hours. Things aren't as desperate as they seem."

"Oh. Then why tell people to retreat?"

"Because we're going to need people rested. Things are still pretty bad, and they're going to get a whole lot worse. We need to start destroying hives all over. We have dozens of confirmed locations in New Montreal's vicinity alone. Thousands across the continent. We've lost contact with some smaller cities already. Truth is, New Montreal is doing really well right now."

"Well, shit," I said.

"We had a lot of additional troops in the city because of the earlier incursion. A good quarter of Canada's cleanup crews were moved to New Montreal in the last . . . you don't need to know all of this. If you and Gomorrah want to take up the job of wiping out the last of the wave, then go ahead, and thank you."

The line went dead and I shook my head. What a weirdo. "Okay, I guess that counts as enough permission for me. Myalis, any idea what kind of fuckery we'll be dealing with?"

More models in ten-to-twenty range, certainly. Possibly early hive structures.

Gomorrah must have been clued in to what Myalis was saying. "Anything we should worry about if we fly over the area and bomb it from above?"

Atyacus was the one to reply, over the coms, though I suspected that Gomorrah heard her own AI in her head the way I heard Myalis in mine.

After observing the area from several camera emplacements overlooking the city, I have noticed fewer flying models than you would usually find in an incursion of this size. Unfortunately, while I have some hypothesis as to why, I lack sufficient data to make a proper analysis.

Myalis added her own two credits a moment later.

That may change. Model twos and other flying models tend to be lighter than their ground-bound equivalents. Their creation rate within a fully grown hive with sufficient biomass is quite rapid.

"So let's bomb them before the skies become inhospitable," I said. "We're taking the Fury?"

"We could jetpack over, but . . . yes, I'd rather take my car. It'll be safer than just being out there without protection. Though . . . I don't know if you'll fit."

I glanced down at myself and my rather imposing armor. She was probably right; unless I was willing to stuff myself into the back seat sideways, there was no way I'd fit. "I can ditch the armor for now. We'll be mostly safe, right? Or I can hang off the rooftop."

"That sounds incredibly reckless."

"I have jump-jets; if I fall I probably won't die," I pointed out. "Besides, someone needs to drop the bombs. Speaking of which, do you think we should combo things again? Your fire, my weird explosives?"

Gomorrah nodded. "Oh yes, I could genuinely go for that right now."

It was a little weird that Gomorrah could "go for" a massive pyromaniacal streak the same way someone else might "go for" a few drinks, but I wasn't going to poke. My favorite nun needed a bit of a break. If that required lighting entire blocks of aliens on fire, then so be it.

Gomorrah called the Fury over, and we hurried up to wait.

It wasn't entirely lost time, though. We had entire combined catalogs to pore over, picking and choosing the kind of personal hell we were about to unleash upon the aliens who had dared inconvenience us.

It was going to be great!

CHAPTER SIXTY-FOUR

CLIMATE CHANGE VIA MASS DESTRUCTION

The average samurai will do as much good for the environment as harm. They'll occasionally decide to ruin an entire corporation on a whim, often the same corporations responsible for Interlewd Four massive environmental disasters (see: BP 2029), and they might provide the tools, expertise, or simple willingness to fix ecological issues.

By that same token, they will often cause massive disasters while attempting to eliminate their adversaries (see: The Lake Huron Incident 2032).

—Excerpt from "An Environmental Analysis
of the Impact of Out-of-Context Actors," 2036

The Fury spun around in a tight circle as it lowered itself to ground level. A few PMCs glanced our way, but we were doing samurai stuff and they mostly knew to mind their own when two samurai were on the warpath.

Also, they'd probably just witnessed the pair of us kill a thousand-odd aliens each, which I imagined was a decent way of instilling a sort of primal respect in someone.

"Are you going to ditch the armor?" Gomorrah asked.

I thought about it for about a second. "I'd rather not. Think I can ride on the hood?"

"That would be exceptionally stupid, but I won't stop you," Gomorrah said. "Try not to scratch the paint, though." She opened the driver's-side door and slid into the car. I hesitated for a second before raising a leg and climbing onto the hood. The muscle-car-like shape of the Fury was coming in handy since it was all sharp, aggressive angles.

"Right, this'll make it easier to fling bombs off the side," I said. I was feeling . . . dubiously confident in my lack of any sort of plan.

Did you decide what kind of bomb you want to use?

Myalis's question wasn't too terrible. "We'll start with those acid-cloud ones I think, right, Gom?"

"It's not a bad idea," she agreed. "I asked Atyacus for ideas for explosives, since those are generally your area of expertise, and he found something interesting. Heat bombs."

"Heat bombs? Is that an acronym?" I asked.

It could be.

Gomorrah probably didn't hear that last comment. "No. They literally create heat. Lots and lots of heat in a small area. It's not exactly fast-acting, which is probably for the best. We want to burn the aliens away, not blow them up."

"I mean, I pretty explicitly want to blow them up," I pointed out as I tried to find better footing on the hood. This wasn't going to work. "Myalis, I need magnets or something."

"We don't want to send bits of Antithesis flying all over," Gomorrah said. "This will kill everything without sending anything flying. It'll create some wind, of course, and . . . likely burn the entire region down, but no explosions."

Myalis helpfully summoned a pair of foot-shaped pads in a box. I placed them onto the hood, then put my feet over them and they clamped on. Suddenly, my feet were locked in place.

"How hot are we talking here? I don't need numbers, just . . . use something my pea-brain can understand."

"Have you ever used an oven?" Gomorrah asked after a moment's pause.

I glanced back toward her, but the Fury didn't actually have a windshield. "Yeah, sure. I've seen them before."

"What about an air fryer?"

"Uh-huh," I said. They had some in the nicer convenience stores to warm shit up.

"Well, those operate at a couple of hundred degrees at most. But the idea is similar here. Only this device pulls its warmth from the sun."

I gestured vaguely toward the sky. "That sun? The warm ball of fire that we can feel way over here, very, very far away from it?"

Technically, not that sun, no. A much larger, less volatile sun.

"Yes?" Gomorrah said.

"Are we going to explode the entire city?"

"No," she replied. "It's entirely non-explosive. It's pure heat and nothing but heat. No fire, no blast, no shock wave. Just a gentle rise in temperature until we shut off the device remotely."

"How gentle? We do need to kill the fuckers, you know?"

"It'll start at boiling and increase until everything melts or lights on fire. Possibly both. I like the idea. A lot."

"Okay, then," I said, surrendering any objections. Let it never be said that I wasn't a great friend. I was willing to support Gomorrah with her weird kink shit in her time of need, and if that didn't make me a good friend, then nothing would. "Let's melt us some aliens. We should start with the acid bombs, though."

I yelped as the Fury jumped up; my knees almost buckled at the sudden movement, but I managed to not make a complete idiot of myself by spreading my arms out to the sides and locking my knees in place.

The car tilted a bit before sweeping out over the battlefield. "Right, Myalis, acid bombs," I said.

Certainly.

Myalis provided, as she always did. No boxes, probably since we weren't in a position where I could open a box up to use it anyway. I underhanded the bomb to the side and grinned as it exploded with a satisfying *blam* and started to spread a growing cloud of green-tinted gas that quickly swept down onto the no-man's-land and the buildings on the edge of the gap.

Gomorrah moved us to the side where there wasn't as much cover, and I flung out a second bomb, then a third as we moved down the line.

The gas was pooling on the ground below, most of it keeping at about waist height.

The few aliens still trying to run across the gap met with a wall of permeating acidic fog that would burn their flesh off and likely ruin their insides. I just hoped it made the job of the people who remained at the barricades easier.

I was in a decent mood until I noticed the number of PMCs pulling out. Laserjack's shit about them needing to rest was all nice and good, but it didn't stop me from wanting to stomp down there and smack some commanders around while calling them cowards.

I put it off. If I didn't have anything better to do later, then maybe I'd trample over some law and order and blow some sense into whoever was in charge of those PMCs. Or I'd just explode them. I wasn't really homicidal, but things would depend a lot on my mood later.

"Last one?" Gomorrah asked as we swung to the far end of the gap.

"Looks like it," I said. I flicked the last of the gas bombs over the side and watched it sail down toward the ground. It burst apart a dozen meters above and started to spread its payload around. "I can't imagine that shit's good for anyone's health."

It very much isn't. Nor is it necessarily good for the environment.

"Well . . . I didn't think I'd be causing any ecological disasters today, but I guess that's part of fighting the Antithesis, isn't it?"

Don't worry. The impact of a few tons of powerful acids seeping into the water table will be nothing compared to the environmental impact of the exotic weaponry Gomorrah has suggested.

"How very comforting," I muttered.

"Are you ready?" Gomorrah asked.

I nodded, then fixed my center of gravity a little lower to make the flight easier. It wasn't too bad. My feet being pinned to the hood and my armor preventing me from being shifted around too much made the ride . . . almost comfortable. It was like surfing. Only I'd never been surfing before, so I wasn't sure if the comparison actually worked.

"The biggest congregation of aliens is . . . about here," Gomorrah said. We slowed down fairly gently, maybe three kilometers from the wall, just over the edge of the now-ruined city clinging to the edge of New Montreal. "I think we can safely drop the bomb here."

I nodded along. "Want to summon it, or should I?"

Technically, it's me who's summoning it. Also, it's not technically a summon at all.

With a slight *whump* of displaced air, a large boxy machine appeared next to me, then crunched down onto the hood. The Fury tipped to the side until Gomorrah corrected for it. "My paint!" she said.

"Calm down," I shot back as I took in the device. The damned thing was the size of a fridge, with dozens of those vents that could fold open all along the sides. It was all bare steel, thick as hell and unpainted. "You can probably afford three new cars after today. Now how the hell does this work?"

The temperature parameters are set. You just need to drop it down to ground level.

"Does it have a parachute?" I asked.

Yes.

"Oh." I shrugged, then grabbed the device from the sides. "Keep the car even," I said before shutting off the magnets holding me in place. With those off, I was able to lift the boxy machine with a grunt of effort, and then I stomped to the side of the car and, with a hard shove, tossed the bomb off the edge.

A trio of chutes cracked open and the sorta-bomb started to gently fall toward the ground.

"That was easy," I said. Then the Fury started to waver under me and I scrambled to get back to the magnets. "What the hell?"

"I think it's just turbulence," Gomorrah said. "From . . . maybe rising hot air?"

I wasn't an expert, but I was pretty sure that wasn't a good thing.

CHAPTER SIXTY-FIVE

RAINING FRIED CHICKEN

Right, I know you've got a cool gimmick going on, and it is interesting,
but just because you could maybe doesn't mean you should have . . . now,
where exactly did you want me to slot your head?
—Recorded discussion between Dial-Up and Lag, 2049

The . . . I supposed it wasn't technically a bomb—started to show its impact
maybe a minute after it dropped. Gomorrah moved the Fury around so that
we were hovering nearby, overlooking the drop zone.

The ground below was teeming with Antithesis, thousands of them
squirming around and doing their thing. I saw plenty of those worm models moving about while others broke into the homes and shops lining the
streets and pulled out anything biological that they could use.

The heat kept increasing, but it was a slow process.

The first signs that it was working came from the advertisements on the
shops nearest the heat bomb. They fritzed out and failed, colorful screens
and hovering holograms shutting off at random.

Then the paint started to peel on the cars abandoned along the road.
One of them had its battery burst, and a gush of fire roared out from the
bottom of the car, catching a few model threes off guard. Not that it hurt
them much.

I continued to watch as the aliens around the bomb started to back away
from it. A few collapsed, and one eventually caught fire, but the flames
didn't seem to last long.

The heat continued to grow. Cars started to warp, their plastic bodies
melting apart. Posters stuck onto the nearest streetlamp burst into flame. A
few wires snapped, and glass exploded. A mirage started to appear over that
entire part of the city, gray reflections shifting and making it hard to see the
asphalt around the bomb turning liquid.

"Damn," I said as I continued to watch. The bomb just kept going. I
could see where the heat had traveled just by following its impact. The

center, nearest the bomb, had the most damage. One of the apartments next to it lit up from within. I imagined that the furniture inside was more flammable than the concrete exterior of the building was.

A clothing store just half a block down turned into a roaring bonfire as everything within it combusted.

The Antithesis ran, but they weren't running fast enough.

The heat was a perfect tool for killing them: slow-acting enough that they didn't seem to understand they were in danger until their eyes were melting and their flesh was catching fire. Those big worms writhed on the ground, sinking into sticky asphalt. Model ones fell out of the air, wings going bright for the few seconds they burned.

And then the first building collapsed. It was right across the street from the epicenter. A big commercial place, store on the ground, offices above, lots of glass and that sort of modern minimalist design that was so popular.

Glass showered down across the city as the heat pushed on. It created an expanding ring of fire. Somehow, though, there was a circle following the ring where nothing burned but everything melted. I imagined that had something to do with chemicals or some scientific bullshit that I couldn't understand.

"This is working out pretty well," I said.

"I'm enjoying it," Gomorrah said.

I snorted. Of course she was. The pyromaniac was probably getting off on this.

"Is the heat going to stop before it causes trouble?" I asked.

"It's already causing plenty of trouble. And I mean that in the sense that this is probably not good for the environment. But yes, we can shut it off before it reaches the gap."

I nodded. Then that was that. An entirely anti-climactic end to this whole ordeal. At least, it was from up in the air. I grinned as I watched the aliens scramble while melting. It must have been a whole lot different for them.

"We should head ba—" I began.

Then the Fury rocked hard to one side and I swung my arms out to keep standing while the car shifted crazily beneath me.

The car spun, losing altitude even as its engine roared to compensate. The loss didn't last long; soon we were leveling off and even rising back up a little. I checked the skies, looking for whatever had caused that.

It wasn't hard to find.

A huge bird was flapping its way higher, a big black thing that was covered in fine scales. A model eleven? "You okay?" I asked Gomorrah as I pulled my Bullcat from the small of my back. I wasn't sure I could nail the bird too easily, but I might be able to annoy it. I deployed my shoulder-mounted rails and let them track the alien through the air.

"Shit," Gomorrah said.

I braced. She wouldn't swear for no reason.

My railguns both fired a split second before the Fury was thrown to the side. I cursed as I felt one foot come loose from the magnet holding it in place. Then I swore some more as I was left hanging perpendicular to the ground while the Fury was on its side.

We were losing altitude, at least until Gomorrah snapped the car back straight.

That sudden motion threw me back.

"Fucking fuck!" I screamed as I stepped back and into open air, dropping off the hood.

I wasn't entirely screwed. My jetpacks all went off at once, righting me in the air just in time for me to crash onto a rooftop with a hard jerk. My teeth clacked together and I was jarred pretty hard, but that was the worst of it.

I glanced up and saw a model eleven clinging to the side of the Fury. "This thing's going to scratch my paint!" Gomorrah complained.

It had done worse than that already. One of the engines that allowed the car to float was ripped apart. I half expected sparks and some fire from the broken parts, but there wasn't anything of the sort.

Guns unfolded from the Fury. First a pair of missiles raced out of the car and rammed into the model eleven above just as it was circling around. Then a flamethrower spun around and hosed the alien clinging on to the car's side until it let go and flew off.

"Where are you?" Gomorrah asked.

"Rooftop, below," I said. I glanced around, then worked my jaw. I found all the missing flying models I was wondering about earlier. Thousands of model ones were taking to the air, slipping out of windows and filling the sky along with dozens of model elevens. Had they been keeping low this entire time?

A lot of them were heading my way, and from the heat I was feeling through my armor, it wasn't hard to guess why. "Ah, shit, Gomorrah head back a bit. Keep an eye on the skies."

"All right," Gomorrah said. "Do you think you can find a place where I can pick you up?"

"We'll find something," I said as I started to run across the rooftop. I reached the edge and leapt off. My jump-jets hissed and I sailed over the gap between two buildings. I caught sight of a nearly empty street below. Just a few lingering aliens who glanced up to watch me slip by.

"Cat," Gomorrah said. "They're heading our way."

The Fury rumbled past above me. The car usually purred as it moved, but now that sound was replaced by a nasty grinding that I imagined meant the car would need fixing.

I landed, still running, and spun around to see behind me.

Gomorrah wasn't wrong. There was a whole flock of birds darting my way, enough to darken the skies. My railguns fired, pinning two model elevens in midflight. Only one of them had the common courtesy to die. I raised my Bullcat and held down the trigger.

Didn't need to aim when there were so many targets.

The birds weren't my only problem, though. I stared as the roof of the building I'd been on caught fire.

Catherine, I would suggest moving with a little more alacrity. You're right on the edge of the temperature range your armor can handle.

"Oh, come on," I said as I spun around and took off sprinting.

I didn't want to get eaten. I wanted to get cooked alive inside my armor even less. I shot over the gap between the building I was on and the next without even needing the boost from my jump-jets. My feet crunched on a gravel-covered rooftop, and I turned hard to avoid a solar-panel setup in the middle.

It was getting warmer.

A black blur zipped past my head and I ducked, even if it was too late.

The model one that had missed me crashed onto the ground next to me, dead, its feathers entirely cooked off.

More of the little models started to plummet down around me, raining out of the sky.

"Gomorrah! It's raining fried chicken here and I'm not liking it!"

"I found a spot," she said, and the Fury lowered itself a few buildings down.

I just hoped I'd make it.

CHAPTER SIXTY-SIX

MOVE FASTER

Q: Can you choose not to be a samurai?

A: Yes and no. A Vanguard can choose to retire at any time. But removing the AI-brain interface is impossible without harming the user.

Q: What are some common mistakes samurai make at the beginning?

A: Either over- or underspending on points. Points are a resource, and learning how to manage them is part of learning how to be an effective Vanguard.

Q: How do AI view each other?

A: Usually with cameras.

Q: Since AI are artificial, are you afraid of dying?

A: Humans are nothing more than lucky collections of stardust. Are you?

—Curated Q&A with Lyvalis,
one of the first Protector AI on Earth, 2026

I had three gaps to clear to get to Gomorrah. That meant two rooftops, then the one the Fury was currently parked on and waiting for me.

The roof I was on at that very moment, though, was melting. It was covered in those cheap flat panes of nonreflective solar paneling. The surface layer of plastic was turning sticky, and each step I took crunched as I broke through the solar cells.

My shoulder-mounted guns spun around and fired behind me. I couldn't see what they were targeting, but I could hear it as bodies thumped onto the ground around me.

You need to move faster if you wish to make it.

"Trying," I grunted between gasps. I wanted to be a little more snarky than that, but snark required breath, and I was all out of that. The air was so hot and muggy that even with my suit doing what it could to regulate things, it was still a chore to breathe.

I came to the first gap and lunged.

My jump-jets fired off, and I sailed across a narrow street, one leg coming up before me to make it so that I'd land at a sprint.

At that moment I had hanging in the air, I glanced down between the buildings. It was interesting to see what the mounting heat was doing. Some windows had burst open and raging fires were burning within, with tongues of flame kissing the sides of the buildings.

Other spots looked nearly intact. Maybe the glass they had was tougher, or less likely to melt. Hundreds of AC units were melting out of the windows they were jammed into. Most were made of cheap plastic, which could very much not endure the kind of heat we were putting on them.

My foot met the next building and I kind of bounced a bit before I really took off. With a grunt, I vaulted over some vents and then cursed as I had to go around an animated billboard that was fritzing out hard.

A couple of model ones slammed into the side of the board, cracking it more than it already was.

My guns thumped again, and I shifted as I noticed the recoil pushing me forward just a bit. "What're you shooting?"

You currently have several large flying models chasing after you.

"Oh," I said. I ducked to the other side of the billboard, hopefully cutting off their line of sight for a bit.

I paused, just to take a breath, but then one of those tower-AC units a few meters away from me burst into flames. A pipe burst on its side and it pissed fire all over. That was my signal to keep going.

My armor was warming up a whole lot. Maybe too much, even.

Disabling passive stealth systems. We don't need to hide your body warmth, and I doubt anyone nearby will be able to hear your suit's cooling systems in your current predicament.

I could hear my suit humming faintly. It didn't feel any cooler, though. I grimaced and continued running. The next gap was easy. I cleared it with barely any help from the jump-jets. The next roof had a damned garden on it.

Probably one of those stupid attempts to "greenify" things. The plants within were smoldering already. They didn't even catch fire so much as they desiccated on the spot.

I jumped again, fired a little spurt from my jump-jets, and used that to hop onto the top of the nearest greenhouse. It wasn't designed to carry my weight, and the metal being so hot that it was likely going soft didn't help any.

Still, it collapsed in such a way that I fell in the right direction and was able to cartwheel my arms around to stay even.

"Graceful," Gomorrah commented.

If I hadn't been out of breath I would have had something snippy to tell her.

I ran to the edge of the roof and jumped. All I had to do was land, then grab on to the Fury. We'd move away, and I'd be nice and safe. Maybe I could reposition myself on it farther out. Or jump out of my armor and into the car itself once we were in a safer spot.

With a grunt, I brought my legs up to clear the edge of the roof.

Catherine! Above!

My railguns fired, but it was just a little too late. My H.I.S.S. activated with a scream, a last-second warning that I didn't know how to heed.

Something heavy smacked into me. It wasn't a direct blow, but it knocked me out of my gentle arc and into a wild tumble. I saw a large feathered body falling past me, feathers on fire and body writhing.

I crashed into and through a window—one of those with bars across the bottom to keep pigeons away—and then I landed on my side in someone's living room. The couch was smoking, the TV was melting, and the carpet was on fire.

"Fuck!" I swore.

"Cat!" Gomorrah said. I heard a whine from above; the Fury was moving. Was she leaving?

I jumped to my feet, then winced. My armor's interior wasn't warm, it was scalding. I could feel the warmth pressing in on me.

Use your points, please.

"Ice! A bomb."

A bomb appeared and immediately exploded in front of me. It sent a wave of white fumes racing across the room with a hiss, and I felt my armor cooling off even as frost covered the walls and floor. But only for a moment. The frost was melting off faster than it could spread.

A whine just outside had me turning to see the Fury lowering itself down, passenger side facing me. The door opened and Gomorrah gestured. "Come on!"

I didn't need to be told twice. I grabbed the edge of the window, placed a boot on the bottom sill, then jumped across the gap.

I didn't fit through the door. Well, most of me didn't fit. My upper body did, and the moment my feet swung out below I kicked up and found something to push my foot against on the car's undercarriage while I held on to the passenger-side seat.

The AC was blasting, I noted idly. Gomorrah used a few non-church-approved words and we shot upward. The car sounded . . . off. I didn't know nearly enough about hovercars to say how, but I knew that a few things were busted with the Fury.

"That was stupid," Gomorrah said.

"I agree," I replied as I kept hugging the seat. "Do you need to drive so fast?"

"Yes."

My railguns deployed, but not to shoot. Instead they reached up and pressed against the ceiling, giving me a couple more points of contact. That was only somewhat reassuring. Gomorrah was flying as if I weren't hanging halfway out of her car, and while I trusted her, my trust in her was only a bit stronger than my grip on the seat.

"Gom?" I asked.

"One second," she said.

We started to slow down, and then I felt us dropping. There was a thumping from nearby, guns going off, and I winced as the Fury shook. An explosion had gone off nearby.

"Just the wall's anti-air," she said.

"Thanks. I was dying to know," I said. "I'm slipping, Gomorrah."

"It's fine," she said.

"I think it's very not fine!"

The car stopped and Gomorrah looked down at me. "Cat."

"What?"

"You can let go. We're hovering over the wall. It's a meter below us."

I paused, considered her words, then lowered my leg until it hit something solid. "Oh," I said before I lowered my other foot and then let go of the seat. I was standing right atop the wall, just a couple of sections away from the gap, which had closed noticeably since we'd left.

Stepping back, I left room for Gomorrah to lower the Fury. Gomorrah stepped out of her car, then walked to the back and inspected the area where the steel was crumpled in. "That's . . . that's not going to be easy to fix," she said.

I shook my head, then patted her on the shoulder. "It's all right. We made plenty of points today; I'm sure all the squished parts are replaceable."

"Might as well replace the whole car," she muttered. Then she rose up and shrugged. "Guess I'll be getting a new one."

"Wow. That was fast."

"That was pragmatic," she said before turning back toward where we'd come from.

The city was melting. Even from the wall I could trace the growing circle of destruction just from the spreading cloud of smoke on the inner edge and the crumbling buildings in the center. "We made a bit of a mess, haven't we?"

"Hmm. Not as satisfying as actual fire," she said.

CHAPTER SIXTY-SEVEN

BECOMING STRONG ENOUGH

How many samurai does it take to defend a city from an incursion?

At least one.

They just need to be strong enough.

> —Menage à Trois, after the Quebec City incursion of 2035

"Now what?" I asked as I looked over the burning city.

Gomorrah shifted. "I've turned off the heat generator. It'll still continue to spread for a while, but without an actual source, it should all slow down."

I nodded along. That was probably for the best. Didn't want to see New Montreal burning down because we'd left the oven on. "I'm guessing all of this is going to have some sort of consequence, isn't it?"

"Maybe," Gomorrah said. "We might have found an effective way of wiping a hive out without too many horrible side effects."

A shorter skyscraper nearer to the middle of the burn twisted, its frame, which was visible since the rest had burned off, bent like cooked spaghetti noodles under the weight of the rest of the building. The rumble didn't even reach us atop the wall. "I'm not so sure about the lack of side effects," I said.

"Oh, we've destroyed half a city, sure, but there's no nuclear radiation, no dangerous biological matter, and once the area cools down in . . . a week or two, then it'll technically be inhabitable again. They might even be able to scrape off the melted metal and recycle some of it."

I hummed. "Yeah, I get it. Can't imagine deploying this kind of thing all over the place, though. Plus most hives will be underground, right?"

Actually, hives in noncontested areas tend to be out in the open. Or nearly so. It makes it easier for Antithesis drones to bring materials to the hive and for the hive itself to collect energy from the sun and wind.

"So, what, we burn the planet, root out the buried hives afterward?" I asked.

Only if you wish to make the planet's environment entirely uninhabitable. The heat bomb you deployed today will increase the planetwide temperature for the day by a sizable fraction of a percent. Not enough to be directly dangerous, but if repeated it may be enough to destabilize the planetary ecology.

"We'll try not to burn the entire planet," Gomorrah said. It didn't sound as reassuring as she hoped, not coming from an obvious pyromaniac. "Why are you looking at me like that?"

"I'm wearing a helmet, you can't see my expression," I pointed out.

"I can read body language," she said. "And no, I won't burn down the planet just to see a big fire. I live on this planet. My favorite things are here. It's also, possibly, against my religion. Though I suppose that part's up to debate."

"Let's not," I said. There were few things I wanted less than that kind of debate. "So . . . now what?"

Gomorrah sighed. "We call Laserjack and get an update on the situation? He should know more than we do about what's going on, or so I hope. Then we find the next fires to put out."

I nodded, and then with a few flicks through my augs I set up a conference call with Laserjack, Gomorrah, myself, and Crackshot Cowboy. He might have missed the last part at the end there, but he'd done his share, and in his shoes I wouldn't want to be left out of the loop.

"Uh, hi?" Crackshot said. He was the first to reply. "Is everything all right?"

"We're fine," I said. "Back atop the wall. Just a bit warmed up." That was an understatement. My armor was still smoking lightly. I think it was mostly just heat dissipating off the metal.

"Hah! I felt that from here. Regret not wearing my sunscreen today," he said, rather jovially for someone talking about a city being lit up. Then again, I guess not being near the burn radius was a good enough reason to be in a good mood.

The line clicked and Laserjack picked up. "Hello," he said. "Sorry for the delay there, I . . . well, you can imagine how hectic things are."

"Hey," I said.

"Hello," Gomorrah replied.

"First, before anything else, I just want to thank you. That was a nice job out there," he said.

"No problem," I replied, smoothing over the fact that I'd nearly cooked myself. "Just happy to see the city a little safer."

"Well, the city will appreciate it, I'm sure," he said. "We had several countermeasures ready to go, but we'll be deploying those farther away from the city now. Jolly Monarch's King drone is about to start a sweep around New Montreal. It should gain us a fair amount of space to work with."

"Wait, do you mean that we didn't need to do that?" I asked.

"Cat's right, I was under the impression that things were dire," Gomorrah said.

Laserjack was quiet for a few seconds longer than I'd expect before he replied. "Honestly, no. Things were never that dire. The city has several decently high-ranked samurai in it. Any one of us could have repelled the horde on our own. I'm sorry if you were unaware. We should have made that clearer; it would prevent the possibility of taking greater risks."

"Then why?" I asked. I couldn't decide if I was pissed or not.

"Because it gave you an opportunity to grow," he said. "The three of you and all the other low-tier samurai in New Montreal. You likely had the chance to earn more points today than in your entire career. With the global situation being what it is, we might all have to rely on *one* of you to protect an entire city. You need that head start and that added experience to be able to do that."

I crossed my arms, but I decided to be the bigger person about it and keep my anger in check, even if Laserjack was pouring water onto my head.

"Think of it as a quick way to grow. Plenty of new points, lots of opportunities to test new weapons and weapons platforms. Even whatever mistakes you made can now be corrected before you're being relied on to secure a city on your own. Gomorrah, Stray Cat, you're both well on your way to being tier-three samurai. I'm afraid you haven't had quite as much time to grow, Crackshot Cowboy, but your time will come."

"Ah, uh, thanks, sir," Jimothy said.

"Anyway. Get some rest. All three of you," Laserjack said. "I can't give you orders, but I can give you advice. You need rest. Things will get worse before they get better, so take the time you can now to catch up on sleep, to buy new gear, and to relax. You'll appreciate it later."

I glanced back and up. The sky was turning to night already. I hadn't noticed it, being so close to the glow of the city and with the many pillars of smoke obscuring the sky more than usual. "So, we get a night off, huh?" I asked.

"No. A day. I've seen your records, what's public at least. You've been a samurai for barely more than a week, with no more than half a day of inaction in that entire time. Your AI hasn't flagged you for burnout or anything of the sort, so I imagine you could keep going for a while, but this global incursion might last longer than that and we don't need you losing your edge before things get really complicated." Laserjack chuckled darkly. "Don't worry. There will be plenty more aliens to kill once you're done."

I wanted to argue. It would feel . . . *wrong* to stop. But then, yeah, I could use a day off. Just time with Lucy, with the kittens, getting used to the new place. I probably had enough points to furnish the whole home in expensive alien stuff.

"Thank you, Laserjack," Gomorrah said.

"I, ah, I think I'm going to stick with the PMCs for a bit," Crackshot said. "I haven't done as much as you two. My bit's not as big, so I won't get tired just yet. I can take it."

"That seems reasonable for now; just remember to take a break before you break," Laserjack said. "Call me if there's anything. If I can't answer right away, well, the world's ending, but I'll call back as soon as I can."

And with that, the line went dead, at least with him. "Nice fella," Crackshot said. "On that note, thank you, ladies, but I've got to run to keep up. I need a minute to buy a few things before we set out. See ya!"

We said our quick goodbyes, and then it was just me and Gomorrah.

"So," I said.

"Yes," Gomorrah said. She reached up, then paused before touching her mask. "My God, I'm going to have to talk to Franny."

I grinned. "I'm sure it won't be too bad," I said. I didn't want to pry into my . . . best friend's love life . . . but I one hundred percent wanted to pry. "If you need help, Lucy's awesome with romance stuff. She's discreet too." Which meant she wouldn't tell anyone but me.

Gomorrah sighed. "Want me to drop you off?"

"Did you want to drive out of your way so that it would take longer to get back home to confront Franny?" I asked.

"Shut up, Cat."

Franny was waffling back and forth between being more angry than she'd ever been before and worrying herself sick. The roiling emotions were twisting around in her gut, and she was pretty sure that if she continued to feel this way, she'd be sick.

The church was too calm, which didn't help. Earlier in the day she had chores to do, tasks that she could focus on to the detriment of all else so that she could push her worries back. The people Delilah—Gomorrah, she supposed—had saved from the sewers still needed help getting sorted, and then the massive incursion had started and the church got to work sorting supplies and getting ready to provide a few temporary shelters.

Those shelters had remained empty for the moment. The incursion had, according to what she'd read, been stopped at the walls.

Delilah had been there, risking her life against overwhelming odds.

Franny had stared at too many drone-cam videos of the waves of aliens charging the gap in the walls. She'd even seen Delilah's flames burning them down. They were hard to miss.

Then the call.

Franny wanted to punch Delilah in the nose.

She stomped through the church, past a few senior nuns who gave her space and then through the familiar corridors of the great building that had been her home and school her entire life.

The worry twisted in her gut again, and this time she wasn't sure if it was just her worrying about Delilah's safety or if it was more worry about the damnable call.

It hadn't lasted long. Delilah had overridden all of Franny's questions, which she supposed was fair. Delilah was a samurai now. She wasn't the cute bumbling girl who followed Franny around like a lost puppy anymore; she was so much more than just that now, even if Franny missed that about her best friend.

Then Delilah had told Franny that she might die, and that she might, maybe, be in love with her.

"Where are you going, young mis—" Sister Margaret froze as Franny locked eyes with her. The older woman might have clued into the naked mix of conflicting feelings Franny was freely wearing. In either case, she shut up, picked up her habit skirts, and walked off in a hurry.

Franny closed her hands into fists, then looked around for a place to calm down.

She had a bad reputation with the sisters already for being something of a hothead and for disregarding quite a few rules. Usually for good reason, but that didn't always excuse her. When she was younger she'd gotten her share of switchings for her attitude. Now she was older and strong enough that last time they'd tried, she'd stolen the switch and given Sister Maeve a real reason to complain.

Grumbling to herself, Franny opened one of the doors in the corridor and peeked within. It was one of the classrooms, one she recognized. They'd done math in here once. The room had a few rows of old presswood desks and windows that would have overlooked the city if they weren't covered in a blurry film.

Franny shut the door behind her, then stood by the front of the room and focused on breathing.

"Delilah," she whispered. The name came out of her with both frustration and longing.

She loved Delilah. Of course she did. For years they were the best of friends. She'd defended and helped Delilah countless times. They gossiped together, they pulled pranks together, they'd cried on each other's shoulders, and they had both seen enough of each other's most embarrassing moments to write entire books about them.

Did she *love* Delilah, though?

Franny growled and kicked the teacher's desk with her very not-nun-like steel-toed combat boots. Right then, she didn't have any sort of love for her blond friend.

"What kind of bitch drops that kind of bomb on someone before jumping to their death," she grumbled as she opened up a news site on her augs. There was a site dedicated to tracking samurai-related news in and around New Montreal. They'd announced the death of Nomad earlier.

Franny was dreading the idea of seeing an article about Gomorrah on there. She didn't know what she'd do if that was how she learned that Delilah was dead.

She had some passing worry for Gomorrah's new weirdo of a friend too, that Stray Cat girl who was clearly insane and probably not the best influence on Gomorrah. Had the confession been *her* idea? That woman was a raging lesbian if Franny ever saw one.

She'd kick her ass too, if she could.

Once, not so very long ago, she'd thought of samurai as basically saints. She hadn't realized how much of the church's Kool-Aid she had drunk until Delilah became one herself.

It was hard to think of someone as a saint when you had vivid memories of that person as a preteen waking you up at two a.m. because they'd had an accident and needed help covering it up.

Franny paused, then kicked the desk again. It felt good.

There was no news about Gomorrah. She groaned. Was it better to have no news than to find bad news waiting for her? She didn't know, and she didn't want to find out.

The door clicked, and Franny spun around, an excuse on her tongue already. She *had* just kicked the desk a few times. She might have been frustrated, but she understood that it was a little immature.

Then Delilah stepped into the room and gently closed the door behind her.

Her friend wasn't in her samurai gear. It was a strange detail to notice, but Franny couldn't miss it. Delilah was in one of the skirts Franny had bought for her: a knee-length dark blue thing that showed off her calves in a way that had made the sisters look on disapprovingly before Delilah became Gomorrah.

She had a blouse on, which was sticking to her skin, especially around her shoulders where Delilah's wet hair was draped down. The blouse was part of their old uniform, with a little necktie and all, though Delilah had left it undone.

Franny stared at her best friend and Delilah, in turn, stared at the floor.

She stepped up to Delilah, then, without thinking, slapped her friend across the face. Then, with a suppressed sob, she hugged Delilah close, squeezing her for all she was worth.

They stood there for a while, Franny holding Delilah close and soaking in her presence. The worry was bleeding off her; she could almost feel the knots in her gut untangling as she held on to her friend. Delilah's scent filled Franny. It was so familiar, so nice and . . .

Franny stepped back from Delilah just as Delilah's hands started to hug her back.

She stared at her friend, who was finally daring to meet her eyes. There was a red mark on Delilah's cheek, but she wasn't moving to touch it. Franny imagined that it stung. She quashed the guilt.

"So?" she asked.

Delilah blinked. "So?" she repeated.

Delilah, for all that she was a bit of a shrinking violet sometimes, had really taken to the lessons they had about good posture and form, and her voice rang out with an authoritative tone. Franny knew better than to just listen to Delilah's voice to read her. The trick was her friend's eyes; they might as well be signboards telling the world what Delilah was really thinking.

At least, they were for Franny.

Franny stared at Delilah, and there was no missing the massive amount of guilt her friend was feeling. Worse, there was an unhealthy heaping of worry there.

Franny didn't have to guess why. Delilah had just confessed before running off to maybe die.

Obviously, she was fine. Probably. She had all of her limbs and didn't look hurt. The smack on her face notwithstanding, Delilah looked okay. She might have had some other injuries, and Franny would have no way of knowing with the way she was covered up, but . . .

No, Delilah wouldn't confront Franny if she was injured. Delilah didn't like confrontations like this one. She wouldn't avoid them forever, but being injured was enough of an excuse that she'd take it and know that Franny wouldn't judge her for it.

It was a weird twist of logic, but it felt right to Franny.

So she crossed her arms and glared at her best friend, her sister in all but blood, the girl she'd go to hell and back for, and who had just . . . "Care to explain yourself?"

Delilah winced. It was just a tightening in the corner of her eyes, but it meant a lot. "I . . . Franny, I didn't know if I would make it. Things were looking bad and . . . and I decided not to die with one more regret in my life. It was selfish. I'm sorry."

"You're sorry?" Franny snapped.

She took a deep breath, and Delilah remained silent. She knew Franny well enough to know that that had just been her venting a little.

"Fine. So you're sorry. Did you mean it?" Franny asked.

Delilah glanced down, then forced herself to meet Franny's eyes. Her cheeks now both had a slight tinge of redness to them. "Yes. I think. I . . . I don't know, but I think so."

Franny raised one of her eyebrows, the sort of judgmental look the senior nuns were very good at. "All right, tell me again."

"Really, Franny?" Delilah asked.

Franny nodded. "Yes, really. I want us to be on the same page here."

Delilah swallowed, closed her eyes for a moment, then shifted slightly to work off some of her nervous energy. Then she took a calming breath and met Franny's gaze. "I love you," she said.

They stared at each other for a long time, the three words floating in the air between them, spoken and impossible to take back.

Franny felt her face warming up. She knew that her freckles would make any amount of blushing she did very obvious. Delilah's cheeks weren't any better.

So Franny decided to switch the focus to something else. "Since when are you gay?" she asked.

Delilah stiffened a little. "I don't know if I am?" she asked.

Franny blinked. "What?"

"I talked to Atyacus about, well . . ." Delilah made a vague gesture between them. She seemed as glad about the change in subject as Franny felt. Then her words registered and Franny felt a pang in her heart.

Delilah came to her when she needed to talk about stuff. That was their thing. They'd talk about their problems, about their silly dreams; they'd gossip and complain together while huddled up on the church's roof, or in the kitchens when no one else was around.

Franny supposed that she shouldn't be too hurt. Delilah could hardly come to her to talk about feeling . . . that way about her. That would have been strange. And the AI stuck in her brain was as good a candidate as any for sharing things with, Franny supposed.

It still stung a little. "What did he say?" Franny asked.

Delilah licked her lips, the motion catching Franny's attention for a moment. "He said that, well, he can see my brain chemistry. And my augs allow him to see out of my eyes. I don't think I'm gay?"

Franny blinked. "You are aware that I'm a woman, right?"

"Yes, I'm very aware," Delilah said. "I think he just said that, I guess the term would be more, something akin to being attracted to, well, you, more than just women in general." Delilah glanced away after that particular confession.

Franny worked her jaw. She wasn't sure what to say to that. It was flattering, certainly. She pretended not to feel the fluttering in her stomach.

"I . . . I'm sorry if I made you uncomfortable," Delilah said. "I can go, if you want. I know it's a lot to spring on you; I shouldn't have—"

"No," Franny said. She sighed. "Damn. You know I'd rather know this than not, right?"

"Yeah, I know you," Delilah said. She smiled over to Franny. Just another, normal smile, like Franny had seen from Delilah a million times. Somehow, though, this one made her feel different.

"Yeah, you do," Franny said. There was a long silence. It wasn't exactly uncomfortable, but it wasn't great either. Franny knew herself too. She was . . . probably not the ideal nun. She was by far too violent, too impulsive by half, and she cared more about helping people than preaching.

She was also, she was willing to admit to herself, a little bit attracted to women.

She stared Delilah up and down. Her friend was . . . well, frankly, Delilah was unfairly attractive. Franny liked women; she loved Delilah like a sister. There wasn't much of a leap to make to go from one idea to the other, smash them together, and make Delilah very happy.

Franny wasn't sure if she wanted to take that step.

Or maybe she wanted to but was worried about what it would mean for her, and for Delilah.

Worse, things had . . . changed.

Franny wasn't sure she wanted to admit it to herself, but if Delilah had confessed just a month or two ago, before Delilah became a samurai, things would be different. A month ago, Delilah still needed Franny. Franny was her protector and friend and more.

Had Delilah approached her then, then Franny could imagine herself teasing and prodding and seeing how far they could go. The idea that it was forbidden wasn't much of a deterrent for her. If anything, it made things more exciting.

Now . . . Now Delilah was the boss, and that made things different in a way that Franny still hadn't gotten used to.

Unless.

Franny swallowed.

She had a very bad idea.

That had never stopped her from carrying out an idea before, though.

"What do you want out of all of this?" Franny asked. She recalled that strange samurai, the cat-themed one, and her equally weird girlfriend. At a glance, it was clear who led the two of them, at least in their private life. Lucy—was Lucy her name? Franny had only really interacted with her the one evening—wore the pants in that relationship, samurai or no.

"I don't know," Delilah said. She chuckled, low and throaty. "I guess I have more wishes than wants, if that makes any sense."

"Wishes?" Franny asked. She was genuinely curious now. Plus it was just tangential enough to what they were discussing before that it didn't feel as awkward.

Delilah glanced up, then back to the ground. "You're going to call me sentimental," she said. "But I want both of us to be happy. Together, preferably, but happy most of all."

Franny squirmed on the spot. The awkwardness had returned tenfold. Now Franny was fighting with something like shame. Delilah loved her. She'd known about the more sisterly love, but this was a lot.

She exhaled hard. She couldn't continue being on the back foot; it was too much for her. So she struck from an angle that Delilah wouldn't expect. "Did you ever do anything about it?" she asked.

"What?" Delilah asked.

It was a fair question; Franny barely knew what she was talking about herself. "I mean. You find me . . . attractive, right?"

"Very," Delilah said without an ounce of hesitation.

Franny sniffed. "Well, did you ever do anything about it? I remember how much of a puritan you are, Delilah. I was always the one trying new things, right? So, did you?"

Finally, Delilah was surprised enough that her visage cracked. A beautiful redness spread to Delilah's cheeks and even across the bridge of her nose. "Franny. I . . ." She shut her mouth with a click, then crossed her arms and looked away. "Yes."

Franny felt her mouth going dry. She didn't actually expect that as an answer. "So, is that something you want? Sex?"

Her friend glared. "I'm not an animal. I want more than just sex, Franny." Delilah hesitated. "But yes. I'll admit that I've had thoughts about that kind of thing before."

Franny saw her chance. It was right there, an obvious, shining moment that she could take if only she wanted it. It was a risk, but she was nothing if not reckless. "And what did you imagine me doing to you in those thoughts?" Franny asked.

"Franny," Delilah complained. "Really?"

"Yes, really," Franny said. "Let's say we decide to see how all of this works out. What then? We go on a couple of dates? Which is basically just us hanging out like we've done a million times before. We share secrets and talk more? I doubt we could. What would actually change?"

"I . . . I guess not very much," Delilah said. She sounded a little hopeful there. "I'm a samurai now. We could go to new places. I'd keep you safe."

Franny frowned. She couldn't fault Delilah for that. "Yeah, I guess you are. So that leaves one big new thing, doesn't it?"

"Sex," Delilah said. "I think there's more to it than that."

"Yeah, of course," Franny said. "I bet love's plenty complicated. But . . . okay, look . . . I . . ."

"You feel like you lost your place in our relationship," Delilah said.

Franny blinked.

"And now you want to reassert it, if only in a limited way," Delilah continued. "You want to be the one who runs the relationship itself. Nothing outside of that would change much. I'll still be the samurai, you'll still be the same old Franny, but in this one big thing, you'd be the . . . the leader again."

"Uh," Franny said. Had she been too obvious? Delilah was good at reading her, sure, but usually Franny had figured out what she wanted to do before Delilah could guess her plans.

Delilah crossed her arms under her breasts and glanced away. "I . . . may have been cheating a little," she said. "I wanted to know what to say, and I wanted to see if we even had a chance of working out at all or if it was all just me being stupid."

Franny understood then. "You asked Atyacus for help," she guessed.

Delilah shrugged a shoulder languidly. "A little. I told him not to violate your privacy, just my own. He analyzed things based on what I'd seen, basically, and what I could guess about you, and . . . yeah."

"Huh," Franny muttered. "Okay. I didn't expect that. I guess I should have. So, what did your AI friend say?"

"Not too much," Delilah said. "Just that there are ways this could work." She gestured between Franny and herself. "And one of the ways where you're happiest is if I just let you take control of things. We go at your pace. Unless I think we're moving too fast, I suppose. Then we slow down, but you *set* the pace. If you want to try something, we do."

Franny chuckled. It just escaped her in a burst. It was such a weird idea. She'd barely even formed her own thoughts on the matter. She didn't have time for that. Then Delilah came around with the perfect solution. Or at least, a solution.

"He really thinks we could work out?" she asked.

Delilah nodded slowly. "He said we'd need to work on things, and communicate, but I think that's par for the course with this kind of thing, isn't it?"

"Yeah, I guess so," Franny said. "So, you're okay with that? We split things down the middle. Like that one time at the camping retreat, the tent with the tape."

"That didn't work out so well," Delilah said.

Franny laughed. "But it was fun."

"It was."

Franny looked at Delilah, and Delilah met her gaze. There was hope there, and acceptance, and a lot more. Franny stepped up, walking closer to Delilah. She'd probably done it a thousand times before, but this was different in a way she couldn't quite describe. "So, if I decide that I want to kiss you right here and now?" Franny asked.

Delilah's breathing hitched, just faintly. "Then that's what we do."

"And if I decide that we go further than that?" Franny asked.

Delilah's face reddened again. "How much further?"

Franny didn't want to be awful. She cared about Delilah too much for that. She might have had permission to set the pace, but there were limits. Delilah had always been a slow and careful person. She took to new things with careful analysis and a clear sort of progression.

Besides, Franny was about as inexperienced as Delilah was. She wasn't sure she wanted to rush things herself.

"Let's start a little slower, then," Franny said. She raised her arms for a hug. Usually it was Delilah who initiated those.

Her friend stepped up and returned the gesture.

Warm and soft, as always. Still, Franny felt like the hug was a little different. There was a *charge* to it. She felt her breasts under her habit pressing into Delilah, and Delilah's pressing into her. The warmth was more than just the comforting warmth of a hug.

Franny hesitated. Were they ready for more?

Was that pushing things too much?

"Okay," she said before stepping back.

They stared at each other from half a pace apart.

Franny wondered if Delilah felt the lack of warmth as keenly as she did.

"That was . . . nice," Franny said.

Delilah nodded. "Nothing too unusual, but . . . okay." She smiled. Franny treasured it. Delilah wasn't much of a smiler. She was always too serious, too broody by half. She'd joked that she had to make up for Delilah's stoicism by being twice as brash before. This smile was a small, private, but happy one.

Franny thought, hard and fast, even if her brain felt a little like mush from the thrill ride of emotions. She realized that she wasn't angry anymore, though; instead her chest hummed with the wild beating of her heart and she was genuinely happy, though it was a weird confusing mess of happiness.

She didn't want to end this here. She didn't want to leave the room without having done more. Without exploring things more. But how could she move on while not making Delilah do something she wasn't comfortable doing already? Even kissing felt a little too far.

Then she had another terrible idea. She was full of them.

"So," Franny said as she considered how to say what she wanted to. She crossed her arms and tried to look a little more stern. "Tell me, Delilah. What have you done while thinking of me?"

Delilah rocked back a little. "You mean, in a sexual way?"

"Yes, obviously," Franny said.

Delilah's throat bobbed as she swallowed. "I . . . nothing much?"

"Oh, okay," Franny said. "Then you wouldn't mind doing what you did while thinking of me again?"

"Um, well, I suppose not," Delilah said. She flushed again. The topic they were dancing around was so ridiculously taboo, it was a thrill just to talk about it.

Franny grinned. "Good," she said, arms squeezing a little around her waist. "Then do it."

Delilah inhaled sharply, just shy of a gasp. "H-here?"

Franny gestured around the room. "Why not? I mean, I guess a bed would be better?"

Delilah's jaw worked and her face reddened from her neck up. "Franny!" she gasped.

Franny laughed, and after her shock passed, Delilah's expression turned to what some would call a pout. A very beautiful pout. "All right, how about we start a bit easier, then?" Franny stepped back over to the teacher's desk, turned, then leaned back onto it. "I'm curious though, how much, ah, experience do you have?"

Delilah sighed. "None."

"None?" Franny repeated.

"Basically none," Delilah said. "What about you?"

Franny shrugged. "I mean, I've got a hairbrush I'm fond of," she said. The way Delilah's cheeks flushed was gorgeous. She was starting to understand the wilder people who were always so flippant. There was a lot of fun in getting someone to react. "But you said earlier that you'd . . . you know, while thinking of me?"

Delilah closed her eyes. She only did that when she was truly embarrassed. Franny imagined that the fact that she continued meant she didn't mind Franny knowing. "I've never stuck anything up . . . there. Ever. I was always saving myself. For the right person."

"Oh, wow," Franny said. "In that case . . ."

Delilah sighed. "The most I've ever done to . . . relieve tension was rub myself on something. I think the first time was in this room."

"While class was on?" Franny asked. Maybe Delilah was a lot more daring than she'd imagined.

"No, after, when everyone was gone. I . . . you know, with the corner of a desk."

"I really don't know," Franny said.

Delilah very awkwardly gestured below her stomach. "It was only once here. I was terrified of being caught, and I never told anyone, obviously. I just went up to a desk and . . . moved against it."

"You humped a desk?" Franny asked.

"Yes, I humped a desk," Delilah said flatly.

Franny grinned. "And that's the most you've ever done?"

Delilah squirmed. "Well, I've tried it with my skirt raised."

She wondered what to say next, before the silence stretched for too long. "Okay, then do that," Franny said. She gestured with a wave to the rows of desks. "It's nothing you haven't done before."

Delilah looked at her, then the desks, then back. "What if someone walks in?"

"What if someone walked in last time?" Franny asked.

Her friend conceded the point with a sideways nod. "I guess. I . . . fine. I suppose this is just a small thing. From everything I've heard this is really tame."

"We're not even touching," Franny said. "We couldn't go slower if we tried."

Delilah chuckled. "I guess not. It still feels fast." She raised a hand to stall Franny, who was about to suggest the stop. "No, it's fine. It's . . . after what I did to you today. Pulling that on you all of a sudden."

"You don't owe me for that," Franny said.

"But I want to," Delilah replied. She stepped around one of the desks so that she was facing Franny from behind it. Franny very much didn't fail to notice that it was her own desk. The sisters sat her in front so that they could always keep an eye on her.

Carefully, Delilah stepped up to the desk, then pressed herself into the corner of it. The rounded edges pushed into her skirt, right at the crotch, and Delilah shifted her hips forward. Her face was practically steaming. Then, very deliberately, she slid back, the corner making her skirt ride up just a little as the material bunched up.

"This is what I did," Delilah said.

"While thinking of me?" Franny asked. Her stomach roiled, and she was glad she was leaning against the desk because her legs felt a little weak.

"Yes," Delilah said simply. "While thinking of you."

"Was that all?" Franny asked. As far as she knew, this was about the most tame sexual act anyone could do. It was barely masturbation at all.

"I . . . sometimes, I'd grab my own chest," Delilah said.

"Do that," Franny said. "I mean, please?"

Delilah sniffed, then raised her right hand to her breast and squeezed. Delilah was always more endowed than Franny. She'd been a little jealous once. More recently, as she grew up, she always admired Delilah's features.

She'd never expected to see Delilah groping herself that way.

"C-continue rubbing," Franny said.

Delilah complied. Her hips moved up, then down. Up. Then down. She added a bit of a roll to her motions, just as if she were tracing a big oval with her hips while the desk dug into the fabric of her skirts.

Her hands didn't remain idle. They squeezed and pinched at her breast, just the one hand, and never fast. Just a careful taunting of flesh through her blouse and bra.

"Franny," Delilah whispered as her eyes closed.

Franny gulped. She felt very warm as she carefully repositioned herself against the teacher's desk. Still, her attention never left Delilah with her slow, careful gyrations.

Delilah glanced up to Franny, a question in her eyes. Did Franny want her to continue? Franny nodded, and that simple gesture sent goose bumps down her spine. There was so much *wrong* with that simple action. She was ordering a saint to do . . . that.

She continued to watch as Delilah rubbed herself, mind whirling. Then Delilah stopped with a gasp.

Franny listened, and then she heard the same thing Delilah must have. Footsteps, coming down the corridor. More than one, even.

Someone opened a door farther down, into one of the other classrooms across the hall, if Franny had to guess.

They'd be caught. Or Delilah would, at least.

Franny looked at the way Delilah was frozen, and then she whispered across the room. "Don't stop."

Delilah stared at her, then at the door. Franny could hear her heart beating over the approaching footsteps.

The desk Delilah was rubbing herself against shifted as Delilah started over. It was slower, certainly, and more tense. They both listened as footsteps grew closer, then continued right by.

Another door opened, closer this time. The classroom right next to this one.

Delilah continued to rub herself, as she'd been told to, and Franny couldn't stop the goose bumps rising across her arms and neck, nor the queasy feeling in her stomach.

Then the door to the next classroom closed and someone walked right by theirs without ever stopping in.

Delilah let out a relieved sigh.

So did Franny. "Did . . . did you ever do more?" she asked.

Delilah paused, but just for a moment. She resumed the rubbing as she spoke. "I did, eventually," she said. "The material . . . you don't feel much through it."

"Oh," Franny said.

Delilah's free hand, which had been holding on to the desk, slid down to her side and started to fist into her skirt. She raised it, bit by bit. Franny kept staring as more and more of Delilah's long legs were exposed. Then Delilah backed her rear up from the edge of the desk long enough to flip the front of her skirt over it.

Franny inhaled sharply. She hadn't seen anything. She could smell something, though, maybe. It might have been her imagination.

Delilah fixed her skirt atop the table so that it wasn't too bunched up, and then her free hand gripped the edge and she paused, shifting her hips as if to realign them.

Franny imagined that without the skirt in the way, it would just be Delilah's panties between her and the desk. Delilah bit her lower lip, then pressed herself forward again. She took in a shaky breath, then pulled back.

The motions started languid and slow, but as Franny watched, Delilah sped up. Her grip on the table turned white as it tightened.

She moved back and forth for a minute. Then two. Her eyes were half-lidded, her mouth open in a little O. Then Delilah started to pick up the pace. "Franny," she whispered again. She undid a button on her blouse and slipped her hand in. Franny didn't fail to notice her bra slipping down, or the way Delilah's nipples were erect under the thin fabric.

Franny continued to watch even as she herself warmed up. The heat traveled down, and she pressed her legs together. There was no ignoring the sticky heat between her legs. It was as if someone were gently pouring her full of warm syrup.

Her reverie was jolted hard as the desk Delilah was using squeaked. The metal-tipped leg screeched across the floor. Delilah was red-faced; even her ears glowed. Her hand pulled out of her blouse and came even with the other so that she gripped the desk on two sides.

Then, to Franny's amazement, Delilah raised a leg up and onto the school chair.

Her perfect posture was gone. She was rubbing herself along the length of the desk, breathing so hard it verged on panting. Her eyes were closed and every hard thrust filled the room with a tiny squeak as the desk was slammed forward.

"Franny, Franny, Franny," Delilah whimpered with every hump.

Franny's entire being froze. She was no more than a drunk passenger who'd fallen onto the tracks, unable to do anything but stare as the train came rushing to her. She caught glimpses of Delilah's breasts bouncing through the opening in her blouse, of her long leg, exposed by the way Delilah had raised her skirts, of Delilah's face, where in her ecstasy and with the repetition of Franny's own name, her dearest friend, always stuck up and proper, failed to notice a thin line of drool next to her mouth.

Her friend squeaked, her back went rigid, and she stopped her hard thrusts. Not entirely, she was still swaying back and forth on the edge of the desk, but the energy was gone.

Delilah panted and her eyes fluttered open.

They stared at each other, Delilah with mounting mortification, Franny . . . she wasn't sure what emotion was on her face, but her mouth was open and her cheeks felt warmer than they'd ever felt before.

Delilah broke eye contact first. She wiped a hand over her face, brought her leg down quickly, then adjusted her skirt with a quick shimmy of her hips.

Her friend paused, and for a moment her face reddened before she bent down, both hands going under her skirt for a moment and shifting about. Did she have to readjust her panties? Franny's ears couldn't hear much over the drumming of her heart.

Franny took in her friend, who was trying to make herself presentable. She pulled her bra back on straight, then buttoned her shirt up and tucked it back into her skirt's waistband. With a quick comb through her hair, it was almost impossible to notice that she'd been doing anything. There was only that lingering scent and . . .

They both looked at the desk. The corner, nearly the entire edge, was wet.

"That was—" Franny started.

"I'm sorry—" Delilah said at the same time.

They stopped. Franny gestured for Delilah to go first, and her friend took a moment to control her breathing. "I'm . . . sorry you saw that. I . . . I lost myself, and I must have looked like some sort of freak."

"No," Franny said. She took a long step toward Delilah, then stopped. There was definitely a lot of wetness clinging between her legs. That was . . . probably not a surprise.

If Franny ever doubted whether she found Delilah attractive, then, well, no, she could put that doubt to rest.

"I mean. I'm happy you showed me that," Franny said.

Delilah's blush returned, and she failed to meet Franny's eyes. "Usually it takes a lot longer," she muttered.

Franny swallowed. Was it being seen that made it better, or Franny's presence? The fact that it was a punishment of sorts? Franny . . . honestly couldn't wait to find out.

"I think," Franny said. "That we've, ah, done nearly enough for one day. Enough pushing, I mean."

"Nearly enough?" Delilah asked. She was as sharp as usual.

Franny nodded and came closer. She breathed through her nose and felt a little light-headed. She *recognized* the smell. From Delilah's own room, no less. Did that mean . . . she pushed those thoughts aside. "Nearly. I think, maybe next time we can do the reverse. Or maybe I can . . . provide something better than a desk?"

Delilah nodded slowly. "But . . . I know I said you would be in the lead, but . . . can we make the first time we go . . . *in* special?" she asked.

"Okay," Franny agreed. If it was special to Delilah, then it was special. Though perhaps she was looking forward to that too.

Then, after a moment's pause to muster up her bravery, Franny stepped right up to Delilah and took her friend's face in both of her hands. Delilah looked at her in shock, but there was trust there, trust and want and maybe some lingering lust.

"I guess that makes us girlfriends, then?" Franny asked. The word, or maybe the position, made her even more light-headed.

"I guess so," Delilah said.

Then she said nothing at all, because Franny captured Delilah's mouth with hers.

CHAPTER SIXTY-EIGHT

GETTING HOME

Samurai are horny bastards, I swear. I think it's all the action. It gets their blood pumping like nothing else.

—Madam Acrais, high-class brothel owner, 2045

I ended up figuring out my own way home. I wanted to ride along with Gomorrah, but there was no way my armor would fit in the Fury unless I hung off the side again, and . . . no, I wasn't in the mood for that kind of thing.

I did want to be close to Gomorrah. She was twitchy and a little worried, even after I tried to reassure her that everything would be fine.

Some things a girl just had to tackle on her own, though, and that included confronting a possible romantic interest. I told Gomorrah that we had extra rooms over at my new place, and that she was always welcome to come over and spend the night, or even just call to rant if that was what she needed.

I didn't want to be a poor friend, so I was going to support Gomorrah however I could. I just didn't want to overstep either. Franny seemed like a good match for Gomorrah, so maybe things would work out. At least, I hoped they would. Gomorrah deserved a good time, or maybe her own version of Lucy. Someone to ground her and for her to return home to.

Speaking of which. I sighed as my bike came around and landed with a thump on the top of the wall. I was a bit bulkier in my armor, so it was tricky to sit atop it, but I still managed to fit. I couldn't get my feet on the pedals without spreading my knees way out, though, so I left the flying to the autopilot and Myalis.

"So," I asked as we took to the air and headed toward New Montreal proper. A new shadow was cast against the suburbs from the massive new wall. "What was all of that worth?"

In terms of experience gained, or in terms of something more quantifiable, like your point total?

I chuckled. "In terms of points, I think," I said as we flew around a sky-scraper. I noted that there wasn't quite as much traffic as usual. More cop cars hovering around too, but they dutifully ignored me as I flew by.

Current Point Total: 98,845

I stared at the number for a while, then shook my head. "Are you serious? Like, twelve hundred away from six figures?"

Had you expended less ammunition firing at the spaces between enemies, you would have just enough points to reach one hundred thousand.

My grip on the handles tightened. "Yeah, fine. I'll practice my aim. Maybe . . . *maybe* get one of those brain implants to learn how to aim. You'll need to work to convince me, though."

Noted. If you want more points, you could turn around and fly back out of the city. It shouldn't be too difficult to find a small pocket of Antithesis to wipe out.

"Nah. Laserjack was right, I need a break." I could feel the weariness in my bones. So much adrenaline, for such a long period. I was burnt out. What I needed was a warm meal and about twelve hours of sleep. What I wanted was a cool room with Lucy's warm body and twelve hours in bed, most of which weren't spent sleeping.

That was the kind of happy, buzzing thought I was entertaining as we flew around a skyscraper and came into view of home.

I'd kind of forgotten that my home was now a giant metal sphynx atop a stubbier skyscraper. The floor just below the sphynx was lined with turrets fixed about a meter apart. Raccoon had been hard at work, it seemed.

I flew around the building, then came down for a gentle landing between the building's forepaws. I swung off the back of the bike and straightened up. The city was plunging into night, but it wasn't much darker than mid-day. Neon ads were a sun of their own, splashing their RGB brightness across the city.

I took it all in for a moment. This was, in a way, what I'd worked to save.

It didn't count nearly as much as what was in my home. With a bit of a pep to my step, I walked in.

There was a shout as one of the kittens—Nose—spotted me in the door-way. "She's back! And she's not dead!"

"Hey! There's my favorite bunch of assholes," I cheered. "One of you needs to toss something in the microwave for me; I'm starving." My armor made it hard to be bowled over, but the kittens gave it a good try anyway. It was mostly the youngest ones. Junior and Katallina were old enough that that kind of display was not going to happen.

"Glad to see you didn't die," Junior said.

"Thanks, I worked hard not to," I shot back. "What have you been up to?"

"Eh, we've been watching you and the others fighting. There's a livestream. But it got boring so we started watching AI-generated Sponge-Bob episodes instead," Junior said.

I laughed. "Yes, I can see why that would be more interesting than seeing the person paying your rent fight not to die."

She shrugged, clearly showing what she thought of that.

"Where's Lucy at?" I asked.

"Oh, she's in the back," one of the Twins said. "With the big machine."

Lucy was playing with the creation machine? I suppose that giving that woman unlimited creative power was one way to keep her busy for a few minutes. "All righty, then," I said.

I gave some heads a few pats, then stood off to the side and started to undo my armor while fielding questions from the kittens. Mostly it was about new gear, celebrities I'd met, and I got to sneak in a few surprisingly unexaggerated stories of killing aliens that I thought sounded pretty badass.

"Okay, don't touch the armor, it's still a little hot. And it's also kind of screwed up. I give it even odds that if one of you climbs into it, it'll lock up and we won't be able to get you out of there without a saw." That wasn't entirely or even partially true, except for the part where the armor was in a rough state. A few scratches were more than paint-deep, and it looked like some of the padding on the inside had melted outright.

I might have to toss the whole thing into the printer's deconstruction bin. I'd bet there were plenty of exotic materials in the armor that might be useful for other crap later.

Tossing my coat onto one of the couches, I walked up to the back of our home and to the vault where the printer was. Lucy was there, sitting on a stack of neatly piled material blocks with a tablet sitting on her knee.

"Hey," I said from the doorway.

She jumped and looked up to me, and in that instant I saw unfamiliar stress lines fading from the corners of her eyes. "Cat!" she shouted before darting across the room.

I laughed and met her halfway with a tight hug. "I missed you," I said.

She hugged me tighter, then pulled back. Her eyes darted across my features, taking me in. "Are you okay?" she asked.

"Tired," I admitted. It wouldn't do to lie to Lucy; she'd just find out and be disappointed. "I really did miss you. It was a long day."

"No injuries?" she asked. Then her hands roamed, but not in a pleasant way; she was just checking to see if I was all there. "Wait, this isn't the same arm."

"Oh, right, this is new," I said with a grin. I raised my new cybernetic hand, then turned on one of its primary features. The room filled with a low buzz. "It vibrates."

Lucy shook her head. I could tell she was amused, but she pushed past that anyway. "What happened to your other one?"

"Well . . . my old armor wasn't up to snuff. I got newer, better armor, but the arm was damaged, so . . . yeah."

The whole story would come out, but I wasn't ready for that.

Lucy, being Lucy—which just meant that she was perfect—caught on. "We'll have to put the new arm through its paces, then. Technically, you're . . . one-sixth virgin now, you know?"

"I don't think that's how it works," I said with a laugh. "What have you been up to? Making stuff?"

Lucy nodded, then skipped back away from me. That almost ended when she tripped over nothing and had to swing her arms for balance. She, of course, pretended that didn't happen, then struck a pose. "What do you think?" she asked.

She was in a T-shirt with a very low hem, almost a nightgown, really. The front said "Cat's Got My Tongue" with a stylized cat head behind it. She was also wearing thick white thigh-highs that stopped a handspan above her knee, right at the thickest part of her thigh. There was a very delicious thigh squish at the top.

"I made both of these," she said with a bit of a wiggle added.

"That's really nice," I said, honestly.

She bounced over, then pulled me down a little so that she could whisper in my ear. "I was going to make lingerie, but you're here already, so these two things are all I made . . . and all I'm wearing too."

"Oh," I said. God, I loved Lucy.

CHAPTER SIXTY-NINE

NICE

Look, I'm not a conspiracy nut, but this whole thing with the mass world-wide incursion? Something's fishy about it. Where are all the big-name samurai? Where are the really strong samurai who can wipe out an incursion solo?

A bunch of them are supposed to be around Mars. Which, all right, fine, they're samurai, they'll go into space and do space samurai stuff, whatever.

Now why haven't any of them come back? And why are so many more of them leaving?

You know what I think? I think they've built a new home for themselves up there. They know Earth's screwed, so they just up and left. Cowards!

—Live comment section of live-world-news-streaming.com, 2057

Lucy and I left the room with the matter printer with rather goofy smiles on. I didn't particularly care. Lucy was clinging to my side, almost hanging off me for support while I absently tucked my shirt back in with my free hand. We hadn't done anything too fun, just a lot of handsy stuff and some kissing. Good kissing. Non-PG-13 kissing.

"We don't have a bedroom," Lucy said suddenly.

"We don't?" I asked. I distinctly remembered a room being for us to sleep in.

"Well, okay, we do, but we don't have a *bed* in our bedroom. Which I think means that it's technically just a 'room' and not much else." She grinned up at me. "Unless you want to sleep on the floor? I'd be down for that, but, like, as a onetime thing."

I laughed and wrapped an arm around Lucy's back to pull her closer into my side. Then, because her head was close, I planted a kiss on her forehead. I regretted it when a curly lock of Lucy's hair got caught on my lips and I had to pull my face away to get it off.

Lucy, at least, thought that was hilarious.

"So, I was checking things out, and I'm pretty sure we can buy enough furniture for the whole place for fairly cheap. You know the matter machine will create blueprints of anything you throw into it? We only need to buy one bed per kitten and then we can print out new ones for all the rest. I'm pretty sure it's piracy of some sort, but I don't think that'll stop us."

"That's an idea," I said. "Or we could just buy everything we need from Myalis. I think I can afford a furniture catalog."

There are quite a few of those available. Some are relatively inexpensive. Most human furniture isn't exactly mechanically complex.

I nodded along. "There you have it," I said. "Myalis can get you whatever you need. I bet she can send things to your augs if you ask nicely."

Do you wish for Lucy to be allowed to make purchases in your stead?

"That's allowed?" I asked.

No, but I can do it anyway. Technically, she'd need to ask your permission for every item, but we both know you'd just say yes to anything she asks for. I do suggest that you set a reasonable budget. Both to keep spending in check and to encourage creativity when it comes to point expenditure.

What followed was a couple of hours of Lucy running around all over our new home, at first while gesturing all over, then later with a tablet in hand. She went from broad strokes to making small changes. Judging by the smile she carried and the contagious excitement that was infecting the kittens, the whole place would be entirely different in a few hours.

I decided to leave her to it and quietly excused myself to go to our—now somewhat furnished—bedroom. I needed a bit of time to think. I wasn't an introspective sort of person, which I think was rather obvious, but the last day or so had been so insanely busy that I had a hard time just keeping track of everything that had happened.

The meeting with the other samurai, which happened just after Gomorrah and I were tossed out of Deus Ex's space station, was just last night. After that, everything was sort of a blur. The meeting with the other samurai led by Laserjack, then Gomorrah and I ran off to that giant gardening place, I could vividly remember not-nuking the place. Then . . . dinner with Gomorrah and Franny and Lucy in our new home.

The next morning, I'd run off to help Jolly Monarch hold off a wave until Grasshopper needed help with the caravan. What had happened after that? The group of survivalists next to that one nuclear reactor factory? Were they even still alive? Gomorrah and I had left soon after to protect the gap in the wall. That building coming down around me . . . that was going to be in a nightmare or two. I still had to find the asshole who'd dropped those shells on my position and give them a piece of my mind.

Had it only been one day? I think I'd experienced more trauma in twelve hours than most people dealt with in a lifetime.

"Being a samurai's kind of fucky, isn't it?" I asked.

It is. Though you are living in very interesting times. Things will inevitably calm down, and you'll be able to enjoy the fruits of your labors.

"The fruits of my labors, huh? Mostly I'm just smashing things and hoping I don't get smashed in turn." I flopped backward onto the bed and stared at the ceiling while I sank into the mattress.

Maybe things weren't so bad. Lucy was happy. The kittens were safe.

I'd do my part to make sure she stayed happy and that they were even safer. I had the resources to spare. I lacked some time, sure, and training, but . . . well, maybe that was something I'd finally get around to fixing.

I closed my eyes and was just considering sleeping—the fact that I was still in dirty clothes be damned—when the door burst open and Lucy rushed in. "Cat!" she cheered. "I'm done!" With that, she jumped onto the bed, knees on either side of my hips, and lowered herself close. "I'm done!"

I laughed, then reached up and pulled her into a hug. "Good. I needed a pillow," I said.

"Cat! No! I wanted to show you around!" She squealed as I rolled over and pulled her down with me.

"But I can explore the place later," I muttered. "What if I want to explore you right now?"

Lucy squirmed. "Cat, you've explored every inch of me before; you won't find anything new."

"You don't know that," I said. "I always find a new thing to be amazed at." I reached around her waist and pinched her side, not hard, just enough to grab on to the slight love handles she had. "Look at what I've discovered here. It's beautiful. Worthy of worship."

She grabbed me by the lapels and pulled me up. She wasn't strong enough to really force me higher, but I helped her along. "I guess I should give New Montreal's big hero a bit of a reward, shouldn't I?" she whispered.

"Hmm? I don't know. I don't think I want to be a hero."

Lucy looked at me, then pulled me into a hug that was a lot more comforting than it was erotic. "That's okay too," she said. "How about you be Cat, and I'll be Lucy, and the kittens can be annoying brats, and we'll pretend that the rest doesn't matter as long as we're here?"

I grinned. "I think I'd like that. Never thought you'd be one to suggest role-play, though."

Lucy snorted, indelicate and definitely not ladylike. "Please, if we were doing role-play it would be a lot more involved. I'm talking costumes and, like, an entire storyline. You'd need to memorize lore."

"Oh? Maybe we can do the brave samurai saving the poor, helpless girl from some scary monsters?"

Lucy nodded. "Sure. I'll be the brave samurai, and you be helpless."

"That doesn't sound hard. I would be helpless without you."

She gasped. "Catherine! That actually sounded kind of smooth. Is Myalis feeding you lines?"

"There weren't any cat puns, so you know she wasn't," I said.

Lucy giggled, and soon we shifted around so that she was at my back, hugging me close while we basically spooned. It was warm and just . . . nice.

Then, of course, Nose barged into the room. "Hey! If you two aren't too busy, there's this weird chick who just got here."

"What?" I asked.

"Yeah, she's just . . . really weird. Said her name was Grasshopper. Might be a samurai. Or a nutjob."

"God damn it," I swore as I jumped to my feet, then pulled Lucy up to hers. I gave her a quick peck on the cheek before rushing to the door. "Come on! You're going to want to meet her. She's nice, if a little loony. Did she say what she was here for?"

"She said you needed a nanny," Nose said before running down the corridor and leaping the steps to the floor below.

I think I might have been cursed to not have a minute to myself.

Grasshopper was keenly aware that the flimsy front door of Stray Cat's home couldn't hold her back. Still, being a samurai was, in her opinion, less about strength and more about knowing when to use that power. Too many samurai forgot that they weren't all that different from the average person on the street.

So, being a polite neighbor and friend, Grasshopper stopped by the door and knocked. Stray Cat's home didn't have a doorbell. She imagined that the young samurai was so busy making her house look like a giant cat that she might have forgotten to add something to let people know she had guests over.

Or maybe that was on purpose. Grasshopper had had to deal with all sorts of rude, unwanted, and rudely unwanted guests, especially when she was newer to the job. Her house wasn't a gigantic cat sitting atop a skyscraper, which afforded her a bit more privacy.

Eventually someone passed by the door on the other side and stopped. It was a young woman, maybe fourteen or fifteen years old. She stared at Grasshopper, who waved, and then the young lady turned and screamed something to someone deeper in the home.

Grasshopper had turned down her audio devices, the systems that allowed her to see through walls, and even her tracking systems. Privacy was a valuable commodity, and even if no one knew that Grasshopper could violate theirs, it was still rude to do so.

It took a minute, but eventually the girl was joined by another who looked to be about the same age. They chatted, looked to Grasshopper, then walked over and opened the door. "Who're you?" the first girl asked.

"Hello! I'm Grasshopper! But you can call me Miss Hopper."

The girls looked at each other, then back at Grasshopper.

She imagined that some of the confusion came from how she was dressed. She really loved her outfit. It was a woman's business suit done up in dark blue with big happy green grasshoppers with itty-bitty guns all over it. She had a big bag too, one of those old medicine bags with an umbrella hooked across the top. It was very similar to the kind of outfit she used to wear at the elementary school she worked at, but the grasshoppers on this one moved.

"All righty, then, Miss Hopper," one of the girls said. "You know this is Stray Cat's place, yeah?"

"I was counting on it." Grasshopper grinned, and she hoped it came out as more sweet than weird. "Can you tell Cat that I'm here?"

"You know her?" the other girl asked.

"We worked together a few times," Grasshopper said.

"Wait, you're a samurai?" the first girl asked. She narrowed her eyes. "Prove it."

"Oh, I can do that!" Grasshopper said. She raised a hand and was about to ask her AI to buy something small when the girl piped up.

"Buy a knife."

"A knife?" Grasshopper asked.

The girl nodded. "A cool one."

"Knives are dangerous," Grasshopper said.

The girl shrugged. "So's living."

Grasshopper couldn't refute that logic. "Okay, but only a small one," she said. With a few stray thoughts to her friendly AI, a box was summoned into her open hand with some sparkles and little pops of glitter.

The girls stared. "When Cat summons shit it doesn't do that."

"I pay extra for the effects!" Grasshopper said, rather proud of the fact. The glitter settled (it was designed not to stick and to be entirely biodegradable within under a year), and Grasshopper opened the box, revealing a little army knife. "It has a knife, two sporks, a little flashlight, and a compass."

"Neat!" the first girl said. She plucked the knife out of the box, and they toyed around with it. Finally, after a moment of obvious reluctance, she gave it to the other girl. "Cat gave me a knife already, so you know, fair's fair."

Grasshopper had to suppress a joyful clap. Sharing!

"Anyway, come on in, Cat's with Lucy. Bet they're banging while thinking they're being all subtle about it."

"Oh?" Grasshopper asked as she stepped in. "Is that a common occurrence?" She made a mental note to add sex ed to her lesson plan. That hadn't come up much when she was teaching in elementary school, but Cat's kittens seemed to cover a wider range of ages.

"Cat thinking she's subtle? Yeah, that happens often enough," the girl said. "I'm Junior, by the way. This is Katallina."

"Hello!" Katallina said. She'd pocketed the knife already.

A dog padded over to them, and Grasshopper was momentarily distracted from snooping around since there was a dog and she had to let it sniff her hand and then it let her scritch its tummy and mostly

Grasshopper was too busy for the next couple of minutes to take care of other things.

That was, until she noticed she was drawing a bit of a crowd.

"Oh, sorry," she said.

"That's okay," Katallina said. "Catkiller seems to like you."

Grasshopper made note of the dog's name, and also that Stray Cat had a dog called Catkiller in her house. She stood up and, with much determination and self-reminders that she was a grown woman, pretended not to notice the way Catkiller's tail stopped thumping as she stopped rubbing his tummy. "That's nice. Is everyone here?" she asked.

The living space in the center of Stray Cat's home was rather open, with a large wraparound couch and a hovering television in the center of the room that was definitely not human tech. She liked it. The space was open and roomy, and she noticed that most of the doors surrounding it led into little bedrooms that were personalized a bit.

"Yeah, everyone who counts," a young man said. He was leaning against a pillar, arms crossed and brows furrowed. He was also, she noted, poking at her augs' security measures. It was a little bit rude, like a mosquito poking its big stingy nose against the side of a battleship, looking for a way to push through the armored hull.

"Wonderful!" Grasshopper said. She clapped her hands together and smiled big and bright. "I'm Miss Hopper, or Grasshopper, whichever you prefer. People refer to me as 'she,' 'her,' and 'oh God oh God where are those shots coming from.' Starting today I'll be your self-appointed volunteer teacher and instructor."

"You're a teacher?" one of the smaller kids asked.

She nodded. "Fully certified and everything," she said.

She kept her teacher's certificate next to her literal license to kill.

"Hey, Nose, might wanna go get Cat," the older boy said. "Just in case, yeah?"

One of the kittens jumped to his feet and ran up the stairs. Stairs that lacked appropriate railings, but Grasshopper wasn't here to inspect the place for that kind of thing.

"School's boring," one of the kids said.

"You're right!" Grasshopper agreed. "But I'm not here for *school* lessons, I'm here to teach! Boring classroom lessons have their place, but when you're learning one-on-one, you can learn so much more!"

"Oh, shit, it really is you," a familiar voice said from the top of the stairs. Stray Cat walked down the steps with a careless slunk. She had a strange way of walking, almost liquid, but also a little janky. Grasshopper wasn't surprised that she'd earned the name Stray Cat; it suited her perfectly. "What're you doing here, and what are you wearing?"

"This is my teaching outfit, and I'm here to teach," Grasshopper said.

Stray Cat blinked slowly, and Grasshopper smiled without showing her teeth. When a cat blinked slowly it was a sign of trust, after all. "Oh, okay. Yeah, I guess the kittens could use some schooling."

"Hello!" a chipper young lady said as she came down the stairs. Stray Cat turned and met her halfway down, then guided her to the main floor. It seemed an entirely unconscious gesture that neither of them really noticed, but it warmed Grasshopper's heart.

"You must be Lucy!" Grasshopper said.

"Aw! Did Cat talk about me?" the young woman asked. She was clearly quite curious, which was one of Grasshopper's favorite qualities in a new friend. She was also not wearing any underthings, which Grasshopper wasn't sure how she should feel about. "Nothing bad, I hope?"

She tried to tamp down any blushing as she shook her head. "Nope, I'm afraid it was nothing but good things from her. I think . . . and pardon me if I give up the secret here, but I think she might be in love."

Lucy giggled, her laughter brightening up the room while Stray Cat glared weakly at Grasshopper. "I might have noticed," Lucy said. "She keeps giving me these looks. She's not exactly subtle, you know?"

Grasshopper nodded along. "I noticed as much, yes."

"All right, all right, enough bullying me in my own home. You're here to bully some knowledge into the kittens, right? Like, math and history and English and such?"

"Oh, not just the kittens," Grasshopper said. "You too! Your education seems a little lacking. But don't worry, my lessons are always super interesting." She bent down, opened her big bag, and pulled out a rocket launcher. "I was thinking we could start with chemistry, trigonometry, and physics!"

She had a lot to teach, and only so much time, but it was okay. The more fun a lesson was, the more it stuck!

ABOUT THE AUTHOR

RavensDagger is a Canadian writer who wants to make people smile. The best way to do that, he has found, is by pecking away at the keyboard and hoping for the best.

Podium
DISCOVER
STORIES UNBOUND
PodiumAudio.com